700

ILL OCT '00

GAYLORD MG

700 B

The Assistant

J. Patrick Law

A NOVEL

SIMON & SCHUSTER

New York • London • Toronto • Sydney • Singapore

SIMON & SCHUSTER
Rockefeller Center
1230 Avenue of the Americas
New York, NY 10020

Simon & Schuster and colophon are registered trademarks
of Simon & Schuster, Inc.

Designed by Leslie Phillips
Manufactured in the United States of America

10   9   8   7   6   5   4   3   2   1

LIBRARY OF CONGRESS CATALOGING-IN-PUBLICATION DATA
Law, J. Patrick.
The assistant: a novel / J. Patrick Law.
p.   cm.
1. Intelligence service—Israel—Fiction. 2. Israel—Fiction. I. Title.
PS3562.A859 A9 2000
813'.6—dc21   00-022208
ISBN 0-684-84261-0

FOR MY MOTHER AND FATHER

sayan assistant; pl., *sayanim*

Ha Mossad, le Modiyn ve le Tafkidim Mayuhadim the Institute for
     Intelligence and Special Operations; commonly referred to as
     Mossad, or the Institute

katsa case officer responsible for recruitment and handling of foreign
     agents in designated countries, including the United States

AUTHOR'S NOTE

Although the *sayanim* exist as an integral facet of the Institute's overall
ability to conduct its operations, the characters in this work bear no rela-
tion to people living or deceased.

   Also, certain details about the Israeli embassy in Washington, D.C.,
have been altered or omitted for security purposes.

The
Assistant

One

THE UNSEASONABLE SPRING STORM crashed down from Virginia's Blue Ridge Mountains and into the Shenandoah Valley. Its tail clipped the distant Alleghenies, but it saved its brunt for the city. Black skies, shot through with green and purple, churned over Washington, D.C., the lightning cracking and roaring like the voices of dueling gods of some long-dead planet.

"I am the Mighty Shazzam and you will never catch me!" a deep, ominous voice called out.

Over a timpani drumroll of thunder, another voice trumpeted, "Yes, I *will* catch you. For I am Sir Elmo, a knight pure of heart and noble of mind!"

Sir Elmo, outfitted in aluminum foil that passed for a suit of armor, dashed after the sorcerer, caught him by the trailing ends of his black robe, and sent him tumbling to the ground.

"Where is the Lady Lucy?" Sir Elmo demanded.

"I will never tell you," the Mighty Shazzam gasped. With that he rolled over and lay still.

"Elmo . . . Elmo, is that you?" came the plaintive cry.

Elmo raced across the floor where, in the corner, the Lady Lucy had mysteriously appeared, leaning against the wall, one hand on her brow.

"Oh, Elmo, you have saved me from the Mighty Shazzam."

"And I promise he will never come between us again."

At which point the Lady Lucy stood on tiptoes and planted a demure kiss on her hero's cheek.

Benjamin Poltarek let three beats go by, then dragged his right foot along the floor. A simple construction of string and pulleys slowly brought down the navy blue curtain on the puppet stage.

Now came the moment of truth. Like any good magician, he had an almost physical connection with his audience, could feel their awe and appreciation crackling in his palm. But these twenty-four spectators, seated in a semicircle around his velvet-draped table, were the harshest critics. You could walk a giraffe past most adults and they'd never see it. Try that with this bunch of four- to nine-year-olds and they would hand you your head.

"Gol-*lee!*"

It was the wheelchair-bound little girl in the third row, with hair like spun corn silk and eyes as blue as cornflowers. Her exclamation broke the spell; all the kids started clapping and yelling for more.

Ben removed his top hat, with THE GREAT ELMO inscribed in gold glitter, and, with a flourish, bowed. The hat was the only unusual piece of his wardrobe. Whether performing for children or adults, Ben always favored dark, conservatively cut suits that hung perfectly on his tall, lean frame. They should have because even after custom tailoring, Ben always added the little touches indispensable to his act: secret pockets, pockets that could be tugged open, seams that hid invisible nylon thread, sleeves that could be stuffed with coins or silks. The teacher who'd introduced him to the magic arts over twenty-five years ago, when Ben was only ten, had insisted that he learn to sew. Over time, a "tailor's notch," a groove, had worn into his left incisor from biting thread.

Instead of a regular shirt, beneath his suit jacket he wore a dancer's blouse with a billowy front and puffy sleeves. The sleeves not only allowed him a wide range of motion, they were necessary to the sleight of hand he was performing as he moved among his young audience. Silks—the more colorful the better—always captivated children. Since ultimately any magic show takes place in the viewer's mind, Ben used his audience's perception to heighten the effect of his tricks. He stopped in front of a six-year-old boy with braces on his legs, and, using an emerald green silk, performed the "Hay poke-through vanish," making it appear that the material he'd poked into his left fist with his right forefinger had disappeared—only to reappear when he slipped his hand around the boy's head and made the silk come out his ear.

As Ben wended his way through and around his audience, his movements, agile and graceful, seemed totally random. They were, in fact, deliberate. He stopped in front of a redheaded girl seated in a soft chair, with an oxygen tank beside it, and watched her eyes shine as he revealed the secrets of his color-changing handkerchief. Two rows away, a boy in a torso cast was mesmerized when the "breakaway fan" opened one way, seemed perfectly ordinary, only to fall apart—much to the magician's embarrassment—when opened in the opposite direction.

"Who wants to help me bake a cake?"

A chorus of "I do!" drowned out the pounding of driving rain against the windows.

Ben went over to a second table that he'd set up before the children had been brought into the playroom. Since he'd focused their attention on the big front table, this smaller one, eighteen inches square with four sturdy legs, had been ignored.

First, Ben removed his hat and set it on its top.

"Recipes, recipes," he muttered, patting his pockets, finally coming up with a piece of paper that he unfolded beside the hat.

"Now, three eggs." He looked around his audience. "Anyone?" Two dozen heads shook solemnly. "Well, let's see. Maybe in this pocket . . ."

One by one, he pulled the eggs out of his right pants pocket—where they'd nestled in three individual, carefully sewn sheaths—and deftly cracked them over the hat.

"Now we need a little flour." Which came out of a jacket cuff. "And some milk." Courtesy of a plastic tube taped to the underside of his forearm. "And . . ." He looked at the kids, puzzled. "Chocolate or vanilla?"

"*Chocolate!*"

"Chocolate it is." Squirted out from the hollow of a large cuff link.

"Now we have to cook it."

Picking up his hat, Ben retraced his steps to the redheaded girl.

"Your hair is so beautiful, just like a rosy campfire. Do you think I can use it to cook my cake?"

The child giggled. *"No!"*

"Well, I think I can. Let's see."

Humming, Ben moved his hat around and around over the girl's head, as if he were handling an omelet pan. He peeked inside.

"Oh, yes. This will be delicious. Can you smell it yet?"

The children bobbed their heads enthusiastically.

Geez, I hope so. Ben had dropped a few odor pellets—gelatin capsules filled with chocolate fragrance—down his pants leg, and carefully crushed them underfoot.

Ben peered into his hat. The ingredients were all gone, having disappeared into the outer pan of a tried-and-true prop called a Cake Pan. Nestled in the smaller inner pan was the cake, which Ben had baked only hours before his performance. Since he had to wear his hat *and* keep the cake in it at the same time, the mix of choice was always angel food or sponge.

"Looks like we're almost ready . . ."

Ben moved back to the larger table, where a pile of paper plates and plastic forks had magically appeared. He frowned. Over the scent of warm chocolate, he caught the hint of another fragrance. The sight of the woman standing with her back to the door almost made him lose focus.

"One and two and three and . . ."

With a flourish, Ben turned over his hat, catching the cake as it slipped out of the smaller pan. He set it down on one of the plates, produced a Swiss Army knife, and cut off a small piece to taste.

"I think it's pretty good," he told his audience. "Who wants to try some?"

The woman at the door was Dr. Rachel Melman and she smiled when the clamor went up. Watching Ben cut the cake into bite-size pieces and pass them around on the paper plates, she felt a rush of love. A bachelor, he was nonetheless a magnet for children and pets, who tended to adopt him on sight. He had the ability to make every child feel special, as though he or she was the sole focus of his attention at that moment. It was this rare gift, above all his other qualities, that had tapped the deep, almost inaccessible wellspring of her love.

Rachel dropped her hands into the pockets of her hospital smock. Her eyes took in the large, pleasant room, with its cheerful colors, cartoon cutouts, and finger paintings on the walls, the huge bin of child-safe toys and games. It was a special place in the Children's National Medical Center, both to its young patients and to its staff. It wasn't unusual for the room to stay open after visiting hours and children's bedtime; doctors, nurses, orderlies, and other staff slipped in here for a quiet moment, to contemplate Barney's goofy grin or absently play with Disney lions, dalmatians, mermaids, a temporary relief from the grim realities just outside the door.

Ben came to the Center twice a month. He did not seem affected by what magicians called hospital performances, the Heartbreak Circuit. He said he came to practice in front of a conjurer's most demanding audience, an audience that, unlike adults, demanded to feel that it was *their* show, mostly. Whether silk, sponge ball, cake, or even a simple piece of string, the magic that sprang from the prop was only for their thrill and excitement. Rachel thought that Ben fibbed a little about his reasons.

"The Great Elmo wanted me to give you this."

Rachel looked down at the blond girl holding up a plateful of cake. "Why, thank you, Cheryl. Will you say thank you for me to the Great Elmo?"

"Sure."

"Do you think he'll do any more tricks for you?"

Cheryl scrunched up a frown. "They're not *tricks*, Dr. Melman. They're ill-*ooo*-shins."

Rachel shook her head. "I'm sorry. Of course they are. I guess I don't know enough about these things."

"Well, you should," Cheryl said primly. "Everyone knows you're the Great Elmo's *girlfriend.*"

Having put the pediatric surgeon in her place, Cheryl rejoined the group.

God help me, thought Rachel. This from a child who, just four days ago, had been rushed into the trauma unit suffering from heart palpitations. After stabilizing her, Rachel had discovered that Cheryl Pulaski had a pinprick of a hole in her heart. Surgery was scheduled for five o'clock tomorrow morning. Rachel had a meeting later tonight with the specialist she'd be assisting, who had flown in from Los Angeles.

She looked at Ben, surrounded by faces that seemed to have lost some of their hospital pallor. Faces that, for the moment, were devoid of the fear and pain the children lived with but did not understand; faces belonging to children suffering from AIDS, sickle cell anemia, or leukemia but who could say only that it hurt here, or there, or all over.

Rachel knew that the end of the show was the hardest time for Ben. It was almost impossible to make a graceful exit, with the applause created by small hands, and eyes that silently pleaded with him to stay. Which was why Ben always ran over his allotted time.

"Gosh, what's that? Did you see something?"

Rachel did. The movement was almost imperceptible, but then she knew what to look for: Ben's fingertips in his pants pocket, tugging one end of the nylon string that had been trailing behind him. Whose other end was connected to one of the puppets behind the curtain of the marionette stage.

"It's the Mighty Shazzam," one of the children squealed. "He's *alive*!"

From behind the curtain came the Mighty Shazzam's deep bass, thrown by Ben, whose ventriloquism skills startled Rachel even now.

"Sir Elmo. Where are you? We are not finished, you and I."

Rachel watched Ben crouch so that he was eye-level with his audience.

"What should we do?" he whispered.

"Save Sir Elmo!" was the chorus. "Sir Elmo and the Lady Lucy!"

The curtain went up and he pulled all of them into the world behind it. There was the Mighty Shazzam bearing down on Sir Elmo, the children shouting warnings at the knight. At the last instant, Sir Elmo deftly sidestepped the onrushing sorcerer and, as though swept along by the cheers of his supporters, dashed up the castle steps to await the Mighty Shazzam's next attack.

* * *

Thirty blocks way, Yossi Tarnofsky clutched the rubber rail of the escalator gliding up from the Red Line subway platform to Union Station.

Tarnofsky was a young man, twenty-eight, battle-tested and very fit. He could admit to himself that the two bullet wounds, one in the fleshy part of his right thigh, the other in the lower abdomen, were serious injuries. He refused even to countenance the idea that he might be dying. Landau had given him strict orders to the contrary: Nobody dies before the assignment is complete. Word in the Institute was that if you pissed off Landau, he would make it his business to follow you to hell, and then you'd wish the Devil had gotten to you first.

In a burst of savage grief, Tarnofsky wondered if that's where Rothman and Bernstein were now, trying to explain to Landau how the Arabs had managed to shadow the tactical incursion team, drop on it like a scythe across wheat. Tarnofsky recalled his last image of his two partners and then he couldn't stand to remember them at all.

Tarnofsky leaned heavily on the rail. He'd always had a problem with tunnels, even in training. The huge concrete-lined cylinder that linked the subway to the train station was, to him, a giant sarcophagus. His breath came in jagged rasps, not so much from the pain of his wounds but from the fear that he might never again see the sky before he died.

The mission . . . Tarnofsky pushed the claustrophobia away, pushed away the pain. He checked behind him. There were five other people on the escalator, all of whom had gotten off his train. Three office girls, a businessman, a student with a backpack. None belonged to the Arabs. He'd have smelled them if they had.

The storm had drenched him so completely that his jacket, sweater, and pants, dark to begin with, were now black, effectively hiding the blood that had seeped into the fabric. Passengers in the subway car had looked at him once, then away. Tarnofsky saw himself through their eyes: a derelict or an addict, doubled over, clutching his stomach. He'd hoped there wasn't a good Samaritan in the car and hadn't been disappointed.

The top of the escalator was coming up. Tarnofsky did inventory, starting with his face. Despite the coolness of the tunnel, his forehead was hot. Fever and blood loss, a potentially lethal combination.

His right arm was still numb where the Arab bullet had cut through it. Every team member carried five small army-issue pressure bandages; Tarnofsky had had to use up three on that wound alone. That had left two for the jagged tear in his abdomen. From the color of the blood, dark and rich, he knew that the bullet had, at the very least, nicked his liver. If the damage was greater than that . . .

There was nothing Tarnofsky could do about the wound in his thigh, but he did not curse his luck. The Arabs had been shortsighted using steel-jacketed ammunition instead of hollow points, which expanded on impact and created an exit wound the size of a child's fist. The bullet had passed through fat and muscle without touching the femoral artery. Each step Tarnofsky took was excruciating, the pain hobbling him, stoking the image of his helplessness. But at least he could keep moving. Because Landau had to know what he knew.

The words branded into Tarnofsky's memory were meaningless to him, but they had been bought at a terrible price, from a man who'd been quite ready to die rather than part with them. Tarnofsky was certain that in the end, the man had given up the truth. Now it would be up to Landau, whose mind was a Rosetta Stone, to decipher the inexplicable and the arcane. No code, no cryptography, no secret pattern or system yet devised was beyond his ability to crack it.

So Tarnofsky willed himself to keep moving, to exist only for that moment when Landau, the high priest, could make him understand the meaning of what burned within him like an unfulfilled prophecy.

He saw the Arab just as the steps of the escalator brought him eye-level with the wide corridor that led to the train station. He was a slim young man with quick, darting movements. Right now he was standing at an angle to Tarnofsky, by the tall, heavy doors to the concourse, looking in the opposite direction. From his vantage point, Tarnofsky could see the angry welt of a scar that ran from the back of the Arab's jawbone and disappeared up toward the eye.

It was an immutable law of nature, Landau's law: Arabs never operated alone. If you saw one, others were close by.

How close? How many?

And how did they know I would be coming to this train station?

The last question unnerved Tarnofsky. After the attack on the safe house, the butchery, and his escape, he had had choices: to make a run for the Israeli embassy or to head for one of two other destinations. The Arabs would expect him to run to the embassy. Tarnofsky didn't know how many of them there were, but it was a given that they would concentrate on the embassy, create a gauntlet that even an uninjured man could not survive. He might get close, but they would tag him and kill him even as he was within hailing distance of his goal.

Nor had Tarnofsky telephoned the *katsa*, the senior Mossad officer at the embassy. That would have gone against standing orders, in effect since the Pollard affair. A Jewish U.S. citizen working at the Intelligence Support Center of the Naval Criminal Investigative Service, Jonathan Pollard had been apprehended and exposed as an Israeli spy. Stung by the incident, American counterintelligence had placed the movements of all Israeli diplomats under close scrutiny. This included electronic eavesdropping and surveillance. It was still safe to talk within the lead-lined concrete walls of the embassy itself or on hardened lines, but no matter how sophisticated the internal communications system, calls coming in from a pay or cell phone could be picked off as easily as a sharpshooter drills a bull's-eye.

"Stay anonymous," Landau had said in the briefing. "The Washington *katsa* doesn't know about this operation. He doesn't know about you. Keep it that way. But if you must make contact, do so in person. Don't even let them know you're coming."

Dragging his wounded leg behind him like a stroke victim, Tarnofsky moved as the Arab moved, always staying in his blind spot. At the same time, he kept scouting the entrances to the train station. So far, only the last straggle of commuters and tourists arriving back from day trips outside the city. No other Arabs. Yet.

Tarnofsky leaned against one of the massive, polished granite pillars. The cold stone felt good against his feverish cheek. He had gotten off at the Union Station stop because here he was virtually guaranteed of finding a cab. He could not afford to expose himself by trying to flag one down in the street—not in this weather when taxis would be scarce, not knowing who might be coming up behind him.

The Arab continued to pace in front of the great glass doors, a sentry guarding his assigned perimeter. He continued to scan the travelers passing him but did so in an almost cursory fashion.

He knows what to look for, Tarnofsky thought. *Someone who is injured. The rest don't matter.*

But still the question: Why here? Had the Arabs seen him disappear into the subway at the Takoma station? Possible, though not likely.

Still, the Arabs had managed to find the safe house. Maybe they recognized the car, too. When Tarnofsky had abandoned that, they had automatically assumed he would use the subway. So they had contacted the rest of the team, strung out a picket fence of agents at the most likely stops. Union Station was an obvious one, as was Van Ness, close to the embassy. Metro Center, where the lines converged, would be another. Tarnofsky doubted that the Arabs could cover more than those stations. Under other circumstances, he might have eluded them, but he was moving so slowly that they had had time to position their intercepts. Still, there was always room for luck.

Decide.

Tarnofsky would go through the Arab, no question about that. It was what came after that he had to be sure about. Landau had given the team two *sayan* contacts—names, addresses, telephones. Both were equally good, places where Tarnofsky could get medical attention, rest, and shelter until Landau came for him. But the key was to avoid leading the Arabs to the *sayanim*. The *sayanim* were civilians. It was a golden rule that never, ever were they to be put in harm's way.

Because of that rule, the choice was clear.

Tarnofsky fell in behind an elderly couple clucking about the miserable weather and used them as a shield to move in on the Arab. His left hand was in his jacket pocket, fingers curled around the butt of the short-barrel .38 Smith & Wesson, threaded for a two-inch silencer. The weapon was American-made, untraceable, as generic as laundry soap.

Tarnofsky felt the hairs on the back of his neck push against his shirt collar. He was vulnerable and exposed. The Arab was twelve feet away now, the elderly couple struggling to pull open the heavy door, the woman looking to Tarnofsky for help.

He ignored her, slipped across the face of the doors just as the Arab was turning to walk toward him.

"*Aiwa!*" Tarnofsky whispered.

The slang salutation made the Arab whirl around. Hearing his mother tongue, he naturally expected a comrade. His eyes widened and his upper lip curled back when he saw Tarnofsky.

It was much too late. Tarnofsky reached out and gripped the Arab just beneath the elbow, squeezing down on a cluster of nerves. The Arab grimaced and in a reflex action, reached for Tarnofsky with his other hand, exactly as the Israeli had anticipated. The move left the Arab's chest exposed. Tarnofsky, his gun already angled in his coat pocket, fired three quick shots into the Arab's heart.

Tarnofsky shielded the Arab with his body, propped it up against the wall until he had a chance to glance over his shoulder. The elderly couple had already gone through the doors. The nearest civilian was more than fifty feet away, standing on the escalator, reading a newspaper. A threesome in army uniforms were buying subway tickets from an automatic dispenser. A pair of giggling teenage girls skipped out from around the corner, their eyes sliding across him as quickly as water over stone. There would not be a better time.

Tarnofsky stepped back slowly, allowing the body to slide down the wall until the Arab was sitting on the floor with his legs splayed. Tarnofsky walked away, not looking back. He gripped the door handle and pulled. When he stepped through, he saw the Arab tilt and collapse to one side, as if drunk.

The glass behind him exploded, pebble-size pieces showering Tarnofsky as he was flung forward. Pain seared through his leg and abdomen but his training took over, making him roll along the cold stone floor until he no longer felt the crunch of glass beneath him. He scrambled to a column and slipped around it.

Tarnofsky heard screams behind him, saw the three servicemen looking around with dazed expressions. But he couldn't see the second Arab, the shooter. The bullet had come from behind him, but at what angle, how far away? Maybe the Arab was a poor shot. Maybe he had been shooting from too great a distance or from a bad angle. Tarnofsky had been a slow-moving, unwary target. He should have been dead.

More commotion now as people strolling in the arcade slowed to look. The three soldiers were hollering for someone to call 911, the transit police, an ambulance. Tarnofsky knew he still had a chance. With more and more people crowding into the kill zone every second, the Arab had lost the advantage of surprise, he could not try another shot without giving himself away. Tarnofsky picked a knot of onlookers, steadied himself, and plunged ahead.

"Hey! Hey, buddy. You hurt?"

And another voice: "Geez, man. Is that blood?"

Tarnofsky moved as rapidly as he could, cursing the leg he was dragging. He used his shoulders to break up the groups of people, felt them brush him, shrugged them off. He was in the arcade now, stumbling past brightly lit shops that would be closing in a few minutes. A knife thrust of pain sent him sprawling against the plate glass of the Great Train Store. Tarnofsky slapped his palm against it to keep his balance, never saw the bloody streak he left in his wake, like some grotesque rainbow.

His breathing was ragged, each inhalation burning a hole in his chest. Glimpsing a pair of transit police rushing down the concourse, Tarnofsky veered into a Sam Goody record store. He didn't comprehend why the clerk, a pimply youth with tattoos and pierced facial parts, kept staring at his hands. Tarnofsky glanced down and saw blood welling from between his fingers where he was clutching his abdomen. The pressure bandages had been soaked through and had fallen away.

"Hey, man, this ain't my scene, you know? Just keep walkin'. Please."

Two things registered at the same instant in Tarnofsky's mind: the youth's desperate plea and the movement he caught in the polished metal disk mounted in the corner where the wall met the ceiling. An antitheft measure. What Tarnofsky saw wasn't a shoplifter but a figure in a dark coat, raising one arm. He shifted his weight onto his bad leg and went down in a heap just as the Arab fired. The bullet passed through where Tarnofsky had been standing and slammed into the clerk. The Israeli never heard the boy fall. He had his gun out, firing, his aim compromised by the waves of pain that cascaded over him. Glass, stone, and wood were splintered, but not flesh.

Tarnofsky pushed himself along the floor to the counter, seeking cover in case the Arab made a frontal assault through the door. Instead, he heard more gunshots, most of them coming from heavier-caliber weapons. Nine millimeter handguns, common American police issue. *The transit officers.*

Tarnofsky edged his way out of the record store. The firing boomed down the concourse, followed by a high-pitched scream, then its echo. Over the stink of hot loads came radio chatter, one of the officers calling in a ten-thirteen.

Tarnofsky cursed silently. How could the Americans have failed to hit their target?

Tarnofsky scrambled out of the arcade and into the main concourse. The vaulted ceiling with its Beaux-Arts dome and rows of stylized Greek and Roman statues stared down sightlessly at the unfolding nightmare. Now the giant space was completely deserted. Tarnofsky knew that Washingtonians, like New Yorkers, lived amid random, sudden violence. They recognized gunshots when they heard them, knew that the only thing to do was to take cover and wait until people with bigger guns arrived. Tarnofsky picked them out, crouching behind giant stone slabs that passed for benches, using overturned tables belonging to the Coco Pazzo Café as shields.

Tarnofsky understood that he had almost no time left. The firing had picked up again. The odds had shifted in favor of the Arabs taking down the police instead of the other way around. When that happened, they would come back for him.

Tarnofsky looked into the recesses of the main hall. The closest doors were below an enormous half-moon window with an inset clock. He estimated two hundred feet of open space. It seemed like miles.

The blood from the wound in his abdomen was no longer seeping but trickling. He couldn't feel his left leg above the knee. If he didn't make it out of there, the Arabs would kill him before any emergency crews arrived. And if by some miracle he survived, there would be the gun and the wounds to explain. Since he was working without diplomatic cover, the Americans would mend him and hold him for as long as they liked. They would have many questions for him. *Too many complications.* Tarnofsky remembered that Landau's loathing of complications was legendary.

Concentrate on the doors. Two hundred feet to the doors. Beyond them, taxis, cars, a way to get out of here. Without leaving your guts all over the floor.

Tarnofsky pulled out his gun. A woman who'd been watching him from behind a café table shrank back. He scuttled past her, over to one of the stone benches, then zigzagged to another. His next goal was a small information stand. Beyond that, a porters' station. Stepping-stone to stepping-stone, he'd reach the doors that opened up to the night and the storm, and from there he could escape, reach a place where he could hide until Landau came for him and lifted the terrible knowledge from his heart.

* * *

Ben Poltarek stood under the awning, the rain sluicing down, spattering the tips of his shoes. In his left hand he held the larger suitcase, containing the dismantled marionette theater and the puppets; in his right was a smaller case, scarred leather with tarnished brass hardware, that held his magic.

"We'll never make it," he muttered. "Never."

Rachel laughed. "The car's right over there. Come on." She fiddled with a flimsy telescopic umbrella and finally managed to open it. "On three. One, two, *three!*"

Rachel was as tall as he and held the umbrella so that he didn't have to crouch. On his fourth step he placed his foot squarely into a deep puddle.

"Shit!"

A gust of wind tore the umbrella from Rachel's grip just as they reached her venerable, lovingly cared for BMW. Rachel fumbled with her keys. The locks popped; Ben shoved the suitcases into the trunk and jumped into the passenger seat.

Rachel, already behind the wheel, reached out, her soft, long fingers cupping his cheek. There was nothing Ben could say or do. She had an ability to make his world stop completely at the most unexpected moments. The wash of the anticrime lights sculpted her face in alabaster, dramatically setting off her thick red hair. He could not let go of her eyes, blue like a glacier under a full moon. Crusader's eyes, he called them, for although she had been born in Israel, he liked to imagine that they belonged to some long-ago knight-errant who had made the holy pilgrimage to Jerusalem and there had lain with a Hebrew noblewoman.

"You're looking at me that way."

"Which way?"

"Like you're going to ask me something and as much as I want to, I'll have to say no."

Ben pushed levers to get the heater going. "We'll talk on the way home."

Rachel knew her side streets and they made good time to Connecticut Avenue. She listened to Ben talk about the show, occasionally stealing a sidelong glance at the slight ridge where he'd broken his nose as a child, the full lips she knew had touched no other woman in the last three years, the long eyelashes and heavy eyebrows that could, in the right light, lend him a mysterious air.

Which was, she thought, perhaps the greatest illusion of all. For there was nothing remotely mysterious about Ben Poltarek. Although his stock-in-trade was mystery, he was utterly without guile or affectation. When they'd first started seeing each other, she had been on the alert to discover the real man, the personality that lay beneath the skin and would, sooner or later, rise to the surface like a brass rubbing. But that had never happened, and slowly Rachel had come to believe that there were men other than the kind she'd attracted before. The kind who loved only to use, whose cool and poise were nothing more than brittle lacquer over dead nerves and a mummified heart.

Ben Poltarek, on the other hand, was one of those rare beings who loved unconditionally, needed to change nothing, accepted any gift that came his way as blessing, not due.

Yet, as much as Rachel loved him, he sometimes gave her pause. The world had taught her that it could be dangerous to get too close to people. You might catch their dreams and in the end their dreams could alter you forever, destroy you.

"Where are your folks tonight?"

"Right about now Sid and Rose should be arriving at the Kennedy Center." Ben often referred to his parents by name, as if they were old buddies, which, given the family dynamics Rachel had witnessed, was virtually the case.

"How are they putting up with you?"

"You make it sound like I'm the houseguest from hell."

"You snore."

"No more than you."

She elbowed him in the ribs.

"The contractors tell me another week."

"That's what they said before you and Sid left for Paris."

"And before that, too."

Ben's townhouse in upper Georgetown, on the fringe of the university, was in the last stages of remodeling. He'd moved into the Poltareks' spacious four-bedroom condominium on Connecticut near the National Zoo for the duration, an arrangement that played havoc with his and Rachel's sex life.

"Have dinner with me tomorrow," he said suddenly.

Rachel was startled by the quiet intensity of his words. There was something behind them, something she couldn't divine.

"Ben, I have surgery tomorrow. Cheryl . . ." She touched his hand. "Ben, what is it? Is there something you want to tell me?"

He sighed. "It'll keep, I guess."

"Tell me about Paris," Rachel said, quickly changing the subject. "What I missed. What you'll take me to see one day."

She loved to hear him describe things. He had the gift of making her see through his eyes, believe that one day she would see everything he was describing through her own.

The pleasure she experienced was not without cost. Not in terms of promises she'd made him and failed to keep, not the experiences she delayed or deferred, not the time she could not offer him and that could never be replaced. All these things, Rachel believed, would come their way one day. It was the tapestry of secrets that kept her postponing that day.

Rachel had never lied to Ben. Not overtly. True, she had been born to an American father and a Sabra mother. The family had returned to the United States when Rachel was five. By the time she entered college, all vestiges of her Israeli heritage had melded into American Jewishness.

The family's circumstances were comfortable until Rachel's father died of a sudden heart attack. Poor investment advice quickly depleted the Melman coffers. Rachel attended Smith on full scholarship, but the money ran out by the time she was accepted at Johns Hopkins Medical School.

With student loans falling short of covering tuition and no collateral to offer banks, Rachel turned to the sponsor of last resort: the government. Specifically, the army. In return for its picking up the balance of her tab at Johns Hopkins, she agreed to give them four years of her life after graduation.

Rachel completed her studies just shy of her twenty-seventh birthday. The next week she found herself at the army's medical training center at Fort Bragg, North Carolina. Six weeks after that, she was assigned to a frontline unit with the Bosnian peacekeeping force.

With ten months' experience to her credit, Rachel was rotated back stateside where she was offered a tour of duty that would knock one year off her military commitment—if she enrolled in the Special Warfare Center and School.

Rachel began her twelve months of training at the Fort Bragg medical lab, where better than half the medics in training washed out in the first few weeks. Rachel, with childhood memories of kibbutz animal pens and ritual slaughter, concentrated on the reason why the baby pigs and goats were wounded in specific areas by a sharpshooter. She and her team then ministered to these animals, learning to treat combat trauma, practicing military emergency medicine, even conducting battlefield surgery. The next day the sharpshooter would shoot fresh animals in different places and the exercises would begin all over again.

By the time Rachel earned her honorable discharge she'd been responsible for saving the lives of three Special Forces officers wounded by friendly fire during training. Off the coast of Sudan, she'd fought to keep two members of her team alive as the unit evacuated the country after a successful attempt to free an American diplomat being held hostage. She finished out her tour at Fort Bragg as an instructor, teaching recruits how much more difficult it was to hold the human body together than to tear it apart.

Ben knew all this, even about the Sudan raid, which the Pentagon had declassified and made the centerpiece of a trumpeting PR campaign. He knew that she'd finished her residency at Georgetown Medical Center and then, because of her experience, had been assigned to the emergency room trauma team. It was there, one night three years ago, that she'd literally bumped into him as he was on his way to perform for the children.

Rachel transferred into pediatric surgery, where she could help those who were most in need of her nimble hands, quick mind, and dearly paid for experience. Once, Ben had said she would make a wonderful mother, and Rachel hadn't dared reply that the prospect terrified her. Ben saw all the joy that a child could bring into their lives; she saw only the dangers, dreaded the day when she would confront something that she could not defeat. Then a child would die. Maybe her child.

Whenever Ben spoke of children, Rachel felt her guilt most keenly. There was a part of her life she had successfully hidden from him—the eight months she'd rolled into her Georgetown residency that actually belonged somewhere else. It was not a place she often visited, and she understood that by refusing to take him there she was betraying him.

But only a little. And for his own good.

Flimsy excuses in the face of the love and trust he lavished on her. Excuses that were barbs on her conscience.

Sometimes, Rachel asked herself what Ben would do if she took him down that road. He would be confused—angry, too. Press for explanations where none could be given. Sickened and overwhelmed, he might retreat from her life. Rachel didn't think she could survive that, not only the shame, but because she didn't know of a single way to bring him back. In the end, it always came down to this: It was better to betray him than to risk losing him.

Through the rapid motion of windshield wipers Rachel saw the flatiron building where the Poltareks lived. She turned off Connecticut, made a U-turn, and parked in the street instead of under the canopy.

"Does this mean you don't want the doorman to overhear you propositioning me?"

"Propositioning you in your dreams. Come here."

Rachel wrapped her arms around Ben, her mouth finding his, tongue probing. She kissed him as though she needed to fill herself with him, to make him remember her, always want her.

"You know Sid and Rose always go to supper after the opera," he murmured.

"I know Rose eats like a bird and they'll be home a half hour after that."

"Still leaves us an eternity."

"Don't do that." Ben was nuzzling her neck, just behind her ear, making her flush. "Honey, please. After Thursday night I'm off for four days. Do with me what you will."

"Words you'll regret."

"I hope not."

Rachel inched the car into the circular drive and under the portico. A uniformed doorman opened Ben's door.

"I'll call you tomorrow," Ben said, getting ready to slide out.

"Love me?"

"So much."

She waited until the doorman retrieved the suitcases from the trunk, then hit the accelerator. The tires spun and the rear end fishtailed, but Rachel regained control of the car. She couldn't say the same about the tears that stung her eyes, washing away Ben's kisses.

*　*　*

The Poltareks' apartment took up the top two floors of the building, which were connected by a sweeping semicircular staircase.

Ben had taken back the room he'd had as a boy. His mother, for reasons she never explained, had changed nothing since the day he'd left for college. Posters of the Four Kings of Magic—Nate Leipzig, Harry Blackstone, John Mulholland, and Thomas Downs—hung on papered walls. Bookcases smelling of lemon-scented wax held his collection of conjurers' texts; award statuettes and framed citations rested on shelves above his bed. The only thing out of place was the framed law diploma from Yale, hung to catch your eye as soon as you opened the door. His mother's small expression of pride.

And the picture of Samuel, his older brother, at seventeen, big and strapping like their father and even taller. Samuel, who had relished contact sports, was good enough to have won a Golden Gloves competition; "the tough son of a bitch Jew," he called himself.

As much a friend as a brother, Samuel had spent hours helping Ben build his magic props, and though his thick fingers could never quite master the strings of illusion, he'd been proud of Ben's abilities. Eighteen years dead, yet as alive today as his last day. Whenever Ben came to that thought, he carefully folded up his memories and made them disappear into that secret place in his heart.

"I miss you, Sammy," Ben said aloud.

Ben deposited the suitcases in their proper place in the closet and padded into the *en suite* bathroom. He stripped off his costume and stepped under the hot shower spray. Through the hot mist and the shower's glass door, Ben glimpsed the box he'd left on the nightstand, a small, black velvet jeweler's cube whose contents were immediately obvious.

He'd been doing what amused the French most about American tourists: jogging at first light, when the streets of the First Arrondissement were still, devoid even of the ubiquitous street cleaners. He was coming back into the place Vendôme, running lightly past some of the most expensive boutiques in the world, when something caught his eye. Behind thick shatterproof glass was a jeweler's display case, empty save for one mannequin hand in the corner, as though it had been forgotten. On the fourth finger was a wedding band, a small marquis diamond accented by a pair of sapphires. The sapphires reminded him of Rachel's eyes.

Now, like found money, the ring was burning a hole in his pocket. He had come up with and rejected a dozen ways to present it to Rachel. The place had to be just right, the timing perfect.

Somewhere over the drumming of the shower Ben heard the telephone. He wrapped a towel around his waist and went into his bedroom.

"Is this Benjamin Poltarek?"

The voice was cool, detached, and unfamiliar.

"Who's this?"

"Detective Priestly, Fifth Precinct. Are you Mr. Poltarek?"

"Yes, I am. Is this about one of our clients?"

"I'm afraid not. It involves your parents."

Ben sat down on the bed. "What about my parents?"

"Mr. Poltarek, I'm very sorry. There was an accident. Happened right outside the Watergate. Look, this sort of thing is hard over the phone."

"I'll be right down. The Watergate . . ."

"No, sir. That is *not* a good idea. There's nothing you can do here. The paramedics tried their best, but . . ."

Priestly's sigh whistled through the jagged hole in Ben's soul. "You're saying they're dead. My mother and father are dead."

"I'm sorry. Death was instantaneous."

Ben knew that police and emergency teams always said that. It was a gentle lie. Rachel had told him that instant death didn't exist. There was always at least a split second of consciousness, the awful realization of what was about to happen, what was about to be taken away.

"I want to see them."

"I understand, Mr. Poltarek. They're being taken to Georgetown Medical—"

"I'm on my way."

"Sir. *Sir!* Listen to me. I'm going to come and get you, okay? It's a lousy night out there. I don't want you behind the wheel. Do you understand?"

Ben was holding the receiver away from his ear. He didn't want to hear any more. He said something before hanging up, wasn't sure if Priestly had heard it, didn't care.

He stood up quickly and was immediately seized by vertigo. He steadied himself on a bookcase. His eyes found the photo of Samuel.

"They're dead?" he asked his brother. "How can they be dead?"

Then he remembered that those were almost the exact words his father had uttered when Ben had told him that Samuel had been in an accident, that he was dead. He saw himself in the mirror, tried to remember if his father had looked like that.

Ben dressed quickly and headed downstairs, collecting his wallet and keys, which he'd tossed on the table in the vestibule.

The doorbell startled him. It had to be the detective; he'd called from his car.

Ben threw the bolts and the door pushed hard against him as a figure staggered inside.

Tarnofsky slapped a bloody palm on the wall to keep from falling. He turned so that his back was supported by the vestibule table and he was facing the young man who was staring at him, his mouth agape.

"Are you Poltarek?"

Ben took a step toward him, then saw the gun. It wavered in the stranger's grip as though he could barely hold its weight.

"I'm Benjamin Poltarek. Who are you? What happened?"

"Close the door." Ben hesitated. *"Close the door."*

"You're hurt—"

Tarnofsky pushed himself off the wall and staggered to Ben, falling heavily against him.

Ben gripped him under the shoulder, half-led, half-dragged him to the bottom step of the staircase. The wounded man leaned back against the edge of the stairs, blood pooling on the carpet.

Ben made a move for the phone.

"Don't!"

He turned, saw the barrel of the gun. "I'm calling an ambulance."

"Too late. Come here."

"You're bleeding!" Ben shouted. "If you don't get help—"

"Closer. Come closer." Tarnofsky's breathing was very rapid. He could feel the siren song of his life in his veins, feel his heart labor as it tried to keep pumping what blood remained. He knew there wasn't much.

He grabbed the young man by the hair, jerked his ear to his lips. "This is for Landau, only him. Understand?"

"Landau?"

"Tell him they are bringing in an American. *An American*. Landau will know what to do."

The gun fell from Tarnofsky's fingers, clattering along the steps to the floor. He couldn't keep his grip on Ben, and now his head rolled to one side.

"What American? What are you talking about?"

"Rothman . . . Bernstein, dead. El-Banna too, I think. But he talked before they hit us. Bringing in an American." Tarnofsky summoned up one last fistful of courage. "Tell Landau it will be an American!"

Tarnofsky began to shake violently as his heart skipped and sputtered. Strong arms embraced him and held him up and he was grateful for the comfort. He was dying in a land far from his own, but he believed, needed to believe, that these arms would eventually transport him back to Israel, where there would be someone to say Kaddish for him.

Ben felt the blood paste his shirt to his skin. He could not tear his eyes away from this stranger, with his fluttering eyelids, soundlessly moving lips, and rapid, shallow breathing. He heard the doorbell again but could not let go, hugging and cradling the stranger the same way as, years ago, he had held his brother.

The door to the apartment opened and a figure cautiously stepped in. Ben saw the detective's shield hanging over the breast pocket of his jacket, heard the sharp whistle of his breath through the space between his large, square teeth, like Scrabble tiles.

Priestly was moving fast toward him, one hand pulling out his radio.

Ben wondered how his voice could be so calm, how strange his words sounded: "He never even told me his name."

*   *   *

Ben Poltarek could not have known then that it would be impossible for him to core out answers to the questions raging within him.

He could not have known that such answers lay not in the broken body that had plunged into his life, but within himself. Or that the first thread of the tapestry of knowledge had not been woven there in Washington, but in an ancient capital five thousand miles away.

Most of all, he never suspected that the truth, and he, were now caught in the gears of the immovable, implacable law of unintended consequences.

Two

TWO WEEKS EARLIER, Benjamin Poltarek had faced his father across the table in the living room of their suite at the Hôtel Ritz in Paris. The tall windows were open to the balcony, and the warm morning air stirred the scents of breakfast—honey; freshly baked pastries; strong, hot coffee—which was set out on the table.

Sid Poltarek was built like a drayman, but he had a classically sculpted face with a Roman nose and a leonine head of pure white hair. His voice had a low, rumbling quality, like the first faint stirrings of an avalanche. Also like an avalanche, the sheer weight of his intellect and personality always followed. Opposing counsel facing him for the first time discovered such things the hard way.

He nodded toward the *International Herald Tribune* that Ben had been reading.

"Anything interesting?"

"Kaiser-Agfa stock was up in Tokyo this morning." Ben tapped the financial page. "The feeling is that either the lawsuit will be dropped or the payout will be minimal—with no admission of culpability."

Sid Poltarek grunted, reached for a croissant, and slathered it with marmalade.

Suddenly, he glanced up at Ben. "Don't look at me like that."

"Like what?"

"Like your mother does when I say yes to a second helping of dessert."

"It's not dessert I'm worried about. You have a week's worth of cholesterol in that croissant."

"If it kills me, sue it. In the meantime, let me enjoy. And don't tell Rose."

Ben popped a strawberry into his mouth. "As if she doesn't know."

"She *suspects*. That's not the same thing." He stared at his croissant, then pushed away his plate. "Now look. You made me lose my appetite."

Ben hid his smile behind the sports page.

Sid Poltarek reached for a piece of baguette and dipped it in his coffee. At sixty-eight he felt as strong and vigorous as a man twenty years younger. His mind was, if anything, sharper than ever. But he could not discount the warning that had come in the form of a mild heart attack. No lasting damage, praise God, but a warning nonetheless. Rose, a woman whose reprimands about his diet and pipe had once been couched in a gentle laugh, now turned to more serious chiding. It was time to slow down at the office, she said. Let Ben start to pick up more of the load, she said. He was ready, she insisted.

Was she right?

Maybe.

Sid chewed on the soggy bread. "What's on tap for this morning?"

"Plaintiff's counsel wants to raise the issue of when they were handed over the last batch of discovery documents. They're crying foul."

Sid grunted—or it could have been indigestion. "What do you think?"

"It's a delay tactic."

One of many that the plaintiffs—220 middle-class homeowners in rural Virginia—had been advised by their lawyers to raise.

Five years ago, Kaiser-Agfa, the third-largest chemical company in the world, with headquarters in Paris, had been sued in a class action by the residents of a tract development called Spring Meadows outside Harrisburg, Virginia. The issue was alleged contamination of groundwater by the company, which, over a period of two decades, had resulted in an unusually high number of birth defects. During the period in question, Kaiser-Agfa had been the lead contractor on an air force development to build the next generation of supersonic interceptors.

Facing a lawsuit whose judgment could run into nine figures, Kaiser-Agfa made inquiries, then had a series of meetings with Poltarek & Associates. Ben had sat in on most of the discussions, taking notes, saying nothing. His contribution began after the firm, with its blue-chip reputation among defense contractors, had been handed the case.

His son had not disappointed, Sid considered. Ben's intellect was married to tenacity and an uncanny ability to ferret out the most arcane and effective precedents. Besides research skills, he had a knack for reading and evaluating opposing counsel. A Kaiser-Agfa executive who'd watched Ben operate had whispered to Poltarek that his son was stealth —the opposition never saw him coming until it was too late.

So maybe Rose was right. Maybe it was time to move Ben into center court. But Sid Poltarek remained uneasy. Ben was not a gladiator, a gunslinger. His engine hummed; it did not burn red-hot. He seemed to lack what a trial lawyer needed most—guts, daring, the desire to tear the jugular. He was not Sid Poltarek. Nor Samuel.

Sid Poltarek thought himself a decent, even righteous man. But because he had loved his elder son more—and still did—he knew that he would never be perfect in the eyes of God.

"Discovery documents." Sid said, "What's your gut tell you?"

"They're grasping," Ben replied. "You were pounding salt up their ass for weeks back in Washington. Plaintiffs' counsel needed to get away, regroup. Someone thought he or she had come up with a bright idea: drag the case to Kaiser-Agfa's home turf. Bring in a French judge. Maybe get some sympathy, at least muddy the waters."

"And you think . . . ?"

Ben leaned forward. "They're ready to settle."

"What would you give them?"

"Give them? Give them nothing."

Sid was pleased. "Why not?"

"Because Kaiser-Agfa didn't do anything wrong. Our experts demolished their experts. We *know* that Agfa cleaned up after itself and that the source of the contamination was the company that moved in after them."

Sid made sure his tone was casual. "I want you to take the lead today."

Ben replaced his coffee cup. "Did I hear that right?"

"Why are you so surprised?"

"Because I'm your water carrier is why."

"You don't have the stones for the job?"

"I didn't say that."

"Then what?"

"Agfa is our biggest client right now. They're paying for all this"—Ben swept his arm around the suite—"because they expect the heavy hitter to deliver. They want to see *you* crush Spring Meadows."

"No. They want Spring Meadows crushed, period. They don't give a damn who does it."

"You want me to do it."

"I'm giving you the chance. If you feel you're not up to it, don't want to do it, fine, tell me."

Ben took a deep breath to still his rising anger. His father had the maddening capacity to give with one hand, then take away with the other; pretend to care, then make it clear he didn't give a damn.

But underneath the porcupine quills that studded their relationship, Ben sensed that the offer was genuine, that in making it his father was extending him a commodity he guarded like a miser: trust. There was a choice to make and Ben wanted to choose wisely.

"I can't do this with you looking over my shoulder."

"Looking over your shoulder? I won't even be in the room."

"You're not coming today?"

"If you'd been willing to settle, I never would have made the offer. But you're not. And in this situation, we can't tag team them; it's a single player's game. You think you can bring it home, I'll stand by that."

"I've never known you to be a gambler."

"I'm not. I bet only on sure things. And if I can't bet on my own son . . ." Sid extended his hand across the table. "Go show those hillbillies—and the French anti-Semites—that Jews can give it to them up the *zudick* as hard as anyone else."

* * *

Sid Poltarek bought a white rosebud from a young flower girl and slipped it into the lapel of his light wool blazer. He moved easily in the crowds that ebbed and flowed along the boulevard Saint-Michel. The women pausing for a quick morning coffee on their way to work noted him as he passed. In his hand-tailored wardrobe, Poltarek cut quite the dashing figure, with a touch of the roué.

Poltarek turned off the boulevard at the rue Soufflot and proceeded up the gentle incline to the Panthéon. He walked around this magnificent sarcophagus that housed Napoleon's tomb and came to the small cemetery of Saint-Etienne du Mont. There, the bustle of the Latin Quarter, with its thousands of students, subsided a little. Poltarek slipped behind the Lycée Henri IV, then crossed the rue Descartes to a small café.

The interior was much as Poltarek had expected: wood panels darkened with age and tobacco smoke, an original zinc counter topped with scarred, pitted marble, framed theater posters that once had been cheap decoration but now were worth a small fortune.

The clientele was made up solely of academics from the Sorbonne and surrounding *lycées* stealing a few moments of peace, reading journals and dusty tomes. Poltarek counted no fewer than twelve different nationalities, three ethnic groups, two genders, and one slim young thing who could have belonged to either sex. This mix was one reason why the café was Manshur's preferred meeting place: strangers were neither memorable nor remarked upon.

"Good morning, Mustafa. It's been some time. You look well."

Mustafa Manshur was a small man given to darting, birdlike mannerisms. His cocoa eyes plucked out customers as they came in or left, then resumed scanning the various customers he'd already accounted for. His slightly baggy suit was too heavy for the climate, thus the perspiration beads beneath his pencil-thin mustache. But the clothes made him look exactly what he was: a professor who aspired to comfort rather than fashion.

"Good morning to you, Sidney," Manshur said. Poltarek could smell cloves on his breath, from his cigarettes. "You are looking well, too—and quite elegant, I must say."

Manshur had learned his English from the British and his speech had a clipped, singsong cadence to it.

"You're too kind. Another coffee?" Poltarek gave their order to the elderly, long-aproned waiter, then settled back and studied Manshur. "Tell me, how is your family?"

Poltarek knew damn well the state of Manshur's domestic affairs, but he listened for as long as politeness dictated, then switched to Manshur's work at the Sorbonne. Technically, Manshur was a visiting professor of physics from the University of Beirut. In reality, he, Lebanese-born and -raised, had become a permanent fixture on the French academic landscape. Because Manshur was very gifted in his field, the Ministry of Foreign Affairs kept renewing his visa regularly and without comment. In the morning he taught introductory physics to semibored, listless undergraduates; in the afternoon, in seminars restricted to individuals who appeared to be a little long in the tooth to be students, he held give-and-take sessions on the more exotic aspects of his work, aspects that had military and national security applications.

Poltarek was aware of this because several years ago he had had occasion to use Manshur as an expert witness. A professional relationship bloomed into a personal one, then deepened into friendship over games of chess via e-mail and dinners whenever either crossed the Atlantic. In such an atmosphere, Manshur eventually let slip that the French were not the only ones who were benefiting from his ongoing residence in Paris. Poltarek pretended not to have noticed the comment. He knew that Manshur wanted to tell him something and that a listener's silence was the most slippery grease on the tongue.

Manshur kept the mandatory circumlocutions surprisingly brief, which in and of itself told Poltarek something. When he finally spat it out, Manshur's wish could be reduced to a single word: insurance.

He was giving the French the benefit of his expertise. But the French had no reason to suspect that the Lebanese was passing back to various Arab intelligence organs as much—or more—information that he was gleaning during his dark seminars. If French internal security ever became suspicious, or the Arabs decided that the arrangement was no longer to their liking, Manshur wanted safe haven for himself and his family. To pay for it, he was willing to share his knowledge of certain Arab operations, some of which he had personally been involved in, and personnel he'd had occasion to meet.

This was communicated to Poltarek in a most delicate way. The lawyer had excellent connections with American defense contractors. That meant political contacts at a reasonably high level. It followed that Poltarek might be able to shepherd Manshur's nebulous offer to ranking members of the U.S. intelligence community.

Poltarek did not disappoint. He did indeed have excellent connections—and not only in Langley, Virginia. But what Manshur never suspected was that Poltarek was operating under false flags.

Poltarek had always made good the promises of his mysterious masters—evidenced by a Swiss bank account in Manshur's name and U.S. passports for him and his family. In turn, the Lebanese had never hesitated to share nuggets he'd ferreted out from the faceless men from Damascus, Cairo, or Tehran who passed through the French capital to pick up Manshur's information and leave behind fresh instructions. It was usually after such fleeting visits that Poltarek received innocuous e-mail whose subtext was a request for a meeting.

Mustafa Manshur eventually completed his rambling discourse on the demise of French education under the current Socialist government.

"Are you by chance familiar with the name Hafez Jamal?" he asked.

Poltarek pretended to study the intricate scrollwork on the tinplate ceiling. What he was really doing was trying to stave off another heart attack. *Hafez Jamal.* Of course he knew the name.

When he was sure he had his voice under control, he said, "No. Never heard of him."

"It is my understanding," Manshur said slowly, "that his current whereabouts would be of great interest to certain people."

Poltarek shrugged as if to say, *How could I possibly know such a thing?*

"This information is very fresh," Manshur carried on, tearing off tiny bits of his paper napkin.

Poltarek called up his most engaging smile. "Tell me."

*   *   *

Sid Poltarek left the university quarter as he'd come, walking down the rue Soufflot to the boulevard Saint-Michel. There he fought the impulse to head for the nearest Métro station and take a train to the rue Rabelais in the posh Eighth Arrondissement. But there was a way of doing these things and he always followed procedure.

Poltarek squeezed into a busy café and, instead of a subway ticket, bought a telephone token from the bartender. The din created by the patrons effectively cloaked his brief conversation.

Then Poltarek was moving again, turning right where the boulevard met the river and proceeding along the quai Saint-Michel. He crossed a short bridge and found himself in front of the Cathedral of Notre Dame.

A squad of paramilitary police in navy blue uniforms and polished jackboots patrolled the perimeter in pairs. Tour buses were angled into parking spaces, well over a hundred tourists, in three groups, milling around their guides and interpreters.

There were also the unescorted travelers, generally younger, in pairs or by themselves. As he strolled toward the cathedral doors, Poltarek tried to pick out the man he'd been told would meet him.

His shoulder was bumped. Turning, he saw a young woman in her mid-twenties, with braided hair, loose comfortable clothes, and sturdy walking shoes. In her hands she had an unfolded map, which she must have been studying when she walked into him.

"Pardon," Poltarek muttered and moved away.

"Gabriel sends his greetings."

Her voice was soft, with a lilt, and an accent Poltarek couldn't identify. He turned around and came back to her, thinking that she didn't look any more Jewish than Christie Brinkley.

Then again, most of them never did.

"My regards to Gabriel," Poltarek said, completing the simple recognition phrase.

The girl stepped over to the parapet and shrugged off her small backpack. Poltarek noticed the red maple leaf emblem prominently displayed. He severely doubted that she was Canadian.

The girl spread the map out across the stone and placed the backpack on it to prevent the breeze from snapping it away.

"Come help me find the way to the Eiffel Tower."

Poltarek thought the girl was good. Even if security glanced in their direction, all they'd see was a prosperous middle-aged man, dressed like a Parisian, helping out an attractive tourist. The policemen's thoughts might turn prurient, but there was nothing going on to raise suspicion.

They bent over the map, heads close together, his finger tracing randomly over the paper.

"Please tell me what Manshur said."

Poltarek had been through this procedure many times. He knew enough to understand that the person he was speaking to was a human tape recorder, and that as a backup she was undoubtedly carrying a real recorder with a sensitive microphone, maybe the Walkman hanging next to her backpack.

He repeated verbatim what Manshur had told him, annoyed that his dry, concise recital crumbled under the excitement when he first mentioned Hafez Jamal. He glanced at the girl to gauge her reaction but saw that her eyes hadn't moved off the map.

Poltarek's account took less than two minutes. "Is there anything you wish me to repeat? Sometimes they ask for elaboration."

"No, thank you," she replied politely, already swinging her backpack over her shoulder, refolding the map.

She gripped his hand and shook it vigorously in the manner of a Scandinavian woman.

"Thank you for your help. Gabriel will be in touch."

Watching her walk off, Poltarek felt deflated. He had wanted someone to share his excitement, offer him encouragement. But nothing like this had ever happened—nor was it likely to. The girl had been exactly the same as every other go-between he had dealt with—polite, efficient, a chameleon.

Poltarek did what he did not for money, medals, or glory. He and his wife had entered this secret world, which lay like a sheen just below their normal lives, because they were believers. In Israel's right to exist, to defend herself, and to endure. They did not much care for the right-wing political parties that were in power in Jerusalem nor for the influence of the Orthodox rabbis, but to them Israel was a beacon, the ultimate refuge, the place where, if you came naked and despoiled, they had to take you in because it was home.

* * *

After leaving Poltarek, the girl continued across the Seine to the Right Bank. She popped the locks on a Vespa scooter parked near the Hôtel de Ville and proceeded along the rue de Rivoli, headed for the Eighth Arrondissement.

A few blocks from the rue Rabelais, she donned goggles and a cap that covered her hair. She stuffed the backpack with the Canadian flag into one of the saddlebags that straddled the back of the scooter. Now she looked like any one of the thousands of delivery people who crisscross Paris every hour. The cameras of the Deuxième Bureau, France's internal security department, would photograph the nose and lips of someone who could have been either a young woman or a shapely boy.

The girl got off her scooter, walked up to the guard post at the side entrance to the Israeli embassy, and placed an envelope on the conveyor belt. The guard behind the bulletproof glass activated the belt; a fluoroscope checked the contents of the envelope as it rolled through. The girl pushed a receipt into the roll-through tray, watched as the guard signed and returned it.

Six minutes later, the tape from the girl's Walkman was being played in a room dressed up to look like a lounge, with soft colorful furniture, good art, fresh flowers. Except that this room was forty feet below street level. Its walls were six feet thick and lined with lead.

The senior Mossad agent, the *katsa*, smoked three cigarettes while he listened to the conversation, in which Poltarek described his meeting with Manshur. He switched off the recorder, popped the tape, and beheld it as if it were a parchment of the Dead Sea Scrolls.

He picked up the phone and dialed the communications chamber.

"Warm up the line to Landau."

"Wait one."

In his mind's eye, the *katsa* saw the commo officer check the computer, which tracked Israel's senior civilian and military policy-makers, for Landau's exact whereabouts.

"He's in the prime minister's office. After that, the two of them are taking the Sabbath—"

"Pull him out."

"Repeat, please?"

"You heard me: Pull him out of the meeting and get him to the commo link."

"There'll be hell to pay—"

"Landau will forgive us when he hears that we have a location on Fast Walker."

*   *   *

Ben left the turn-of-the-century office building on the boulevard des Capucines and proceeded toward the Opera. The sun felt good on his face. Better still was the glow of satisfaction that put a spring in his step.

The depositions had gone better than he could have hoped. Attorneys for the plaintiffs had put on a brave front, but their slash-and-burn tactics had not impressed the French referee, a tiny woman who could have been Dr. Ruth's twin and who ruled over the proceeding like a nun with a sharp ruler.

By noon, the referee called a break and recommended that the plaintiffs strongly consider wrapping up the proceedings. She ventured that their coming to Paris to offer French expert opinion against Kaiser-Agfa had, at best, been an ill-advised fishing expedition. If they persisted in their course, her report to the American court would include her opinion that the plaintiffs were deliberately stalling.

Before reaching the Opera plaza, Ben ducked down a narrow side street and checked the storefront windows until he came to La Tour de Magique.

Like divers, golfers, and chess enthusiasts, magicians have a loose, worldwide affiliation, guided by the International Brotherhood of Magicians. A magician, amateur or professional, can walk into any magic store in the world and be assured of a warm welcome, a chance to catch up on that city's magic community, trade shoptalk and gossip.

Speaking passable French, Ben spent a pleasant half hour with the proprietor and several clients who stopped by. He purchased biographies of two of France's most eminent godfathers of magic, Joseph Buatier and Louis Comte, who in the early 1800s was known as "the King's Conjurer." Ben signed the visitors' ledger and handed out several business cards.

Promptly at half past twelve, he entered the Café Odéon and was shown to a table under the striped awning four rows from the sidewalk. His father was already seated, nursing a citron pressé.

The restaurant was full, the waiter impatient to take their order. Both men chose the *plat du jour.*

"So? How did it go?"

"Whupped their collective asses."

"Did you now?"

Sid sat back, straining the cane-backed chair. His body language brought to Ben's mind a potentate waiting to be amused.

Ben sipped his cocktail and leisurely recounted the morning's events.

"Where does this leave us?" Sid asked.

"Plaintiffs' side will have to hang in there for a few more days—to save face *and* justify the expenditure of dragging this thing across the Atlantic. But they'll tread carefully, given that the referee is standing on their collective necks."

Sid raised his eyebrows. The combative, aggressive tone in Ben's voice was something he hadn't heard before.

"You want to handle the show tomorrow?"

"Sure. Why? Do you have something else going on?"

Sid shook his head. "It would be nice for me to sit and take notes for a change."

The waiter deposited hot plates of boudin blanc before them.

Ben watched his father slather the tripe with hot mustard. Ever since he'd gone into business with his father, not once had Sid Poltarek failed to have at least a hand in a deposition. He lived for verbal sparring.

Ben felt his appetite ebb. His father had something on his mind. Something that, clearly, was important enough to hide from his son.

Three

THE HADAR DAFNA BUILDING, an office tower on King Saul Boulevard in Tel Aviv, is remarkable only in the severe way in which it offends one's eye. Constructed of drab, gray concrete, the building's ugliness astounds.

Inside, Hadar Dafna is spartan, the hanging artwork an afterthought, the security desk and cameras standard. This is an effective front. The wall behind the security desk has a large rectangular two-way mirror. Behind it, twenty-four hours a day, sits a team of two men armed with submachine guns. They are part of the real security.

Beside them is a scanner, the kind used by airports to screen carry-on luggage. After an employee walks past the lobby security, he has no option but to turn left and disappear behind the screen. There, whatever he's carrying is X-rayed and his ID is checked.

Ever since the Institute, the building's sole tenant, moved in, there have been only three attempts to breach security, all involving Palestinian suicide bombers. What the would-be killers never saw or knew about was the security *outside* the building.

At any given hour, a trio of young men and women can be seen loitering away the day in the café across the street. Each is wired to security inside Hadar Dafna; each is a walking arsenal; each has a photographic memory imprinted with the faces of those who belong in the building.

Besides acting as spotters of approaching strangers, the trio is also a rapid-reaction team. Not one of the three suicide bombers even cleared the doors before the team challenged them, spooked them into revealing themselves, and mowed them down.

Now the spotters stirred again, but this time their hard expressions softened into incredulity. Ezekiel Landau was a short, trim man who glided rather than walked. His features were unremarkable and not distinctly Semitic. He could pass for an American or a northern European; with a deeper tan, a Spaniard or South American.

At age fifty, Landau could bench-press two times his own body weight. He was lethal with his hands and a host of weapons. The exact number of confirmed kills to his credit was a secret, but rumor had it that before Landau had become head of the Institute, and so had to leave field operations, he had single-handedly eliminated 30 percent of those whose names appeared on the prime minister's Execution List. At the time, the List had 104 names.

The spotters in the café were taken by surprise. Landau was supposed to be with the prime minister all afternoon. One spotter radioed in the likelihood of a snap inspection.

All three watched as Landau mounted the steps, paused, and scratched the crown of his head. A chuckle circled the group. Few things were known about Landau, but one fact was legendary: Landau was a religious man. When he operated abroad, it was impossible for him to wear a yarmulke. He'd solved that particular problem by carefully shaving the crown of his head and fashioning the hair into a makeshift cap. If anyone noticed, it would simply look like a bad hairpiece.

Landau did not break stride inside the lobby, nor did he pause at the checkpoint behind the screen. He missed nothing and could see that the spotters had relayed word of his visit. Internal security looked very sharp.

Landau stepped into an elevator that descended four floors and opened onto a room that very much resembled the *katsa*'s lair in the Paris embassy. It should have, since it was the blueprint for identical rooms in Israeli embassies around the world.

"Shalom, Landau. How is our prime minister?"

The speaker was a handsome, fifty-year-old, chain-smoking woman with hard, intelligent eyes and forearms that could wrestle a Brahman bull to the ground. Her name was Bella and Landau had inherited her when he took office. Bella was a fixture because her knowledge about the Institute was encyclopedic—as it should have been, since Bella was family, the granddaughter of the Institute's founder.

"Shalom, Bella. The prime minister sends his warmest regards. He also asked—very delicately, mind you—why you humiliated his brother-in-law at the fund-raiser last night."

"Because he is a thief—a horny thief at that. He tried to feel me up under the table." She flicked her wrist and sent a manila envelope gliding down the long conference table to Landau. "The son of a bitch has been taking kickbacks, and none too discreetly, either. Our august leader might want to have words with him before he reads about it in the *Jerusalem Post.*"

Landau read the one-paragraph synopsis and sighed. "Thank you, Bella. I'll bring it up at the appropriate moment."

"You mean when you need something from him," Bella shot back.

Landau blinked. "Of course. Why waste it before then?" He flicked the file back across the table. "So what's this uproar from the Yahalomim?"

The literal translation of the term is "diamonds." In the Institute's parlance, it refers to the communications department.

Cigarette smoke trailed in her wake like the smoke from the stacks of a magnificent ocean liner. Bella handed Landau the traffic from the Paris *katsa.* She watched his eyes narrow as he read the brief, decoded text.

"Fast Walker," he murmured. "Our old friend Jamal."

"Whose acquaintance you've been wanting to make for a very long time," Bella observed dryly.

A smile creased Landau's lips. True. Jamal was, in a way, his *Doppelgänger,* an evil twin. For years he'd been head of Al Fatah's Revolutionary Council, a splinter group supported by Iraq, Iran, and Libya. While Yasser Arafat had been busy transforming himself from terrorist to statesman, Hafez Jamal had been tending his garden of munitions experts, infiltrators, and suicide bombers. Year after year his crop had been bountiful, and the soil from which it sprang was continually nourished by Israeli blood.

To Landau, Jamal was not only a target; he was a crusade. Year after year, using dearly paid for intelligence, Landau set forth to prey upon whatever lair the terrorist was holed up in. From Cyprus to Lebanon, to the wastes of the Sudan, as far afield as Morocco and Mozambique, he struck again and again. But each time Jamal had eluded him. Landau would bag his lieutenants and field soldiers, their weapons and explosives, but the quarry he so desperately sought always managed to slip away.

A month or two after one of Landau's raids, Jamal would announce himself again, and Israeli bodies would be shredded at bus stops, department stores, and restaurants.

One time Jamal had even made it personal. He kidnapped three people whose last names were Landau, bound them with plastic explosives, and drove them to a public square in Tel Aviv. After pushing them out of the van like so much garbage, he waited until passersby rushed to their aid, then calmly flipped the detonator switch.

This from a man who had medical degrees from universities in France and Switzerland.

"Landau?"

"I was thinking."

"You were salivating. It smells good, doesn't it? Herschel in Paris is sharp. He would not pass on dreck."

"What about the originator, this Poltarek?"

Bella had the file in hand. "He's been a *sayan* for over thirty years. Spotless record. Hasn't turned down one request. And his information is always CLEAR grade."

Meaning "reliable," Landau thought. Very *reliable.*

He reached for a TV-type remote control unit and a backlit topographical map of the Middle East descended from the ceiling. The blue dots belonged to known terrorist camps; the red, to suspected ones. Landau went to the map and traced his finger from Tel Aviv, across the Golan, into Syria, stopping at a red dot next to the small town of Juba. He tapped the dot with his fingernail.

"Why Juba?" he said aloud, but speaking to himself. "Jamal has no history there. He's never used it as a staging ground or refuge."

"Maybe that's exactly why he's going there, because he has no connection to Juba."

"Is there any supporting intelligence?"

Bella ground out her cigarette. "I thought you might want to handle the requests yourself."

She was right. Only Landau could pick up the phone and get the leaders of AMAN (military intelligence), APAM (intelligence operational security), and PAHA (Department of Hostile Sabotage Activities) on the line instantly. Matters would proceed swiftly from there because when it came to Hafez Jamal, interdepartmental bickering and withholding ceased.

"The others don't have this information," Landau said abruptly. "I would have heard if they had."

"Maybe it will come down to how much you believe Herschel."

Landau believed the Paris *katsa* plenty. Before taking up his post in the French capital, Herschel Jacobsen had been a squad leader in the Sayret Metcal, the intelligence reconnaissance group that regularly performed small miracles like the raid on Entebbe, or more recently, the spiriting away of six of Saddam Hussein's in-laws.

Bella watched Landau turn back to the map. His eyes burned with religious fervor as he tracked across the geography, weighing risks, options, possibilities. Bella imagined the scene that must have been fixed in his mind: a brace of the newest, American-made Apache attack helicopters descending on Juba like the horsemen of the apocalypse.

She understood that Landau would not flinch from inflicting devastation even though he knew that innocents, with whom terrorists invariably surrounded themselves, would also die. He would open the gates of hell for Jamal and not let them close until Jamal was behind them.

"Contact the Green Man in Damascus. Tell him that Juba is pleasant this time of year. There are things to hear and see."

Landau said all this in a flat monotone over the beating of a raging heart. The Green Man was his principal agent in Damascus, the best Landau had ever recruited. For six years he'd been providing a steady stream of class-A intelligence. Landau had never demanded product that would put the Green Man at risk, had never exposed him to other, less secure contacts, or sent him to places where his presence would arouse suspicion.

But Juba was not that far from Damascus. The Green Man could arrange a convincing excuse to be absent from the Syrian capital for a day or two. Jamal was worth the risk. He was worth moving the Green Man out of his sanctuary.

Bella knew that Landau had one option. She was not surprised that he would use it; she was sad. Sometimes she wondered if the people Landau used as human chess figures—and sacrificed—ever visited him in his sleep.

"The Green Man," she said, giving him one last chance to change his mind.

"Yes."

Landau snatched up the phone and began to speak quickly to his opposite number at the air force. Bella overheard mention of Apaches fueled and armed, of crews being held in ready rooms, of how much fighter cover to provide and how to coordinate it. After all these years, even she was still amazed at how quickly operations took on a life of their own, genies that could never be put back in the bottle.

Four

THE ROAD THAT MEANDERS south from Damascus to Juba continues all the way to the Fertile Crescent. It was a trade route even before the days of Moses. The Romans had come and laid stone upon it. Later, the Crusaders had dotted it with religious way-stops that stood until they became tired of fertilizing the desert with the blood of their warriors and went home.

Juba flourished and stagnated with the vicissitudes of fortune. In the best of times, its population never exceeded a few thousand. These were not the best of times. The map of the Middle East had been drawn and redrawn. Trade was carried by ship, rail, and plane. Decade by decade, the desert weathered the Roman stone until it became sand and the road was all but invisible. Driving it today, one might believe it had never existed at all.

Like the stone, Juba's population had eroded to less than four hundred. Even with a fragrant oasis, the land could support no more. The younger men, the few who remained, dreamed of following their brothers and cousins to the cities to find work. Tending sheep and goats, growing dates, and pressing palm oil was women's work.

Hafez Jamal had chosen Juba precisely because the rest of the world had forgotten about it. He had arrived there several days ago via a circuitous route that had taken him from Tripoli to Valletta, on the island of Malta, on to Beirut, then across the border to Iraq, only to double back into Syria. By the time he crossed the Euphrates, Jamal was certain that neither the Israelis nor the Syrians were aware of his whereabouts. All to the good. The Israelis wanted to see his head on a pike; the Syrians claimed he was behind in his payments for the sanctuary they provided.

Landau had said that Jamal had no reason to be in Juba. It was one of the very few things he was wrong about. Unknown to anyone, Jamal had kin there, a cousin twice removed. He had kept this a secret because by definition, a secret remains one only if those who become privy to it also become dead. Juba was Jamal's bolt-hole, his refuge of last resort, where he might craft his next creation.

And what a creation it would be! Seated under a yellowing palm tree at the back of his cousin's house, vacated before his arrival, Jamal cast his thoughts across time. A hundred plans had been conceived and ultimately discarded. But he had persevered, toiled in silence and solitude, shared nothing with anyone. With the blind certainty of the fanatic, Jamal knew the answer would come to him, perhaps in a vision or a dream. He would know it was the right one when he felt its awful glow in the pit of his stomach as it consumed him.

The dream had been long in coming, but it had revealed itself to him during a restless sleep on a flight from Malta to Beirut.

During his days in Juba, Jamal had crafted and perfected the plan as meticulously as a glassblower shapes his fragile creations. He was a patient man by nature, meticulous by training. It was his habit, when he was lost in thought, to contemplate the calluses on the tips of his fingers, the result of working with detonator wires the width of a hair. Beneath the object of his concentration, another consideration was being examined. Hafez Jamal had fond memories of his time in European colleges and hospitals. But his thoughts about what he could have been invariably made him sad. Then rumination would become the slippery slope of anger, and without being the least aware of it, he would plunge into the psychosis that threaded its way through his mind like a tapeworm.

But for the moment the worm was still. The project had been thought through. Its framework was very strong, yet as light as an aerialist's ropes. There had been contingencies, of course, but those had crumbled one by one under his laserlike concentration.

Then, when it was done, Jamal took a metaphorical step back and focused his considerable powers on destroying his creation. He found some minor cracks and details that needed a little shading, but overall the edifice would not fall. He was ready. The monument to his vision of holo-caust was ready.

Jamal had unpacked the smallest of the three suitcases he'd come with. Nestled in protective sponge was a powerful transmitter married to an encryption unit. The transmitter operated via a satellite launched by the Chinese for the Libyans. Jamal had received permission from Khadafy himself to use it.

The message was capsulized in a microburst and lasted a tenth of a second. After Jamal repacked and put away his equipment, he settled down to wait.

The man to whom the message had gone had been expecting it. Even though he had a wife and child, he would be ready to travel. Two days, maybe three, no more.

In the interim, Jamal seldom left the house. The woman who cooked and cleaned for his cousin came and went about her business in silence. She recognized hard men and was painfully familiar with what they could do to her and her family. She carried out her chores with downcast eyes, even when Jamal was outside, his back to her.

Jamal did not think much about his magnificent edifice. There was nothing he could do to improve it. But he had one last task to perform before the man and woman arrived. He went to the market and used one of the two working pay phones. The connection to Damascus was scratchy, but his words got through. Words that were bait for the traitor he hoped to snare. He would know soon enough if it'd been taken. In fact, he was counting on it, for a traitor's act was to be part of the foundation of his terrible palace.

Now, sitting beneath the palm tree, Jamal heard only the hum of insects and the scuttle of small lizards along the stone walls. They enveloped him as a lover would and lulled his fevered imagination. Still, he heard the footfall by the front gate, though he pretended not to.

"*Ai,* Hafez. We could have been Jews coming for you."

Issim Hassan was two heads taller than Jamal, with bronzed skin over cables of sinews, black laughing eyes, and teeth so white that when he'd fought in the field, he'd had to rub them with charcoal.

Turning to his boyhood friend, Jamal thought, *He is the paragon and I, with my hairy body and coarse lines, am the dwarf.*

Anyone who saw the two men side by side immediately had the same thought. It did not matter that Jamal was the smarter of the two, the learned cosmopolitan who possessed the genius of both saving life and taking it. Hassan was the charismatic. The gift of leadership is both elusive and eternal. If a man is born to it, he cannot give it up, no matter how much he might want to. The standing joke about Hassan was that he was so handsome that he could have run for a seat in the Israeli parliament and won. It was also rumored that the top Palestinian commanders, including Arafat, were more than a little afraid of Hassan's magnetic personality, which was why he had never been promoted to the inner councils.

As he rose to embrace his friend, Jamal knew that none of this mattered to Hassan. He was not oblivious to his gifts, but neither was he ruled by them. Once, he had used them to lead men in the field. Now, he turned their considerable power to politics, to the hard task of wrestling a Palestinian state out of an increasingly intransigent Israel. The warrior had become a peacemaker. In Jamal's eyes, Hassan had lost the purity of his vision, then abandoned it altogether. Jamal believed he knew exactly when this had happened—when Hassan had become first a husband, then a father. The two combined to make him a traitor.

Jamal wrapped his arms around Hassan. Beneath his cheek, he felt the great muscles of Hassan's chest quiver like those of a racehorse at the starting gate. Then he stepped around him, toward the woman who, like a Hebrew siren from the Torah, had stolen Hassan from the movement. *From his destiny.*

"Manar . . ."

The woman was as tall as her husband, but younger. Although she wore the robe and the veil, her eyes, emerald pools flecked with gold, belonged to youth. Even the garments could not entirely hide her shapely figure—and that after a hard birthing.

"Where is the boy?" asked Jamal. "I have a present for him."

"He will see it later. He is asleep in the truck."

Jamal thought her voice was rich and throaty, and he often wondered what it would be like to lie with her.

Jamal had had beautiful women, but he had always paid for them. He wondered if Manar, who had beguiled the most beautiful of men, could see beyond his misshapen flesh. Was she truly as exceptional as Hassan claimed? Jamal was counting on that.

Jamal prepared the table with food, bottled water, and sweet Jordanian wine while Hassan carried in his two-year-old son, Naji. The boy, who had his mother's eyes and light complexion, never stirred as the father lay him on the couch.

Hassan and Manar were hungry after their long drive, but Jamal ate sparingly. He already knew what Hassan had come to say, and this had robbed him of his appetite.

The ax fell after Jamal had poured them sweet Turkish coffee.

"The committee has come to some conclusions," Hassan said. "New directions."

Jamal nodded but remained silent.

Hassan leaned forward, as though by lessening the distance he could speak softly and so spare his old friend pain.

"We have been fighting the Israelis for better than forty years. We have won some great victories but we have also eaten ashes. We have used up our youngest and finest men until we have had to recruit children. We are tired, my brother. Who would have thought blood could weigh so much. But it does, upon the Israelis as much as upon us."

Hassan accepted the cigarette Manar lit and handed to him.

"You and I," he continued. "We have been the stilettos, striking again and again at the Israelis. Believe me when I say that I do not regret anything we have done. Our actions, and those of our comrades, were responsible for herding the Israelis to the bargaining table.

"But now the talking is done. The Israelis have given us their best and final offer." Hassan pushed across a thick sheaf of documents. "The American President has promised to guarantee the terms—and our rights—as soon as we sign."

Jamal's expression did not betray his revulsion. He merely took the documents, excused himself, and went to the couch. For the next hour, while he read, he absently reached for Hassan's son, still asleep, and stroked his hair.

"It seems we have fought long and hard for very little," he said when he returned to the table. "And these guarantees the American President is to sign, they are secret protocols, appendices no one will ever know about. If the Israelis change their minds, if the Americans renege, who will speak for us then?"

Hassan's nostrils flared as his world-weariness whistled out of him.

"Trust has to begin somewhere, Hafez. For us, the Israelis, the Americans. You may not know it, but the Israelis resisted very hard. Only when the American secretary of state made clear her displeasure did they relent."

Oh yes, my brother. I know how much they relented. But Jerusalem still belongs to them, does it not?

Jamal touched the documents lightly, as though they might be contaminated. "Does Arafat agree to this?"

"Arafat would have agreed to less. I, and others, had to remind him how much blood had already gone into this bargain."

Jamal noted that there was no pride or preening in Hassan's voice. Certain parts of him were utterly without guile. The idea of taking credit, even when it was his due, would never have occurred to him.

"And you, Issim. If you had to sign, would you?" *Knowing you could enforce nothing?*

"Yes, I would."

Jamal pretended to consider the flame in the lamp between them. In his heart he had been hoping that his sources in Damascus were wrong. He had hoped that Hassan would bring him meat, not gristle. He was neither angry nor disappointed that this had not happened. He was resigned. A man who has anticipated the worst, who has not been lulled by false hope, can afford resignation. Jamal was such a man. He could afford to be because he still had his beautiful, terrible dreams.

When he spoke, it was to both Hassan and Manar.

"Try to think of it as I do. You have been married to a woman for many years and then one day she leaves you. You cannot, on that day, cease to love her, no matter the pain. Nor can you turn a key in your heart and begin to hate her. Until you accept new realities, you live with ancient sentiments.

"That is how it is for me and Jews. I have fought them and hated them, and even though I understand compromise, I cannot embrace it. Accept it, yes. But to come to terms with it, I need time, and your patience and wisdom." Jamal paused. "I suspect there are many like me, even among Israelis."

More than you could imagine, Issim.

He felt Hassan's strong fingers around his forearm, saw his tears of relief. He listened to his assurances and promises, but secretly he was saying a prayer for him. Hassan believed, but this time in the wrong things.

Jamal rose from the table. "When do you return to Beirut?"

"Arafat expects me the day after tomorrow."

"Have you sent the message?"

Jamal thought he saw the shadow of shame flit across Hassan's eyes.

"All the brigades I command have been ordered to stand down. As of now, there will be no more retaliatory attacks against Israel—in any form." He looked at Jamal. "Will you now send the same message to your fighters?"

Jamal let him wait. "Yes," he said finally, "I shall do this. You have my word."

"Tonight?"

"Tonight, but later. When we reach our destination."

Manar spoke. "Destination? Where are we going?"

Jamal smiled. "Under the circumstances, this may be an unnecessary precaution. But old habits . . . I never spend more than a few days in any one place. Here, my time is up. Arrangements have been made in another place, where I have means to contact my men."

"What is the name of this place?" Manar asked.

"You may have heard of it. It is called Samarra."

* * *

The drive in the aging Land Rover took three hours. There was no road as such, but Jamal navigated by memory and the stars. Along the way, the boy, Naji, awoke, and Manar sang songs to him that were lifted by the night wind to the constellations above.

It was almost midnight when they reached Samarra, nothing more than a hamlet, forty miles west of Juba. Another refuge awaited them and, tired by the drive, the three adults and the child quickly settled into their beds.

Out of habit, Jamal was the last to fall asleep, listening to the night, accounting for every movement, sound, and smell. When he deemed that all was secure, he closed his eyes and allowed himself to drift off, hoping to dream of the green fields and the honey of Paradise, the virgins and the cool, still waters. After tonight, such dreams would be all he'd have to sustain him.

Five

JAMAL'S CALL TO DAMASCUS did not stay with the first man who listened
to it. Within the hour, its substance was relayed to a second individual, who in turn dialed Mustafa Manshur's number in Paris.

Placing international calls from Damascus is a treacherous business.
Connections take time, and internal security monitored the lines constantly. Even a brief conversation, larded with references to recent
surgery regarding a family member, might not fully disguise the essential
text, and in this case, a name and a place had to be mentioned without
the cloak of code.

Mustafa Manshur was trembling when he replaced the receiver in its
cradle, as much from fear of the risk the caller had taken as by his message. Hafez Jamal had not survived so long because he was careless. So
what had possessed him to use an open line to relay the message that he
was leaving Juba? Manshur would never know and perhaps it was of no
consequence. What mattered was that the information he had passed on
to Sidney Poltarek was now out of date. And God only knew with whom
the American lawyer had traded or what decisions had already been
framed on the strength of Manshur's intelligence.

Manshur glanced at his watch. Although it was only six o'clock in the
evening here in Paris, there was no answer in Poltarek's suite at the Ritz.
The concierge informed Manshur that the American and his son had
gone to the Georges V for cocktails.

Manshur called the hotel and was put through to the lounge. Poltarek sounded jovial, as if he'd had a good day and was looking forward to an even better evening. His tone changed abruptly as soon as Manshur spoke.

"Are you absolutely sure?" Poltarek asked.

Poltarek listened to Manshur's desperate assurances.

"Don't get worked up over nothing, Mustafa," he said soothingly. "I'm glad you told me this, but please, don't worry."

Another fifteen minutes went by before Poltarek finally calmed the Lebanese. The clock in the lobby tolled the hour and he cursed under his breath. The Israeli embassy was closed for the day. Yes, he had an emergency number, but did Manshur's updated information justify using it? And had the Israelis already done something with what he'd passed along? Did they need the update?

Poltarek decided. He called the embassy's night number and spoke to the duty officer. He gave the man his name, asked to speak with a certain individual, and was politely told that the person in question was unavailable. Poltarek left the name of the restaurant where he would be dining and the time at which he would return to his hotel.

"Everything okay, Pop?"

Sid was surprised and shaken to hear his son's voice behind him.

"That was Marty. Just some crap about the Hensen case. He'll be calling back. Come on. Let's go back in."

As he followed his son into the lounge, Sid thought that the relaxing evening he'd been looking forward to had proved to be a fool's dream.

* * *

Before leaving for the day, Herschel Jacobsen, the Paris *katsa*, always provided the duty officer with three things: phone numbers and places where he could be reached, and a list of people, who, if they called, the *katsa* was to be notified at once.

Sid Poltarek's name had not been added to the list. The *katsa* believed that the American *sayan*'s job was finished. As far as he could tell, there would be no need for further contact, and Landau had said nothing to change that opinion. He went home for the night.

It was four o'clock in the morning in Tel Aviv, three o'clock in Paris, when the *katsa* arrived at the embassy to check for special overnight commo traffic he'd been expecting. As he stopped at the duty officer's desk, he happened to glance at the computer screen showing the call log.

"This one—Poltarek. Did he say what he wanted?"

"Just to speak with you. He left contact numbers."

"Pull up the record."

The duty officer tapped the keyboard. The *katsa* checked the times and swore softly. A *sayan* doesn't leave a telephone trail around the city because he needs his hand held.

The *katsa*'s first instinct was to call Poltarek at the Ritz. Instead, he told the guard to have his car brought back up.

Twenty minutes later, the *katsa* was speaking to the night manager. Despite his misgivings, he ended up having to produce his diplomatic credentials before the man would inconvenience a guest. The manager spent more time apologizing than relaying the message.

Fifteen minutes later, a puffy-eyed Poltarek shuffled into the lobby. The night manager delivered him to an alcove where the *katsa* waited.

"I regret waking you up at this hour."

Poltarek was still a little woolly, but he was sure there was no apology in the *katsa*'s voice. His kind never expressed regret over anything, Poltarek thought sourly.

Then a cold, bony claw clutched his stomach: *What the hell is he doing here at this hour?*

"Something's wrong." It was his first thought and he couldn't help blurting it out.

"Nothing is wrong, Mr. Poltarek," the *katsa* said calmly. His voice was soft, modulated; the eyes were very hard, as if they were restraining something that was battling to get out.

"You called, saying you had a message for me."

Poltarek remembered Mustafa Manshur's fevered words. Was it possible that Manshur had known how critical this new twist was to the original information?

"Do you want me to tell you, here, now?"

The Israeli looked around and shrugged. "We are alone. Now would be a good time."

Poltarek hunched forward and, dropping his voice, delivered his brief message.

"You are sure that's all that was said?" Jacobsen asked.

Poltarek thought he sounded disappointed. "That's everything."

The *katsa* leaned forward and squeezed Poltarek's forearm. "Thank you."

He rose and had taken two steps when Poltarek's voice stopped him. "Was it important? Does it change things?"

The *katsa* almost took pity on him. A man dragged from his bed in the middle of the night without explanation deserved something better. Unfortunately, the *katsa* was not in a position to give it to him. Poltarek's words were like a branding iron upon his heart. He had to reach out to Landau immediately. Maybe it was not too late.

The *katsa* doled out crumbs. "Change things, Mr. Poltarek? Maybe. Is it important? Everything is important to someone sometime, isn't it?"

*   *   *

At the same time as the *katsa* was leaving the Ritz, four Apache attack helicopters lifted off their pads at an air force base south of Haifa. Israeli military air traffic made sure there was nothing else in the skies, allowing the helicopters to run without lights. In less than thirty minutes they were approaching the Syrian border.

In the command and control office in the Hadar Dafna Building, Landau focused on a backlit, electronic map that currently displayed four red blips closing in on Syrian territory. To the left of the board was a digital clock that had started up the second the first helicopter lifted off. The operation was thirty-two minutes, eleven seconds old.

As was his habit, Landau was alone in the room. He had no need of assistants or runners. He liked it this way—a tight control over an operation that was limited to the minimum number of people needed to plan, approve, and execute it. In this case, Landau, the prime minister, who had signed off on it without protest or argument, and the four two-man Apache crews.

At precisely thirty-five minutes into the mission, the helicopters crossed into Syrian airspace. They were flying low, using a terrain-hugging navigation system, and were equipped with the best antiradar equipment available. Those two factors, coupled with the Apaches' silent-running ability, meant that in order to detect them, the Syrians would need to actually see them. Since the attack route did not go near any Syrian military posts, the likelihood of discovery was minimal.

At thirty-eight minutes, the red blips veered sharply to the south. They were now nine minutes from Juba.

Landau sipped his coffee, looked around the C&C. During other operations—Entebbe, the raid on Iraq's Osrik nuclear reactors—the room had been full of people's sweat, cigarette smoke, and desperate hope. Landau preferred the way it was now. The space and the silence made the room feel larger, allowed him to pace, to hold a quiet dialogue with himself, some of which actually made it past his lips. Landau's habit of talking to himself was never remarked upon in the Institute.

"The Green Man . . ."

There had been unforeseen problems where he was concerned. The Green Man had not been able to leave Damascus until yesterday morning, which meant he'd have arrived in Juba at noon. Precious little time to scout for Hafez Jamal. Even less to exercise the elaborate precautions that preceded a transmission to Israel.

Landau wanted the Green Man to confirm that Jamal was in Juba. Not that he didn't believe the American *sayan*'s account. He was sending nine men into a combat zone that could turn hot in an instant. Their lives were his responsibility; ultimately, the quality and veracity of the intelligence that had sent them there was his, too.

But there was nothing from the Green Man, and the Apaches were six minutes to target.

The hard line to the commo desk buzzed as if Landau's very thoughts had conjured up his agent.

"Sir, you need to hear this—now," the commo officer was saying. "It sounds very strange, but—"

"What's the source?"

"Juba."

"Encrypted?"

"That's just it, sir. The message came in the clear—sort of. It came over a telephone."

"A telephone."

"Public pay phone in Juba."

"Play it out."

Here was the call, broken up by shards of static, the speaker in Juba arguing with the international operator in Damascus that he'd been put through to the wrong party. No, he *didn't* want to talk to any camel-fucking Jew in Tel Aviv. He was calling Samarra. No, there was no one here to help him. *No one here.* Couldn't the operator get that through his ugly skull? *Samarra!*

Then silence.

The commo officer was back on the line but Landau shushed him. The voice in Juba belonged to the Green Man. The audacity! For whatever reason, the Green Man hadn't been able to use his transmitter. But he'd found out what Landau needed to know, had to get the information to him. A pay phone. A call to the international operator in Damascus, rattling off a number. Connections being made. Then the fake outrage as the commo officer picked up, and hidden in the diatribe, the message for Landau: Jamal was gone. To Samarra.

Landau jabbed at buttons on the communications console.

The pilot of the lead Apache had Juba in sight, a dark smudge under a starlit night. He was about to order weapons hot when Landau's words crackled in his headset.

This was not the pilot's first mission over Syria and he knew something about such operations. For instance: that they could be changed or aborted at the last second.

The pilot confirmed the orders, then checked his fuel gauges. Plenty.

Fifteen seconds later, the formation wheeled around sharply and headed south. In Juba, goats brayed and old men stirred uneasily in their sleep, as though they sensed something lethal hovering close. Then silence closed over Juba again. The angels of death had been called to another appointment.

In the bunker, Landau lit a fresh cigarette and muttered a phrase that an American Special Forces captain had once used: "Fortune favors the brave." *And the lucky.*

The phone rang again. Landau glanced at it warily, malevolently. He did not believe in *too* much luck.

It was the Paris *katsa*, speaking rapidly, not wasting a word. The American *sayan*'s update on Jamal. Yes, the *katsa* considered the information reliable, but he had no supporting intelligence.

"But I do, friend," Landau said gently.

He hung up and turned his attention to the pulsating red dots on the board. In minutes, the monster would be his.

* * *

The desert was cool in the minutes before dawn. Manar dug her bare heels into the mare's flank and gave her her head. The wind whistled through the thin fabric of her robe and veil, cleansed her of sleep, and made her heart race. Manar imagined that she could taste the ocean on the wind.

The taste was especially sharp because it seemed to melt the dry, fine-grain sand that, despite her clothing, managed to find its way into her skin and down her throat. Manar was a child of the ocean, and Samarra was as far from the sea as one could get. Like Juba, it was built around an oasis, but it was even poorer and more desolate. *Exactly the kind of place Jamal would pick*, she thought dryly.

Not that she held a grudge against Jamal. The journey from Juba had been hot and tedious but necessary. Manar had been Hassan's wife for six years; she understood the rigors of security, the need to move often. The life of the one she cleaved to depended on it.

Manar slowed the mare and turned her around toward the splinter of light on the horizon. This was the time she cherished. Alone in a wilderness that had not changed in millennia, she could witness the dawn of creation. Each new day gave her hope, and of late it seemed that her prayers had been answered. Somewhere beyond the light, almost in reach now, was peace. A peace that would return her husband to her, return him from the wars he had been fighting ever since he was a boy. Peace for her son, who might grow up in a world where people were not torn apart by death from the skies or at the hands of men who came silently in the night and departed with blood on their knives. Peace for her, too, who had made her husband's cause her own, who believed his beliefs, who had plotted and planned with him, but then had to stay behind and wait to see if he would ever return home.

Home . . . The word sounded both foreign and delicious at the same time. Sometimes, Manar had given up hope that such a thing might be hers. She had vague memories of another place, another time, when she'd had a home. But she had been a different woman then, weak and indecisive, timid. Hassan's love had changed all that. She had been taught to believe, to fight and sacrifice for that belief, never to let go of the vision that one day she and the cause she was wedded to would prevail.

Manar slipped some sugar and salt from her robe, reached around, and felt the mare's rough tongue on her palm. *Was today the day?* she wondered. *Or tomorrow?* Perhaps not. But the guns were to be laid aside. Soon the day of peace would come and its promise swelled her heart.

Manar sensed rather than saw the other rider. She scanned the horizon and picked out a moving dot. Instinctively she dropped her hand to the automatic rifle in the sheath beside the saddle.

The rider was in no hurry. Manar was looking into the growing light and could not make him out until he was close.

"*Aiwa*, Manar!"

"*Aiwa*, Hafez!"

He reined in his mount before reaching her so that the kicked-up sand would not blow on her, then walked the horse to her.

Jamal whipped off his scarf, threw back his head, and laughed loudly at the sky.

"A day to behold, Manar!"

Behind her veil, Manar smiled. She had accepted Jamal because of Hassan's love for him, but in the beginning she'd had difficulty with him. In a world of secretive men, Jamal was stone. His bulky, awkward body made Manar think of a frog matted with thick hair. His eyes, always moving, watching, weighing, unnerved her. There were other moments, too, when she felt those eyes on her in a different way, examining her as a woman, not as a competitor for Hassan's affections. It was only much later, when she had worn away his suspicion, that she appreciated and responded to his dedication, intellect, even moments of brilliance. That made it easier to be in his presence. But at the same time, she discovered hints of Jamal's darkness, saw the vultures and hyenas in the sudden explosions of his anger. When he sent men to die or received word of an unsuccessful operation, she glimpsed savage things rising from the well of his hatred.

Could a man like that ever learn to live with peace? In peace? Could he bring himself to love and desire it? Her husband said yes. Manar was not so sure. To her, Jamal was a damaged vessel. His only safe harbor was violence.

"You're frowning," Jamal said. "I have offended you by intruding on your solitude."

"No. I was daydreaming."

"It is written that dreams are answers to questions we haven't yet asked."

Manar was startled. The frog was a poet.

"We have asked many questions over the years. We deserve answers. We deserve our dreams."

"I wish that for you, Manar. For you and your son, and Issim. Who knows? Maybe he is right. Maybe peace will not elude us this time."

"Do *you* want peace?" she demanded suddenly.

Jamal looked directly at her. "I want to see Issim grow to be an old man surrounded by grandchildren. I want your son to bring pride to his home and name. I want you to watch your son and the other children you will surely have flourish in the sun. If that is peace, Manar, that is what I desire."

The horses sensed it first, stamping, jerking at the reins. The eyes of Jamal's stallion rolled until Manar saw the whites.

"The devil—"

Jamal's words were lost to the shadows that raced across the ground, then obliterated the sun. The Apaches were overhead, then were gone before the muted sound of their engines ever touched the sand.

"Hafez!" Manar screamed. She stared after the airships into the glare of the rising sun. "I can't see their markings."

"They need none!" Jamal shouted as he jumped back on his mount. "They're Israelis!"

Manar wheeled her mare around, but Jamal reached out and seized the reins. "We are too late!"

Her eyes reflected savagery and stark terror. Samarra was a mile away, a jumble of houses backlit by the sun. Then the sun was consumed by something brighter and hotter. Manar heard the telltale whistles of the missiles as they streaked from their pods, the rattle of uranium-tipped ordnance spat out by Gatling guns, shredding everything in its path.

The four helicopters hung over Samarra like giant, carnivorous crows jabbing and stabbing at a carcass. Then just as quickly as the raid had begun, it was over. Three helicopters peeled off and came into formation. The fourth continued to hover over the village as the smoke cleared, then turned a lazy circle over its target, sniffing for anything that might still be alive. Finally, it lifted higher, joined the others, and all four disappeared to the west.

Manar broke Jamal's grip on the bridle and whipped the reins across her mare's haunches. The wind shifted, carrying black smoke toward her, enveloping her. Somewhere beyond the thunder of hooves she heard cries and screams. Then, breaking through the smoke, she saw villagers rushing out of their homes. There were bodies scattered in the streets, human and animal, buried among burning carts and wagons that had been reduced to kindling.

They cannot be dead. They cannot be dead. They cannot . . .

The litany shrieked in her mind as she reined in the mare, jumped off, and ran to the house where she had slept with her husband and child. For an instant, she thought she was in the wrong street. The house wasn't there.

She let out a choking wail as she realized that she was wrong. There was the house, now a pile of rubble, with flames snapping through what remained of the walls and windows.

"Manar, don't!"

She ignored Jamal's warning, kept pushing her way past the people crowded in the street. She clambered over rubble, saw an opening, and, taking a deep breath, disappeared inside.

Racing up to the house, Jamal threw himself to the ground as a wall crumbled. He staggered to his feet, swaying, thinking that no one inside could survive. Then he heard a high-pitched scream and pushed forward.

He was scrambling over fallen timbers to get to what was left of the entryway when he saw Manar. She glided like a sleepwalker, oblivious to the flames that licked at the hem of her robe. In her arms she held something small and black, something that once might have been a child.

Jamal plunged inside, clawing his way past debris, falling, the heat searing his lungs and the smoke burning his eyes. He staggered ahead like a blind man, his bleeding fingers tearing at the rubble.

Jamal did not know how long he'd spent inside the ruined house. But it was only by the guidance of Allah's invisible hand that he found Hassan.

Gasping, his knees buckling, Jamal emerged into the light, silently calling on Allah to give him enough strength for one more step, one more . . . Then he was in the street and Manar was at his side. Jamal fell to his knees and gently lowered the body of Issim Hassan. He lay on the ground as though asleep, his features and limbs miraculously untouched and whole. There was even a hint of a smile on his lips, as though his last thought had brought him pleasure and peace. Only his head was not right, resting at an impossible angle.

Jamal drew back as Manar reached for her husband. Her fingers trembled above his eyes and lips, then finally touched them. It was as though an electric current had galvanized her, and she fell onto the body, wailing, pounding the earth with her fists, cursing and swearing vengeance upon a people she couldn't even see.

* * *

Landau sat very still in front of the communications console. His eyes tracked the Apaches' return as he listened to the engagement relay coming in on the encrypted channel.

The pilot reported that the house at the end of the street, the one next to the olive grove, had been leveled. Nothing could have survived the barrage. Nothing had.

Landau knew something about the firepower the Apaches carried. The ordnance from one would have done the job; four would have given Jamal a prelude to hell.

Which was where Landau hoped the terrorist was now. He pulled out a cigar.

Landau was so cautious a man as to seem almost superstitious. He never celebrated victory until it was absolutely certain. Even then, he first counted the casualties with which it had been bought. He knew that Jamal was dead, felt it in his bones. Within the hour, maybe sooner, the Palestinians would broadcast their outrage and grief. The prime minister would come under attack, both from the domestic opposition and from the Americans, for having jeopardized the peace process. Landau disdained politics, but for once there would be a clear, succinct reply: Hafez Jamal and his terrorist wing had *not* signed the armistice. They had vowed to pursue their dream of destroying Israel. They had been condemned, made outcasts, by everyone who had come to the peace table, even Arafat.

Landau appreciated the subtleties of the Arab mind. By ostracizing Jamal, Arafat and the others had pushed him out from under their protective umbrella. Which in turn made him fair game. To the Arabs, Jamal was a thorn and an embarrassment, a killer who'd tasted so much blood that he could not live on anything else. Sooner or later, he would have to be put down. And if the Israelis got to him first, so much the better. Arafat would carp and scold, but in the end he would be quite relieved that Jamal wouldn't be coming for him in the night.

The helicopters were almost at the Israeli border. Syrian military traffic was full of questions, but since Samarra was not close to any Syrian forward staging areas, the interceptors remained on the ground.

Landau drew on the cigar, savored it, mused on the fortunes of war. If Jamal had left Juba for any place other than Samarra, the operation would probably have been canceled. But Landau, who knew Jamal better than any man alive, was aware of the terrorist's connection to the village. Samarra was the birthplace of Jamal's father. Over the years, Jamal had made pilgrimages to honor his father's memory. The Green Man had said Samarra; the American *sayan*, the same. There was only one place Jamal would go—to his father's house at the end of the street, next to the olive groves.

Without warning, fatigue crept through Landau. His body had stopped manufacturing adrenaline. It was telling him to rest.

Instead, he pulled himself to his feet and headed upstairs to the communications room that monitored Arab commercial news broadcasts. He walked like a man sure of himself, with no misgivings. But he wanted to hear about Jamal from the Arabs' mouths.

Six

HAFEZ JAMAL DID NOT STOP to mourn his fallen comrade and the child. Nor did he allow the newly stricken widow to do so. His operation depended on precise timing and a deliberate sequence of events, the first of which had now occurred.

Jamal pried Manar off Hassan's body and carried it to a small army truck. It had once served as a frontline Syrian ambulance and still had stretchers inside and a fading red crescent on the panels and roof. Despite its appearance, the vehicle had a finely tuned engine and a second gas tank.

Jamal laid Hassan out on one of the stretchers, then returned with a blanket for the child. Manar was standing, mute, over the charred remains. When Jamal knelt down, she brushed him away and wrapped the blackened figure herself. Only when she was done did she turn away and let loose her sickness.

After placing the son beside the father, Jamal returned for Manar, grabbed her by the elbow, and half-walked, half-dragged her to the truck. He was glad she was in shock; it was easier to handle her.

"Where are we going?" Manar asked suddenly.

Jamal pressed the starter button and the engine roared. "To a safe place."

Her next words cut and humiliated him: "*This* was supposed to be a safe place."

Under different circumstances, Jamal would have beaten her for such words. He may have learned the ways of cosmopolitan European society and aped its mores, but at home, centuries-old instincts prevailed. A woman was always subservient and deferential. She had no opinions, questioned nothing.

But this was not just any woman.

"I don't know how the Israelis discovered us. But I will find out. On my life, I swear it."

Manar stared straight ahead, unblinking. Her voice was thick and hard. "Keep your life. Others have already paid for what you will find."

Jamal bit his lip until he tasted blood. He could not lose his composure now. Let Manar insult and savage him. It would serve only to whip her anger. She would be denied rest or sleep until exhaustion dropped her. Then, when she awoke to find herself still in the nightmare, the grieving would begin.

But the anger would remain. Every day Manar mourned, it would grow, spawning new pustules that would eventually break open, become the breeding ground for more. Until anger became hatred, which, like lava heaved out of a volcano, would begin to cool. Cool until hatred became stone, pitiless and opaque.

Hatred would be the forge in which he would mold her. She would cry out for, crave, revenge, and he would give it to her a spoonful at a time, the way one feeds an addict.

He would give her what she most desired—just not the way she expected.

*   *   *

Jamal drove without pause through the morning and into the hottest part of the day. At the border, he had bribes out and ready for both the Syrians and the Jordanians. The corpses in the back of the truck were explained away as relatives being returned for burial.

At the outskirts of Amman, Jamal turned south toward Petra. He drove until he was within a mile of the ruined capital of the ancient Nabateans and its archaeological treasures.

At the end of the Gulf War, the Jordanian army fell upon the last remaining Palestinian camps and herded their occupants to Syria or across to the sliver of the embryonic Palestinian state that hugged the Mediterranean. Promoting the country's ruins and temples instead of

Arab solidarity, the Jordanian monarchy set about the business of re-
plenishing its war-depleted coffers. Word spread quickly among travel
agents that Jordan was open for business—cheap, exotic, and, above all,
safe. The baths, markets, and the magnificent treasury of Petra quickly
became important cogs in the money-printing machine.

The Israelis had watched this transformation and were pleased. It
meant one less potential battlefront to worry about. They never suspected that something else might have spirited its way to the ruins on the
tourist caravans.

Hafez Jamal had been the first to recognize that although Jordan was
lost as a terrorist staging base, it could function very well as a refuge. Provided that the force was small, well disciplined, and independent, its
members could easily blend with the ever-increasing workforce that
sprang up around the archaeological wonders. The ruins themselves—
the minor ones that were too badly weathered or too insignificant to be of
interest—served as perfect places to cache armaments, communications
equipment, and men. Best of all, the suicide squads and machine gunners were a stone's throw from Israel, facing a border that, over time, had
become porous. And once the killers reached Jerusalem or Tel Aviv, who
was to say where they'd come from?

Jamal skirted the hastily constructed apartments, cubes piled one
on top of another, built for the tour guides and administrators. The
truck bounced madly as he swerved into a byway that was little more
than a rutted path. Now came the shanties and hovels that housed the
poorest of the poor, the excavation laborers who toiled fourteen hours a
day, picking at the mountainsides as if they were decay in giant teeth.
After them came the stonecutters, and finally the sweepers, until, after
centuries of darkness, forgotten ruins were once again warmed by the
sun.

There, among the dispossessed, Jamal had built his nest. The workers
were a silent, peaceful lot who kept to themselves, so visits by the Jordanian military or security forces were rare. They were also a people who
had developed a very selective eyesight. Jamal and his force of thirty
fighters who lived on the fringe of the shanties might be strangers, but
they were also kinsmen.

Jamal parked the truck behind a wooden shack that was bigger and
sturdier than most. He was immediately surrounded by his lieutenants,
to whom he gave a brief but graphic description of the events at Samarra.

When he spoke of the death of Issim Hassan and his child, the men's eyes grew moist and their hands dropped to their weapons.

Jamal did not give them the luxury of grieving. He pointed to Manar, still seated in the truck's cab, and described what had to be done. In minutes, the women of the camp were clustered around her, cooing as they led her away to be bathed, dressed in fresh clothing, and plied with food.

After a quick outdoor shower, Jamal retreated to his tent and, from under his bunk, pulled out a footlocker. Unlocking it, he brought out a sophisticated laptop computer, which he plugged into an electrical outlet connected to a gas-powered generator.

The scope of the Internet never ceased to amaze him. There, in a setting that was several thousand years old, he was able to gather the world unto himself with a few simple keystrokes.

Jamal sat erect on the edge of the cot, the computer on his knees. He closed his eyes, saw the letters swirling behind his eyes like cosmic nebulae, gradually forming whole sentences, complete thoughts, until the entire message blazed in his mind.

With eyes still closed and a smile tugging at his lips, he let his fingers fly.

* * *

The hours crawled by and still there was no hard word that Hafez Jamal was dead.

Landau's fourth cigar, smoked down two-thirds of the way, lay cold in the ashtray. The milk in the coffee had curdled, though Landau could not have known this because he was dozing. Sleep had come like a saboteur, ambushed him, as he listened to the news cycles on CNN because he was getting nothing from his own people.

Landau thought he heard someone calling him. He looked around at the landscape of his dream but saw no one. Then he opened his eyes, blinked at the harsh light, and heard the sound again. The voice coming over the speakerphone belonged to the commo officer.

"Yes?" His voice was raspy.

"We have a report on the Syrian news."

"Punch it up."

Landau stood, placed his hands on his kidneys, and leaned back, vertebrae and joints popping.

On one of the television monitors was a dour-faced Syrian anchorman staring at the camera, not even bothering to shuffle the papers in his hands. He was reading the censor-approved text about a savage aerial assault on a peaceful village, Samarra, that had left three dead and six badly wounded. The raiders remained unidentified, but army experts who were examining the shell casings identified them as the kind favored by the Israeli Defense Forces.

Landau snorted. On "black" sorties the usual American or homegrown ammunition was replaced by rounds used by Arab forces. Shell casings would tell the Syrians nothing.

Landau continued to listen as the Syrian droned on. *Three dead. Give me a name. Jamal was important enough. Unless his face was blown off.* Given the damage he saw on the videotape, that was a distinct possibility.

The voice on the speakerphone had to call his name twice before Landau answered.

"What is it?"

"Turn to CNN, sir."

Landau dreaded the commo officer's hesitant, almost fearful tone. He'd heard it often enough from countless lips to know that it was the harbinger of misfortune or defeat.

There was the pretty American anchorwoman silhouetted against pictures of Hafez Jamal and Issim Hassan. Landau began to feel sick even before the woman spoke.

"A predawn raid on the village of Samarra, in southern Syria, left at least three people dead and six badly wounded.

"Positively identified among the dead are Issim Hassan, a ranking delegate to the recent round of Middle East peace talks, and his two-year-old son, Naji.

"The third victim was an elderly man, believed to be a lifelong resident of Samarra."

Landau had laced his fingers together and was pressing them hard against his stomach, as though straining literally to hold himself together.

Disaster.

The word tolled like the mournful notes of Kaddish.

And where is Jamal? What happened to him? It's possible for the Americans to identify Hassan so quickly. But his son?

The commentator provided the answer.

"Syrian government spokesmen are on record as saying that only Israel had the means and motive to carry out such an attack.

"In Tel Aviv, the prime minister's secretary flatly rejected the Syrian claim, calling it slander of the worst kind.

"But only a few minutes ago, CNN received information that may well bolster the Syrian claim.

"The following segment was sent to our Tel Aviv bureau over the Internet and will be run in its entirety."

Landau's lips curled back when Hafez Jamal appeared on the screen, very much alive. He sat on a cot, a laptop on his knees. The lighting was such that nothing of the background was visible. Jamal could have been in a bedouin tent or in one of Saddam Hussein's palaces.

When Jamal spoke, his words were clear yet somehow heavy, as though something was dragging them down.

He wants the world to see him grieve.

"People of Israel, people of America, people of the world . . . This morning I was witness to an atrocity perpetrated by commandos of the Israeli Defense Forces against innocent civilians and men of peace.

"This unprovoked attack resulted in the slaying of, among others, Issim Hassan, a delegate to the peace conference, and his son, Naji, only two years old.

"People of the world, I *saw* the Israeli helicopters fly past me. To my shame, I could not reach my friend in time; I could only watch as his house was surrounded and, without warning, destroyed.

"This was not war. It was premeditated murder.

"I call upon the nations of the world to condemn the Israeli butchers who talk out of the sides of their mouths. Today, something more than flesh and blood died in Samarra. Peace was also a victim.

"We Palestinians have long believed that peace was possible, in our time, for us and our children. We have made concession after concession in order to achieve it. We have agreed to put down our weapons and set free the dove."

Landau heard the phone ring. It was the direct line to the prime minister's office. He ignored it. Jamal's body language had changed. He was sitting forward, his fingers gripping the laptop. The lighting caught a thin line of perspiration along his brow, the flare of his nostrils.

For you, this is better than sex, Landau thought. *You have something to tell us, don't you? Maybe more than you intend.*

"Now the dove is no more, slaughtered by the Israelis at Samarra," Jamal continued, his voice rising. "If, before the week is out, the Israeli gangsters have not publicly admitted their role in this atrocity, if they do not offer such compensation as is possible, *and if they do not recognize the legitimacy of the Palestinian state*, then blood will be spilled again.

"People of America, hear me. I have no wish to anger or hurt you. But I must have your voice, your help. Use your power so that Israel delivers unto the Palestinians that which is theirs by treaty and by right.

"But know, too, that if nothing changes, the future will be very different from what you imagine.

"Praise be to Allah. Farewell."

Even as Jamal's last words died away, Landau was on the line to the commo officer.

"The prime minister was—"

"Was anyone able to pinpoint the transmission?" Landau snapped.

"No, sir. We've been talking to CNN. The transmission was relayed halfway around the world on the Internet before it reached their Tel Aviv bureau. There's no way to determine origin."

Landau tasted ashes in his throat. He had told the prime minister that this would be an *ain efes*—a no-miss operation. Now Israel was saddled with a disaster that would cost her dearly.

Landau's legendary victories were like thorns in his flesh. None of them counted anymore, especially his thirty-three confirmed kills off the Execution List. It was all worthless because he had accepted promotion instead of sticking with the job he did best: cleaning up the List.

Landau closed his fists and jammed them into his eyes, the way a mourner might lose his composure at a grave site. Even if at that moment he'd been granted absolution, one fact would continue to damn him forever: Hafez Jamal had been number thirty-four on the List.

*   *   *

Hafez Jamal watched with rapt attention as his image flickered across the four-inch screen of the palm-size television. At the last minute, he had decided to have one of his men videotape his message instead of just sending it out on the Net. A camera had been found and lights prepared, and Jamal had delivered his address. Now, watching it on each successive news cycle, he thought it a stroke of genius. He came across as a man wounded and torn, proud and defiant, eager to achieve peace but always prepared to reach for the sword. With a series of keystrokes, he had made himself the most famous terrorist in the world.

Jamal emerged from the stifling heat of the shanty into the cool of the night. He inquired about Manar and was told that she was sleeping, worn out by exhaustion, helped along by twenty milligrams of crushed diazepam that she didn't know had been mixed into her tea.

"Good," he said aloud. He was pleased that, for a while at least, she would not intrude on his concentration.

Jamal glanced around the camp. His men were gathered around a large fire, smoking cigarettes, talking in low, urgent tones. He sensed their impatience, their need to act. Seeing their leader on television had given them a new sense of self-worth and resolve. Old passions stirred and ancient grievances began to chafe.

Jamal called out softly and a boy, no more than sixteen, disengaged from the group and ran to him.

"Go to el-Banna. Say that I have sent for him and that he should come at once."

The boy's eyes glowed like those of a deer. Jamal watched him disappear into one of the shanties, then come out with a bag. Now he looked like any one of a thousand orphans in search of work and shelter, carrying all his worldly possessions over his shoulder.

Jamal reckoned it would take el-Banna no more than a day to get there. His chief lieutenant, his eyes and ears in the outside world, had a thriving nursery in Amman, where he grew big Jordanian roses for the upscale flower shops of Europe. His business caused him to travel a great deal, place many international calls. The cover was one of the best Jamal had ever devised for his execution squad.

Jamal lit a crumpled French cigarette. What he would have given to be in Jerusalem right now! No price was too rich if it meant he could bear witness to Landau's shame and defeat.

Jamal considered that the bloody fiasco might end Landau's career, and with it, the constant threat to Jamal's life. But perhaps not. Landau had been in the game a long time. He knew how to protect himself.

From his own kind, maybe, Jamal mused. But Landau had no shield from the Americans, whose wrath, by the time Jamal got through with them, would be terrible.

Jamal knew that America was slowly disengaging itself from Israel. Already there were discreet protocols in place calling for a gradual reduction in both foreign and military aid.

The Jewish lobby in Washington had marshaled considerable forces against these cuts; its fight had been impressive. In the end, the lobby had succeeded in stemming the bleeding, but not the private opinions and reservations of a great many American lawmakers.

Jamal had a much more persuasive way to deal with such obstacles. One way, really. That would horrify and infuriate America. Yet retaliation would be futile because the man responsible was stateless, belonging to a people who did not yet have a nation.

But after Jamal played his hand, they would have that nation. Arafat and all the other soft men would be swept aside and forgotten. A nation can have only one father, and Jamal intended to be it.

As long as the Americans thought along the exact lines that he expected them to.

As long as their outrage did not cloud their judgment.

As long as they had assurances that their humiliation would never be paraded in front of the world.

Jamal exhaled smoke, watching as it became gossamer upon the night and stars. Yes, he thought, he could satisfy the Americans on that last point.

Seven

LANDAU WAS ADMITTED into the prime minister's office at half past nine that morning. After a shower and a change of clothes, he cut an elegant figure in his quiet tan suit and polished loafers.

The same could not be said of the prime minister. Yakov Admony looked like he'd grabbed the first clothes within reach and put them on in the dark, which was almost the case.

Admony was an ex-paratrooper, a big man, who claimed whatever room he happened to be in. Now his eyes were red with fatigue and anger, unshaven jowls pulling his face down, close-cropped hair spiked in clumps. To Landau he appeared unpredictable, even dangerous.

"Coffee, Landau?" The words came out on a burst of cigarette smoke.

"No, thank you."

"Then sit."

The prime minister looked across a desk no less littered than a battlefield. The image brought memories of his service with Landau, dangerous, exhilarating times when things seemed more defined. The fight had always been righteous. The cause was always the preservation of Israel. By contrast, peace and diplomacy were a messy business.

"The American President has been on the hotline all morning." Admony gestured at his telephone console. "He was not pleased that his state dinner for the Chinese was so rudely interrupted. He wanted to know what really happened at Samarra—and why." Admony waited a beat. "So, Landau. What happened?"

"Hafez Jamal was not where he was supposed to be."

"That much I already know. *Why* wasn't he there?"

Landau shook his head. "I'm checking. Our intelligence was very good on this. Remember, Yakov: *two* sources, one of them being the Green Man."

Admony was familiar with the Green Man. His information was so exceptional that the prime minister insisted on reviewing it personally. It was the reason he'd green-lighted the operation. "Who was the other source again?"

"An American *sayan*. An old hand. Always reliable."

The prime minister crushed out his cigarette. His words lunged at Landau.

"So why wasn't Jamal there? Is it possible that the intelligence became garbled, that the Green Man and the *sayan* thought you wanted the whereabouts of Hassan?"

"This operation was not put together by spit and shoestring, Yakov," Landau said quietly. "You saw every piece of information I had before you signed off. There were no discrepancies. The fact is that Jamal, not Hassan, should have been at Samarra. And died there."

"Instead, we have the corpses of a Palestinian terrorist who saw the light and embraced peace, his two-year-old son, and an elderly man. Not to mention the wounded, some of whom, I'm told, are in pretty rough shape.

"The Americans are hounding me, Landau. The rest of the world is not far behind. Across the street, the knife grinders are plying their trade for my political opponents. If that weren't enough, the peace conference is about to collapse and talks designed to hammer out the treaty are in shambles. With one breath the Arabs call me a murderer; with the other they wail in mourning."

"Do you want my resignation?" Landau asked. "If that's what it'll take to get the hyenas off your back, you have it."

"I want *answers*! Explanations I can offer the Americans. They don't want the whole loaf, Landau. They'll settle for crumbs. But right now I can't even give them that much." The prime minister hesitated. "I can tell them our intelligence was solid—that we had a chance to surgically take out Jamal and we took it. I'll have to eat a mile of shit, but the President might come around to holding the conference together."

"You can tell him that, Yakov," Landau said coldly. "And after using you for a punching bag, the President would probably herd everybody back to the table. But you'd be wrong."

"What the hell are you driving at?"

Landau possessed an uncanny ability to compartmentalize disparate things. One part of his brain might be consumed by fury and remorse; another would be calculating what had gone wrong; a third would be choosing the best method of revenge.

Landau had had enough time to turn the facts over and over again, to play the probabilities and factor in discrepancies. When all other answers crumbled and fell away, the one left standing had to be the truth.

"We liked Hassan, didn't we? Maybe not enough to break bread with—not after the Jewish blood he'd spilled—but we could do the business of peace with him. He, not Arafat or anyone else, could guarantee that there wouldn't be any more suicide bombers strolling in our department stores or boarding our buses.

"So Hassan was important to us. Which means he was dangerous, or an obstacle, to someone else. *Cui bono*, Yakov? Who benefits from his death?"

Admony's mouth fell open. In a reflex action, he glanced at one of the television monitors. It was dark but he imagined the face on the screen.

"Jamal!"

"Yes, Jamal. Who is spinning political gold out of Hassan's sudden status as a martyr."

"Are you saying that Jamal knew we'd be after him in Samarra and that somehow he persuaded Hassan to be there?"

"Exactly so."

"Then where was Jamal when the Apaches came?"

Landau spread out his hands. "He told us, Yakov. He told the whole world: He was watching it all come down, the man who was just a little too late, a little too far away to help his 'brother.'"

The prime minister slumped in his chair. "It makes sense. Perfect sense. But you have no proof. Nothing that I can show the Americans."

"Not yet. But Jamal isn't quite finished. He didn't walk Hassan into the slaughterhouse only to usurp his position among the Palestinians.

Everyone knows Jamal considered the talks and treaty a betrayal of the Palestinian cause. He was the lone holdout among the groups that were ready to put down their weapons. No, Hafez Jamal still has things to attend to."

"What things?"

"If you can buy me time, if you think you can survive the fallout for a few weeks, maybe a month, I promise I will find out."

The prime minister brooded. "Can you do this, Landau? Can you bring me proof that Jamal betrayed Issim Hassan?"

Landau became very still. "Let me loose, Yakov."

Silence descended between the two men. Landau counted off thirty seconds and left, carrying Yakov Admony's wordless answer.

*   *   *

The tribunal that would sit in judgment over Hafez Jamal's dream assembled in a small dusty room in the warrens of Cairo's Department of Public Works. The raid on Samarra, coming only twenty-four hours earlier, was very fresh in their minds.

The two men and one woman were high-ranking members of the Iranian, Syrian, and Libyan governments. They had been chosen because each had the ear of his or her head of state.

Cairo had been selected because it was neutral ground. The Egyptians had declined to participate, but they turned a blind eye on proceedings while providing a suitable, discreet venue. The members of the tribunal played their part. In spite of their influential positions, each looked and dressed like any one of the four hundred clerks who scurried throughout the building.

Hafez Jamal entered the room, followed by a muscular young man in his late twenties. He was startingly good-looking, with features that might have been stamped on a Greek amphora. His thick hair fell in waves to his shoulders; he walked with his shoulders back, stepping lightly on the balls of his feet. In the street, people often mistook him for a star soccer player. In fact, he was Jamal's prized assassin, Samir el-Banna. Number 41 on the Execution List.

"Welcome," said the woman seated behind the desk.

Jamal recognized the Libyan as well as the two men flanking her. This was not his first time before them.

But the first time without Issim Hassan.

Previously, Jamal had stayed in Hassan's shadow, mesmerized by his eloquence, the force of his personality, which irresistibly drew to him all that he desired. Now Jamal would stand alone. Already he felt nervous and hot, and despised himself for it.

"Our condolences on your loss," wheezed the fat Syrian. "Hassan was a great leader. He will be missed."

"A tragedy," Jamal murmured.

"Yet you say it can be turned to our advantage," said the Iranian, a scholarly-looking man with a trim beard.

"I believe so, yes."

"Please elaborate," the woman said.

"Hassan was betrayed."

Jamal noted the eyes widening in surprise, the exchange of quick glances.

"The question is, who knew that Hassan, his family, and I would be in Samarra at that time? I move around a great deal. Hassan and I were in Juba, where I had already spent several days. Preparations had been made for all of us to travel to Samarra." Jamal paused. "The number of people who knew my itinerary and whom I would be traveling with is small."

"What is the exact number, please?" asked the woman.

"Three. I have gone over exactly what each individual knew and when he knew it. One can be eliminated immediately because I spoke with him about this matter in Jordan. A second cannot have been involved because he was in the presence of my adviser"—here Jamal indicated el-Banna—"at all times. There was no opportunity for him to slip away and alert the Israelis."

"The third man . . ." the Syrian said laboriously.

"In Damascus, currently under loose but effective surveillance twenty-four hours a day. He will not be going anywhere, at least not until he and I have talked." Jamal paused. "Perhaps you want his name?"

"That won't be necessary," the Iranian replied. "But a thought occurs: How can you be certain that Hassan, not you, was the target? After all, you would have gone to Samarra whether or not Hassan was traveling with you, yes?"

Jamal nodded. "The man I believe to be the traitor could have sold me out anytime. Why not while I stayed in Juba? It is closer to the Israeli border, equally as isolated as Samarra. The Jews could have sent their helicopters then. But they didn't. They waited. For Hassan."

"Yes, I see," the Iranian mused. "Still, the Jews were pleased to have Hassan at the peace table. Why kill him?"

"Not *all* Jews were so happy," Jamal corrected him. "I'm sure your own intelligence will support that. Clearly, the faction that wanted Hassan dead prevailed and the helicopters were sent in. We have seen such a strategy before from Tel Aviv, have we not? First, coax forth your enemy under the guise of reconciliation. Then, when he is plainly exposed, destroy him. Why? Because you never really believed that he would cease to be your enemy. Better to kill him now than wait for an opportunity that might never come again."

The Syrian shrugged, his body language saying that he found the theory acceptable. The Iranian's expression was openly skeptical. The woman appeared neutral, uncommitted.

"Whatever the internal politics, the fact remains that Israel launched a raid in which Issim Hassan was destroyed," the woman said. "You have come to us with a proposal to remedy, at least in part, this outrage. We are listening."

Jamal realized that all his life he had been preparing for this one moment. He had rehearsed his address so many times that the words rolled off his tongue. There were no hesitations or awkward pauses. He knew exactly which points to emphasize, which aspects to play directly to each of the three listeners. Jamal was not an orator, nor did he have Hassan's charisma, but he delivered his words with a powerful combination of startling clarity and cool dispassion.

There was a moment of silence when he finished. The woman spoke.

"Thank you, Hafez Jamal. Now, would you please wait outside?"

Jamal did not take offense. It was procedure. The tribunal's decision had to be unanimous. Jamal thought he had convinced the fat man and the woman. The Iranian bothered him.

In the waiting room where a secretary would have sat, el-Banna lit a cigarette and said, "You were magnificent."

Jamal stared at the frosted glass set in the door that opened onto the hall. Every few minutes, a shadow would flit across the glass as office workers hurried by.

"But did I convince them?"

"Absolutely."

"Even the Iranian? He seemed not to listen."

"He was listening the hardest. Don't worry about him."

The two men stared out the window at the never-ending din and the traffic that clogged Cairo. The scene reminded Jamal of a giant bazaar that never closed.

"Can you do it—if they say yes?" Jamal murmured, not taking his eyes off the street.

"Of course. The preparations are well under way. Damascus and Beirut can be handled quickly. Paris is a little more intricate, but nothing to worry about."

El-Banna, with twenty-two confirmed kills to his credit, might have been discussing a shipment of machine parts.

"America?"

El-Banna's perfect teeth flashed behind his smile. "Did you not know? I am an Italian flower-grower coming for a month-long business trip in New York. Visas, letters of potential buyers, everything has been arranged."

"Let us hope you get the chance to use them."

The two men lapsed into silence. The little room had no air-conditioning and the window was painted shut. It was better not to speak, to sit still, with eyes lightly closed. Both Jamal and el-Banna had a great deal of experience with waiting.

A half hour passed, then a little more, before the door to the tribunal room opened and the woman silently bade them to enter.

When she was seated, she said, "We have approved your plan in its entirety subject to one condition: We must see the individual you intend to use."

Jamal expected nothing less. He nodded to el-Banna, who left the room and walked to the hotel across the street. He was gone for twenty minutes.

During that time, Jamal answered questions put to him by the Syrian and the Iranian. They centered on the issue of deniability. The countries that the tribunal represented had to be shielded by a fire wall from any link to what Jamal would carry out. The Americans would be outraged. Every intelligence resource would be marshaled. They would dig deep and hard and wouldn't care whose toes they stepped on. If they discovered a hard link between the perpetrator of the act and any country that might have helped him, the bombers and cruise missiles would fly.

Jamal took great pains to explain exactly how the operation was compartmentalized. Each stage involved a different individual or team that would disappear after completing its mission. Further, only Jamal and el-Banna knew the entire sequence of events that was to unfold.

A knock on the door interrupted Jamal. He went over and opened it, stepping back to allow Manar, the widow of Issim Hassan, to step silently into the room.

Jamal was pleased that the tribunal appeared puzzled. He had expected as much. In Arab lands, the woman walks behind the husband, both physically and metaphorically. It was common knowledge that Hassan had been married, but no one had ever asked about his wife. She was never mentioned in conversation, nor did she ever accompany Hassan on political business. Her photograph had never been taken, at least not in the role of his wife. The few who were close to the Hassan clan could be trusted to take her real identity to their graves.

"Hafez," the Libyan said softly, her tone carrying an unmistakable demand for an explanation.

Jamal turned to Manar. "Show them, please."

Manar came before the table. She reached around and undid the folds of her robe so that it fell to the floor. Then she stripped away the veil and, finally, the headdress.

The three tribunal members could not believe it: Before their eyes, the traditional-looking Arab woman had been transformed into a white woman with golden blond hair, looking chic and sophisticated in a navy blue business suit.

Jamal stepped forward. "May I present to you the American I was talking about."

Eight

THE EVENING CONCIERGE at the Ritz was working on his end-of-shift log. He heard the slap of rubber on marble and looked up at the young American walking quickly through the lobby.

He smiled indulgently. *"Bonjour, monsieur."*

Ben waved. *"Bonjour."*

The concierge watched his guest go through the revolving door and disappear outside.

Ben warmed up as he jogged through the place Vendôme, lengthening his stride when he hit the rue de Castiglione. He caught a green light at the rue de Rivoli and crossed into the Tuileries Gardens, turning right toward the Jeu de Paume.

Crushed rock crackled beneath his shoes. He breathed deeply of the fresh morning air, tinged with the scent of oranges, cooled by mist. A third of the way into the Gardens, his heart rate reached its optimum level. His legs became pistons and he felt himself running effortlessly, floating. The sounds of light morning traffic faded from his consciousness. He became intensely aware of the lightening color of the sky as day cleared away the night. Exhilaration poured into him.

With his body looking after itself, Ben thought of Rachel and found himself smiling. This was the time he missed her most, in the mornings, missed the curve of her hip next to him, the warmth of her skin, the way her hair spilled across the pillow in a crimson tide. Love was slow and gentle in the mornings and he missed that, too.

Ben kept her image in front of him as he ran the length of the Gardens toward the place du Carrousel. The image, swaying just out of reach, was very much like the woman, desirable, coy, not quite accessible. After three years, Ben still found himself strolling in the halls of her character and coming across a twist or turn he never knew existed. She always had the power to surprise him, keep him slightly off balance, making his discoveries a delectable treat that she offered at the most unexpected moments.

Whether she was complex or complicated, Ben wasn't sure. In the end, it didn't matter because he understood that he was a simple man. Rachel was the woman he loved. She was the one he was destined to marry. A long time ago, he had read somewhere in the Torah that God provides in the land in which ye dwell. God had provided him Rachel, opened his heart to her and hers to his. Nothing more needed to be said or done.

Rachel's face rode before him like a kite on an invisible tether. Then, as if a gust of wind had snapped the line, she floated away, replaced by thoughts of business.

It would be the final day of depositions, with plaintiffs' attorneys making one last stab at his expert witnesses. *Good luck*. Ben was sure that the judge, who by now had had her fill, would move things along quickly. They might even be finished by noon—a pleasant thought. Ben hadn't seen very much of the city on this visit. A half day's wandering across the Left Bank had stirred memories of his first visit here, thirteen years ago. It had been his first trip outside the United States and the experience was imprinted upon him like some extra gene. Just as a gosling adopts as its mother the first creature it sees, so Ben believed that the first city a traveler visits becomes special forever. For him, Paris was that city.

He kept up the pace as he turned off on rue Saint-Honoré, with its chic clothing boutiques, gourmet shops, and wine merchants. Every so often, he veered into the street to avoid the dog shit that the tiny green-and-white vacuum trucks had yet to pick up.

A few minutes later, Ben saw the entrance to the place Vendôme. He loped easily into the ancient square, staying on the sidewalk, glancing at the polished granite and thick glass cases of the most expensive jewelers in the world. Something blue winked at him and he pulled up hard.

Ben bent over, hands on knees, breathing deeply to lower his racing pulse. He stood erect and cautiously approached the window. Just velvet-lined displays that in a few hours would be decked out with necklaces, rings, bracelets, and earrings. He'd seen nothing except a trick of the light.

No. There it was, tucked away in a corner, forgotten either by design or error. He took one look at the marquis diamond, a queen attended by two ladies-in-waiting, the sapphires, and imagined that the ring had been left out for him to see. Because such a ring could grace the finger of only one woman.

Back in the hotel lobby, Ben corralled the concierge and asked him to call the jeweler as soon as the store opened and have him set the ring aside.

Returning to his suite, he stripped, showered quickly, and donned a freshly pressed navy blue suit. He knocked on the door to his father's bedroom. Receiving no response, he opened it and discovered that Sid Poltarek was gone.

"Yes, monsieur, your father departed the hotel twenty minutes ago," the front desk clerk informed Ben when he called down. "No, he did not mention his destination." There was a hesitation on the line. "However—"

"Did someone call him?"

"Perhaps, monsieur. However, late last night he received a note by special messenger."

Note. Ben hadn't been looking for anything like that.

He thanked the clerk, hung up, and checked his father's room. Nothing on the desk or night tables. The wastepaper basket was empty.

In his father's bathroom, Ben discovered a damp bath towel, his father's toothbrush, bristles still wet, perched in a water glass.

And in the basket under the vanity, a small card, torn in half.

Nothing on the card to indicate who the sender was or a return address.

Ben placed the two halves of the card on the vanity, pushed them together, and read the few words written in elegant penmanship.

Someone wanted to meet his father at the Gare Montparnasse railroad station, located in the Sixth Arrondissement, close to the boulevard of the same name.

Sid had a meeting he'd forgotten to tell him about. Nothing more to it than that. Ben knew how his father was about clients. He never even came close to breaching the confidentiality, or on occasion the anonymity, of his clients.

But that was before Ben had taken the bar oath to uphold that same trust. From the day he'd started working in his father's office, he believed he was entrusted with everything that passed through the office doors. Sid Poltarek had never given him reason to think otherwise.

Until now.

There was something else: The way Sid had handed him the lead in the depositions. Sid's distracted reaction when Ben had told him the results. The way he had looked away when Ben asked him if anything was wrong. *Holding back something.*

Ben picked up the phone next to the wall-mounted hair dryer and dialed the bell captain. At this hour, taxis would be hard to come by.

*   *   *

Landau had said it was a priority matter. *"Extremely urgent"* was how he'd phrased it. The Paris *katsa* had heard about the botched raid on Samarra; the embassy staff talked of nothing else. He could only imagine the intense pressure Landau was under—for answers, results, corroborating intelligence. But the *katsa* had his own problems. In the wake of the raid, and the Arab outcry, French internal security had tightened their surveillance of embassy personnel. They did not want their oil-rich trading partners to think that France would allow Israeli atrocities to be hatched on their soil.

Whenever he left the embassy, the *katsa* felt French eyes on him like a noose. Landau was clamoring for an answer, but the worst thing the *katsa* could do now was to allow himself to be followed to Sid Poltarek. It was a matter of responsibility. Poltarek was a civilian, a volunteer with experience but no formal training. As astute and intelligent as he was, he would be no match for French interrogators who, if they snared him, would eventually trip him up.

Landau was in a hurry; the *katsa* had to protect Poltarek, himself, and, by extension, the entire delicate Israeli network strung out across the country. Landau would have to wait. He would gnash his teeth but he'd understand.

The day of the Israeli raid, the *katsa* led his French watchers on a typical day across the city. In the morning he went shopping for his wife's birthday present. He arranged to have lunch with a senior official from the Trade Ministry, an obnoxious fellow who the *katsa* knew was an anti-Semite. Good. Let internal security see that son of a bitch breaking bread with Jews and investigate *him*. In the afternoon, the *katsa* attended an intergovernmental seminar that had been on his calendar for months.

That evening, he escorted his wife and daughter to a fund-raiser hosted by the Israeli ambassador at the Hôtel de Crillon. Given the number of guests and the grand size of the hotel, it was easy enough to slip around the corner into the Ritz.

Poltarek was waiting for him in the hall outside his suite.

"Monsieur Poltarek. It is pleasant to see you again."

Poltarek eyed the man's black tie. He had received the telephone message to meet that afternoon. He had watched the CNN updates on Samarra. He hadn't been surprised by the summons.

"Come, let us walk," the *katsa* suggested.

He did not wish to talk in Poltarek's suite on the slight chance that it was bugged, or the greater risk that they might be interrupted by his son. The hallways were not bugged and were not covered by security cameras, which wasn't the case inside the elevators. This way, they looked like two men on their way out, talking last-minute business.

"It's about Samarra," Poltarek said bluntly.

The *katsa* ignored him. "Are you absolutely certain that your source said it would be Jamal who'd be in Samarra?"

"Positive."

"And you had no reason to believe he was lying? Or perhaps intentionally misleading you?"

Poltarek snorted. "One and the same, aren't they? The answer is no."

At the elevators, both men murmured good evening to a heavily rouged dowager with a hideous Pomeranian on a leash. They waited until she turned the corner, then the *katsa* touched Poltarek's elbow and they walked into another wing of the hotel.

"Did your man seem nervous at all? Unsure of his facts? Maybe he elaborated a little, wanted to impress you?"

Poltarek shook his head irritably.

"And he never mentioned the name Issim Hassan?" the *katsa* asked softly.

"I would have told you if he had. Look, I know the shit's hit the fan. Why don't you just tell me what you want me to do."

To Poltarek, it seemed that the *katsa* was fascinated by the wallpaper pattern. The man couldn't tear his eyes away from it.

"Yes, maybe that would be best. Do you think you might arrange for me to meet Mustafa Manshur?"

"He's not going to tell you anything different."

"I'm sure that will be the case. Still . . ."

"All right. A meeting. When and where?"

"As soon as possible. At a location of his choosing."

"He likes the area around the Sorbonne."

The *katsa* already knew that, but said, "So do I, monsieur." He added, "And please, when you vouch for me, just say that I'm an old friend, yes?"

The two men returned to the elevator. While waiting, Poltarek said, "It's not good, is it? That business in Samarra."

"Things could always be worse," the *katsa* replied lightly. "Bonsoir, monsieur. I'll expect your call in the morning."

Poltarek stared at the elevator doors after they had closed. Shaking his head, he returned to his suite, thinking he'd had enough of this bullshit. Israel he loved; some of its citizens he could live without.

Ten minutes later, he had Mustafa Manshur on the line. Poltarek assumed a casual, nonchalant tone. Using the pretext of having to leave Paris soon, he asked for another meeting.

"Does this have to do with Samarra?" the Lebanese asked.

"Mustafa, please. Not over the phone."

"Tomorrow is impossible. I can't cancel any of my engagements."

"The day after, then. Maybe early in the morning."

Poltarek heard the rustling of pages being turned, imagined Manshur tracing his finger along the lines of his appointment book.

"Very early. Seven o'clock."

"Where?"

"Let me think about that. I'll send a note to your hotel, with directions."

"Mustafa—"

"I must go now. Tomorrow, Sidney."

Which was how Sid Poltarek came to be sitting on an uncomfortable stool at a filthy round table outside a fast-food concession in one of the city's busiest railroad stations.

Morning commuters swirled around him like dirty newspaper pages swept helter-skelter by the wind. The metallic tones of computer-generated announcements made his head ache. A layer of silky soot and diesel film seemed to coat everything that he touched.

Poltarek took a sip of his coffee, made a face, and pushed the cup away. He had bought two cups, an excuse to commandeer a pair of stools.

He continued to scan the crowds, searching for Manshur's familiar face. The *katsa* had asked him to set up a meeting. Fine. He would do that. But he had questions of his own for Manshur. The name of Hafez Jamal had never been mentioned in conjunction with the casualties at Samarra. Later in the day, Poltarek had understood why: There was Jamal, braying to the world about Israeli war crimes that had claimed the life of his brother-in-arms. Rank bullshit propaganda, but it still hurt Israel. Poltarek was keen to know how Manshur had committed such a monumental error. Was it bad information or a deliberate lie, designed to mislead Poltarek and everyone else down the line who accepted it as truth?

To clear his conscience, Poltarek had to know. And he sure as hell couldn't rely on the hard, quiet Israeli to share whatever Manshur might tell *him*.

"Sidney?"

Poltarek whirled around to find Manshur standing behind him, blinking furiously.

"I'm sorry if I startled you, Sidney."

The little Lebanese was much more nervous than usual. His eyes darted across the faces that swept by. Like a small fish seeking safety in the reef, he edged up to the table, pressing himself between the stool and the American.

"What's going on, Mustafa?" Poltarek asked, trying to keep his tone light. "Going out of town for the day?"

"No, Sidney, nothing like that. Nothing is open around the university at this hour. This was the only place I could think of."

"Fine," Poltarek assured him, pushing his stool closer.

Manshur's eyes were red-veined with exhaustion, the skin underneath them dark and deeply creased. The Lebanese couldn't have gotten more than a few hours' sleep. He was weak and vulnerable, and Poltarek wasted neither time nor words.

"Jamal was not at Samarra." It was a statement, not an accusation, spoken reasonably. Poltarek did not want Manshur to withdraw into himself.

"I don't know what to tell you, Sidney," the Lebanese replied miserably. "He *should* have been there. My information was good."

"Who gave you that information?"

Manshur wet his lips with a small, pink tongue, like a cat's.

"Sidney . . ."

"You're my friend, Mustafa. I won't betray your confidence."

"I . . . I have relatives. In Damascus. Beirut. They tell me things."

Poltarek noticed that Manshur had begun to shred a paper napkin.

"Their information has always been accurate, hasn't it?"

"Oh, yes, Sidney. You know that."

Poltarek shrugged. "Not necessarily. But I take it on faith because I trust you. Still, this situation at Samarra—it's caused a great deal of embarrassment, concern."

"I know! I know! But it wasn't my fault."

"I'm not saying it was," Poltarek said soothingly. "I believe you. I want others to believe you."

"I know you said you would be leaving tomorrow, Sidney. Maybe you could stay an extra day, just until things quiet down."

The desperation in the Lebanese's voice cut Poltarek. He felt sick about the way he was manipulating Manshur. Such things were not his responsibility.

"I have to return to Washington," he said, then threw the bone. "But someone I know wants to speak to you about Jamal."

Poltarek was pained by the hope of vindication that fired in Manshur's eyes. He bulled through the rest of his words.

"He is an important man, a good man. He is aware of your past contributions. He appreciates them. Now he needs to talk to you himself."

Poltarek could see that Manshur was torn. He considered Poltarek his friend. Everything that had ever passed between them was grounded in that relationship. Now Poltarek was leaving, but at the same time offering Manshur another contact, someone who represented the same insurance.

"Do you know this man, Sidney?"

"Yes. He is a strong man. I can vouch for that."

Poltarek loathed himself. He felt dirty.

"Then I will see him. I think the café by the university would be best."

"Yes, of course," Poltarek said faintly.

"I will tell him everything I can about my information on Jamal and Samarra, Sidney. Maybe by then I will have other things, too."

Poltarek couldn't stand this anymore. He pushed back the stool.

"I'm going back to the hotel. I can drop you off."

Manshur shook his head. "I can take the Métro. It is faster."

"Good. Well, then—" Suddenly, Poltarek clamped his hand over Manshur's arm. "I want you to call me after your meeting. I want your impressions."

"Of course, Sidney. Besides, we have to continue our chess game. I have discovered a move that will astonish you."

"I'm sure you have."

Manshur was more composed now, relaxed even. Poltarek had given him no reason to question his faith in him.

As the two said goodbye, neither noticed the young man who had been wandering through the concession stands and had just spotted them.

Ben was fifty feet away, standing next to a large map of Paris mounted behind scarred plastic. Through the pedestrian traffic he saw his father embrace a Levantine-looking man, then quickly walk toward the exits.

Ben made to follow him when he noticed another man, with distinct Arab features, disengage himself from the crowd at the news kiosk and fall in behind the Levantine as he headed for the subway entrance.

It's all wrong, Ben thought. *What's Sid gotten himself into?*

* * *

Ben did not get an answer to his question when he met his father for breakfast in the hotel at eight o'clock.

"Good morning, Pop."

Newsprint crackled as Poltarek deposited the *Herald Tribune* in the extra chair. "Good morning. You're looking good. Got some color. Did you run?"

"Uh-huh."

While they ordered, Ben scrutinized his father, thinking that he was wound a little too tightly. His voice, which normally carried, was sub-dued. It was as though Sid Poltarek did not wish to draw attention to himself. *As if he's afraid* . . . Ben had never known his father to be afraid of anything or anyone.

Who is that Levantine you were with? Is he the cause of all this? What were you doing with him?

But words would not follow the thoughts. Instead, Ben heard himself say, "Did you sleep all right? You look a little peaked."

Poltarek waved his hand as if he were batting away an annoying insect.

"Fine, fine. I'm just tired." He paused. "I'm thinking that maybe we should go home early. This afternoon, even. This morning's session isn't going to go past noon, is it? Be a nice surprise for your mother."

You're bullshitting me, Pop.

"Yeah, we'll wrap it up by lunchtime," Ben said carefully. "More than enough time to make the American flight into Kennedy." He waited a beat. "Provided you don't have anything else to do."

Poltarek appeared fixated on the soft-boiled egg the waiter placed in front of him. "What would I possibly have to do?" he asked mildly, then raised his spoon and delivered a sharp rap to the shell. "That you're run-ning the case so well is the reason I'm bored." He peered over a spoon-ful of egg. "That's a compliment."

"Thanks. I got it."

I also got that you're not going to talk to me about your little rendezvous this morning.

Over the years, Ben had learned that little if anything was achieved by confronting his father. Chipping away worked some. Patiently waiting for him to come around and offer an explanation was always the best route.

Ben stirred his oatmeal and berries like a fortune-teller seeking an-swers in thrown bones. His father was a tough man, difficult to love sometimes. But Ben never doubted Sid's love for him, could not remem-ber a time when he would have jeopardized Ben's love for him by a lie.

Let it go. It's not worth the fallout.

Ben thought he could get past his anger. It was Sid's fear that contin-ued to nettle him, that and the fact that he didn't have enough confi-dence in his son to confide in him.

Because I'm not Samuel.

*   *   *

The Arab's name was Hatem and he was an expert in trailing people. Or tracking them down. Mustafa Manshur was almost too easy, a man who seemed oblivious to almost everything around him. He never looked back, stopped abruptly, or suddenly changed direction or speed. He was a sheep that never sensed the thing watching him from the shadows beyond the pasture.

Hatem followed Manshur up the rue Erasme, up the wide stone steps of the Physics Building, and down the vast, cool halls until Manshur disappeared into his office.

Hatem pulled out a cellular telephone.

"He's in the pen."

The voice on the other end belonged to a man Hatem knew well, yet it still had the power to chill him. The instructions were concise: Stay with the Lebanese until his guest arrived.

Nine

THE WOMAN KNOWN AS MANAR opened the shutters, then the balcony doors, and let Cairo assault her senses. The apartment she was in was low enough for her to smell the scent of cumin, allspice, and saffron drifting up from the stalls. The bleating of livestock and the squawking of fowl mixed with the aroma of grilling meats. Hawkers stirred as the first caravans of tourists appeared, herded along by guides who would haggle for them. Manar had once lived in Cairo. She knew there was an unspoken agreement between the guides and the hawkers: The tourist would be fleeced just enough for both parties to make a decent profit while allowing the tourist to brag to his friends that he'd struck a good bargain.

Manar gazed down at a culture and a people she had embraced as her own and asked herself if she would ever see any of it again.

"If Allah wills it, you shall."

She turned toward Jamal. He was sitting in the small living room furnished in Sears Americana, legs crossed, watching her.

When her husband had first introduced her to Hafez Jamal, Manar had felt uncomfortable in his presence. He had the uncanny ability to appear where she least expected him. She swore that he could read her thoughts whenever he wished. She recalled asking Issim if Jamal was a witch or a demon, and how Issim had thrown back his head and laughed, embraced her, comforted her.

Who would hold her now? Where could she turn for succor? Not to Jamal. Never. Manar had come to respect him, but her fear of him never completely dissolved. She understood how he looked at her, how he desired her. That he could not hide. But he would never give rein to his feelings. Jamal had worshiped Issim and would never transgress by coveting his widow.

But Issim is gone and this is the man who rules my life now.

Manar stepped back into the cool room. Everything about it was strange to her. She detested the hard lines and sharp angles and the antiseptic smell. Yet, these things, and others she had all but forgotten, would surround her in the place for which she was destined.

Manar moved to the kitchen and made tea on a gas stove instead of an open fire. She put the silly-looking steeping pot on a tray, added the cups, saucers, and sugar, and carried it to the living room. She was about to kneel and serve Jamal when he held up his hand.

"No. Serve the way an American woman would serve."

Her lip trembled and her eyes swelled with tears, but she did as he bade, standing and bending from the waist to give him his cup. She sipped her tea and almost gagged because the city water made it taste so foul.

"You must be strong," she heard him say softly. "For Issim."

Manar's eyes flashed. "My husband and child lie in unmarked graves hundreds of miles away. I have been a widow for less than a week. I have been denied my grieving. You ask me to be strong, Hafez. You do not know the strength I need just to take my next breath!"

Jamal said nothing. He was a very astute student of human nature and behavior. Manar was suffering under an enormous amount of guilt. Her husband and child had died; she had lived. Because that morning she had risen earlier than they had. Because she loved to ride into the dawn. Because no matter how fleet her mount, she could not have outraced the Israeli helicopters to share her family's fate.

Jamal understood that Manar would carry this pain for the rest of her life. It would be her Christian stigma, a wound that would never cease to bleed.

Yet from that same blood he had fashioned his most perfect weapon.

Jamal glanced at his watch. "It is time. Please go and dress. There are still things to attend to before we leave."

Manar paused before rising because she did not want Jamal to mistake her acquiescence for obedience. When she stood, she was tall and proud, forcing her shoulders back, holding her head high. Nothing less would be expected from the widow of Issim Hassan.

In the bedroom, Manar removed her robe and veil and headdress. It would be a long time before she wore them again. She went into the bathroom and stood under the shower for as long as it took her to spill the last of her tears. There was no room for them where she was going. Tears could betray her.

Back in the bedroom, she reached mechanically for each garment laid out on the bed. The bra felt tight and confining; the business suit, the same one she'd worn before the tribunal, offended her by its new-garment odor.

She stepped out and gazed straight ahead as Jamal examined her handiwork.

"Do you approve?" she asked, not looking at him.

"It is not a matter of approval. You must fit in. You do not need makeup, but some will be helpful. I'm sure that with a little practice it will be as perfect as the rest of you."

Jamal gestured at the documents spread out on the coffee table. When Manar sat down opposite him, he pushed across a piece of thick paper, folded four times, the folds brown with age.

Manar opened it. Judith Nancy Sawyer, born July 12, 1967, Laguna Beach, California. Kaiser Permanente Hospital. Attending physician: Dr. James Kendall. Parents: Lester and Joanna Sawyer.

Judith Sawyer. It had the feel of a stranger's name. And why not? She hadn't used it in almost a decade, had all but forgotten it.

An image darted out from behind the curtain of the past. A skinny little girl playing on the beach, racing into the surf after friends. Her mother, wearing huge sunglasses, laughing as her father waded in waist-deep, picked up his daughter, tossed her in the air, dunked her . . .

With one finger, Jamal pushed across a thin leather sheath, the kind that would hold a driver's license or a Social Security card.

Judith's eyes blurred. It was a photo wallet. Pictures of her mother, a formal studio shot. Her father standing in front of a Christmas tree. Without thinking, Judith turned the photo over: "New York, Xmas 1979."

Had the Lester Sawyer in the photo known that he had only three more weeks to live? Maybe he did. Because by then the trial was well under way and the portents were becoming darker with each day's session.

Judith remembered peeking into the kitchen. The wonderful smell of baking holiday cookies cut by the liquor in the tumbler. Her father sitting at the little table, her mother busy at the sink, her back to him. Her husband couldn't see the tears; Judith did, in the reflection in the window over the sink.

Lester Sawyer was—had been—a vice president in a prestigious Wall Street brokerage house. He was an honest, decent man, and such men should never be the ones to stumble upon transgression. In this case, it was a giant Ponzi scheme run by a handful of senior partners.

Lester Sawyer saw his way clear. He went to the government watchdogs, gave them evidence and testimony. He was lionized, praised, and promised his just rewards.

Until the tape surfaced, implicating him, making it appear that he had been in on the scheme from the start. Then Lester Sawyer was said to have tried to blackmail his partners. When they wouldn't truck to his demands for more money, he'd kept what he had and turned state's evidence.

The fabrications were flawless, the logic inescapable. Lester Sawyer went from accuser to accused. He lost his good name and was vilified by the same people who had applauded his courage and honesty.

On that cold January day, Lester Sawyer went to the federal courthouse one more time. He took the stand, prepared to endure the slurs and humiliation he knew would fall upon him. He let the attorney ask a few questions, then rose in the witness stand and reached into his suit coat. It was all one fluid motion—pulling out the gun, bringing the barrel to his temple, applying pressure to the trigger.

Only at the last second did Lester Sawyer hear the scream and see his daughter, who he had never imagined would be there. It was either the relentless momentum of his movement or the shame and horror of seeing Judith that made him complete his act.

Lester Sawyer, beloved husband of Joanna, loving father of Judith, dead by his own hand at age forty-two.

Jamal watched Judith close the photo holder and put it by her birth certificate. He had been a spectator to the grisly film that had played in her mind.

It had been rank cruelty to give her the photographs, but he'd been certain that the result would be exactly what he had wanted. Judith had never been able to make the world believe that her father had been innocent. The bullet that had killed him had also condemned her as the daughter of a thief and coward. To rub salt into the wounds, all the guilty parties had been acquitted. Revenge was something that Judith craved but had never savored.

Now, years later, her carefully reconstructed life had been torn apart by the murders of the only two people in the world she had allowed herself to love. Jamal was certain that when Judith had watched the helicopter rockets vaporize the life she'd made for herself, she'd seen her father's image in the inferno.

The only difference, as Jamal had whispered to her, was that this time vengeance *could* be hers.

He pushed forward an American passport.

"It's been renewed," Judith remarked, glancing at the first page.

"We have certain resources." He placed two official-looking documents beside it. "Work authorization from the Labor Ministry, your employment certificate issued by the Cairo Museum. You came here, placed your education and training at the disposal of the Egyptian people. Your offer to further the nation's historical excavations was gratefully accepted."

"You sound like a bureaucrat."

"I am quoting from the Museum director's glowing references on your behalf."

Judith did not touch the documents. "Those are forgeries."

"Of course. But the seals and signatures are genuine. If anyone cares to check, their queries will be routed to someone who will vouch for you."

"The truth is not good enough?"

"The truth is dangerous."

Judith picked up her passport. She hadn't seen it in years but didn't remember it being so worn. Of course it would have looked like this if she'd been carrying it around in a backpack from dig to dig. The pages were suitably weathered, a few stained by tea or some other dark liquid.

She flipped to the front page and didn't recognize the pale, unsmiling face of the woman staring back at her. A mannequin's face, but with fear pushing against the eyes, if one looked closely.

The first visa was dated ten years ago. A lifetime ago, when she was twenty-three, a doctoral candidate in Columbia's Middle East archaeological studies. A dormouse subsisting on government loans, college grants, slivers of departmental largesse. She had had to sleep with one of her tutors before he put her name on the list for the next expedition to Egypt. He would take her along not as a colleague or because of her expertise, but because the desert nights were cold and white women scarce. Judith later learned that it was not unusual for expedition leaders to include pliant females on the list of "must takes." In terms of importance, they ranked somewhere below a good guide but slightly above the dray animals.

Judith had swallowed her revulsion and pretended that the arrangement was nothing more than a temporary business agreement. The tutor got fucked; she got a long-term visa and access to some of the best Egyptian minds in archaeology.

Curiously, it was the Egyptians who respected her knowledge and cultivated her expertise. They were the ones who eventually made it possible for her to leave her college's expedition and join the indigenous digs.

Judith remembered how flummoxed the tutor had been, outraged—until the Egyptians took him aside and explained the infinitely slow, laborious, and often unsuccessful process of visa renewal.

She remembered, too, the man who had come to her with the offer to stay. The man who had sparked fire in her and left her breathless. Who, when he asked her to stay, was not speaking only on behalf of the Museum. It was the first time she'd set eyes on Issim Hassan, yet that was all she needed to realize that her life could never again be the same.

Judith set aside the passport. She sensed Jamal's impatience but would not allow herself to be hurried. So many things she did now, would do in the coming weeks, she might be doing for the last time.

"Your original Social Security card," Jamal said, then on top of that laid an Illinois driver's license, library card, credit and bank cards that had expired long ago.

"The driver's license and charge cards can be renewed quickly enough." He added a bundle of well-thumbed American bills. "To get you started. When you have a bank account, call this number. A wire transfer will be forthcoming—money you saved during your time here."

Jamal didn't bother mentioning such things as tax considerations. Judith wouldn't be staying long enough to merit the attention of the IRS.

He handed her a modest purse, along with a new wallet, and watched her put away the items on the coffee table.

"The last thing," he said, reaching beside him.

There were six thick notebooks, held together by rubber bands. Judith remembered them from her days at the excavations. Very clever of Jamal. If anyone bothered to look, the notebooks bore witness to places she'd been, things she'd participated in. An academic log in her own handwriting.

But there were also years the notebooks could not account for. She raised her eyebrows at Jamal, who held up a small, hard plastic carrier. He popped open the lid to reveal thirty computer floppies.

"Cheap technology has enabled even money-strapped archaeologists to record their notes on disk."

Judith ran a fingertip over the collection. "Someone did a lot of homework for me."

"You can review it on the plane. The flight is a long one."

Judith didn't think she'd need to, but she nodded. She had many other things to think about in the time left to her.

Jamal packed her notebooks and the disk case into a carry-on. Two mildly bruised suitcases stood by the door, bulging with clothes, archaeological tools, mementos. A lifetime built on falsehood, a lifetime that had nothing whatsoever to do with what she was abandoning.

The telephone shrilled.

"Your driver is downstairs. Come."

Jamal carried the suitcases to the elevator. Neither spoke on the way down. A man dressed in black pants and a white shirt stained with sweat hauled the bags to an ancient Mercedes idling at the curb.

Judith did not bother to ask if the driver was one of Jamal's men. Of course he was. Otherwise, Jamal would never have allowed him to see his face.

"Do you have his bracelet?" she asked suddenly.

Jamal had anticipated this, but he was still debating how to respond.

"Yes."

"May I have it?"

"It is a very fine, very distinctive piece of work. People might ask you about it. Why create such an opportunity?"

"Hafez, I have nothing of his. Not one ring, not a picture, nothing. I understand why. But a bracelet, it's meaningless to anyone but me." She paused. "Let me take it. Please. There may come a time when I will need his strength."

That thought had occurred to Jamal. If she'd wanted the bracelet as a lover's souvenir, he would have denied her. But he understood and believed in the power of a talisman.

He fished in his pocket and dropped it in her upturned palm.

The chain was cast of soft, yellow gold, the links thin, the clasp almost invisible. But Judith could open it in her sleep. She dropped to one knee and secured the bracelet around her bare ankle.

"See. No one will even notice."

Jamal shook his head. "Your loss does nothing to hide that you are a woman. Remember this and act with discretion." He hesitated. "But it does look beautiful. I remember the occasion on which he gave it to you."

"On our fourth wedding anniversary," she said coldly. "Who knew it would also be our last?"

"Go now," he whispered. "Go and know that you will not be alone for long. When I get there—"

Jamal was startled when she put a finger to his lips, silencing him. "When you arrive, everything will be ready. I promise."

He stood rubbing his finger across his lip as she walked quickly to the taxi. It was as though she'd branded him.

Jamal returned to the apartment and locked the door. From the bedroom, he brought out a garment bag and a small hard-shell carrying case. He took the latter into the bathroom and opened it on the vanity.

The carrying case yielded a full theatrical makeup kit that included a mirror ringed with small but powerful battery-operated lights.

Thick padded cotton strips went on first, around his waist, thighs, and hips, adding twenty-five pounds to his frame. A very expensive wig gave him a silver mane. Rubber pads placed between cheek and jowl filled out his face. Contacts turned his black eyes to a deep brown.

Jamal carefully scrutinized his appearance, made a few subtle alterations, then put on a suit that would fit over his new, bulky frame. The last item was a pair of black-framed glasses with thick but clear lenses.

Jamal picked up his suitcase and exited the apartment, leaving the door unlocked. In less than a minute, men in cleaners' overalls would come in and scrub down the unit, removing all traces of his transformation.

The bus ride to the airport took forty minutes. Jamal got off at the international terminal and made his way to the TWA gates.

El-Banna was in a café, chatting up a Swedish flight attendant when Jamal strolled by.

"You look like a prosperous fig merchant," el-Banna remarked. "Even I had to look twice."

"What of Manar?" Jamal asked.

El-Banna gestured toward the closed door to the Jetway then out the panoramic windows where a TWA 767 was pulling back from the gate.

"I watched her board and waited until the gate closed. She had no problem at check-in, which means the passport was properly handled." El-Banna knew that Jamal had been worried about the ability of their embassy contact to obtain the proper magnetic strip. "She had a coffee, bought two magazines, some perfume at Duty Free, then boarded. At no time was she approached nor did she talk to anyone."

Jamal was pleased. TWA was one of those airlines that flashed their passengers' passport numbers to U.S. Customs and Immigration at the port of entry. Had there been a problem with the passport, American authorities would have alerted Egyptian internal security. They in turn would have frozen the flight until Judith Sawyer had been removed, along with her baggage. As it was, she would now clear customs without incident. The weapon was en route and safe.

"What about your departure?" Jamal asked.

El-Banna indicated the wide hall that linked the gates.

As they walked, the two men spoke French in soft tones. Details that had been committed to memory were reviewed one last time, lost in the cacophony of the airport.

El-Banna stopped at the EgyptAir gate. He gripped Jamal by the shoulders. "I expect to hear from you soon."

"You shall. When you do, be prepared."

The two men embraced, and el-Banna strode toward the Jetway. He gave the flight attendant his first-class ticket, along with a heart-stopping smile, and disappeared into the cocoon.

Jamal hurried along the concourse to the Air France section.

The pretty flight attendant at the ticketing counter glanced from his passport to his face, stamped the security code on his ticket, and in a mechanical monotone, wished him a pleasant flight.

Walking to the jetway, Jamal chanced to glance at his reflection in the tall windows. He would never deny that he had envied Issim Hassan his charisma and coveted el-Banna's bedroom charms. Yet there was a great deal to be said for the plain and unremarkable. Jamal's old enemies had never seen him coming. Neither would this one.

As Jamal's Air France flight lifted off from Cairo, Ezekiel Landau was boarding a private jet at the far end of Tel Aviv's Ben-Gurion International Airport.

The plane belonged to a well-known Israeli electronics firm that did a substantial amount of business in France. Its designation numbers were familiar both to air traffic controllers and to French immigration. Flight 61 was always tagged for discreet, courteous handling.

No sooner had Landau settled himself in than the jet began to roll. Five minutes later, it was climbing high over the Mediterranean.

Landau got up and went into the tiny galley. There was never a flight attendant on board when the plane was on loan to the Institute.

Landau sipped orange juice from the Haifa groves and double-checked the paperwork that Bella had delivered to him at the last minute. On this occasion, he was the electronics firm's new president of marketing, a post senior enough to rank the privilege of not flying commercial. He also had use of the corporate apartment but didn't think he'd be taking the firm up on that particular perk. He wanted to be back in Tel Aviv by tomorrow morning at the latest.

The prime minister had given Landau one chance to redeem both of them for the fiasco at Samarra. Landau had been on a safe link to the Paris *katsa* even as he was being driven to Ben-Gurion. The *katsa* had assured him that the American *sayan* had already set up the meeting with Mustafa Manshur. The Lebanese was prepped to expect a high-ranking American who wished to know more about Jamal and Samarra.

Landau had passed for an American in places where Americans were scarce. To the Institute's knowledge, Manshur knew only one American: Poltarek. Landau would be coming in as someone Poltarek had indirectly vouched for. Trust should not become an issue.

Landau hoped so—for his sake and Manshur's. Landau needed to know where Jamal had been at the time of the raid on Samarra, where he'd disappeared to afterward, where he was now. It would be best if Manshur accepted Landau's impersonation and gave him what he needed. If the Lebanese suspected that Landau was deceiving him, if he hedged or balked, Landau would have no choice but to do it the hard way. It would not be pleasant for Manshur, but necessary for Landau. Landau was convinced that Jamal had sent the man he professed to love above all others into a deadly trap. What could merit such sacrifice? How did Jamal intend to capitalize on it? If Hassan's murder had been the springboard for an operation, how far along was it? Who or what was the target?

Landau could not afford to leave without answers. With Manshur, he would try the gentle way first. But if the Lebanese tried to mislead him or lied outright, Landau would demonstrate what true pain felt like. And he wouldn't have to lay a finger on the man. Just show him a copy of *Al-Ahram*, the largest daily newspaper in the Arab world, show him the front page where tomorrow or the day after, soon, Manshur's picture would appear, alongside a story detailing his long-standing relationship with and contributions to the Jewish state.

T en

A T THE CONCLUSION of the deposition, Benjamin Poltarek, metaphorically, neatly folded the hides of the two opposing counsel and
stowed them in his briefcase.

The morning session had been a complete rout. The other attorneys
stayed just long enough to mutter goodbye before beating a hasty retreat.

"I'm heading back to the hotel," Sid Poltarek said as they stepped out
of the building onto the avenue de l'Opéra.

Something in his father's tone made Ben stop short.

"What's wrong?"

Poltarek, who'd gone ahead a few steps, turned around. Ben had put
down his briefcase, the anger in his eyes spoiling for a fight.

Just like his mother.

Poltarek drew his son to the side of a newsstand.

"What are you talking about?"

"Don't use that on me. You never ask a question without knowing the
answer. We took those guys to the cleaners. Kaiser-Agfa will be doing
handsprings. But you're acting like you've just come from sitting *shivah.*"

Don't push me, Ben. Don't force me to lie to you.

But there wasn't any other way.

"I'm tired. Okay? I don't know why, but I didn't have my heart in this
case—at least not this aspect of it. Nothing tragic. You get those feelings

from time to time when a case has been running as long as this one has."
He paused, then added the balm: "Besides, you did one hell of a job. I'm
proud of you, kid. I should have said so before."

"That's not what I'm talking about," Ben said. "I mean, thanks for the
vote of confidence but—"

"Your old man's getting old. Don't make anything more out of it than
that. Now let's get going. Our flight leaves in a few hours. I still have to
pack and make a few calls."

Silently, Ben fell in step with his father. *Calls to your strange pal, Pop?*

When they reached the place Vendôme, Ben touched his father's arm.
"You go ahead. I have something to pick up." He gestured toward the
jewelry store.

"You and Rachel . . . ?"

"You never know," Ben said lightly.

The concierge at the Ritz had been as good as his word: A saleswoman
was expecting Ben. The item was ready for his inspection.

The ring was even more startling up close. Ben accepted the jeweler's
loupe and gazed into a cosmos of brilliant, fiery constellations. It was
done.

While the saleswoman handled his credit card, Ben idly perused the
other offerings in the display cases. His eyes passed over a selection of
tiny gold figurines set on thin chains, and suddenly froze. Resting on a
velvet display was a small Star of David, crafted from reddish-hued Rus-
sian gold. Ben had seen such a piece only once before. But this couldn't
be the same one. The one he was thinking of had been resting on his
brother's chest when the casket lid closed.

"Is there something else that interests you, monsieur?"

Ben glanced up, startled. "Nothing, thank you."

The woman smiled hesitantly, then returned to writing up the bill.

Ben could not tear his eyes from the pendant. He shifted to get a better look at it.

Identical.

Images of Samuel lying in the casket assaulted him. Others followed,
as they always did, grabbing hold and spiriting him away to places where
his conscience could never be at peace, pricked and prodded by memories he could never be rid of.

The end of summer at a camp in upstate New York where Ben and

Samuel had been going for years. It was Samuel's last season. He was seventeen, a senior counselor. After his freshman year at college, he would be traveling in Europe.

Ben was six years younger, thin and wiry, clumsy at sports, a boy whom girls had yet to discover. He'd had a fight with Samuel. Ben was not a good swimmer, but he had practiced hard all season. Two miles from the camp was a wide river, gentle at the near shore where the beach was located, swift and unpredictable on the other side, where one had to climb directly out of the current onto big, slippery rocks. Ben had promised himself that before going home he would conquer the river.

On the second-to-last day there was a big barbecue on the beach. While the charcoal heated up, everyone went into the water. Ben watched as Samuel, who had a drawerful of ribbons in sports, swam effortlessly to the other side, pulled himself up on the rocks, and lay back in the sun.

Ben turned to his friend. "Let's do it."

David Perlmutter was Ben's age, just as skinny and inept. The two were always the last to be picked for the baseball and volleyball teams. This knowledge that they were not really wanted became a powerful bond—and an overwhelming incentive to prove themselves. Before the summer was out, they had vowed that they, too, would bask on the rocks on the opposite side of the river.

"I dunno, Benny. It looks awfully fast today."

"Chickenshit."

"No, I mean it. Look at Jerry. He barely made it."

"Chickenshit."

Ben saw the hurt in David's eyes. He wasn't old enough to recognize the fear.

Ben stepped into the water, swirled the mud and wood chips with his foot.

"If you don't come, I'll tell Michelle you wimped out." Ben paused for effect. "On second thought, I won't have to tell her anything. She's sitting right over there." Ben waved at a tall black-haired girl who sat with her friends, all of them watching and giggling at the two boys.

"You're a jerk, Poltarek," David said miserably.

"Maybe. But I'm not the one who's been pullin' the old pud at night, thinking of Michelle."

David crimsoned, balled his hands into fists, and charged after Ben, who skipped away, dove into the water, and began doing a reasonable facsimile of the Australian crawl. Fifty yards out, he looked over his shoulder; there was David, flailing in his wake.

Ben had gone over and over the route he would take. "Never fight the current," Samuel had drilled into him. "Use it. Start well to the right of the place you want to end up in, and toward the end, let the current take you in."

Except the end was farther than Ben had anticipated. A lot farther. His arms were tiring just as the current was beginning to make itself felt. He redoubled his efforts, kicking hard with his legs. In the center of the current, he switched to the dog-paddle and thrashed furiously for the rocks.

"Ben!"

He jerked his head up, saw Samuel standing on the rocks, staring at him.

"Ben, what the hell—"

"I'm okay!" he shouted. *Yeah, sure. Shut up and keep paddling!*

With a last surge of energy he passed through the worst of the current. His fingernails scraped the algae off the rocks before he had enough faith to reach out with one hand and grab an outcrop. The rest of his body slid by but his grip held.

Awrite, bube! You de man.

Arm over arm, Ben pulled himself up, flopped over on his back, and let out a whoop that echoed clear across the river. Which was why he didn't hear David until the second time he screamed.

"Ben!"

Startled, Ben almost lost his footing on the slippery rock. Carefully, he got to his feet, in time to see David caught in the grip of the current, his thin arms slapping down on the water as he tried desperately to stay afloat.

"Ben, help me!"

Ben froze. The image of him taunting David to come in the water smashed into him.

"David, hang on! I'm coming!"

Ben took one faltering step, then froze again. The black water surged just a few feet below him, hissing as it swept through the cracks and crevices of the rocks. *I can't do it.*

"Ben, don't move!"

He felt steel fingers clamp down on his shoulder and pull him back. He stumbled and fell hard on his bottom. Samuel loomed over him, the Star of David swinging on its chain, catching the sunlight.

"Don't move!" he repeated.

Before Ben could say a word, his brother turned and dove into the river.

David was screaming wildly, trying to heave himself out of the current, slapping the water as he strained to reach the rocks. Ben watched his movements become weaker and weaker as the current held him fast, then sucked him under.

Ben inched his way down the incline until the water was only a few inches below his toes. He reached out with his arm as far as he could. David's face flashed by, his puckered fingertips a good six feet from Ben's. Then the river pulled him under.

Ben screamed, saw his brother surface, and gestured wildly in the direction where David had disappeared. Samuel jackknifed beneath the waves.

The midday sun was so strong that it illuminated the water down to about twenty feet. There was an underwater outcrop, littered with logs, branches, and debris. Ben saw the glint of a tin can. And something else—Samuel, kicking strongly toward David, who was tumbling over and over, like an astronaut whose tether to the capsule has been severed.

Samuel grabbed David's ankle and pulled him close to the outcrop and then to the cliff face. The two of them hung there, out of the current.

"Come on, come on!" Ben whispered. "What are you waiting for? Get him out!"

Then he saw it. Samuel held on to David with one hand. With the other, he reached down to his ankle, caught between the V-shaped boughs of a huge tree trunk.

Ben watched as Samuel continued to pull, but he couldn't free himself. Then he drew David tightly against him, and pressed his mouth to the boy's.

He's giving him air . . .

Samuel pulled back and sank into a crouch, holding David under his arms. In one smooth motion, he propelled himself upward.

That's it! Come on!

In his mind's eye, Ben saw his brother rocketing to the surface. But that's not what happened.

The tree trunk refused to let Samuel go. At the same instant as he was jerked back, he thrust David straight up.

David came at Ben kicking for all his legs were worth. One arm came out of the water. Ben reached out as far as he could. His fingertips grazed David's, then caught, and held. Using every ounce of strength he had, Ben slowly dragged David out of the current and onto a flat rock just above the waterline.

"David! David, are you okay?"

David was throwing up, waving back at the water.

"Samuel? *Samuel!*"

His brother was bent over, both hands working to free his foot. But the boughs of the tree were either too slippery from the algae or too thick to be broken.

"Someone help me!"

Other swimmers had heard and seen the commotion on the other side of the river and were racing across.

Ben stared in horror as Samuel's motions became slower and slower until the current was the only thing that caused him to move, back and forth, back and forth.

A brilliant shaft of sunlight pierced the depths and lit up his lifeless face, the lips slightly parted, the eyes open wide, unblinking. The sunlight shifted, wavered over the gold chain, reflected off the Magen David, and was gone, leaving Ben screaming into blackness.

"Monsieur, are you sure there's nothing wrong?"

Ben pointed to the Star of David. "I'd like that, too."

The saleswoman was struck by the pain in his eyes. "Of course. Perhaps monsieur wishes something to drink?"

It was too late to hide his tears, but he turned away to salvage what privacy he could.

The anniversary of Samuel's death was next month. This year, instead of placing a stone on the marker, Ben would offer Samuel this gift.

* * *

Mustafa Manshur's three-bedroom apartment was in the rue des Irlandais between the Lycée Henri IV and the Curie Institute. The *katsa* thought it a pleasant enough neighborhood, filled with bookstores, cafés, and small, inexpensive restaurants. It reminded him a little of

Cambridge and its Harvard Yard, good memories of his tour of duty in America.

The *katsa* glanced up at a revolving electric clock over a drugstore's green-and-white cross. Landau's jet should be touching down at Charles de Gaulle Airport in less than an hour. Customs and immigration would be a formality; the drive into the city, at this time of day, wouldn't take more than forty-five minutes.

The *katsa*'s arrival at Manshur's building ahead of Landau was deliberate. Sidney Poltarek had vouched for Manshur, and true, in the past the Lebanese's information had been very good. Although the *katsa* had a deep background dossier on the man, he could not smell him. He wanted to see where the physicist lived, who his neighbors were, what kind of building Landau would be going into. So the *katsa* spent a leisurely half hour checking all the entrances and exits, walking up and down the streets, pausing to look into shop windows, taking snapshots of the people around him. The environment measured up to the image the *katsa* had had of it. As for the apartment building, it was a standard prewar affair with half a dozen ways in and out.

The *katsa* crossed the street to Manshur's building. The normal-size door, cut into one of two garage-size double doors, was open, so he stepped in and found himself in a small courtyard with a circular flowerbed surrounding a small fountain. On his left, the door to the concierge's small apartment was open. The *katsa* heard the sports announcer on television, saw the board with apartment keys hanging from tiny hooks. The scrape of leather on cobblestone made him turn around.

The man was an Arab—Algerian or Moroccan—the *katsa* guessed. He wore a blue workman's jumpsuit stained with grease, and a tool belt around his waist.

"Can I help you?" he asked in a surly tone.

"No. I was calling on a friend."

The workman thumbed in the direction of the foyer.

The *katsa*'s next move was instinctive. He reached for the key rack and ran a finger over the apartment numbers, hesitating only briefly at 6, Manshur's flat.

Then something slammed into his consciousness. The workman's shoes. Workmen wore boots, not thin-soled, highly polished loafers.

The *katsa* whirled around, his hand disappearing into his jacket for his gun. But the Arab was well into his attack. The wrench in his hand arced, cut down, and crushed the soft muscle tissue of the *katsa*'s neck, just below his ear.

* * *

Inside the silent apartment, with its expensive Oriental rugs, Persian antiques, and riot of potted plants, Mustafa Manshur paced. He stopped in mid-stride as the clock chimed the hour, then resumed, working against the nap of the silk rug, slowly destroying the delicate fabric.

He paused to pluck a cigarette from an inlaid ivory case and snapped a lighter three times before getting a flame. He inhaled deeply and the nicotine calmed him for a moment. He tried to reassure himself that there was nothing to worry about. His wife and children would be out until dinnertime. The maid had been surprised and grateful when he'd given her the day off, with pay. Sidney Poltarek had assured him that his visitor would be prompt.

Manshur checked the clock again. Fifty-five minutes. He should have insisted that Poltarek's American boss come earlier. Waiting around like this was intolerable. Poltarek had said that he'd tried to bring the meeting forward but the logistics had made it impossible.

What logistics? If the American was traveling—as Manshur assumed he must be—couldn't he have left an hour or two earlier?

He was crushing out his half-smoked cigarette when there was a knock on the door. Manshur checked his appearance in the full-length mirror in the foyer closet. It never occurred to him to check the peephole. Even if he had, he would not have been suspicious.

He flipped the lock and turned the handle. A split second later, the door slammed into the smile he'd put on to greet his guest, knocking out three teeth and tearing open his upper lip.

The Arab in the blue overalls was Hatem and he moved like a dancer, not missing a beat. He had his forearm around Manshur's neck and was dragging him to a straight-back chair with a padded seat.

Hatem sat Manshur down, grabbed a fistful of hair to keep the Lebanese from toppling over, and reached into his tool belt for the roll of duct tape. Within seconds, Manshur was bound to the chair. Hatem tore off a short strip of tape and glanced at Hafez Jamal, who surveyed the handiwork while a third man, al-Rahim, stood by, holding a submachine gun.

"No," Jamal said. "He will want to talk to us."

Jamal walked into the kitchen and returned with a glass of water that he held up to Manshur's ruined mouth. The water turned soupy red and Manshur gagged as it hit the open blood vessels. A piece of tooth spiraled down to the bottom of the glass.

"Do you know who I am?" Jamal asked in a conversational tone.

Manshur knew well enough, but he wasn't about to admit as much. He shook his head.

"I realize you are in pain," Jamal told him. "But it is nothing compared to what you will experience if you do not talk."

With great effort, Manshur raised his chin off his chest.

"I know of you," he said in a tortured voice, wincing as he cut his tongue on a jagged tooth shard.

"Always pleasant to hear the truth. There's no reason for us to have met before now." Jamal paused. "Because you never tried to betray me—before now."

Manshur knew he was not a brave man, but he was shrewd. In a blinding moment of lucidity, he thought he might have found a way to spare himself torture and even to save his life. He said nothing until he was sure that his silence had condemned him.

"So you do not deny this," Jamal said. "Good. Tell me, were you acting alone?"

"No."

"The names of your henchmen?"

"Abdul Muhsain and Wadi Ghusha."

"Yes, of course."

Jamal produced the front pages of two newspapers and held them in front of Manshur's face. One was the Damascus daily, the other from Beirut. Each had a prominent story about the horrible mutilation and killing of two prominent businessmen. The accompanying photographs induced Manshur to vomit.

Jamal went to the kitchen and returned with a bag of scented cat litter. He proceeded to pour the contents over the mess.

"Those men were . . . ?"

"Cousin . . . wife's brother."

"Were they the ones who told you I would be in Juba?"

"Yes . . ."

"Then Samarra?"

"Yes . . ."

"And how did they learn that?"

Manshur looked up at Jamal with the limpid eyes of a dog that knows it's about to be beaten.

"I don't know," he croaked.

Jamal was neither angered nor surprised. It was he who had called Abdul Muhsain in Damascus. Muhsain, who knew him by another name —and rank, since Jamal had led him to believe that he, Jamal, was an officer in Syrian intelligence looking to trade tidbits for hard currency. As matters turned out, Muhsain had been a prompt and generous payer.

From Muhsain, the information had gone to Wadi Ghusha in Beirut, and from there to Manshur. Jamal had stumbled across this treasonous cabal two years ago, but had neither reported it to authorities nor dealt with it personally. Having a preexisting pipeline might be valuable, if only for blackmail purposes. As matters turned out, not only had Jamal been able to use the trio's activities to insure Issim Hassan's death, he had also delivered proof of their complicity to the tribunal, proof that had prodded the tribunal to authorize retribution.

Now he also had a souvenir to send back to the tribunal, evidence of just how right he'd been.

Jamal flicked his wrist. Hatem disappeared and returned, dragging the barely conscious *katsa* behind him. He dropped the body at Manshur's feet.

"Who is this man?" Jamal asked quietly.

Manshur's eyes rolled back, revealing the red-veined whites. "I swear I do not know," he whispered.

"He knew *you*, Mustafa," Jamal observed. "He was downstairs, waiting to come up, when we introduced ourselves."

"Please . . . I am telling you the truth."

"Are you?" Actually, Jamal believed that Manshur was doing exactly that. It was something else that intrigued him.

He pulled out a laminated plastic card and held it up for the Lebanese.

"No." Manshur spoke as if he were being garroted.

"Oh, yes, Mustafa. This pile of dung at your feet is a Jew. A special Jew. Who works at the embassy. 'Commercial attaché,' it says here. But you know that this is a cover. We have a child-killer here, Mustafa. Mossad."

The stench of waste rose in the room as the Lebanese soiled himself.

In Jamal's mind, this, more than any protests, spoke to Manshur's innocence. Truly, he did not know who this man really was.

"Let me speculate," Jamal said. "You were passing information that your treasonous kin were moving out of Syria. You had a contact. Not this scum. Someone else. Now, I cannot believe that you would *willingly* work for Jews. Would you?"

Manshur shook his head furiously.

"Which means that your contact misled you, lied to you, duped you because you are a gullible fool." Jamal came very close to Manshur, ignoring the foul stench. He had smelled far worse. "Tell me, Mustafa, about the man who came to you. Was he American? British? Someone like that, yes? Someone you believed could protect you. Tell me, and I will be merciful. Otherwise, I will trade your wife into slavery and your children into a harem."

Tears mixed with rivulets of sweat. "I will tell you . . . everything. Just don't . . ."

Jamal ran the back of his knuckles along Manshur's cheek, a lover's gesture. "Tell me."

"His name is . . . is Poltarek."

"Poltarek, yes. Please, continue."

* * *

The American Airlines DC-10 was on the taxi apron when Ben noticed a trim blue-and-white corporate jet touch down on the runway.

"Must be a VIP flight."

Sid Poltarek looked up from his magazine. "What's that?"

Ben tapped the Plexiglas. "That jet. Usually, they shift private traffic to Le Bourget."

"Maybe whoever's on it thinks this is closer to the city."

Ben studied the aircraft as it taxied by. He had flown a good deal and, out of boredom, had memorized the international designations of various aircraft. The numeral 4 followed by the letter X indicated that the jet's home base was Israel.

* * *

Two men were waiting for Landau when he came out of the immigration office, quiet, reserved men in expensively tailored suits befitting assistants to a globe-trotting executive. They opened the back door to the

Mercedes sedan. One got behind the wheel, the other slipped into the front passenger seat.

"Where's Jacobsen?" Landau asked.

"Staking out the apartment building," the passenger replied.

He flipped down the panel that covered the dashboard cavity meant to hold the air bag. The bag had been removed, the interior gutted to make room for the submachine gun.

"Get him on the line," Landau said.

The agent flipped open his cellular phone. Landau was looking out the armored glass window when the agent said, "I can't reach him. Either the battery is dead or he's turned off the phone."

Landau's nerves trilled. *No, not turned off. Not Jacobsen.*

"Step on it," he said.

The vehicle had diplomatic plates, so even if a motorcycle cop had been inclined to stop the speeding sedan, issuing a ticket would have been meaningless. The driver was very good, slowing the car only when he turned into the warren of streets around the Sorbonne. Halfway down the rue des Irlandais, he came up against a traffic jam.

"An accident," the passenger said.

In front of Manshur's building? No. That's too convenient.

Landau was out of the car and walking fast, the bodyguards covering his flank. He shouldered through the crowd, saying, "Doctor. I'm a doctor. Let me pass, please."

"Too late for him," a voice in the crowd called out.

It was. Mustafa Manshur lay sprawled in the street, his arms outflung, his legs at odd angles to his torso. Flies swarmed around the corpse and over the blood pooling between the cobblestones.

Within seconds, Landau was in the building's courtyard, flanked by his men. He ran past the fountain, wrenched open the door to the foyer, and took the marble steps of the staircase two at a time. Somewhere outside, he heard the telltale "hee-haw" klaxon of a police car.

The door to Manshur's apartment was ajar. Landau and his men crouched, then burst into the flat. The foul odor made them gag, but neither that nor the sight on the rug in the living room slowed them down. Each room was thoroughly checked before they regrouped, standing over the fallen *katsa*.

One of the men let out a choking sob.

"Not here," Landau said harshly. "We do not mourn here. When we get him back . . ."

Landau kneeled and removed Jacobsen's wallet, already halfway out of his jacket pocket. *Like someone wanted to draw attention to it.*

Landau fished out the *katsa*'s commercial attaché ID, made sure that that was all he'd been carrying.

"His gun's missing," one of the agents said dully. "Jacobsen never left the embassy without it."

Enraged, Landau stared at the red mass. Jacobsen had been his friend, a fellow warrior when they had been young men. Landau had been Jacobsen's best man. Now Jacobsen was a heap of raw bleeding meat. The precise Y incision from sternum to groin had opened him up, then the skin had been peeled back across bloody tissue, the entrails spilling out as the knife sliced. Jacobsen had died slowly, in great pain.

Landau clamped his hands on his men's shoulders and pushed them out of the apartment. Leaving Jacobsen behind, to be gazed at and prodded by strangers, sickened him. It was no different from leaving a fallen soldier on the battlefield. But Landau had no choice.

Stumbling, the trio made their way down the servants' staircase and into the alley where the garbage containers were lined up.

"Bring the car around," Landau told the driver. "Go ahead. Bring it around."

The klaxons were closer now, caroming off the sides of the buildings. Landau turned to the remaining agent.

"Jacobsen chose you to work with him because you were the best. I need to know what he knew—every step he took, every call that he made, every person he spoke to."

It was a bald lie. Landau could have gotten that information himself. But he understood that leadership is a coarse gift, often wrapped in deceit.

The agent nodded. "We'll find—"

"Yes, we'll find who did this. You have my word."

Another lie. Because Landau knew who the killer was. That particular style of evisceration had been Hafez Jamal's trademark for years.

Landau was on the car phone most of the way to the embassy. He spoke carefully and only of those things that would give nothing away. By the time the car turned into the rue Rabelais, he'd learned that the ambassador was attending a reception for the Israel Philharmonic. Good. Landau did not want to deal with politicians. The Institute's liaison to the embassy would be saddled with that.

The head of station was waiting for Landau when he entered the underground bunker.

"We've already heard from the French," he told Landau. "They're screaming for an explanation."

"Where did they take Jacobsen's body?"

"To the central morgue."

"Send a team to get him. I don't want some French butcher handling him." Landau hesitated. "And prepare a casket. He will not arrive in Israel in a garbage bag."

Landau glanced at the big desk, strewn with everything that had once been in Jacobsen's office. He noticed that the computer was on, gestured at it.

"We have Jacobsen's itinerary and calender. This was to be his first direct contact with Manshur."

"Set up by?"

"The American *sayan*."

"Get Washington on the line. Tell them I want everything they have on Poltarek in their *sayanim* register." Landau waited a beat before delivering his next words. "What do you have on Jamal's presence in Paris?"

The communications officers at their consoles, the agents at the computers, the two secretaries who tended to the head of station, all fell silent, as though Landau had uttered an obscenity in a holy place.

"What?" Landau demanded. "No one knew Jamal was here?"

The head of station motioned for everyone to return to work.

"We had no clue that Jamal might be here," he admitted quietly. "And the French couldn't have known either. We have sources . . . Do you want a search?"

Each head of station maintained an up-to-date list of locations that terrorists had used, ones they might favor, the names and addresses of their sympathizers.

"Jamal is gone," Landau said flatly. "He's done his work and left."

"He wasn't here only to kill the *katsa*," the head of station observed. "Maybe he was looking for the American *sayan*."

Damn right, maybe. Now, for sure.

Landau understood that Mustafa Manshur would not have been de-fenestrated until Jamal had extracted every piece of information he could.

Jacobsen would have held out longer, maybe long enough for Jamal to feel he was running out of time. But then Landau recalled the *katsa*'s corpse and knew that Jacobsen had talked, at least a little.

The head of station was very sharp. He'd been following Landau's silent reasoning.

"Jamal might know about the American *sayan*."

Landau did not respond. He had to assume that. Which meant that Poltarek was in harm's way.

"Do we know where Poltarek is right now?"

The head of station consulted Jacobsen's computer screen. "Accord-ing to this, he and his son are on an American Airlines flight to Dulles. It left an hour or so ago."

Landau nodded. At least for the next five hours, the *sayan* would be safe.

"Do you want me to contact Washington and arrange for him to be covered as soon as they land?"

That's what I should *do*, Landau thought. *The decent thing. Because it is part of our code that we do not jeopardize the lives of civilians who help us.*

On the other hand, Jamal was still out there. Would he be after the Poltareks? Were they somehow unwitting players in his plot? If so, Lan-dau needed to know. If he threw a protective blanket over the *sayan*, Jamal would never come close. He'd take one look at the security and disappear.

But whatever he was hatching would continue to incubate. That *wouldn't disappear.*

No, Jamal had to be allowed to approach the Poltareks unmolested. He wouldn't kill them—at least not right away. He'd want to talk to them first. If he took them to a location he thought was secure and did his work there, Landau could learn a great deal before dropping on them like the wrath of God.

And if he could take Jamal alive, then he could pry open, eventually, whatever horror was born in Samarra. Crush it.

"When does the next Concorde leave for Washington?"

"Sir?"

"The next Concorde."

The head of station was a humane man. It took him a moment to catch on.

"It leaves Charles de Gaulle in two hours."

"Make sure I have a seat."

"Shall I call Washington and arrange for cover?" the chief of station said forcefully.

Landau was aware that heads had turned. "No. No protective cover. Tell Washington to have a car waiting for me."

For a moment, Landau thought that the chief of station would argue—or even take a swing at him. In his shoes, Landau would have wanted to do that.

But the impulse passed. The head of station gave the commo officers their orders, then gave Landau his back.

Eleven

"Benny! Did I mention that Rachel called to say she couldn't make it?"

Rose Poltarek's mezzo soprano carried all the way up from the kitchen to Ben's room.

Ben poked his head out in the corridor and hollered back, "Yeah, Ma! You told me—three times."

It was as if she hadn't heard him. "Come down, for heaven's sake. The soup is getting cold."

Ben finger-combed his wet hair, then stuffed his shirt into his jeans.

Rachel. Her name drew his eyes to the two little jeweler's boxes on the dresser. Ben opened the wrong one, saw the Magen David. He glanced at the picture of Samuel.

"Be seeing you soon, kid," he whispered.

The table was set for three, Sid Poltarek pouring the wine.

Rose, holding a soup tureen in her plump arms, bustled through the swinging door to the kitchen, pausing just long enough for Ben to give her a peck on the cheek.

"Love your 'do," Ben said, raising his eyebrows at the platinum-colored curls that erupted from Rose's scalp. She could have been Little Orphan Annie's mother.

Rose primped. "Really? The girls say it's me."

"It's you, it's me, let's eat," Sid Poltarek grumbled.

Over dinner, Rose peppered her men with questions about Paris. Ben found it odd that he ended up fielding most of them; his father was the raconteur in the family.

"Sid? Something wrong?"

Nothing ever got by Rose.

Poltarek speared a cabbage roll and helped himself to gravy. "Jet lag."

Rose glanced at Ben with a raised eyebrow.

Mother and son carried on a lively discussion all the way through dessert. Ben loved sparring with her. Rose had been an economics professor at Georgetown and a consultant to the governors of the Federal Reserve. She knew Washington cold, had been—and still was—courted by some of the capital's most powerful figures. Information is power, and Rose Poltarek had thirty years' worth of facts, background, and gossip to mine.

"I'm going to catch up on the mail," Sid announced.

"Fine," Rose told him. "But only one cognac. I want you to get a good night's sleep so that you can enjoy the opera tomorrow."

"As if such a thing is humanly possible," he mumbled, retreating to his study.

"What about you, Benny?"

"Going out."

Rose nodded knowingly. "Take your jacket. The nice brown leather one. It's still cold at nights. And give Rachel a hug for me."

Grabbing his jacket, Ben stole a glance at the velvet box on the dresser. The ring. *Yes? No?*

He shook his head. Wrong time. Wrong place.

The perfect moment would suggest itself, probably when he least expected it.

* * *

Ben Poltarek was not the only one with an appointment to keep that evening.

El-Banna had arrived on the New York–Washington shuttle several hours before the Poltareks. Now he was settled in a fine room at the Ritz Carlton in Tysons Corner, halfway between Washington Dulles International Airport and the city, waiting.

El-Banna had gone directly to his room and unpacked his laptop computer. As expected, he had e-mail. But the message from Hafez Jamal in Paris was not one he'd anticipated.

Jamal wrote that he'd had a lengthy dialogue with M.M. El-Banna snorted. He could imagine exactly the kind of "dialogue" Jamal had induced from Mustafa Manshur.

It appeared that Manshur had passed the information regarding the Samarra raid to an American lawyer, Sidney Poltarek. Poltarek, accompanied by his son, had been in Paris on business. Manshur used this and other visits to feed American intelligence.

But Manshur had been duped. Poltarek was working not for the Americans but for the Israelis.

So that's how they had known where to strike, el-Banna thought. He was familiar with Mossad's use of Jews around the world. Clearly, this Poltarek was a *sayan*. His son, too, probably.

The introduction of Poltarek had caused a complication, Jamal continued. Minor, but one that had to be dealt with.

Clearly, Poltarek had passed along Manshur's information on the Samarra raid to the Israelis. But Poltarek had no reason to believe that his actions might have had unintended consequences for Manshur. If Poltarek did not already know, he would soon learn of Manshur's death— and that it had not been from natural causes. This would prompt Poltarek to contact his Israeli handlers to obtain details. But Poltarek might have another motive. He might have *other* information from Manshur that he hadn't passed along, things that Manshur might have mentioned about Jamal.

Another possibility was that when the Israelis heard about Manshur's demise, *they* might want to have a long, quiet chat with Poltarek to see what else besides Samarra he and Manshur had talked about.

Either way, Poltarek—as well as those he might confide in, such as his wife and his son—was a liability if not an outright threat.

Jamal's e-mail closed on the note that el-Banna was extremely successful when it came to eliminating such threats.

El-Banna smiled at the compliment. However, there was a problem. His job in the United States was to pave the way for Manar to reach her target. In order to do that, he was obliged to establish and maintain a discreet profile. Going after Poltarek ran against the grain.

El-Banna e-mailed back, acknowledging receipt of the message. Then he called an Arab bakery in Bethesda and placed an order with the proprietor.

While waiting for delivery, el-Banna found the Poltareks' home and business addresses in the directory. The work number was listed, but not the one for the house. No matter.

The Internet is a wonderful tool for one who is curious about the comings and goings of people in the public eye, which, as el-Banna soon discovered, the Poltareks were. Husband and wife were active in charity circles—for both Jewish and non-Jewish causes. Their names appeared regularly in society and business columns. There was even a small piece about the son, who was an amateur magician.

El-Banna found that tidbit useless, but there were others. Particularly about Rose Poltarek's love affair with the opera. She was on the Kennedy Center committee. There was a gala scheduled for tomorrow night. The work to be performed was *La Bohème*, with Freni and Pavarotti, and Zubin Mehta conducting.

Poltarek had bought a table for the reception afterward. Twelve chairs, two thousand apiece. Such largesse would guarantee the Poltareks' presence.

El-Banna turned off the computer. For the next hour, he made handwritten notes on hotel stationery. The plan unfolded with startling clarity. It had all the necessary elements: simplicity, surprise, speed, and certainty. El-Banna reviewed it thoroughly, playing devil's advocate, but found no flaws.

When the doorbell sounded, he gathered up his notes and the top three blank sheets on the pad, tore them up, and flushed them down the toilet.

El-Banna's guests were two well-dressed men who were often mistaken for Arab diplomats or businessmen. In fact, they were trusted longtime associates of el-Banna and Hafez Jamal. By day, they oversaw a chain of coin-operated laundromats in Baltimore; at night they went home to their families. On April 15, they paid their taxes.

But on very special occasions, their mundane lives became a little different. Graduates of el-Banna's school for assassins, they quietly maintained their skills, never losing their edge, knowing that one day these talents would be called for.

When they looked into el-Banna's eyes, they realized that such a day was at hand.

* * *

In Washington, Landau, too, was tending to business. Before leaving the Paris embassy, he had closeted himself in the communications chamber. Now, the call he had made was bearing fruit over drinks with an elegant woman at the Four Seasons hotel in Georgetown.

FBI Special Agent Kaelin Reece was in her late thirties, slender, with hair the color of blond jarrah wood and eyes as gray as the arctic mist. She had spent fifteen years in the field before voluntarily switching to the Bureau's administrative side. Currently, she was the number-two person in the FBI's antiterrorism division.

If Landau had to meet people in public, the Four Seasons cocktail lounge—a large atrium, really—was the best venue. The tables were spaced well apart; side-by-side seating on the banquettes allowed a discreet sweep of the room every now and again.

"It's nice to know you still remember to take a girl out for a drink," Reece said. Her voice carried a slight smoker's rasp.

"You were at the top of my list," Landau replied gallantly. "After all, it's been a while."

"You mean nearly two years."

Landau offered up his most dazzling smile. "I am contrite."

Reece sighed. Landau was a character. Slippery, dangerous, but a character. And he had taste: the champagne was a rare Louis Roederer. In terms of information, he gave as good as he got. Reece wondered if that was true of him in bed.

"You mentioned that this concerns our friend, Jamal," she said.

Landau always couched his intentions in an angel's-hair nest of lies. "Yes. We're interested in him, given what happened at Samarra."

He knew that Reece had almost as much information on Samarra as he had. He would dole out additional tidbits as required.

"Your people screwed that one up royally," Reece observed.

"Please, don't spare me. Tell me *exactly* how you feel."

"For heaven's sake, Landau. You went after a rat with a sledgehammer and took out a good guy." She noted his arched eyebrows. "Okay, not exactly a saint, but someone you were at least talking to."

"From the world reaction, you'd think we'd burned Gandhi at the stake."

"Enough. What's he done? Why are you on his ass?"

"You don't know?"

"Let me guess: Paris, about sixteen hours ago, one Mustafa Manshur takes a header out his window. You think Jamal was in on it."

The first of the lies appeared now, delicate and soundless, like a string of ballerinas gliding along the stage.

"The French seem to think so. They called *us*."

Reece frowned. She hadn't heard that particular take. But it made sense: The French toadied up to the Arabs every chance they got. Pissing them off was bad for business. Better to hand the mess to the Israelis and tell them to settle it somewhere far, far away.

"And your take is . . . ?"

"That Jamal and Manshur were in business together." A pause for effect. "That this business may have brought him over here."

"Recently."

"Very."

Reece stole a glance at the sealed manila envelope on the banquette beside her. *Not yet.*

"Any thoughts as to why?"

"Nothing we can put our finger on yet."

"Nothing that would be of interest to us?"

Landau feigned hurt. "I have never withheld anything like that from you, Kaelin."

That was true—and it was the only reason why she now placed the envelope on the table.

"Immigration control photos for the last twelve hours, covering JFK, Dulles, Boston, Chicago, Atlanta, and, on the off chance, LAX. I didn't see Jamal in there, but like all of us, he's getting older, maybe had a nip-and-tuck. You'd know better than I would."

"About nip-and-tucks? I don't think so, Kaelin."

"Oh, piss off." Suddenly, her eyes went cold. "Listen to me. If you spot something in those pictures, I expect you to share. I heard Jamal's graveside speech like everybody else, except I tend to think more the way you do."

"And how is that, Kaelin?"

"This son of a bitch is no Issim Hassan. He's not going to change his spots. I don't think it'd be a loss to humanity if he fell off the edge of the universe."

"Kaelin, Kaelin. Policy-making is for politicians—"

"Save it for the virgins, Landau. Policy is what gets done after the likes of you and me have finished." She raised her flute, and Landau thought that her voice was almost as sad as her eyes. "Shalom, Landau."

When Landau returned to his room, three men were waiting inside. He was not surprised, merely annoyed that they had raided his minibar.

"Don't they serve dinner on planes anymore?"

Yossi Tarnofsky spoke through a mouthful of peanuts. "Only an hour and ten minutes from Ottawa. The Canadians have switched to crackers."

Landau embraced each man in turn. In the Institute, the agents were referred to as Landau's boys and girls. He might send them into harm's way, demand sacrifices or even their lives. But not for a second would he hesitate to walk alongside them on the same road.

Tarnofsky and the other two agents, Bernstein and Rothman, slouched against the walls. Landau put on some jazz for background.

"No trouble coming in?"

The three men shook their heads.

Organizing a Sayret Metcal operation that relied on a three-man tactical team was difficult even with sufficient lead time. In this case, Landau had to have the unit on site and ready to move by the time he arrived in the American capital. Using embassy security personnel was out of the question. Landau was under no illusion as to the fallout that would ensue if the Americans, who monitored Israeli movements in the capital, caught wind of a developing operation.

The only solution lay in raiding the talent in the Israeli embassy in Ottawa. A few years ago, Landau had deliberately overstaffed his Canadian contingent for just such an eventuality. His men had the best credentials—partners in a high-tech firm that did a lot of work with a company in Virginia. The free trade between Canada and the United States made the infiltration virtually risk-free.

"Who's the target?" Tarnofsky asked quietly.

Landau passed around photographs and bios of the Poltareks.

"They are *sayanim*."

Landau had no idea that with these three words he had committed a terrible error. Nothing in the way they rolled off his tongue alerted him. Later, as he gazed upon the wreckage, he would try to remember if he had been a little overtired, too anxious to get to the meat of the briefing.

"We think that Hafez Jamal has taken a special interest in them," he finished.

The mention of Jamal's name hardened the faces of the men listening. The terrorist had the blood of their comrades on his hands.

Nor did they flinch when Landau described how the Poltareks were to be used as bait. Morality held no sway here, not if it meant that Hafez Jamal might be taken.

"I'm not sure that Jamal is in the country," Landau continued. He ripped open the envelope that Kaelin Reece had given him, spilling black-and-white 8x10s across the bed. "Maybe these will tell us."

Ten minutes later, one of the pictures did.

"El-Banna," Bernstein said in a monotone. "Jamal's prize calf."

The four men stared at the overhead shot of a chic young man with a ponytail presenting his passport at the immigration counter.

"The Americans didn't pick up on this?" Rothman demanded.

"They weren't looking for el-Banna." Landau looked at his men. "And there's no reason to educate them."

The agents nodded. El-Banna's presence in the United States meant that Jamal was definitely running an operation. If the Israelis shared this information without knowing the details, the Americans wouldn't wait. They'd run el-Banna to ground, then let his lawyer cloak him in his constitutional rights. El-Banna would remain silent until the FBI ran out of patience or a judge ordered his deportation. Nothing would have been learned, and Jamal's operation would remain on track.

"However," Landau said softly, "if you were to pluck el-Banna *before* he gets near the Poltareks, you might induce him to discuss his current business. He might even care to share his thoughts on Jamal's role and whereabouts."

"Do we care about el-Banna?" This was Tarnofsky's way of politely asking if, after the interrogation, Landau wanted to haul the assassin's carcass to Tel Aviv.

"I doubt that even his mother cares about him," Landau replied flatly.

"The Poltareks," Rothman said. "Who is el-Banna most likely to target?"

Landau tossed him another tin of cashews and made stiff drinks for everyone. The glasses were drained by the time he recounted the events in Paris, the murder of Mustafa Manshur and the Paris *katsa*, Jacobsen.

"Sidney Poltarek," Landau said. "He was Manshur's go-between. He's the one el-Banna will focus on."

"Do we have details on his movements, habits, that kind of thing?" Tarnofsky asked.

Landau passed him the *sayanim* register's file on Sid Poltarek that he'd been handed via the Paris embassy just prior to boarding the Concorde.

"Read."

* * *

The nurse at the admitting desk at the Children's National Medical Center looked up and waved at Ben as he came through the doors.

"Long time no see, Ben. Still doing the show for the kids tomorrow night?"

"You bet."

The nurse smiled flirtatiously. "Know where to go?"

"By heart."

Her laughter followed him down the halls, empty now that visiting hours were over and the children had been put to bed.

Ben passed the physicians' lounge, where a trio of doctors in surgical greens sat drinking coffee. A fourth doctor was immersed in the bulldog edition of the *Washington Post*.

Beyond the lounge were the supply closets, then the changing rooms. One of the doors was marked with a lightning emblem, indicating that it was the electrical room. Ben tested the handle, then went inside.

The smell of antiseptic and floor wax was replaced by spice—cinnamon—from a pair of candles on the narrow shelf above the single bed. Ben was still getting his eyes accustomed to the dim light when a pair of arms snaked around his chest, nimble fingers working quickly to unzip his jacket.

"You're wearing way too many clothes, Mr. Poltarek," a husky voice whispered.

Ben felt warm breath on his ear. His head was filled with cloying perfume. His breath came in gasps as clothing fell to the floor.

"No. Don't turn around. Not yet."

Ben felt her breasts push against his back, her nipples already aroused.

Her thigh slipped between his, her pubic hair teasing him as she reached around and took him in her hand, caressed and fondled him.

Slowly, so she wouldn't let him go, he turned around and fell into her eyes, buried his fingers in the masses of her red hair, covered her mouth with his. His hands trailed over her body, gliding, squeezing, making her whimper and gasp until she led him to the bed.

"I love you, Ben."

"I love you, too, Rachel."

His lips slipped over her breasts, across her taut stomach, down the insides of her thighs and then back up again. He cupped her buttocks and raised her slightly so that he could taste all of her, lose himself in the roar that filled his head.

After an eternity, he felt her tug hard at his hair and understood what she wanted. Rachel's legs parted for him as he covered her. Her fingers guided him into her, and with a sharp cry she raised her hips to meet him, tightening herself around him, rocking all the while, whispering his name to the universe.

* * *

"So, Poltarek. Who'd you sleep with in Paris."

Rachel finished hitching up her baggy khaki pants and faced Ben with hands on her hips.

"Excuse me?"

"You heard me the first time. You did things to me you've never done before."

"That's so bad?"

Rachel leaned forward and kissed him hard. "Nope."

On the way out, Rachel removed the lightning emblem tacked on the door by a Velcro strip. She left the emblem at its designated place behind the nurses' station. The night was young; someone else was sure to use the DO NOT DISTURB signal.

Rachel slipped her arm through Ben's as they walked down the hallway. The overhead lights brought up the half-moon swirls where a floor polisher had buffed the tiles.

"Are you still coming to do the show tomorrow?"

"Absolutely." He paused. "Maybe we can have dinner after."

She looked at him curiously; Ben couldn't hide anything from her.

"A special occasion?"

He reddened. "Maybe."

Rachel laughed. "I'll check my rounds, let you know. Okay?"

They held the kiss even after the elevator doors opened.

"Drive carefully. It's supposed to start raining."

"I'll call you tomorrow."

Ben slumped against the wall of the car, slightly giddy, happily exhausted. The image of the ring on Rachel's finger burned in his mind.

The admissions area was still quiet. Ben raised his hand to wave goodbye to the duty nurse when a faint voice got his attention.

Opposite the admissions desk was a reception area with a dozen soft chairs, coffee tables with magazines, and a wall-mounted television. Without fully understanding why, Ben was drawn to it. The CNN announcer's drone became more distinct.

". . . Paris earlier this afternoon, a Lebanese-born scientist, Dr. Mustafa Manshur, was killed after falling three stories from his apartment window."

The monitor showed a split screen: the chaotic scene in a Paris street and a passport-style photograph of the victim.

"Shit, no!"

The man on the screen was the one Ben had watched his father talk to at the Gare Montparnasse. Ben would swear to it.

"Everything okay, sweetie?" the duty nurse called out.

"Sure. Fine."

According to the announcer, the police were treating it as a robbery gone bad. The body of another man, presumed to be the assailant, had been found inside Manshur's apartment.

The station went to a commercial.

Ben felt the nurse's eyes on the back of his neck. He forced himself to smile as he passed the admitting desk. Outside, he moved off to the side, away from the light.

Coincidence? *It can't be!*

Was it really the same man who'd been talking with his father? *Absolutely.*

Ben had always had a good memory. His training as a magician had honed it to an excellent one. No question that the man at the train station and the one on the screen were one and the same.

Does Pop know?

Ben dug into his pocket for his car keys. A cold wind had come up, pushing heavy clouds ahead of it. Rain was on the way. After starting the engine, Ben fiddled with the heater.

He drove carefully through the traffic on Michigan Avenue, skirted the McMillan Reservoir, and made a left on Seventh Street. It wasn't until the traffic thinned that he noticed the big sport utility vehicle two cars behind him.

The same one he'd seen out of the corner of his eye as he'd left the hospital? Ben cursed softly; he should have kept his mind on driving instead of on the image of the dead man in Paris. It might be the same one, distinctive because of the rack of roof-mounted floodlights.

Ben turned into the right-hand lane. The truck followed suit.

Ben slowed until he came to the next corner, then made a hard left and goosed the accelerator. He was halfway down the block before his rearview mirror exploded with light, momentarily blinding him.

Instinctively, Ben hit the brakes, the rear end of his car drifting left. Now the lights from the SUV filled the interior. Even with the windows up, he heard the roar of a custom-tuned engine.

Ben wrenched the wheel to the right, but that sent him into a spin. Now his car was facing the truck as it bore down on him. Ben threw himself across the center console and got his feet out of the well. The shriek of metal shearing metal filled his head. Something snapped, like a rotten tree limb, and clattered away into the night. A rush of air like that created by a locomotive rocked the chassis of his car.

Cautiously, Ben raised himself up. The truck was gone, so was one of his side mirrors, and he was pointed in the wrong direction. Traffic crept by him, people staring at him through rolled-up windows, mouthing obscenities he couldn't hear. He got back behind the wheel and pulled into a handicap parking space.

Slumped over the wheel, a single word reverberated in his mind: *carjacking*. He'd heard about it on the news, read about it in the paper, but had never come close to appreciating the terror it could bring on. It made sense: The fancy truck—probably stolen—the "follow home" tactic. If he hadn't spotted the truck, its occupants might have trailed him all the way to the condo building.

Ben took a deep breath and started the engine. This time he drove quickly, constantly checking the rearview mirror.

The doorman whistled at the damage. Ben told him he'd been sideswiped in the hospital parking lot.

The apartment was silent when he entered. Even his father's study was dark.

Tomorrow, he thought wearily. He would ask him about Manshur tomorrow.

Twelve

W HERE'S POP?"
    Ben entered the country-style kitchen and kissed his mother on the cheek.

Rose Poltarek, wardrobe and accessories by Chanel, glanced up from the *Wall Street Journal*.

"Not even a 'good morning'?"

"Good morning. Where is he?"

"He left early. Breakfast with a client."

Ben poured himself some grapefruit juice and tried to think who the client might be. His father had cleared the rest of this week, thinking he wouldn't be back from Paris until the weekend.

"Where are you headed?" he asked.

"Alan wants to have a chat."

Alan was Alan Hirsh, the current chairman of the Federal Reserve.

"Tell him for me that interest rates are too high."

Rose looked at him slyly. "You might want to think of refinancing in the next month or two."

They left the apartment together. Fortunately, Rose's car was brought up first, so she didn't see the damage to Ben's vehicle.

Looking at the ugly scrapes along the driver's door, Ben was angry with himself that he hadn't been quick enough to get the truck's plate number.

The offices of Poltarek & Associates were located on C Street near the tip of the Federal Triangle. Mary, who'd been with Sid Poltarek for twenty years and ran the business with Teutonic efficiency, hugged Ben as he stepped out of the elevator.

"Welcome home, honey."

Mary was a full-figured, Earth Mother type, a dervish propelled by good cheer. She was the closest thing to an aunt that Ben had.

Ben slipped her a flagon of perfume he'd picked up at Duty Free.

"Ooh! This'll make Steve crazy! You're a doll."

"Do we have the *International Herald Tribune* somewhere?" Ben asked.

"On Sid's desk."

"Speaking of Sid, where did he go this morning?"

"The Martel brothers heard he was coming back early. They were all over me to shoehorn them in. Something about pending antitrust legislation. They're talking about it over at the Hay-Adams Hotel."

Ben stopped by his father's office and plucked the *Herald Tribune* off the top of an array of newspapers and journals. Settled behind his desk, he switched on CNN, then began going through the paper.

There it was, on page 4, complete with a picture of Manshur's building. Ben paused from his reading as the news cycle came on, but there was nothing about the murder in Paris.

The *Herald Tribune* was long on speculation, short on facts. The police had no clear evidence or any eyewitnesses to substantiate that Mustafa Manshur had been murdered by the dead man, still unidentified, who'd been found in the apartment. Manshur's wife, resting in a Paris hospital, had not been able to provide any explanation. The physicist's colleagues at the Sorbonne weren't aware that Manshur might have had enemies.

A physicist.

What the hell had Sid been doing, skulking around a train station with a physicist?

Ben mentally ran down the list of his father's friends and acquaintances around the world. It was a long one and he went through it twice to make sure he hadn't missed anyone. The name Mustafa Manshur did not resonate.

Which didn't necessarily mean anything. Given Sid's penchant for discretion, Ben reckoned there were a lot of characters whose names had never been mentioned—especially if they worked for governments.

Here was another tack: Manshur had been an academic. Governments and private industry often recruited from colleges or had professors on their payroll, sometimes on a sub rosa basis. If Manshur had been involved in combined college and industry research, or had been moonlighting, the French media hadn't made the connection.

Ben tossed aside the newspaper and killed the picture on the monitor. The connection between his father and the dead man continued to nettle him, but the stacks of files on his desk beckoned. He had been away too long.

*　*　*

The morning after he had activated his tactical incursion team, Landau walked in unannounced and took over the Israeli embassy.

The only warning the officials had was a frantic radio transmission from the two plainclothes security men who patrolled the sidewalk in front of the tan brick bunkerlike structure on International Drive.

Ambassadors in the service of Israel knew about Landau's unbending principle: He did not go to Canossa, a reference to the Italian castle where Henry IV of the Holy Roman Empire, dressed like a peasant, had prostrated himself at the feet of Pope Gregory VII in 1077. Meaning he bowed to no one. When Landau came to an embassy, everyone, from the ambassador to the janitor, answered to him. The few diplomats who insisted on querying Landau's presence learned the error of their ways.

The ambassador to Washington was an old hand. He greeted Landau politely, then left for a meeting at the State Department. Landau proceeded to commandeer the secure room in the subbasement and had the *katsa* bring him three of his best people: a *bodel*, the courier who runs messages between the embassy and the Institute's safe houses; a *marats*, an expert in languages and dialects; and a communications specialist.

After the three were assembled, the secure room was deemed off-limits. The communications officer made contact with Landau's hunters in the field. The *marats* was standing by to translate or explain any unusual dialogue the incursion team might come across. The *bodel* waited in the wings in case Landau needed to get information or matériel to the team's safe house.

The house was the best of the Institute's Washington real estate—a nineteenth-century cottage built of fieldstone and timber, in Dent Place, between Wisconsin Avenue and the Georgetown University campus. Its thick walls had been padded with soundproofing material. Inside was a small but well-equipped medical dispensary, two bedrooms for nonofficial visitors such as the incursion team, a sophisticated communications station, and the requisite safe room that doubled as an interrogation chamber.

The whole cottage was riddled with "slicks"—hiding spots, easy to reach but hard to spot, where weapons were stored.

"What are the unit members' designations, sir?" the commo officer asked.

Landau ignited a cigar. "Larry, Moe, and Curly."

There were discreet smiles all around. Landau was said to have a fondness for slapstick, although this had never actually been verified.

The commo officer sent out his digitally scrambled bursts. The replies came back instantly.

"The blanket has been secured, sir," he reported.

Landau examined the plume of his cigar smoke. "Now we wait. Anyone for gin rummy?"

No one dared to refuse even though it was well known that Landau was a ferocious cheat.

* * *

At noon, Ben put a call into the Hay-Adams. The switchboard operator informed him that there was a call block to the Martels' suite. Ben dug their private number out of the files. The secretary who answered told him that the brothers and Sid Poltarek were in conference and could not be disturbed for anything short of a genuine emergency.

Ben had had it with the runaround. He'd talk to Sid tonight, before he and Rose went to the opera.

The first raindrops spattered against the windowpanes. Ben looked at the files strewn across his desk and asked Mary to call the deli for a tuna fish on wheat. The rain would create a traffic nightmare. By working through lunch, he'd be able to leave early. His performance suit was still at the cleaner's, and he had to make a stop at Wanda's Witchcraft and Magic Shoppe on Vermont Avenue to pick up a cake baking pan.

* * *

Samir el-Banna welcomed the rain. It made people keep their heads down, mind their own business. It was harder to identify faces and features, vehicle tags and models. El-Banna smiled as the dark clouds lined up on the horizon, comforted by the camouflage and anonymity the rain would bring him.

It was half past five in the afternoon and he was sitting in one of the public rooms at the Hay-Adams, with a view of the elevators. The area had a direct line of sight to the concierge's desk. Not that this mattered to the assassin.

El-Banna's wardrobe consisted of a beautiful, handcrafted Zegna suit finished off by a Rolex and Gucci loafers. For a prop, he had a slim black leather briefcase with brass trim.

The sitting area was serviced by the staff who worked in the lounge. El-Banna had ordered an aged bourbon from a fetching waitress who turned just so to display a formidable cleavage as she placed his drink on the table.

El-Banna flirted with her, spoke knowledgeably of the flower business, and hinted that if the rain canceled his shoot, he might return to the hotel when she finished her shift.

Satisfied that the waitress's gossip would soon reach the concierge— and, via him, hotel security—el-Banna enjoyed his drink. There was no reason not to, since Poltarek had not left the seventh-floor suite he'd entered early that morning. El-Banna knew this because there was a microtransmitter in the handle of the fruit basket that had been delivered to the suite, allegedly compliments of the manager. Across the street, in a small van parked by Lafayette Park, one of el-Banna's associates monitored and recorded the conversation. Had Poltarek been preparing to leave, el-Banna would have been on him like a cheetah on a peccary.

The pager in his pocket vibrated against his thigh. Poltarek was moving.

El-Banna finished his drink, then went to the pay phones at the entrance to the men's room.

"The wife?"

"On the other side of the city," the second killer responded. "She is at home. The dry cleaner delivered an evening gown."

El-Banna told him what to do next, then returned to the foyer in time to fall in step with Poltarek, who'd just exited the elevator. He watched the lawyer step into a cab and was close enough to hear the address he gave to the driver.

Unexpectedly, Poltarek was going back to his office.

* * *

Landau's tactical incursion team had picked up Poltarek when he'd left his condo that morning. They'd followed him to his office and had just settled down to wait when they saw him reemerge and hail a cab. There was a terse exchange between Yossi Tarnofsky and Landau until it became clear that Poltarek's destination was the Hay-Adams.

Landau called Poltarek's office, identified himself as a court clerk, and learned that the attorney would be out for the rest of the day—at the Hay-Adams. Landau passed this information to Tarnofsky, who proceeded to set up surveillance.

The Israeli embassy has a number of vehicles in its garage, all of them with interesting modifications. The black Lincoln Town Cars driven by each member of the team were heavily armored, equipped with radio scramblers and assault weapons. The markings on their bumpers indicated that they belonged to a livery fleet.

Tarnofsky, Bernstein, and Rothman were dressed in dark, conservatively cut suits. Completing their chauffeurs' uniforms were visored caps. They had parked their cars in the street in front of the hotel. In a city filled with limousines, they drew no attention from the hotel's doormen and valets or the police who regularly cruised the area.

However, in spite of the team's vigilance, two mistakes had already occurred.

The team did not realize that one of el-Banna's killers—the one who had delivered the fruit basket—had already been in the hotel and left. Because el-Banna was reputed to be a solo player, the possibility that he might have backup was not considered. Even if the team had been on the lookout for an accomplice, they had never been shown a picture of the terrorist who'd entered the hotel.

The second mistake related to el-Banna himself. The team's primary responsibility was not to protect Poltarek but to shadow him. The team knew there were other entrances to the hotel, but they couldn't cover all of them continuously without drawing suspicion. Luck was running against them: El-Banna had been able to slip in undetected through a side-street door. The first glimpse the team had of him was when he emerged through the front doors, a few steps behind Poltarek.

"Shit, shit, *shit!*" Tarnofsky stepped over to his car. His arm snaked through the open window and grabbed the radio mike.

A few feet away, Rothman watched the terrorist close in on the lawyer. "He can kill him right now."

Tarnofsky had the mike in his hand when Bernstein touched his shoulder. "No, he won't. El-Banna doesn't like close-in work. He favors the long gun. He'll follow."

Tarnofsky counted off the seconds. *"Baruch hashem!"* he whispered, watching Poltarek get into the cab.

"We can take him now," Rothstein said.

"That would make Landau very happy."

Tarnofsky's call interrupted what would have been another winning hand for Landau. All thoughts of the game vanished as he listened to Tarnofsky.

"Everyone stays with el-Banna," Landau said. "If you get a clear shot, bag him."

And this was the second error, strung like a bead along the string of failure.

Landau was thinking this way: The safety of Poltarek and the successful abduction of el-Banna were mutually inclusive considerations. As long as the team had the assassin in their sights—or better yet, in one of their trunks—Poltarek was safe. There was no need to further concern himself about the lawyer.

But what Landau didn't know—because his team had not picked up on it—was that el-Banna had his own protection. Fifty feet from the Hay-Adams's valet station, a big sport utility vehicle with a rack of rooftop lights idled at the curb. Through the metronomelike swish of windshield wipers, two men watched the black Town Cars swing into traffic after the taxi carrying el-Banna.

* * *

Sid Poltarek entered his office just as Mary was closing up for the day. "How did it go?"

Poltarek waggled his fingers. "So-so. With the Martels, it's always the same. They wait until they get their *schwantz* in a wringer, then scream for help."

"Your black tie is in the closet. Rose called, said she'll take a taxi to the Kennedy Center. And Ben's been looking for you."

Poltarek stared glumly at the rain sluicing down the windows. "Why can't I just go home, have a nice dinner, make a fire . . ."

"Don't be such a *schlemiel,*" Mary said.

Poltarek never failed to be amazed by Mary's command of Yiddish. "When's curtain time?"

"Eight sharp." She handed him the tickets and pointed to the door. "Give yourself plenty of time to get there."

"Thank you, thank you," Poltarek muttered. "What about you?"

Mary shot him a wicked grin. "Steve's taking me to see *Showboat.*"

"Sure you don't want to trade?" Poltarek sighed. "I'll even throw in dinner."

* * *

"El-Banna is not going after Poltarek," Tarnofsky said into the radio mike. "At least not now."

Landau's voice crackled through the tiny speaker. "Where is he headed?"

"Just turned onto Virginia."

"That would take him straight to the Watergate Hotel or the Kennedy Center," Landau said.

"Do you think—?"

"That he knows the Poltareks will be at the Kennedy Center tonight?" Landau finished. "Of course."

"How?"

"Maybe you can persuade him to share that with you when you have your little talk."

Tarnofsky was two cars behind el-Banna's cab. Rothman was up ahead, in another lane. Bernstein found himself right next to the taxi.

"The son of a bitch just looked at me," he reported. "Cold, like a snake."

"Keep him boxed in," Tarnofsky said.

El-Banna's cab dropped him off under the portico of the Watergate Hotel. But instead of heading inside, the terrorist unfurled an umbrella and began walking in the direction of the Kennedy Center. The driving rain made him appear nothing more than a gray shadow.

"Where's he going?" Rothman asked as the three Town Cars crawled through the downpour toward the loading-dock ramp, reserved for transport trucks that ferry in the huge, prefabricated sets.

"He has a roost all set up," Tarnofsky said. "If he gets inside, we might lose him. Bernstein, you stay with the cars. Make sure your engine is running. We'll be coming out fast."

* * *

Samir el-Banna had figured out exactly how he was going to kill the Poltareks and the method had nothing to do with his formidable skills with a rifle.

El-Banna entered the Kennedy Center complex through the doors leading to the Hall of States. He closed his umbrella and strolled past the elevators where couples in evening dress waited to be whisked up to the Roof Terrace Restaurant or the Curtain Call Café for pretheater dining.

He took an escalator down to the sublevel, walked past the gift shop, then stepped on another escalator that carried him to the Hall of Nations. From there, he went outside and, standing under the protruding roof, checked the swirl of roads and highways that spun off the E Street Expressway.

He studied the traffic flow for a few minutes, then walked the length of the Center until he could see the Watergate complex across the street. Special-event parking was available at either the Columbia Plaza garage on Virginia Avenue or at the Watergate. The Poltareks were sure to meet at the Watergate. El-Banna had taken the time to check Poltarek's car. In the bottom left corner of the Jaguar's windshield was an orange Watergate parking sticker.

Which meant that the Poltareks would have to cross the street between the Watergate and the Kennedy Center, an artery that carries traffic off Rock Creek Parkway, a busy, dangerous intersection.

El-Banna spent fifteen minutes watching the increasing traffic flow, looking for and finding the exact spot where he wanted his men to position themselves. Then he pulled out his cell phone and made a brief call, giving nothing except coordinates and everyday markers—a trash can, a flagpole. He spent a little more time describing the crosswalk and exactly how long the light held up traffic for pedestrians.

El-Banna was about to make a second call when a gust of wind sprayed him with rain, forcing him closer to the white marble walls. He never heard the splash of footsteps in the puddles behind him.

El-Banna's phone dropped from his hand as a hammerlike blow paralyzed his arm. A second caught him just below the left ear, causing his knees to crumple. Someone grabbed a fistful of hair and shoved his head forward. El-Banna felt a needle prick the back of his neck. Then he went limp.

Tarnofsky scooped up the phone and jammed it into his pocket. The syringe disappeared into a plastic tube which also went into his pocket.

Rothman had el-Banna propped up against the wall. Tarnofsky glanced around. There were no passersby near them. Even if someone was watching them from a distance, all they'd see were three men trying to stay out of the rain.

El-Banna's head rolled back against the marble. Tarnofsky gripped it with one hand; with the other he checked the killer's eyes. They were glassy, but the pupils were not dilated. The drug, a synthetic paralytic similar to curare, was working perfectly. Tarnofsky also checked the pulse at el-Banna's carotid artery and listened to his breathing.

With their arms under el-Banna's, Tarnofsky and Rothstein half-carried the terrorist down the exterior staircase that led to the tour buses' pickup and drop-off area. Bernstein saw them coming and skidded forward thirty feet, the trunk already open. El-Banna went in like a sack of potatoes and Bernstein sped off.

As Tarnofsky hurried to his own vehicle, he felt exultant. Inside the car, he waited until his heart stopped racing before reaching for the telephone. Landau was going to be very pleased.

Even if Tarnofsky hadn't been thinking of Landau, it was unlikely that he would have noticed the sport utility vehicle trailing him a few cars back on Virginia Avenue. The rain, the gathering darkness, the SUV's height, all meant that it could maintain a discreet distance between itself and the black Lincoln. Which it did, all the way through Georgetown, up Wisconsin Avenue, and into the warren of streets to Dent Place.

Thirteen

THE ASH ON LANDAU'S CIGAR glowed like a rocket's afterburner.

"That was Tarnofsky," he announced to his little group. "We have el-Banna."

Exclamations and congratulations filled the air.

"Will you be conducting the interrogation, sir?" the *bodel* asked.

Landau grimaced. There was nothing he'd like more than to sit down and have a long chat with Samir el-Banna. But that pleasure would have to wait. Tarnofsky was an expert interrogator. He would crack open the terrorist at least as quickly as Landau could.

There was a second consideration: El-Banna's presence in the capital meant that Hafez Jamal was close by. Tarnofsky had said that el-Banna had made a call just before he'd been taken. Among other features, el-Banna's cell phone had a last-number-redial feature. Tarnofsky had said that the call had gone to the Willard Inter-Continental.

Who would el-Banna have been calling at a hotel that was less than two blocks from the White House?

Hafez Jamal.

And what would Jamal be doing so close to the seat of American power?

Landau's blood ran cold just flirting with the possibilities.

Landau picked up the phone and spoke to the *katsa*. He explained about el-Banna's call.

"It went to the switchboard, not to a particular room. Get a team over to the hotel. Make sure each member has seen Jamal's photograph. Send one man inside to make discreet inquiries, the other two hold back in cover positions."

"How hard do you want our man to press?"

"Not hard enough to make him memorable. If Jamal was in the hotel when the call came in, he's certainly gone by now. More likely the call was picked up by a cutout."

"And if we do get a specific room for the call?"

"Position your men by the door and tell them to wait for me."

As it turned out, Landau was half-right. Jamal had been at the Willard Inter-Continental, but not as a guest. El-Banna's call had been routed into the bar where Jamal was still sitting. The second call had not come through the switchboard, but directly to his cellular phone. Now Jamal was in the hotel's spacious lobby, watching himself in an enormous gilt-edged mirror, making sure that his expression remained absolutely neutral. Given what he had to listen to, it was a difficult feat.

Samir el-Banna, Jamal's best, had been taken. But el-Banna's shadows had followed the Israelis to their lair. That was something.

If Samir fights the drugs, doesn't talk . . .

It was a vain hope, because the man who won't talk under torture, eventually, has yet to be born.

Still, something could be made of this. Jamal had firsthand experience with Israeli interrogation techniques. If Landau's men stuck to procedure, it would be a while before they went to work on el-Banna in earnest.

And why not wait? The Israelis were in a safe house; they believed they had nothing to fear. El-Banna's two men had been smart not to hang around in sight of the house once it had been positively identified.

Jamal thought he had some time. He would put it to the best possible use. The Poltareks still had to die. Jamal was all but certain that the lawyer had talked to his handler about Manshur. In the Hadar Dafna Building in Tel Aviv, alarm bells must have sounded when Manshur's body was found—along with that of the Mossad handler. Landau would have wanted to know why the killings were necessary. It was logical that he had turned to Poltarek.

And made him the goat! Jamal thought suddenly. Of course. That's how

Landau would do it—bait a trap and see who came to take a sniff. That's the way Jamal would have arranged matters.

Were you hoping that I would come? The thought must have been very exciting to you . . .

But Jamal had not survived this long because he took foolish chances. If another man could do the job, why *not* send him? Pity that it had to be el-Banna.

El-Banna's accomplice had finished his report. Jamal replied softly in Arabic, using a code that referred to airline schedules. The connection was broken.

Jamal looked around at the prosperous, pampered people who criss-crossed the lobby. Since it was not yet the tourist season, most of them were Americans. A savage hatred boiled up in his blood. These self-satisfied fools, who believed they could dictate terms to the rest of the world, needed to be taught a lesson in humility. Jamal was very glad that fate had chosen him to be the teacher.

The Americans no longer feared the long-range missiles and bombers of other nations. It was the single man with a device in a suitcase that they were terrified of, someone who could plant a nuclear or biological weapon in the heart of a great city and be three thousand miles away when the device went off.

Yes, it would be a single man. But not the way the Americans thought. To destroy a city meant to unleash the kind of revenge the world had never seen before. The man who committed such an act would be hunted for the rest of his days. No government would protect him, no cause or movement would hide him.

But to *humiliate* America, that was something else. To force her to change decades-old policies would be better than a thousand victories on the battlefield. Jamal would do what no other Palestinian or Arab had yet achieved: he would give birth to a new nation. America, rich, bloated, would be compelled to act as midwife. And once the knot was tied, no dagger would ever be able to sever it. The new nation would endure. America would guarantee its existence and prosperity because she knew that if she did not, what was about to happen once could happen again.

"Bigger than Arafat, bigger even than Hassan had he lived . . . I shall be bigger than all of them."

"You say something, sir?"

Jamal's head snapped up. One of the bellboys was standing a few feet away, his expression uneasy.

"Do you need something, sir? I heard you say—"

Jamal shook his head. "No, thank you."

The young man shrugged and walked off.

Had he said something aloud? Was his vision so powerful that it had forced its way between his lips? Jamal smiled. In the desert, visions and talking to the wind were hallmarks of great men confronting and embracing their destiny.

Jamal would have felt grievously insulted if someone had told him that these were also manifestations of madness.

In the gathering darkness, Jamal left the elegant hotel, a dollar bill in his hand for the doorman who would hail him a taxi.

In the north end of the city, Benjamin Poltarek placed his magician's case on the passenger seat and ducked behind the wheel, on his way to the Children's National Medical Center.

In the stone cottage in Dent Place, Samir el-Banna, still groggy, heard a voice say, "He's ready for us now."

* * *

A dim light snapped on. El-Banna squinted at the fieldstone wall, dark with moisture. Something scurried in the dark corner, tiny claws scrambling along metal. He shivered and realized how cold he was. *A cellar . . .*

The face of the man standing a few feet away was cast in a hood by the angle of the light. He wore a short-sleeve shirt. Now el-Banna knew it was the drugs that made him so cold.

His arms were bound around the back of the chair, his legs fixed by chains to the chair legs. He tried to pull his wrists apart and felt the plastic fasteners, the kind airlines use to attach baggage tags. Except these had razor teeth embedded in the plastic. The harder he pulled, the tighter the fasteners became, the deeper the razors bit.

El-Banna knew then who had him. He shuddered and almost choked on his terror. He had killed many Jews and he had sent other men to murder even more. All his successes had cloaked him in a sense of invincibility, lulling him into the belief that he was too clever, too ferocious, for the Israelis even to try to take him.

Now that they had him, el-Banna was terrified, not so much of what secrets he would be forced to part with, but by the awful certainty that the interrogators would take great pleasure in breaking apart his beautiful face. His only hope was that his men had witnessed his abduction and had managed to follow the Israelis to this cave. If that were the case, then Hafez Jamal would have been alerted. Hope stirred in el-Banna as smoke curls from a bed of leaves.

He never sensed that there was someone behind him. The burlap sack came down over his head with great force. At the same time, a drawstring tightened the rough fabric around his neck.

El-Banna screamed until he realized he could still breathe. There were jagged openings cut into the burlap for his nose and mouth. He realized too that no one had struck him. That meant his screaming didn't matter. No one would hear him.

But it was not over yet. Hands fumbled with the zipper on his pants. El-Banna shrank back in the chair as coarse-skinned fingers curled around his penis and testicles and pulled them out.

El-Banna heard the unmistakable sound of a knife being unsheathed and screamed again. He rocked as much as he could, felt his private parts swinging back and forth.

"Feeling comfortable?" a guttural voice called out. Laughter followed. "Maybe if you're a good boy, we'll send you a shepherd to suck your cock."

Something cold and hard struck his penis. For one terrible instant, el-Banna thought it was a blade. The image of his severed manhood, of blood pouring out of the stump, made him faint.

Later . . .

An hour? Two? El-Banna could not say. When he regained consciousness, he understood that he was still alive. Maybe his penis hadn't been severed after all.

El-Banna's lips were pricked by the sharp burlap threads as he moved them in silent thanks.

"Talking to Allah?" The voice could have come from anywhere in the room. "Samir el-Banna. I am addressing you. Are you praying?"

"Yes," el-Banna managed.

"Because I have not cut off your dick? And don't lie to me. I will know it if you do."

The admission made el-Banna nauseated. "Yes. For that."

"Good. As long as you tell the truth, you will keep your dick. Does that sound fair to you? *Don't lie!*"

"Yes . . . It is fair."

"Are you thirsty, Samir el-Banna?"

"Yes."

"Drink. No, drink. It is not poison."

Tarnofsky thrust the straw of a plastic sports bottle between the terrorist's lips. He did so roughly, to make el-Banna believe that this gift was given grudgingly.

Carrot, stick. Carrot, stick. The principles of interrogation were as old as the Institute's biblical motto: "By way of deception, thou shalt do war." Tarnofsky would give his prisoner sweet water in return for something sweet from him. If used properly, the method was virtually foolproof. Time was always on the interrogator's side. To the prisoner, it seemed like an increasingly fast current that he had to keep fighting.

El-Banna was a strong man, physically. But he had never spent time in Israeli hands, had never even been arrested. He knew captivity in theory, but not in practice. Plus, his psychological profile indicated a very vain man.

Tarnofsky believed in time; he believed in profiles. But he was in a hurry and so placed most of his faith in the two hundred milligrams of hydrocodone bitartrate he had dissolved in the sugared water.

In concentrated doses, the drug could drop a robust ox. The way Tarnofsky had mixed it, the effects would creep up on el-Banna. Little by little, he would start to feel good about himself, his chances for survival. He would put this down to his prowess as a warrior. He would feel very, very "up."

And then he will talk, Tarnofsky thought. *He won't be able to help himself.*

He jerked away the sports bottle, making el-Banna dribble his last mouthful into the burlap. Now the fabric would chafe even more. Good.

"Do you like white women? Blond, white women?"

El-Banna was surprised to hear himself laugh. The water was refreshing and tasted perfectly normal, so ice-cold that it was sweet.

"Of course I like white women."

"Good-looking man like you, you must pick them up at hotels all the time, hmm?"

"Hotels, sure."

"What about your pals? You share with them?"

"Scraps. That's all I give them."

The drug was working faster than Tarnofsky had anticipated. He kept the conversation light until, twenty minutes later, he felt the chemicals had saturated el-Banna's brain.

"The Willard Hotel, Samir. Is someone you know staying there?"

To his horror, el-Banna heard himself say, "Not anymore. Hafez—"

"Yes, what about Hafez?" Tarnofsky saw el-Banna's lips press together so tightly that they were white. "Samir. You and Hafez have come such a long way. Come now, tell me: What is it that brought you to this wonderful city? Come, Samir, share with me."

*　*　*

Outside, a hard spring shower had turned into a bitter storm, although there was no way Samir el-Banna could be aware of this.

Sid Poltarek, on the other hand, realized it all too well.

"I should have parked in the Center," he said gloomily, staring at the rain through the glass doors of the Watergate complex, where he had met his wife.

Rose tapped his arm in a tut-tut gesture.

"It's only a few steps. The umbrella is big enough for both of us. We'll be fine."

Her soft tone made Poltarek ashamed of his grousing. Looking at his wife, so splendid in her evening finery, stirred both love and lust in him. With Rose, everything was always fine. It could not be any other way, had been that way ever since they'd met. Each day, she reminded him that gratitude for what one had, and humility in the face of one's good fortune, were two of life's sturdiest pillars. Fortune and fame might crack and splinter, but the goodness two people brought to each other, that could move mountains.

"Sid?"

"Sorry. Daydreaming. Come on. Let's go."

Rose smiled. After forty years of marriage, she knew exactly what her gruff bear had been thinking.

The Poltareks were not the only ones who had parked across the street. The Watergate courtyard became a field of swaying black mushrooms as couples took a deep breath and stepped out from under the overhangs and awnings. Everyone kept an eye on the traffic signals so that they wouldn't catch a red light at the crosswalk.

Poltarek hunched his shoulders to keep the umbrella low so that it covered his wife. With Rose keeping a tight grip on his arm, they reached the corner just as the orange blinkers cautioned motorists to stop.

All but one did.

The driver of the big sport utility vehicle had been parked in the Watergate turnaround. The doorman had made a fuss until a hundred-dollar bill shut him up. The driver did not care that the doorman had seen his face. He would be out of the country by midnight.

The windshield wipers had swept back and forth methodically, giving the driver a clear view of the Poltareks standing behind the glass walls of the Watergate lobby. The husband had said something; the wife had smiled, responding. The husband had unclipped the snap on the umbrella, the concierge stepping out from behind his desk to push open the heavy glass door.

The driver lost them for an instant, when Poltarek unfurled the umbrella. There they were again, both looking in the direction of the crosswalk. He read their thoughts perfectly, shifted gears.

The Poltareks were on the sidewalk on his right side. The sidewalk paralleled the exit driveway, both of which dead-ended at the street. To get to the Kennedy Center, the Poltareks had to cross the street. The driver had a choice of turning left or right.

He noticed the couple had stepped up their pace, and added a tiny bit of pressure to the accelerator. Now his light was turning red. The dual orange crosswalk lamps began to blink, indicating that it was safe to cross.

The Poltareks believed the lamps. They stepped off the curb.

The driver dropped the SUV into first gear and mashed his foot down on the accelerator. The pounding rain drowned out some of the engine roar, and the roof-mounted halogen lights froze the Poltareks when they finally looked up.

The grille-mounted bull bars were not the tubular type but sharp-edged. One row hit Rose Poltarek just above the breastbone, almost severing her head at the neck. Because he was taller, Sid Poltarek took the brunt at center chest. He was dead even before he was flipped in the air, coming down as the truck swerved, its fender shattering his left hip.

It was over before anyone could scream. Only the black umbrella, miraculously unscathed, pursued the fleeing SUV, tumbling over and over like some mad avenger.

*   *   *

At the Children's National Medical Center, the young audience oohed and aahed as Benjamin Poltarek, to the drumroll of thunder, presented his magic cake. . . .

Six miles from the Center, Yossi Tarnofsky stared into the crazed eyes of Samir el-Banna.

Had the chair not been bolted to the floor, el-Banna would have lifted it and himself off the floor. Tarnofsky had ripped off the burlap cover, but there was nothing he could do about the greenish white sickness dripping from el-Banna's mouth. Whether an allergic reaction or an accidental overdose, Tarnofsky couldn't say. Whatever it was, he could not lose el-Banna now. The terrorist's last words had frozen his heart.

They are bringing in an American.

What American? Who were "they"? Jamal? Of course! But someone else as well, working with Jamal. When? *Why?*

Tarnofsky wiped away some of the mess and drew back his fingers just as el-Banna's teeth snapped at them.

I'm going to keep you alive! Tarnofsky promised silently. *You're going to tell me everything about the American—*

This last thought was severed as the explosion buckled Tarnofsky's knees, pitching him forward.

*   *   *

Hafez Jamal had carefully considered which explosives to use.

After arriving at Dent Place, it did not take him long to spot his killer, almost invisible behind the dark windshield of the sedan. The Arab told Jamal that no one had come out of the stone cottage since the Israelis had hauled Samir el-Banna inside. Jamal was not surprised. He imagined the Israelis were quite busy.

The storm and the darkness were Jamal's allies. They kept people off the sidewalks and reduced traffic to nothing. Jamal suspected that the stone cottage was not as innocent as it appeared. There would be cameras, motion sensors, and lights. But he did not have to get that close. There was enough light from the sodium arc city lamps and the occasional fork of lightning for him to see what he needed without leaving the sidewalk.

There was news when he returned to the sedan.

"It is done," the Arab told him.

Jamal's eyes glinted like wet stones as he listened to the all-news radio station. Here was the announcer talking about a hit-and-run that had occurred a short time ago near the Kennedy Center. Two people were presumed dead. Police and emergency vehicles were on the scene.

Ten minutes later, the big SUV nosed down the street. Jamal softly congratulated the driver on his execution, then explained what he believed to be the situation inside the house. There were at least three Israelis. They would be armed. But the raiders would have the advantage of surprise, because the Israelis would be preoccupied with el-Banna. The details were quickly outlined and the weapons readied. Then Jamal made his call.

Twenty-five minutes later, a rattletrap Honda fishtailed up to the stone cottage and double-parked, blinkers winking. A young man, probably a student, slipped out holding a hot pack that contained the large pizza Jamal had asked to be delivered.

The delivery boy jogged up the short walkway and rang the bell. He thought he heard something rustling in the bushes, but put it down to the wind.

Inside, Rothman heard the bell. He had one hand on his gun, the other pushing away a corner of the curtains that covered the bulletproof picture window. He saw the double-parked car with its triangular neon ad on the roof. He knew damn well that no one had ordered a pizza.

Then he checked the closed-circuit security monitor and saw the boy, drenched, holding the pizza in one hand.

"What is it?" Bernstein called out.

"Pizza delivery. The schmuck has the wrong address."

Rothman used the intercom to tell the boy to go away. He wouldn't. If he didn't get paid for the pizza, the cost would come out of his pocket.

"Come on, man. I'm drowning out here."

Rothman looked at Bernstein, who shrugged. "I could eat."

Rothman buzzed the electronic lock, then threw the deadbolt. He was holding his gun with one hand, behind his back; in the other was a twenty-dollar bill.

Bernstein was in the parlor with the submachine gun, out of sight but with a clear view of the door.

Rothman pulled back the door a few inches. For a split second, he saw a face before the bullet from Jamal's silenced automatic blew apart the delivery boy's head. He heard but never saw the concussion grenade being tossed into the parlor, bouncing and spinning as its timer counted off two seconds.

Bernstein's finger tightened around the trigger, but the burst from the submachine gun went wild as the force of the blast exploded his eardrums.

Jamal and the two Arabs were inside. Rothman was taken down first, by a bullet into his throat. The fact that he continued to thrash saved Bernstein's life, momentarily.

The Israeli had plenty of experience with stun grenades. He clawed through the shock, grabbed the submachine gun, and unleashed a devastating barrage. One Arab was torn in half, but Jamal and the other took cover behind armchairs and returned fire.

Bernstein was very tough. He had a bullet lodged near his spine and no way to reach for his spare clip. Still, his fingers found the commando knife tucked into his boot. As the Arab charged, Bernstein swung his arm in a wide arc. The blade sliced through fabric and flesh and into the warm, wet nest of the Arab's abdomen.

Bernstein was still carving when Jamal ran around and shot him in the head. Since the Arab was alive but beyond saving, he left him curled up on the carpet.

El-Banna.

The force of the concussion grenade had done no more than to knock Tarnofsky down and make him realize that something terrible had happened upstairs. He'd grabbed his gun and pounded up the steps, listening to the barrage. Then suddenly everything was quiet. And he slowly opened the door.

Jamal was in the short hallway leading to the kitchen, cursing silently because the stone cottage had so many doors. Any one of them could lead to the basement. He did not have time to try them all.

He didn't have to. He saw the door beside the kitchen sideboard push open. The barrel of a gun appeared, then a hand, finally a questing head.

Jamal forced himself to wait until the Israeli was halfway out the door, poised to race for cover by the refrigerator.

Tarnofsky released his coiled muscles and sprang into the room. He never heard the first bullet that struck him, on the inside of his thigh when he was in mid-flight. But the other two registered, microseconds before he felt the searing pain in his abdomen and across his arm.

Tarnofsky fell, firing, the nine-millimeter slugs gouging out wood and plaster. In a reflex action, he shot away the lock on the back door, then laid down a fusillade into the hallway.

A chip of plaster screamed across Jamal's cheek, drawing blood, cutting off the adrenaline rush. The last gunshot echoed away before he dared snap a glance into the kitchen.

And saw the open back door being batted by the wind.

Hafez Jamal dashed out into the lashing rain, staring around wildly. The Israeli had vanished.

Now lights on back porches and patios began coming on. Even the ferocity of the storm hadn't camouflaged the gunfire from the stone cottage.

Jamal hurried back inside and locked the door. He clattered down the basement steps and froze at the sight of Samir el-Banna chained to the chair. One look at his comrade's face, frozen in a psychotic rictus, told Jamal that el-Banna was beyond redemption.

"They shall pay!" he whispered as he stepped behind the prisoner. "I promise you they shall pay."

Then he fired a single bullet into the base of el-Banna's skull.

Upstairs, Jamal sifted through the pockets of his slain gunmen. He didn't think they would be carrying anything that could identify them, but he had to be sure. Besides, one of them had something that he needed.

A moment later, Jamal was at the front door. He hesitated just long enough to set the timer, then tossed the phosphorus grenade onto the couch and bolted. By the time he was inside the sport utility vehicle, the stone cottage parlor was ablaze.

Jamal eased the SUV into the street. The roof-mounted lights lit up bushes and trees, but not a running man. As he drove, Jamal dialed a number that, after bouncing off two satellites, rang in the heart of the embassy of the United Arab Emirates. When a soft voice answered, Jamal identified himself by code and explained exactly what it was he needed in order to find a wounded, probably dying man.

*   *   *

Israel is not the only Middle East country that keeps a well-trained security force capable of operating incognito in the American capital. Over the years, Arab nations have learned much from their historic enemy and have themselves become quite proficient.

The United Arab Emirates enjoys a polite and comfortable relationship with its host government. Since it is a tiny nation, with no armed forces to speak of but a great deal of oil to protect, it relies on the kindness of strangers—in this case, the United States. And because the UAE is so small and dependent, it does not cast even a blip on America's counterintelligence radar. Thus, it is the perfect home for a team of highly trained Palestinians who live within its walls and who are tolerated as the shark tolerates its ramora.

Fifteen minutes after Jamal's call, three limousines pulled out of the UAE embassy garage. This traffic attracted no special interest from the occupants of the D.C. police patrol car who were accustomed to seeing Arabs drive off in groups.

The cars traveled at a sedate speed, discreetly dropping off competent-looking men in foul-weather gear at various locations around the city.

Jamal had a huge advantage that now came into play. The missing Israeli was hurt, perhaps badly. Since he was probably unaccredited personnel, and wounded, he was not likely to go to the police or a hospital. There was, in fact, only one safe place for him—the embassy.

Following Jamal's instructions, five of the Palestinian commandos were dropped off in the immediate vicinity of the Israeli embassy. If he came that way, the running man would find himself facing a gauntlet he could not possibly survive.

The rest of the team was let off at the major stops along Washington's Metro system. It was possible that the Israeli did not have a car near the safe house. Or else his wounds would preclude him from operating one. In which case, his only alternative was the subway.

Calls filtered into the SUV as Jamal drove the back streets of Georgetown, his lights probing and poking into dark corners. One by one, the men reached their destinations: Van Ness, Metro Center, Union Station.

The idea that the Israeli might have an alternative destination to the embassy never even occurred to Jamal, not even when he heard the urgent reports about the shooting at Union Station.

*　*　*

Train stations all over the world share one common feature: It is always possible to find a taxi nearby.

Yossi Tarnofsky staggered through the downpour and wrenched open the door of the first cab in the line. The ceiling light went out even as the driver turned around to look at him.

"Hey, brother. You all right? Wet out there, huh?"

Tonight everybody is asking me if I'm all right. The thought struck Tarnofsky as absurdly funny.

"Connecticut," he rasped. "Up to Woodley Road. I'll tell you where to stop."

Tarnofsky picked up the odor of an inferior grade of marijuana.

"Connecticut it is, my man." The driver edged out of the line and made a slow turn. "Say, you know what that fuss was all about inside? Sounded like people screaming."

Tarnofsky felt his insides slosh around as the cab hit a pothole. He was grateful for the darkness. The driver wouldn't see the blood seeping onto the plastic-covered seat.

"Don't know," he mumbled. "Just having a drink. Too many drinks . . ."

"Amen to *that,*" the driver replied. "You just settle back. I'll get you home okay."

The driver's singsong voice lulled Tarnofsky. The passing lights were like giant exploding galaxies. He felt himself floating, floating.

He must have lost consciousness because the driver, turned around in his seat, had his hand on Tarnofsky's shoulder. Only the Israeli's instant realization that he was not in any danger spared the driver's life.

"My man, you *did* have a few too many," the driver said, drawing back.

There was something in his passenger's eyes that made him nervous, the terrible angry pain of an animal with its leg caught between the steel jaws of a trap.

"Woodley," the driver said. "Like you wanted."

Yes. Tarnofsky could see the distinctive wedge shape of the condo building. Carefully, he reached into his pants pocket, leaned forward, and jammed the crumpled bills into the driver's hand. When the driver looked down to peel the bills apart, Tarnofsky quickly got out of the cab.

The driver lowered his window and called out, "Hey! Hey, man, you gave me all twenties."

Tarnofsky didn't bother to turn around but kept walking up Connecticut. *One foot in front of the other, one in front of the other . . .* The way he'd done it in the infantry, hundreds of miles. Thousands. All he had to do was focus on the lights of the building. It was his oasis, his new Jerusalem.

Tarnofsky leaned heavily against the pillar that supported one half of the wrought-iron gates that guarded the entrance to the driveway.

The portico was blazing with lights. There was the uniformed doorman opening the car door for an arriving tenant. A valet dashed out from around the corner, hopped behind the wheel, and proceeded to roll the car into the garage.

Move!

Tarnofsky knew he would have only this one chance. The pounding rain was draining away the last of his strength and he was very, very cold. Going in the front way was impossible, with all the lights, the doorman, the inevitable concierge in the lobby. The garage was the only option.

A short, bitter cry escaped Tarnofsky's lips as he lurched after the red taillights of the sedan. At the top of the incline, he slipped, lost his footing, and rolled down through the yawning entrance. He lay there for a moment until he heard the clatter of the steel-barred door closing.

The garage was warm, smelling of concrete and exhaust fumes. Tarnofsky slipped along the walls, ducking behind thick yellow-painted pipes when he heard the valet approach, getting up and moving after the boy's footsteps died away.

Tarnofsky staggered to the elevator, jabbed the button, and the doors parted. He checked the lighted panel, pressed P and slumped into a corner. If the elevator stopped at the foyer, it stopped. If he was discovered, so be it. Tarnofsky had no strength left to care.

The elevator did not stop until it reached the penthouse level.

Tarnofsky crawled out of the car and used the marble foyer table to haul himself to his feet. He whipsawed down the carpeted hall like a drunk.

When he reached the number he was looking for, he uttered a grotesque laugh, then mashed his palm against the lighted buzzer.

Tarnofsky thought that the young man who opened the door had the face of an angel. *Am I dead?* Tarnofsky reassured himself by staggering into the foyer, bracing himself against the wall, beseeching the young man.

"Are you Poltarek?"

Fourteen

"Y̲O̲U̲ ̲D̲O̲N̲'̲T̲ ̲K̲N̲O̲W̲ ̲H̲I̲M̲?̲"

The homicide detective, Priestly, had played tackle for Georgia Tech. His ruined knees cracked when he crouched.

Ben Poltarek was slumped in one of the two Louis XV chairs that framed the equally ornate secretaire in the foyer. He looked across at the body, felt hot bile churn up his throat, and turned away.

"You're sure you don't know him?"

Ben looked down at the detective. Priestly's eyes were a washed-out blue, his thick nose sprayed with freckles, steered left, the cartilage fragile as chalk from countless punches. His words reached Ben on puffs of nicotine.

"I told you, no."

Ben wondered how long Priestly could stare at him without blinking. It was an uncanny ability.

"Mr. Poltarek, try to see it from where I'm standing." Priestly's voice was coaxing, almost cloying. "I come through the front door of your parents' apartment and find you sitting on the staircase with a dead man in your arms. A man who, I figure, has at least three bullet wounds in him.

"Now, you don't smell like you've fired a weapon, but you've got blood all over you—"

"*His* blood!"

"Okay, okay. I know you're not hurt. But like I was saying, if *I* was the one holding the guy and telling you I didn't know him, would *you* believe me?"

"I don't know who he is," Ben repeated after a moment. "Now, I want you to tell me what happened to my parents."

Priestly leaned heavily on the secretaire, leaving a sweaty palm print on the fruitwood when he lifted his hand.

"Let's stay with this for a minute, okay?"

"No, it's *not* okay! I already told you—"

"You're sure he wasn't a client?"

"No!"

"Maybe a recent one? Someone you wouldn't have met yet?"

Ben shook his head. "I would have known."

Ben was not consciously lying when he said this. Part of it was true: He'd never seen the man in the law offices. But his thoughts were too scattered for him to recall that Sid Poltarek had always had his secrets.

The doorbell sounded, followed by the staccato roll of knuckles rapping on wood. Priestly opened the door and Rachel Melman burst in. Ben rose and was rocked on his heels when she flew at him, her arms hugging him tightly. Her tears were hot on his cheek.

"I heard . . . I heard on the radio on the way home. Then you called."

For an instant, Ben was puzzled, then he remembered: Priestly had let him make a call.

"Ma'am?"

Rachel looked over her shoulder. She did not release Ben until she noticed the badge draped over Priestly's breast pocket. She wiped her eyes and rummaged in her bag for her hospital ID.

While Priestly examined it, she turned back to Ben. "You're not hurt?" He shook his head. Rachel looked at the body. "Who's that?"

"That's what we're trying to find out," Priestly said, handing back her ID.

Rachel stooped and pulled back the throw rug, grimacing when she saw the wounds. "He's lost a lot of blood."

"Which obviously isn't here," Priestly said. "But that doesn't explain how he got here."

"He's been out in the rain," Rachel murmured, ignoring the detective. "Soaked . . ."

"What are you getting at, Doc?"

"He would have died from exposure if he hadn't made it this far."

But that's not what she meant at all. Rachel knew that the man had fought enormous pain to get to the Poltareks' home. Why?

"Yeah," Priestly said. "One of the other things that bothers me is how he got up here. For sure he didn't stroll past the doorman and the valets."

"The garage," Ben murmured. "He could have gotten into the building if the doors were open for a car." When Priestly raised his eyebrows, he added, "It's a security problem that was brought up at the last owners' meeting."

He looked at Rachel. "I need to see Sid and Rose. Tell him I have to do this."

Rachel cupped Ben's face in both her hands. "Give me a minute."

She put pressure on his shoulders and made him sit back down in the chair. Priestly caught her slight nod and followed her around to the other side of the staircase.

"The bodies. How bad?" When he hesitated, she added, "I'm a pediatric surgeon. I've seen kids come in who've been pulled from car wrecks."

"It'll have to be a closed-casket funeral."

Her eyelids fluttered. "No question it's them?"

"You think we would've released the names if we weren't sure? I know, I know. You had to ask. But listen, the kid's in no shape to see the remains." He paused. "Did *you* know them?"

"Very well. If need be, I'll make the positive ID." She paused. "Ben's in shock . . ."

Priestly shook his head. "I still need to talk to him."

"I imagine you already have."

"Dr. Melman, I don't want to butt heads here. I'm asking for your help. Your friend says he hasn't a clue who belongs to the body. Now, I don't think he murdered this guy in a bathtub, then dragged him out to the hall so I could trip over the two of them. But that doesn't change the fact that I have a homicide on my hands. The gunshot wounds you saw were not exactly self-inflicted."

"What do you want me to do?"

"Talk to him. You're his friend—"

"Fiancée."

"Even better. Ask him what happened. I need to know. Meantime, I've got to get the crime-scene unit up here."

"Ben will still want to go to the hospital. Even if he doesn't view the bodies, he'll want to take their personal things. That's the only way he'll really know it was them."

"Your call. But when he steps out that door, you're responsible for him."

For a moment, Rachel was puzzled. Then she recognized Priestly's gruff kindness. He could have insisted that a detective accompany her and Ben to the hospital.

Rachel drew Ben into the kitchen. She poured orange juice and made him drink it.

"I want to see them," Ben said flatly. In spite of the juice, he felt a metallic coating on his tongue.

"Ben, listen to me. It was a very bad accident. You don't want to see them like that."

"Like what? What're you saying, Rachel? That they're all broken up? I already know that!" He drew himself up. "I need to do this."

Rachel knew that she could fight him—and win. Ben was like a boxer who'd taken ten too many punches. He was blocking out everything else because he had only enough strength to focus on one crucial thing: seeing his parents. This need was all that sustained him. But she also understood how weak he was, how persuasive she could be.

Instead, she said: "All right. We'll go together. Where's your jacket?"

"In my room."

"I'll get it."

While Rachel went upstairs, Ben returned to the foyer.

"We're going to the hospital," he said. Priestly, sitting in one of the chairs, nodded absently. "I want you to believe me. He didn't tell me anything."

The detective shifted. "I'm beginning to think he didn't. But that doesn't mean my job's done. This guy belonged to someone. We'll run prints, see where that gets us. Thing is, he didn't come here to harm you—at least I don't think so. Depending on what we find—or don't—I'll want to look at your father's records, calendar, talk to his secretary."

Ben nodded. "Client records are confidential, but I'll help where I can."

"That won't be necessary, if the computers do our legwork for us. Maybe they will." Priestly pulled out cigarettes. "Do you mind?"

"Yes," Ben replied sharply. "My parents don't allow smoking in the house."

*   *   *

Landau's first hint that something was wrong in Dent Place came when Rothman missed his hourly update from the safe house.

A few minutes later, the embassy's commo office, which routinely monitored the police channels, called down to report that D.C. units were responding to calls of shootings and possibly a fire at Dent Place.

Landau raced out of the bunker, heading for the garage where a car, driver, and security escort were waiting.

The safe house was a third of the way down Dent Place, which was blocked off by police cruisers at both ends. Landau had the driver park far enough away so as not to attract attention. He turned up his collar against the rain and sloshed his way to a white minivan with a roof-mounted satellite dish and a local television station logo on the panel. A young female reporter, holding an umbrella, was moving her lips while she reviewed her notes.

Landau sidled up to her, flashed a smile. "What's going on?"

The reporter sized him up and dismissed him as a lookie-loo. "Sorry. I'm busy."

Landau held out a business card. It identified him as the director of business affairs for CNN at the Atlanta headquarters. Landau had a number of such cards, each one different.

He kept smiling pleasantly. "Shall we start over?"

The reporter cursed silently. A guy from the CNN tower was someone worth knowing, especially since she was looking to move.

"Look, I'm really sorry," she simpered. "It's just with the rain and all . . ."

"I know. Why don't you fill me in."

Landau kept his smile even as the reporter's words pumped dread into his heart. The rain had helped the firefighters with the blaze. They had found four bodies. According to the coroner, two looked Arabic, the other two—who knew?

"I heard there was shooting," Landau said. "What was that all about?"

According to her police sources—which were *very* good—there must have been one hell of a firefight inside. Shell casings all over the place. The cops were thinking a drug deal gone sour.

Landau knew better, but he had to ask, "Are you sure the count was four? I heard there might have been five."

The reporter inched closer.

"Listen. This is my exclusive, okay?"

"Absolutely."

"I mean, if CNN wants in—"

"You call me first thing, day after tomorrow."

The reporter smiled; the deal had been struck.

"Okay. There *was* one other guy. They found him in the basement chained to a chair, hands tied up with plastic, his dick hanging out. Someone had blown away the back of his head."

El-Banna. Jamal had been here. He could not take el-Banna with him so he killed him.

"I like your style," Landau told the woman. "You'll go places."

Back inside the car, Landau got on a scrambler line to the embassy *katsa*. He watched the expressions of his driver and escorts mottle as he outlined what had happened at Dent Place.

"We have one man out there," he told the *katsa*. "Since he hasn't come in, assume that he's wounded. I want security to sweep the embassy neighborhood. If they spot Arab watchers, we'll know they're looking for him, too."

"What about the watchers?" asked the *katsa*.

"Leave them alone. We don't need to alert them."

Landau continued, ordering that agents be standing by when he got back to the embassy. He had pictures to show them.

Bernstein, Rothman, Tarnofsky? Which one of you survived?

A thought occurred: "It's possible our man may be headed for a *sayan*."

The *katsa*'s voice was hard with disbelief. Protocol demanded that he be informed of any *sayan* activity on his turf—Landau or no Landau.

"Who would that be?"

"Sidney Poltarek."

Silence on the other end of the line, broken only by the faint ticking of the scrambler sending pulses into the ether.

"Poltarek," the *katsa* said heavily. "Have you not heard?"

"Heard *what?*"

"He and his wife were killed by a hit-and-run driver outside the Kennedy Center earlier tonight."

* * *

The hospital committed to police emergencies in the Kennedy Center area is the Georgetown University Medical Center. Rachel held out her hospital ID for the guard and brought Ben in through the employees' entrance.

Ben had been silent during the drive. Images of his mother and father kept tumbling through his mind like cards falling in slow motion. He could not stop them, could not pluck out a particular one from the deck.

"You might want to think of refinancing in the next month or two."

Were those really the last words Rose had said to him? He couldn't remember any others.

And his father, squirreled away all day at the Hay-Adams. That morning, gone before Ben had had a chance to ask him about—

Manshur.

The image of the Lebanese drifted through Ben's mind, then disappeared. Manshur was not important now.

Tears welled in his eyes as Ben thought that the last time he and his father had spoken was at the dinner the day they'd arrived home from Paris. So little had been said, nothing meaningful. Then Ben had left to go see Rachel. . . .

The last words of Rachel's question hung in the air. Ben scrambled to remember what they were.

"Yeah, okay," he said.

She looked at him curiously. "You understand that I'll make the decision. If they're too badly hurt—"

"I said I understand. And they're not hurt, they're dead. Let's go."

The morgue was in the basement. Rachel had phoned the pathologist from the car, but she still took him aside, leaving Ben in the viewing room, a small barren cubicle of painted cinder block and linoleum tile.

The pathologist was a tall, thin man, balding, with a hyperthyroid condition that made his eyes bulge. He reminded Rachel of a predatory stork, yet his voice was very soothing.

"Is the son here?" He indicated the one-way viewing window, which was, for the moment, covered by a flower-patterned curtain.

"Yes. May I see them, please?"

The pathologist stepped over to two ceramic tables rolled side by side. He lifted the sheet that covered the first body and folded it neatly at the base of Sid Poltarek's chin. Then he did the same for Rose.

Rachel was struck by how peaceful they looked. Then she looked closer, discovered the faint brush marks where the pathologist had scrubbed away the blood and touched up the skin with Pan-Cake.

"Thanks," she said.

"It was nothing." He handed Rachel a sealed brown envelope. She didn't have to ask what was in it.

"He may want to see more."

The pathologist frowned. "I wouldn't."

He drew Rachel's attention to the terrible scar at the base of Rose's neck, hidden by her artfully arranged hair. The head was barely connected to the torso.

Sid Poltarek's body was in even worse condition, if scales for judging such things existed.

Rachel took a moment to compose herself before returning to the viewing room. Ben was standing in front of the window, his hands clasped in front of him.

"Ben?"

"I'm ready."

Rachel tapped on the glass and the curtains parted.

They look fine.

This was Ben's first impression and he did not consider it absurd. He even thought he detected the ghost of a smile on Rose's lips.

Then he realized that truly they were dead and that his first reaction had been relief because they hadn't been disfigured. It never occurred to him to ask to see the entire corpse.

He turned to Rachel. "Okay."

She was very close to him, filling him with her scent. She rapped on the glass again and the curtains were drawn together.

"What happens now?" he asked.

"They'll stay here until that detective—Priestly?—says they can be released."

"Priestly is in homicide. Isn't an autopsy required?"

Rachel had missed that. It was true: If death occurs under suspicious circumstances, an autopsy is mandatory. She finished her thoughts aloud.

"Why would a homicide detective be involved in a hit-and-run? Maybe Priestly knows—or suspects—who did it."

"If so, he never mentioned it to me."

"Or he might have been the closest cop to the scene." Rachel paused. "There's really no need for an autopsy. The cause of death is clear. An autopsy won't add to what Priestly already knows—or doesn't."

Ben took her hand and started for the door. "I don't care about Priestly. All I know is that he's not going to desecrate my parents to help along his investigation."

What Ben didn't add was that his mention of Priestly's being in homicide stirred up questions. Could it be that the death of his parents *wasn't* an accident? Priestly had never raised that possibility. Nor had he dwelled on the still-anonymous driver.

He asked a lot of questions, but told me jack shit!

That idea angered Ben. Yes, he had been overwhelmed by events, but he was an experienced attorney. Somehow, somewhere, he should have summoned up the concentration to ask Priestly questions that needed answers. He would do that very soon.

They were back in the bowels of the hospital's physical plant, ducking pipes and fittings. Ben was glad when they reached the harshly lit corridor that led to the employees' canteen.

At the door, Rachel took Ben's arm and pulled him aside. She tugged out the brown package the pathologist had given her and held it out to him.

Things metallic clinked as Ben hefted it. He knew then what the package contained.

When he started to open it, Rachel said, "You don't have to do it here."

He stared at her. "I don't know if I'll be able to do it later."

Ben sat on a battered couch next to a row of vending machines. He tore open the flap and slowly poured the contents of the envelope into his lap. Watches, rings, wedding bands, bracelets, a billfold, keys—the mundane and the meaningful.

Ben let his fingertips graze over the golden metal and calfskin leather. He felt like a pirate who'd just opened a treasure chest but was fearful of raising vengeful ghosts by disturbing the contents. So delicately was he approaching his duty of going through his parents' effects that he never heard the doors to the street open, nor Rachel's soft gasp as she turned and saw Landau standing there, like the devil the storm had blown into her life.

* * *

"You outta here, Jack?"

Priestly was struggling with his overcoat, heavy because it was soaked through and through. He gave up, draped the coat over one arm, and turned to the chief of the Crime Scene Investigation Unit.

" 'Less you need me for something."

"How about the guy who found the stiff." The chief jerked his thumb in the direction of the corpse, which had been rolled into a body bag. "Might help if I could have a talk with him."

"He doesn't know squat."

"Come on, Jack. You know better than to cut loose a material witness."

"I didn't cut him loose. I let him go to the hospital to see his parents—what's left of them."

"And where's he going next?"

"You mean spend the night? Probably with that doc, his fiancée. I sure as hell wouldn't come back here." He paused. "Don't worry, I know where she lives."

The two men moved out of the way as the coroner's assistant rolled the body into the corridor. The photographer followed, saying he had all the video and stills he needed. The fingerprint team was putting away its brushes and powder into hard-shell cases that resembled fishing-tackle boxes, with plastic pullout trays divided into small compartments.

"Do me a favor, would you, Jack?" the chief was saying. "Get me a report and make the guy—what's his name, Poltarek?—available in case I need him."

"I should have let Burke take the squawk," Priestly replied sourly.

"True. But you're too good a cop to do that."

"Keep blowing smoke up my ass and you'll see just how good."

Priestly felt the weight of the night on his shoulders as he leaned against the elevator wall. When the doors opened on the lobby, he saw the doorman, valet, and evening concierge gossiping.

"Don't bother," Priestly said when the doorman made a halfhearted turn toward the doors.

Standing under the portico, Priestly lit a cigarette. He took two deep drags, then walked swiftly to his car. He eased the vehicle into the turnaround, then turned into the street and made a left. A big sport utility vehicle, lights out, swung in behind him.

The storm was dying. Priestly didn't have to turn around to hear the rumble of the SUV's engine. He kept driving up the street, one hand on the wheel, the other reaching for his shoulder-holstered gun.

Without warning, the rack lights on the SUV came on. The truck roared around Priestly's sedan and cut him off, forcing him to swerve and brake hard. When his sedan stopped rocking, Priestly found himself wedged between the SUV and a parked car.

A door slammed and shadows wavered in front of the sedan's headlights. Priestly flicked on the brights, braced his arm on the steering wheel, and trained his gun on the man emerging through the sheets of rain.

The window of Priestly's sedan had been lowered about an inch to allow the cigarette smoke to escape. He had no trouble hearing the voice over the rain.

"You won't be needing that, Detective."

Priestly had the gun pointed at the passenger window, beyond which loomed a figure in a dark jacket. If the situation warranted, he could put a hole the size of a melon into the son of a bitch.

"Your truck's blocking me," he said through the opening. "Tell your bozos to move it."

The man came around, slapped the roof of the SUV, and it roared away.

He then walked around the front of the sedan and calmly got into the passenger seat.

Not bad, Priestly thought, looking at him. The man wore a heavy weatherproof jacket with a high, turned-up collar. A seaman's woolen hat was stretched over his scalp, hiding his hair. Large wraparound sunglasses concealed the upper half of his face; a thick beard and mustache, undoubtedly fake, covered the rest.

Priestly could swear in the confessional that he would never be able to identify the man.

"There has been a great deal of commotion, Detective Priestly," Hafez Jamal said. Rubber pads used to puff out his cheeks also helped to thicken his speech. "Perhaps you would care to enlighten me?"

"The money first."

It was in a letter-size envelope, given over by a gloved hand to avoid leaving fingerprints. Priestly knew it was bad manners to check the count in front of the buyer and couldn't have cared less. He wet his thumb.

Priestly didn't know this man and didn't want to. Over the last six years, he'd met a dozen like him, each one different physically, but identical in terms of his job description. Priestly had been born and raised in Belfast. He knew something about terrorists.

It was an Irishman who'd recruited him. By the time Priestly realized that the Dubliner had been a stalking horse—someone who recruited, ensnared, then disappeared—it was too late. There were certain investments that Priestly could never adequately explain. He was in the Arabs' pocket, like it or not.

At least the Irishman hadn't lied about the one important thing: Priestly never had to take risks or put his job on the line. The Arabs used him only when they were certain that he could deliver without giving himself away. Like tonight.

Earlier in the day, Priestly had received a call from someone who, after supplying the appropriate code word, suggested that Priestly be very close to the Kennedy Center at a given hour that evening. Other, more detailed, instructions followed. Priestly didn't ask questions, made sure he was in position, and when the hit-and-run squawk came, he picked it up.

He followed procedure, telephoned the victims' next-of-kin, then went up to interview Ben Poltarek. Finding the kid holding a body was not what he'd expected.

Priestly finished counting the money and put it away.

"The commotion, Detective?" Jamal asked.

"As soon as the victims were positively identified, I called the Poltareks' home number," Priestly recited in a monotone. He outlined the scene that he'd walked in on.

Jamal held up his hand. "The dead man, the one the boy was holding. Can you describe him?"

Priestly did, adding as a disclaimer, "He was pretty badly shot up."

"Just so, Detective," Jamal murmured. "Just so."

The description was close enough to fit one of the Jews his men had seen kidnap el-Banna. That made three for three.

"And this man was still alive when he reached the apartment, yes?"

"That's what the kid told me."

"The question is, did he tell *the kid* anything?" Jamal's mimicry of Priestly was quite good, but Priestly didn't pick up on it.

"Poltarek says no. I tend to believe him."

"'Tend,' Detective?"

"Poltarek was in shock. You'd be, too, if a dead man drops out of the sky on you."

I might surprise you, Detective.

"Anyway, what I *am* sure of is that Poltarek had no idea who the guy was—and still doesn't."

"But it's *possible* that he may have said something to Poltarek."

"Possible, but unlikely."

How unfortunate for young Mr. Poltarek.

"By the by, who was the corpse?"

"No one important."

Priestly snorted. "In that case, you've overpaid me."

"On the contrary. Your duties regarding Mr. Poltarek are not yet complete. I must ask you to keep an eye on him for the next little while. If you would report any and all contacts, I would be grateful."

"I won't be able to tail him," Priestly warned.

"Not to worry."

"Right. What about his fiancée? She'll probably end up baby-sitting him."

"Are they close? Very close?"

"Like white on rice."

"Then if she happens to be present when you do your follow-up interrogatories with Mr. Poltarek, I would like to hear what she contributes to the conversation."

Jamal caught Priestly's hesitation. "Yes, Detective?"

"This . . . situation. It's not like the others. You've got a dead body on Woodley and five more in Dent Place. All in the same night. That's a little too much, even for D.C."

"What are you saying, Detective?"

"That this thing could get very hot. If that happens, the feds will want in and they'll edge me out."

"That is not likely to happen," Jamal said, making a move to get out of the car.

"But if it does, I want you to know it wasn't my fault. That I didn't let down my side."

Jamal smiled at him. "Such a thought would never cross my mind where you're concerned, Detective Priestly."

Fifteen

EXCEPT IN HIS IMAGINATION, Landau had not set eyes on Rachel for three years. Looking at her across a space that smelled of antiseptic and stale fatigue, he thought she appeared even more beautiful than he remembered her in Israel. A time when he had known her so well. A time when, after she had returned to the United States, he had used her so effectively.

Until the Howe affair.

The canteen swelled with traffic as a new shift drifted in, doctors, nurses, and orderlies stopping for gum or a snack. Coins jangled in the vending machines as the outgoing exchanged greetings with the incoming.

Ben was oblivious to the people around him, his fingers gently examining the objects in his lap. He opened his father's billfold and was slowly going through its contents when he felt a hand on his shoulder.

"Excuse me for a minute?" Rachel was saying. He thought he saw her nod in the direction of the washrooms. "Will you be okay?"

"Fine."

"Don't go anywhere, all right?"

"Where's there to go?"

She glanced back at him, sitting lost in a world of exploding memories. Ben would be okay. But Landau had disappeared. She couldn't spot him anywhere in the canteen. Had he been an illusion? Was she so exhausted that she had allowed him to creep into her mind's eye?

"Dr. Melman."

A man with a low, hoarse voice bumped her gently. He was tall and very hard and had a finger-thick scar on his throat, across the voice box.

Rachel followed his gaze outside, where she saw Landau in three-quarter profile, standing under the portico.

Rachel took a deep breath of the rain-laden air. Oblivious to the puddles, she walked quickly to where Landau had moved, away from the entrance, into shadows.

His natural habitat . . .

"What do you want?"

Landau drew on his thin cigar, the glowing tip illuminating his fine-boned features. Rachel remembered his face in another light, in another time, and immediately felt shamed.

"After four years, that's what you have to say to me?" Landau asked gently. "Not much of a greeting, Rachel."

"You said you would leave me alone. I took you at your word."

"Yes, I said that. But I added that I would come to you as a last resort." Landau finally looked at her. "So here I am."

"I can't help you," she said. "There are things—"

"I know about those things. Why do you think I'm here?"

Involuntarily, Rachel glanced toward the employees' entrance. She could not see Ben from this angle.

"What do you mean?" She caught the resignation in her tone and realized that Landau was aware that she already had the answer to her question.

"The Poltareks were killed tonight," Landau said. "But you already know this, yes?"

Rachel's face was stone.

Landau continued in that same soft way, as though she had answered him.

"Sidney Poltarek was a *sayan*. His wife, too. When Poltarek was in Paris, he stumbled across something very valuable, very dangerous."

"Samarra," Rachel said softly. "When I read about Samarra and heard Jamal on the news, I thought of you."

"I'm flattered. Samarra, yes. Where things went wrong—even after the raid. Poltarek turned out to be in danger after he returned home. I had three men on him. Even they couldn't prevent the Poltareks from being killed."

"You're lying. A squad of terrorists couldn't get past three of yours. They would have died pushing the Poltareks out of the way at that crosswalk."

"They died anyway," Landau said, using harshness to evade her accusation. "They got their hands on the cell leader, were interrogating him before they were ambushed. Two died quickly—"

"The third survived long enough to reach the Poltareks' apartment."

"Yes, he did. In fact, his body is resting in this hospital. Since he was not carrying any identification, it will be delicate work getting custody."

Hope spiked Rachel's heart. "Is that what you want me to do, help you get the remains out of here?"

Landau looked at her with what another person would have mistaken for genuine regret.

"Would that it were that simple, Rachel. No. You see, we knew that our man on the run would go to only one of two places."

"*Sayanim,*" Rachel whispered.

"Yes. He had been given your name and that of the Poltareks."

"But he was one of the people watching the Poltareks. He'd have known they were dead—"

"Not necessarily. He wasn't watching *the Poltareks.*"

Rachel's throat tightened as she realized what Landau was intimating. If the Israelis were around the Poltareks but not watching over them, that could only mean that Ben's parents had been bait.

"Bastard . . ."

"One man got out of the safe house alive, Rachel. He was wounded, frightened. He had no way of knowing that the Poltareks were already dead. That's why he ended up at their apartment."

Landau paused. "And the door opens, a face my man doesn't know, but which he's certain must belong to a *sayan,* appears before him. You can imagine the rest. It was in your young man's arms that my agent died. *He mistook Benjamin Poltarek for his father.* Yet Benjamin was not one of them. I doubt that his parents ever shared any details of their . . . extracurricular work with him.

"Unfortunately, my man probably lived long enough to say something to Benjamin. He had come a long way, in a great deal of pain. He wouldn't have done that just to find shelter. He had something that had to be shared before he died."

"How can you be so sure?"

"I told you, my people had gotten hold of the cell leader. Circumstances lead me to believe he disclosed information—"

"He was tortured," Rachel said flatly.

"—information that my man thought was vital. If he had just wanted sanctuary, Rachel, he would have run for the embassy."

Landau slipped in this little lie and saw that it was swallowed.

"I need a minute," Rachel said, and without waiting, walked back into the hospital.

Ben was still sitting on the couch next to the vending machines, absorbed by what looked like a letter.

Rachel returned to Landau. "What do you want? Tell me quickly."

"What do you know about the events at the Poltareks' apartment?"

Rachel told him what the detective, Priestly, had talked to her about: questioning Ben, Ben protesting over and over that he didn't know who the dead man was.

"Did Poltarek admit to being *told* anything?"

Rachel's eyes flashed. "No! Priestly was after the same thing. *He* wanted to know why a dying man would come knocking, whether he'd told Ben who he was, or why he was there."

"Did the detective believe Poltarek?"

"Why shouldn't he?"

"Do *you?*"

Rachel stepped very close to Landau. "Yes, I do. And I want you to leave him alone!"

Landau appeared completely unfazed by her words.

"Listen to me, Rachel. The terrorists who were after my man? You had best assume that they know exactly where he ended up. I would. Which means they know about Poltarek. Even if they *hadn't* trailed my man to Woodley, they would have *surmised* that the son was involved. After all, they had just murdered the parents."

Landau looked at her keenly. "Sad to say, but Arabs think the way I do. They suspect my man lasted long enough to tell Poltarek *something.*"

"Why? Why should they *suspect* that?"

"The Arabs—this one in particular—are no fools. We snatched one of theirs. They appreciate that not even the bravest or the strongest can remain silent in the face of certain chemicals. They will believe that whatever he said, my man passed it on."

Landau paused. "Jamal has an operation running in this country, Rachel. What you should fear is that I do not know what it is. Maybe Poltarek has an inkling, maybe he has more. Maybe he's suffering from shock and can't remember. Maybe he's deliberately hiding something.

"I know you don't give a damn about me, Rachel. But you're keen on Poltarek. So know that as of this moment, he has a bull's-eye on his chest. Find out, for his sake, if he knows anything. If he does, you can get me at this number, anytime."

Landau leaned forward as if to kiss her. Instead, he murmured a number, then suddenly drew back. He kept looking over his shoulder as he walked into the night, and she after him, until he disappeared in the rain and blackness.

* * *

"You were gone for a while."

"I needed to be alone. I thought you did, too."

They were in Rachel's car. Ben held the envelope in his lap, his fingers tracing the stiff, rough fiber, moving over the ridges and valleys created by the objects inside.

"I don't want to go back to the apartment," he said quietly. "I can't."

"I'm not taking you there. We're going to my place."

She took his silence for acknowledgment and felt a little better. She wanted to do so much for him, to take away the hurt and the horror, to reverse destiny and give him back his family, to confess and beg his forgiveness.

But tonight she would settle for standing watch over his sleep.

The hiss of tires on wet asphalt coiled around Rachel's thoughts, drawing them and her to that black hole she skirted only in her nightmares.

Four years ago . . . a time before Ben.

She had her army discharge in her hand and tickets to Israel. She had always wanted to go because she took the phrase "Next year in Jerusalem" literally. When she got there, Jerusalem captured her soul and a quiet, handsome stranger her heart.

The first time Rachel saw Landau was in the atrium of a café in Herzilya Street in Tel Aviv. She was sitting alone, drinking lemonade, her feet aching pleasantly from the morning trek around Masada. He walked in off the street, saw her, then stopped and took off his sunglasses to get a better look. He asked if he could join her, and Rachel heard herself saying yes.

They had lunch and, that evening, dinner. Landau, who insisted that she call him by his surname, knew exactly where to take her, offering her a smorgasbord of tastes, scents, music, and people. He was a conjurer who could distill the essence of a place and offer it to her one golden drop at a time.

When they went out the second night, Rachel let herself drink a little too much wine. They ended up at a beachfront café, dancing until they were the only ones on the floor. They, a sleepy guitarist, a half-empty bottle of brandy, and a moon so full that its bone white reflection on the Mediterranean hurt Rachel's eyes.

Landau's apartment was nearby and Rachel didn't see much of it until the next morning. Sleepy and sated, she padded toward the kitchen for juice, but never got there. Framed photographs, agonizingly graphic in their intensity, covered the living-room walls. The horrors, triumphs, and defeats of war were so raw that she could almost smell the blood.

She jumped when Landau came up soundlessly behind her and said, "Israel." As if what was on the wall was a simple, self-evident truth.

Later that morning, he took her to the Hadar Dafna Building and revealed who he was and what he did. Shaken and more than a little awed, Rachel accepted everything he said.

"Why are you telling me all this?" she asked when they were in his office.

"So that you know exactly what it is I do and why I cannot give you more than I did last night."

"I didn't expect more."

"I thought I owed you more. Besides, I would feel offended if you considered me just a one-night stand."

Rachel smiled at his gentle attempt at humor. "And how should I consider you?"

"I know little about you, Rachel Melman, except what you have told me," Landau said. "Before we go any further, I need your permission to do a background check."

"For?"

"For the possibility of offering you a job."

Rachel was stunned.

"It's not what you think. And certainly not in Israel. That's all I can say for the moment."

"What if I don't give you permission?"

"Then I hope you will let me buy you dinner before you leave."

Rachel had never understood why the words came so easily: "By all means, check."

They did not sleep together that night, but the next morning, at dawn, Landau picked her up and took her to the beach. They spread out a blanket, ate fruit and warm breads, and drank a thermos of coffee, while Landau's bodyguards kept their vigil between the surf line and the boardwalk.

"You are a remarkable woman, Rachel Melman. Your army record is exemplary."

"Thank you. Does that mean you're offering me a job?"

"It means I will tell you things. You decide if you want to hear the offer."

Landau explained about the *sayanim*, the kind of people they were, the roles they played. He went on to describe a slightly different "friend of Israel," an individual who takes a more active role in operations, who might be called on to serve for a longer period of time, weeks or even months.

"I understand the principle," she replied. "Tell me where I fit in."

It took a long time for Landau to do that. When he finished, he said: "That is the job. No pay, no fringe benefits, but you make a contribution, a difference. The kind very few people could make. What say you, Rachel Melman?"

"I say yes."

A week later, Rachel was back in Washington starting her residency at Georgetown University Medical Center. Four days after that, she had her first "brush."

Like the other "friends of Israel," Rachel was not privy to any details concerning the individual she serviced. She did not know the person's age, appearance, occupation, nationality, not even gender, although she assumed it was a man.

Landau was very patient when he walked her through the tradecraft; his quiet consideration made it seem that he did not repeat himself.

Rachel was aware that he did, but his manner was so smooth and understated that she did not take offense. Still, her imagination stirred occasionally. She pictured the invisible, anonymous man somewhere in the pell-mell of Washington, a foreigner, probably an embassy worker or official, most likely an Arab, for what other national could be so important to Landau? Yes, an Arab diplomat, with a quiet demeanor and a soft smile, beads of perspiration along his hairline and palpitations of the heart every time he stole whatever he stole, then walked it out of the embassy, carrying bounty for Landau along with his own life in his hands.

The first month, Rachel made two brushes, picking up an envelope that was waiting for her either on top of a trash bin or behind a stone, usually close to a Washington landmark with a good deal of tourist traffic. Landau had told her that the brushes would never take place inside buildings, even though the Smithsonian and the Air and Space Museum had plenty of nooks and crannies. Guards in such buildings were more suspicious of unattended packages than of visitors.

By the fifth month, Rachel was up to three brushes per month. The exercise had become routine, her movements and actions automatic. Although she meticulously obeyed the protocols Landau had laid out, the sense of anticipation and adventure, the frisson of possible danger, had melted away. Rachel felt as though she were on a long, comfortable train journey, the destination unknown and mysterious, but the scenery beginning to blur into monochrome. She had no inkling that the flashing pinpricks up ahead were warning lights.

Howe's first name was Jezekiah, although in his thirty-eight years no one had ever called him that. He was good ol' Jesse, who had a joke for any occasion, who always bought the first round at the Black Horse Tavern favored by navy personnel stationed in Washington. He was rumored to have charmed the pants off two admirals' daughters, both of whom still pined for him. He was said to be a perfect gentleman and something else between the sheets.

What was never said of Jesse Howe, or even suspected, was that he might be Jewish and a spy.

All-American in appearance, Howe worked for the Intelligence Support Center in Suitland, Maryland, a branch of the Naval Criminal Investigative Service. He also had duties at the Antiterrorist Alert Center in the NCIS's threat analysis division. In his head, he carried a great many things that would be of interest to a great many people. Instead of reaping a small fortune, Howe passed his secrets on to Israel. He was Landau's greatest creation—a high-level, virtually undetectable mole.

Landau had planted Howe in America when he reached college age. He deftly nurtured Howe's career, steering him into the paths of men whose patronage could assist his progress. It helped that Howe was charming by nature and very, very bright.

Howe provided Landau with intelligence that Israel could not have gotten any other way—information that was withheld even though the United States shared more intelligence with Israel than with any other nation. It enabled Israel to continually peek into the secret lives of its Arab neighbors, to update and alter her plans for first strike and retaliation.

And Howe was only in the first stages of his career. There was no end to the ranks he might achieve. In his private moments—but only to himself, for he shared Howe with no one—Landau wondered how he might fashion Howe into a presidential candidate. Such thoughts were not altogether idle speculation.

Landau handled Howe as he did no other agent. No Mossad personnel—not even the *katsa*—was aware of, much less had any contact with, Howe. Landau knew that the Americans spied on everyone. He could not risk that a random FBI tag on some embassy runner would lead them to Howe.

Instead, Landau used *sayanim* to service Howe—from a seventy-five-year-old grandmother who'd survived Belsen, to a nineteen-year-old Georgetown sophomore whose two brothers, both U.S. fighter pilots, had flown for Israel; a factory foreman from the Newport News shipyards; a retired bus driver; and a mildly famous oncologist. Now, he added Rachel Melman to his roster.

Rachel's final brush with Howe took place at the D.C. War Memorial, close enough to the Mall's public restrooms to attract constant foot traffic. It did not go off smoothly and had unintended consequences.

It was the week after Labor Day, but there were still plenty of tourists around, along with food vendors hawking ice cream cones, soft drinks, and pretzels lathered with mustard. The trash bins, set in green metal baskets, were half-full by noon. Rachel walked along the edge of the reflecting pool and carefully dropped a candy wrapper into the bin. The distinctive yellow-and-blue envelope she'd been told would be there wasn't.

The protocol Landau had drilled into her was clear: If a brush goes wrong, if the material isn't there, walk away. Go back the next day at the same time.

Rachel was about to do that when she noticed a dark-haired, good-looking man hurrying along the path. She would have overlooked him had she not glimpsed the yellow-and-blue envelope he carried—and dropped into the bin. It was then she looked at his face closely and imprinted it in her memory.

Rachel hurried across the grass toward the Memorial. It was a loose heel on her left sandal that saved her. The heel dug into a piece of soft turf, twisted, and broke off, causing her to stumble.

Rachel examined the damage. Like it or not, she would have to walk barefoot until she found a shoe store. Then she looked up and saw the dark-haired man walking away from the Memorial. She got to her feet and started in that direction when a half-dozen men suddenly materialized and swarmed over their target. Within seconds, the dark-haired man was surrounded and hustled to a waiting sedan on Independence Avenue.

Rachel, holding both sandals by their straps, looked on in disbelief as a federal agent plucked the blue-and-yellow envelope out of the trash bin. For an instant, the agent stared directly at her. Rachel made a show of examining the broken heel, then turned and walked away. With every step she took, she expected to feel a heavy hand grip her shoulder.

Rachel reached out to Landau on the designated secure contact, but it was a CNN news cycle that answered her questions.

The lead story was the arrest of one Jezekiah Howe, a federal employee at the NCIS's Intelligence Support Center. According to the FBI, Howe had been a spy for Israel for the last ten years. Specialists were still assessing the damage he'd caused.

At the White House, the President was said to be "shocked and very disturbed" by developments.

The prime minister's office in Tel Aviv had no comment on the matter.

It was almost midnight when Landau knocked on her door. Rachel was wide awake. She let him in and, when he turned, slapped him hard across the face.

"You never told me Howe was a traitor!"

Landau pressed his fingers to his cheek, as though they might absorb the sting of her fury. He sat down in Rachel's living room with its fine antiques and security-company stickers on the windows.

"How did you recognize Howe?" he asked. "You were never supposed to see him."

"But I did—by accident."

"Did he notice you?"

"No."

"That much, at least, is good. He will not be able to identify you when they interrogate him."

Rachel pulled up an ottoman, her knees almost touching Landau's.

"Howe was betraying his country. *My country.*"

"He was a patriot—to you and us. What Howe gave us helped protect the peace."

"You might be able to justify it like that. I can't!"

Landau pinched the bridge of his nose. The chaos and fallout in Jerusalem, the long plane ride, fielding calls and faxes throughout, all this had sucked away his energy and patience.

"You can't," he parroted. "Well, I'm afraid you must. Consider yourself damn lucky that the FBI didn't pick *you* up."

"I have to go to the authorities," Rachel said. "I have to tell them what I know."

"Which is what, exactly?" Landau replied, his words rich with sarcasm. "That Howe is a spy? They know that already. Besides a confession, what could you give them? You never saw any of the material Howe passed on. You know nothing about him—his contacts, methodology, and so on. The only thing you would be doing is confessing that you were an accomplice—a minor one at that. The FBI would parade you in front of the cameras to show what vigilant spy-catchers they are, and you would end up in federal court on espionage charges. Is that how you want to throw your life away, Rachel?"

She looked away. "The life I have feels very dirty."

"I am not your confessor," Landau said coldly. "Nor the keeper of your conscience. I can only tell you that there is no need for you to feel guilty."

"Don't presume to tell me what I should or should not feel!"

Landau rose. "You must excuse me, but it is late and I am very tired. From here on in, the days will be very long."

Rachel stopped him with these words: "How was he caught?"

"Someone made a mistake. I don't know who, yet. Maybe Howe himself, maybe someone else."

"And what happens to me?"

"Why should anything 'happen' to you? Go on with your life, Rachel. You have important things to do."

"I want your word that you will never contact me again."

Landau shook his head. "It doesn't quite work that way. I can tell you that I will not reach out to you unless you are my last option."

"What if I refuse to help you then?"

Landau became very still. The moon slipped out from behind the clouds and leeched his face of color.

"You said it yourself, Rachel: Having helped a traitor makes *you* one. For the time being, you and I are the only ones who know this. I sincerely hope there will be no need to share our secret."

And that was how it had been left between them when Landau walked out of her life in the early hours of that morning.

Lights of oncoming cars washed across Rachel's face. She was glad that Ben was preoccupied and didn't notice that her eyes glistened.

That was the part of her life she had thrown down the black hole, the time she'd worked for Landau, the time it had taken to pull herself together. Before Ben, she had been able, for the most part, to push it out of her consciousness. His coming into her life had blotted out most of the jagged memories.

But one plucked thorn had been replaced by another. The more involved she became with Ben, the more she came to love him, the harder it was to maintain the lie. Not that Ben or his parents had ever focused on that particular period of her life; in fact, Rachel had done such a good job of rolling it into her residency that the time discrepancy never became an issue.

Still, the thorn pricked her heart, made her bleed shame and stole her sleep. Rachel would lie beside Ben, watching him sleep, and mouth the confession that she prayed would bring her peace. She tried to convince herself that his ignorance of Landau and her involvement with him was a harmless secret. As long as she never had to look him in the eye and lie directly, Rachel thought she could endure the thorn. In time, it would wither up and fall away.

As Rachel turned into her street, she heard her conscience mocking her. Her secret no longer slumbered: It threatened to metastasize and destroy both Ben and his love for her. If she had never crossed Landau's path or become involved with him, she could have helped Ben. Now, if she was to save him, she would have to deceive him, betray him, and keep him ignorant of Landau while at the same time trying to woo from him whatever it was he knew.

*   *   *

"Good-looking son of a bitch, isn't he?"

Kaelin Reece glanced at the female pathologist who'd escorted her to the D.C. morgue. The two women were standing beside the body of Samir el-Banna, laid out on an autopsy table. Reece wondered if the woman was depraved or simply jaded.

Reece had her tools ready: a tiny pot of fingerprint ink, the size of a blush container, and a 4 x 6 index card. Deftly, she took the fingerprints of el-Banna's right hand.

On a lab table next to the cutting instruments was a portable fax Reece had deputized from a second-floor administration office. She fed the card through to the Bureau's NCIC and Terrorist Profile Program computers.

"So what did the pretty boy do?" the pathologist asked, firing up a Lucky.

"He killed people. Are you allowed to smoke in here?"

"Honey, it's not like anyone's gonna complain about secondhand smoke."

The pathologist laughed and Reece thought she sounded like the accordion Reece had found under the tree one long-ago Christmas.

The machine beeped to get her attention. Whoever the dead Arab was, he was on somebody's hit parade. This was exceptionally fast for a fingerprint ID.

Reece understood why when she read the fax.

Samir el-Banna. Well, well, well.

"Someone you know?" the pathologist asked her.

Reece smiled. "I'll have to ask you to leave. This is a federal security matter."

For a heartbeat, it looked like the pathologist might spoil for a fight, but something in Reece's eyes made her back down. When she reached the door she said, loud enough for Reece to hear: "Bitch!"

Reece wasn't listening, too busy pulling up her storehouse of knowledge on el-Banna. There was a lot to sift through.

Reece had been called to the Dent Place scene because a sharp-eyed firefighter had discovered a Jordanian passport sewn into the lining of a jacket on one of the dead men and had taken it to his battalion commander. The commander had a brother in the intelligence community. He knew from terrorists.

Reece hadn't held out much hope of anything when she interviewed the battalion commander at Dent Place. But she knew better than to discard a lead before checking it out completely. Now she was coming up sevens.

Reece's thoughts about el-Banna snagged on the fact that he had never before operated on American soil. *At least not so's we know.*

Landau is in town, she remembered, and then it all fell into place. *Oh, shit! Arabs and Israelis. It's high noon at the O.K. Corral. Jamal's here, too. Gotta be. Landau, you son of a bitch! What else didn't you tell me?*

*   *   *

Rachel pulled her car into her postage-stamp–size driveway and killed the engine. Ben got out and looked at the front of Rachel's home with its glowing carriage lantern by the gleaming black door, a sprig of spring flowers tied to the decorative lion's-head knocker. From the first time she'd brought him here, he'd felt as much at home here as anywhere.

"Thanks."

"For what?"

"For being here."

Her lips felt like down against his ear. "As long as you want me."

Inside, Rachel turned on the lights, drew the curtains, and reset the alarm.

The shower was running by the time Rachel came upstairs. The bathroom was filled with steam. She stripped and stepped into the shower, hot and stinging, into Ben's arms. They stood like that, arms around each other, for a long time as the water pounded their flesh.

"Do you want something to help you sleep?" Rachel asked as she dried his back.

Ben shook his head. "I'll be okay."

They slipped under the covers, Rachel lying in the crook of Ben's arm, listening to his heart slow, slow, until its beat was steady and she knew he was asleep. Only then did she turn off the night-light.

One hundred sixty feet away, behind a garage-roof parapet, an Israeli marksman whispered into his radio, then pressed his eye against the rubber tip of the scope and resumed scanning the perimeter.

Sixteen

BEN'S EYES SNAPPED OPEN and he was awake instantly. He knew he'd been dreaming, but he retained none of the images. Which was just as well.

Rachel was fast asleep and he was careful not to wake her. He kept a change of clothes in Rachel's closet, was dressed and out the door in fifteen minutes. The smell of last night's rain lay heavy on the predawn overcast.

Ben walked down to Dupont Circle, where he flagged a cab that took him to the Federal Triangle. He walked the rest of the way to the law offices, nodded to the sleepy security guard in the lobby, then stepped into the elevator.

Moving quickly, Ben crossed the reception area and entered his father's office. He turned on the lights and focused on the desk. He didn't dare look around. There were framed photos everywhere.

Sid Poltarek had embraced computers enthusiastically. All possible bells and whistles had been integrated into his IBM system. As a precaution, he'd shared the necessary passwords with Ben.

Ben brought up the client list, failed to find Manshur's name, and proceeded to the expert-witness file.

A thought continued to prey on him like a circling vulture: Why hadn't he told the detective what the dying man had said to him?

In the cool light of day, Ben could not understand this. He could not hide behind the excuses of shock or terror. Yes, he'd found himself in the middle of a bloody, inexplicable situation, but that didn't mean he'd been unable to think. What alarm had the detective inadvertently set off that had caused Ben to lie?

He replayed those terrible moments, conjuring up the detective, Priestly, the questions he'd asked, how insistent he'd been.

Maybe that was it. Priestly had been pushy, overeager to know something that, to Ben's way of thinking, was at best peripheral. Faced with a dead man and a bewildered, frightened bystander, Priestly had focused not on what had taken place but on what the dead man might have told Ben. Where was the sense or logic in that?

The computer beeped to inform him that its search was ready. Ben ran the cursor down the list and clicked on Manshur's name.

Mustafa Manshur, Lebanese, a resident of France, a professor of physics at the Sorbonne. Employed by Sid Poltarek to serve as an expert witness in *Marbella Industries* v. *Lockheed*. Sid Poltarek's chess opponent— a good one, too.

That's it?

Ben sat back in the high-back leather chair. Why would his father have been meeting a man he obviously respected, and whose company he enjoyed, in a seedy train-station café? And lie about it to his son? There had to be more to Manshur than was contained in this particular entry.

Ben brought up the Marbella Industries case and reviewed it. Nothing. Manshur had been one of six physicists his father had used. There was nothing compelling or unusual about the Lebanese's testimony.

Ben examined the sequence of events from another angle. First Manshur dies, an alleged suicide. Then his parents are killed by a hit-and-run driver. The two incidents occur at different times, in different cities, thousands of miles apart. What possible connection could there be?

Ben willed himself to become still, to allow his mind to drift rather than try to force an answer from it. There was something about Manshur's death, something he wasn't seeing.

Or remembering.

Manshur had not been alone when he died. The body of another man, still unidentified, had been found in the apartment. Someone who had come to see Manshur.

Just like someone came to me: "Are you Poltarek?"

Ben examined this connection as gently as he might a glass figurine. He reached for the phone and was punching in the number when another possibility slammed into his consciousness. The dying man had whispered, "Are you Poltarek?" Not "Are you *Benjamin* Poltarek?" Had the stranger been referring to, looking for, his father?

*　*　*

"She calls herself Kaelin Reece of the FBI. She says she knows you. She's at the guard post."

The *katsa* eyed Landau over a coffee mug emblazoned with the logo of Israel's fiftieth anniversary. He thought Landau looked all right for a man who'd slept only a few hours, his clothes rumpled because he hadn't had a chance to change or clean up before the *katsa* brought him the news about Reece.

When Landau stretched, his spine cracked.

"Get her off the street," he said. "Baby-sit her until I get cleaned up."

Twenty minutes later, a somewhat refreshed Landau entered the room where visa applicants waited for interviews. He nodded to the *katsa*, who seemed glad to leave.

"Good morning, Kaelin. You're up early."

"You look like shit, Landau."

"Please. Spare me nothing."

"Why didn't you tell me about el-Banna?"

"Would you like some coffee?"

"I'd like an explanation."

Landau saw how well turned out Reece looked, rested, fresh, and for a moment he resented that.

"What kind of explanation would you prefer, Kaelin?"

"How about something out of the ordinary—like the truth? Dent Place was one of your safe houses. Sometime earlier in the day you snatched el-Banna and took him there. Even the pro-Israel congressmen would have lost their breakfast if they'd seen el-Banna in your basement."

She paused. "What really tears me is that I was the one who gave you el-Banna. You recognized his picture from the pile I showed you, but you didn't say word one. Kept it to yourself, ran him to ground, and tried to make him talk.

"Did you succeed? Of course you did. Now it's time to pony up."

"Kaelin—"

"Do not fuck with me on this, Landau. No one knows how big a fool I've been, but you know? I don't give a shit if they find out. Because if you don't share, you'll be taken to Dulles in leg irons and this story will be plastered all over tonight's news."

"Can I offer you coffee?"

"You can, but I don't want it. Fess up."

Landau called on his best, soft, inclusionary tone. "I recognized el-Banna from the photographs you showed me."

"How did you track him down?"

"You're aware that we have resources in this city, Kaelin. But don't think for a minute that I would serve them up to you."

Kaelin accepted that. If the tables were turned, neither would she.

"Once you had him, why didn't you call me?"

"Like you said: We had him—and that's all. No information."

"But you made him talk."

"Yes. But I don't know what he said."

Reece puffed out her cheeks, exasperated. "Just when we were doing so well. Landau—"

"Listen to me." His intensity was almost physical, made her start. "Two of my men died in that house. El-Banna's watchers followed them back and blew them apart."

"So what they knew—"

"Died with them?" Landau laughed bitterly. "Not quite. There was a third man, the interrogator. He managed to escape."

Quickly and concisely, Landau outlined how Tarnofsky had come to be at the Poltareks' home. He was counting on the possibility that Reece had not yet connected Dent Place to the Poltareks and he was right. His giving her information she didn't have was currency in Landau's account.

When he was finished, Reece had to take a moment to absorb the details and to settle herself.

"El-Banna and his troops came to this country to murder Sidney Poltarek? Maybe his entire family?"

"That would be part of the operation, yes."

"Your man—Tarnofsky—he made it to the Poltareks' apartment but didn't realize the husband and wife were dead. You suspect that whatever information he had, he passed on to the kid, Benjamin."

Landau nodded.

"Now the elder Poltareks would be *sayanim*, correct?"

"Yes." The notion of *sayanim* was nothing new to the FBI.

"But not the boy."

"Young man, actually."

"Sitting duck, *actually*. If he knows what you think he knows. Does he?"

"He says no. Tarnofsky never said anything."

"But you don't believe him."

"I don't think he's deliberately hiding anything. It's probably the shock. In time, he'll remember."

"Where's our friend Jamal while all this is going on?"

"Probably very worried. Consider: He loses el-Banna, his best killer, plus two expendable gunners. He *knows* el-Banna gave up something before he died. But what? How much?"

"To whom?"

Landau shook his head. "If Jamal could trail my men to a safe house, then he's smart enough to have figured out that there's a connection between the survivor, Tarnofsky, and the Poltareks. Now the situation mutates: The Poltareks die as per schedule. Fine. But then el-Banna is taken. Everything becomes an ungodly mess. Tarnofsky escapes. If *you* were Jamal, where do you think Tarnofsky would run?"

"To the surviving Poltarek."

"Exactly."

"Which is what makes him a sitting duck."

"A *protected* duck. I've had a team on him since last night."

Reece looked away, feeling claustrophobic in this crappy waiting room, wishing for a window so that she could see the sky.

"What's Jamal after?" she asked, not looking at him.

"I don't know."

"Then I don't have any choice. I have to take this to Mitchell."

Bruce Mitchell was Reece's boss in the antiterrorist division. Landau thought he was marginally competent, but no more than that.

"Don't do that, Kaelin."

"Come on, Landau! We have Arabs taking down American citizens in the nation's capital. I can't sit on this."

"I'm not saying you should. But if you go to Mitchell, he'll push every red button he can. He'll assure you that the press won't get wind of an antiterrorist operation, but you know that's nonsense. And when Jamal feels the hunt, he'll burrow so far down we'll never find him."

Landau paused to let her digest this, then finished, "There is another way."

Reece agreed with Landau's assessment of Mitchell's actions. He was a by-the-book guy, with predictable results.

"What do you have in mind?"

Landau had thought through this contingency measure hours ago.

"My boss talks to your boss."

"The prime minister to the President?"

"Right. We make this a tight—*very tight*—joint operation: you, me, and your troops if and when we need them."

"Let's not forget *your* troops."

Landau ignored that. "Mitchell is kept in the loop out of courtesy, but you and I run the show."

Reece did not need a vivid imagination to picture how Mitchell would react to this arrangement. Still, how much choice would he have if word came down from the President directly?

"Say you can pull this off. What's our objective?"

"To find Jamal and snip his operation."

"'Snip.' You mean interrogate him until he gives up the details."

"We don't know what Jamal is running here," Landau said quietly. "It's not likely that the threat is nuclear. But biological, chemical? That's possible. He wouldn't need much of a crew to help him with that. For all we know, el-Banna had already done the groundwork."

Images of Department of Defense videos filled Reece's mind, sheep and cattle collapsing like cardboard cutouts after a device the size of a baseball was opened in a contained environment.

"How long will it take to set this up?" she asked.

"Not long," Landau replied. "Let me get you that coffee."

* * *

It was still too early for any of the staff to have arrived, but the chair across from Ben's was occupied.

Henry Blake was a rail-thin black man who wore, whatever the weather, a black wool three-piece suit with a fob watch in the vest pocket. The cowboy boots and black diamond cuff studs rounded out the image of an 1890s riverboat gambler.

At fifty-three, Blake was the oldest detective in the D.C.P.D. He had been Sid Poltarek's friend for over a quarter of a century, going back to the time when Poltarek had represented the department's black officers in a landmark civil rights action.

"I sure am sorry 'bout your daddy," Blake said. His voice was as soft as his caramel-colored eyes. "I don't think it's all that good for you to be sitting here by yourself, Ben."

"I need your help," Ben said.

"That's what you said on the phone. That's why I'm here."

"I need to see the police report on my parents' deaths."

"Why would you be needin' that?"

"I have to know exactly how they died." Ben hesitated. "If it really was a hit-and-run."

"Why wouldn't it be?"

"Henry—"

"No, Ben. If I'm going to help you, I have a right to ask. I may be Internal Affairs, but like every other detective, I leave a silicon trail when I call up a report. If I'm going to be asked later why I did that, I'd best have a good reason."

"I can't give you anything solid."

"Was Sid in trouble? Was he being threatened by somebody?"

"No. If Sid and Rose's deaths relate to anything, it's the business in Paris."

Ben sketched out the events in Paris and how Mustafa Manshur had figured in them.

"Sounds a little thin," Blake opined. "Still, helluva coincidence, all these people dyin' one after another." He glanced at the ceiling. "What did you say the name of that detective was?"

"Priestly."

"The report will be filed under his badge. Why don't you and I trade places."

Blake's fine-boned fingers danced over the keyboard. Not five minutes had elapsed before the printer clicked on.

Ben and the detective read through the report, a compilation of eye-witness accounts and memoranda from technicians and crime-scene experts. Included were computer-generated diagrams detailing a likely sequence starting with the time the crosswalk light turned orange and the Poltareks stepped off the sidewalk.

Ben's eyes burned when he got to the part about the SUV striking his parents, how fast it had been going, how hard they'd been hit. When he looked up, Blake was watching him.

"I'll get through this," Ben said.

"I know you will, son."

"Something's not right," Ben said. "Something's out of whack."

"Meaning?"

"Look at the diagrams. If you start at the point where . . . where Sid and Rose were hit, and play the sequence backwards, here's what you have: In order for them to end up where they did, the techs say that the truck had to have been going at least forty miles an hour. Now check the distance between the impact point and the corner where the truck turned. The way the math works, the driver would have to have hit the gas just after he turned the corner in order to reach that speed before impact."

"You figured this out in your head?" Blake asked.

"I'm a magician. Magic is smoke, mirrors, and math. Angles, planes, horizons."

"Okay. Let's assume you're right with the numbers. What do they mean?"

"Back it up some more. We know the truck couldn't have been idling at that corner—too much traffic. A cop would have moved him along. So the driver would want to reach the corner a few seconds before the cross-walk light goes on and my parents step off the curb. Question is, if his window of opportunity is so narrow, where is he waiting? It has to be close enough to the corner, but not so close that he'd attract attention." Ben raised his eyebrows at Blake.

"The Watergate," the detective said softly. "In the turnaround area. The driver could have slipped the doorman a fifty to idle."

"Yes. And my parents park at the Watergate when they go to the Kennedy Center. They would have come out the front doors where the driver would have seen them." The last words caught in Ben's throat, tasted bitter.

"After that, all the bastard had to do was fall in behind them. At the corner, he needed a little luck, not to get stuck too far behind. He got it. They didn't."

Ben wiped away the tears. "Son of a bitch!"

"You know what you're saying, don't you?" Blake said quietly.

"Yeah. That it wasn't a freak hit-and-run. Sid and Rose were murdered."

"Don't go down that road, Ben."

"What do you mean? The facts—"

"Facts you made out of math. You think that the interval and distances can't be played with? I can feed those same numbers into a game machine and come up with a dozen scenarios. You know that."

"Maybe. But that doesn't mean this one's wrong."

"No. But it is only one."

"What about Paris? Everything that happened there . . ."

"It's a reach, Ben. Paris is a long way off. Here, all you have are circumstantial details—not even evidence."

"What does your gut tell you, Henry?"

The detective sighed. "I've seen your magic, Ben. I know what you can conjure up out of thin air. But some of the things you said, well . . . I want to think about them. Okay?"

"Okay." Ben went into the galley and got coffee going. When he returned, he asked, "What do you know about Priestly?"

"He's been on the job for twelve years," Blake replied. "Not a cowboy, not a slacker. Very steady. Methodical."

"Do we want to run my thinking by him?"

"Not yet. Like I said, let me turn this over." He paused. "And I want your word that you won't go off half-cocked until I talk to you."

Ben smiled faintly. "I wouldn't know where to go half-cocked, Henry." He paused. "Thanks for coming down, hearing me out."

"Wouldn't have it any other way. You let me know if you need any help with the funeral arrangements."

The phone rang. Ben was tempted to let it go until he thought it might be someone calling about Sid.

It was Rachel, her tone frantic, then filled with relief as she scolded him for leaving without telling her.

Through the open door, Ben saw Mary come in, her eyes red and puffy. When she saw Ben, she dropped her purse and briefcase and rushed toward him.

"Rachel, I gotta go. I'll be at the apartment later."

Ben rose and allowed himself to be gathered up in Mary's tearful embrace. Over her shoulder, he saw Henry Blake standing looking out the window, his hands together in front of him, already a mourner.

Seventeen

I MUST SAY, MISS SAWYER, your credentials are very impressive."

The Reverend Winslow Garrett spoke with a mid-Atlantic accent. He was in his early sixties, a scarecrow in gray, with a freckled scalp and tufts of hair that trailed out from inside his ears like overgrown ivy.

His office was a dusty affair, texts and manuscripts piled on a frayed Oriental rug, potted plants waning from neglect.

"Thank you," Judith said. She wore a conservative beige suit she'd bought that morning.

"Yes, very impressive," Garrett repeated. Judith heard the soft clatter of his dentures. "Tell me, Miss Sawyer, what was it that brought you back home after these"—Garrett squinted at her résumé—"eight years?"

"To be honest, I was homesick." Judith gave him a misty, low-wattage smile. "My parents passed on when I was doing postgraduate work. I had the opportunity to do research in Egypt and took it. I stayed not only because of the work but because I loved the people and the culture." She paused for effect. "There really wasn't much for me here at the time. But I suppose you can't stay away forever. At least that's what I realized. I want to put down roots."

"Meet a young man?" Garrett asked kindly.

"I'd very much like a family," Judith said quietly.

Garrett closed her folder and crossed his hands on top of it.

"Miss Sawyer, from what you've shown me, I think you are qualified to teach at any school in this city. Almost overqualified for our little Sunday school. Not that we wouldn't love to have you. Unfortunately, we don't have an opening in our K-to-six section. Miss Buffett, who teaches geography and history, has been with us forever and she's still a year or two from retirement."

Judith smiled wanly. "I understand. Mr. Garrett, do you keep a list of qualified teachers, in case a vacancy comes up?"

"Of course. And I would be happy to add your name to it, if you wish."

"Please."

"However, I'm sure that by the time we require your services, you will have been spoken for."

I don't think so.

Judith gathered up her things and let Garrett walk her out of the office.

"One thing I forgot to ask you, Miss Sawyer. What denomination are you?"

"Episcopalian."

Garrett beamed. "Of course."

The wood floor, slightly bowed with age and smelling sweetly of lemon wax, creaked under her shoes. The fine crown moldings and the soft honey-colored walls reminded Judith of the kind of school she'd gone to in that California seaside town so long ago. She lingered at the open door to a classroom and took in the familiar sight of one-piece desks lined up in rows. Between the blackboard and the teacher's desk was the American flag.

Although the classroom was vacant, her mind was filled with the sounds of children. Except they sang and shouted in Arabic, not English, and all of them had faces that belonged to her dead son.

"Miss Sawyer?"

Judith caught herself. "I'm sorry. It's just that it's been so long since I've seen such a beautiful, well-preserved building."

"We do try to keep it up," Winslow Garrett said proudly. "After all, it is an historic landmark. Dates back to 1815." Judith nodded. She'd seen the plaque out front.

"Perhaps you'd like to see the church itself?" Garrett offered.

"I really don't want to take up your time."

"Nonsense. Take the next left. That'll lead us to the connecting corridor."

When they reached the end of the hall, Garrett squeezed around Judith to get at the lock. A set of stairs took them down to another hall, a short one, to a door that opened on the basement, which was used as a storage room.

"So many nooks and crannies in these old buildings," Garrett said, puffing his way up one more set of stairs.

"Aren't there though," Judith remarked. She'd been counting on that.

"Here we are," Garrett said, hauling himself by the banister the last few steps.

Following his direction, Judith turned right, instead of going up to the second level. She found herself in a small foyer with several red-cushioned chairs and some scarred end tables that could have come from a yard sale. Below the small built-in bookcases, ancient radiators gurgled and clanged.

Garrett ushered her around the corner, and she found herself standing at the back of St. John's Church.

Unlike the school next door, the church had not been renovated for some time. A musty odor mingled with the strong scent of beeswax candles; dust motes were illuminated by wall sconces. Judith noted that the odor became more pronounced as Garrett led her down the aisle. She thought it came from the faded red-and-white cushions built into the seats and backs of the pews.

On her left was a crypt carved of marble, with candles, a floral arrangement, and a crucifix above it. In a recessed panel, inscribed on a marble plaque, was the *in memoriam* to the Reverend William Hawley, a nineteenth-century rector.

The sacristy was dominated by a large three-paned stained-glass window depicting scenes from the Bible. The altar was in an open area bordered by two thick granite pillars.

"Isn't it magnificent?" Garrett said proudly.

"Breathtaking."

Judith thought the Reverend Garrett was not a well-traveled man if he ranked this little house of worship, albeit quaint, among the Seven Wonders of the World.

"I suppose you know what is somewhat special about our little church," he said after showing her the choir loft.

Judith did, but wanted him to tell her. "No, I don't."

Garrett waggled his finger. He walked up the aisle until he found pew 54, where he pointed to the floor. There, below the shelf that held the hymnals, was a row of knee cushions, one foot square, six inches thick. On each of the plum-colored velour covers was sewn the presidential seal and the name of the chief executive who, during his term in office, had worshiped there.

Judith read the names Ronald Reagan, Jimmy Carter, and Gerald Ford.

"This pew is reserved for *every* sitting president, isn't it?" Judith asked.

"You know your history," Garrett replied.

On her way out, Judith stopped in front of the collection box. She made sure that Garrett noticed the ten-dollar bill she slipped through the slot. It was a generous amount for a schoolteacher, and the man of the cloth would remember her for it.

Winslow Garrett bade her a warm goodbye and wished her well in her quest for a job.

Instead of leaving, Judith tarried in front of the church. To the casual eye, she was just another tourist photographing an unprepossessing landmark.

Judith framed the pseudo-Grecian columns and the bell tower above them. She then photographed the office building next door, which was being gutted. Of particular interest to her was the long waste chute that ran all the way from the top floor to the Dumpster below.

Judith went around the corner to H Street. Between the church and the school was a street-level connecting passage, framed to look like a tiny house. In front of the passage was a delivery area large enough for two cars or a good-size truck. On top of the city's NO PARKING sign was one in black: RESERVED CLERGY PARKING ONLY.

Judith took pictures of everything.

She went back to Sixteenth Street and photographed the bulletin board encased in glass and wrought iron. Now she had the timetables for the Sunday services.

Off to the side was a smaller board:

EDUCATION PROGRAMS

SUNDAY

NURSERY 8:45 TO 12:00

FORUM 10:00

CHURCH SCHOOL 10:00 TO 11:00

Back in Cairo, she hadn't believed Jamal when he'd told her how easy the first steps would be. Everything was out in the open, he'd said. One had only to know where to look.

Judith crossed H Street, went into Lafayette Park, and bought a snow cone.

She had been in Washington for only a few days, but she was acclimatizing fast. At first, the pace of the city had bothered her. After the endless silence and sweep of the desert, Washington seemed like a giant anthill. Judith forced herself to think of Cairo and the other cities of the Middle East she'd visited, and then the noise and crowds didn't bother her.

She had spent her first night at the Comfort Inn on Twelfth Street. After sleeping off her jet lag, she'd moved to a residential hotel near the National City Christian Church. She'd paid for a month in advance, and the clerk seemed not to care that she offered cash instead of a credit card. The hotel housed a lot of young women who'd saved their waitressing money then got on the Greyhound bus at small-town stations throughout the South and Midwest.

Judith had opened a bank account, applied to have her credit cards reinstated, then stood in line half the morning at the DMV. She'd used the Yellow Pages to find the locations of midrange department stores, bought a map of the city, and begun walking. At the end of the day, she had a wardrobe. Tomorrow her new bank account would be fattened by a deposit from the National Bank of Cairo.

Looking at the people she passed in Lafayette Park, Judith thought America hadn't changed very much at all. There were more homeless around—and police, too. The tourists were no different from the ones she'd sometimes chanced to see at archaeological sites or in the great cities of the Middle East. They were, for the most part, humorless and grim, determined to squeeze a memorable moment out of each dollar spent.

Behind her sunglasses, Judith felt invisible, as though she were a ghost in their midst, leaving a kiss of cold air on their cheeks as she drifted by. Deep in her heart was an ache she could not still, memories that would never dissolve in the sharp acid of time. She told herself that the ache was there to remind her why she had traveled so far, and of all the things she had yet to do. It whispered to her that she didn't have to hate these people who were no longer kinsmen but not quite strangers. She had no reason to level their cities or cause them to die like flies. They had absolutely nothing to do with the fight she had brought to their shores. They couldn't possibly change or influence what she needed to cause.

Judith was so lost in thought that she was surprised to suddenly find herself at the edge of the park, on the Pennsylvania Avenue side.

There it was, right in front of her. The White House. Where Charles Woodbridge lived.

Judith went to a souvenir stall. Here were coffee mugs with Woodbridge's image on them, T-shirts, and flags. Even a life-size cardboard likeness that tourists could pose beside and show to the neighbors back home.

Judith thought the years had been kind to Woodbridge. Even in these bad reproductions she saw a man fifteen years younger, big and rangy, with flashing white teeth and dark, thick, curly hair. A man who had many faces—the seducer of juries; the contemplative scholar seeking justice; the sly, tenacious inquisitor who could twist a witness's words to mean anything he wished them to mean.

Her father's words. Judith watching as Woodbridge, then lead counsel for the investment firm her father had allegedly robbed, picked apart Lester Sawyer's truth like so much carrion, then turned around and hammered accusations like nails into a crucifix.

Charles Woodbridge, hailed by most of the world as the best President in fifty years, loved by his people, was to Judith a monster who devoured the innocent. But Woodbridge's real sin lay not in the destruction of Lester Sawyer but in the fact that as a brilliant legal technician, he had to have known that Sawyer was innocent.

Still you went ahead and destroyed him.

Judith heard the gun as it went off in her father's hand. She saw the rooster's plume of blood spraying high in the air, as the bullet tore apart her father's head.

Woodbridge, blood-drenched, crouching, ducking, then looking up to find his witness sprawled in the box like a broken puppet. Judith remembered that those who rushed up had gone to Woodbridge first, to see if he was injured. Only the deputies, charging into the room, went after her father, their guns drawn.

Did you think you had washed that blood from your skin? Did you believe you could ever do it?

Judith thought Woodbridge did believe this. Here was a man so callous and blind that he'd never even sent a condolence letter to his victim's family. No apology, no remorse, no plea for forgiveness. Nothing.

He probably doesn't even remember, she thought, staring at the grand house.

Woodbridge's career had not been impacted in the least by that sensational moment. If anything, the incident lionized him. Later, it became part of the Woodbridge legend, how he'd stood up, unarmed, to a deranged gunman, having only words to defend himself with.

But he will remember. On a Sunday. As he sits in pew 54. I will come for him then, I will look into his soul and he will remember, and the prayer in his mouth will become one for himself.

Eighteen

B EN GOT OUT OF THE ELEVATOR and walked down the hall to his parents' apartment. He had steeled himself for this moment, thought he could manage it if he got through the door.

There was yellow barricade tape across the door and a police seal along the seam. Suddenly, the image of what wouldn't be waiting for him on the other side of that door poked him in the throat.

Through a haze of red, Ben reached out and ripped away the seal and the tape, fumbled with the key as the gummy underside of the tape stuck to the sole of his shoe.

The body of the man he'd held in his arms had been reduced to a cartoonlike figure outlined with white tape. The figure lay in such a position that Ben would have to step over it if he wanted to go upstairs.

He didn't need to do that right away.

Now that he was home, the things he had only idly wondered about became real. He would have to clean out his parents' closets. What about the personal mementos, the pictures and paintings and sculptures and a lifetime's worth of bric-a-brac? And then there was the furniture, their bed . . .

Ben realized he was close to hyperventilating and shut off the seemingly endless demands bearing down upon him. One thing at a time. First, he needed to do what he'd come for.

Ben fired up the computer in his father's study. Swiftly, he pulled up the references to Mustafa Manshur, but found nothing more than he had in the office files.

Not good enough.

Ben went on the Internet, seeking anything that might cross-reference with the physicist. In a few minutes, he had his answer, courtesy of the abbreviated, English version of Cairo's *Al-Ahram.*

The day before Manshur died, two other men had also been killed: Abdul Muhsain in Damascus, Wadi Ghusha in Beirut. The first had been Manshur's cousin; the second, his brother-in-law.

Ben sat back, staring at the three-inch newspaper column. He was lucky that Muhsain and Ghusha were prominent Middle Eastern businessmen; otherwise the newspaper would never have printed the story. So now there were *three* men, all related, all dead within forty-eight hours of one another. Plus the dead man in Manshur's apartment and the one who'd died in Ben's arms. The last two were not related to Manshur, at least not by blood. But could they be related to *each other?* Had someone come to warn Manshur or pass on information just as the anonymous man had whispered to Ben, "Tell him they are bringing in an American."

And something else! Suddenly, Ben remembered that the dying man's message hadn't been for him.

"This is for Landau, only him . . . Tell him they are bringing in an American . . . Landau will know what to do."

Ben shivered as he recalled the desperation and intensity of the dying man's words.

Who were you? he asked himself. *Who is Landau? And the American?*

Landau . . . Ben knew he needed something more specific than the name in order to run a search.

There were other things, too, names the stranger had managed to get out. Ben closed his eyes and called up the scene in his mind, him holding the man, the stranger gasping as the life was pumped out of him.

"Rothman . . . Bernstein, dead!"

Ben scribbled down the names. One more. There was one more.

Benny? Bunny? Beignet? L. Something . . . Dana? Bana. L. Bana. Albania? No.

He typed in "L. Bana." The computer searched, then requested more details.

Ben drummed his fingers on the edge of the keyboard.

The way the stranger had spoken, his accent . . . Middle Eastern? A tie-in to Manshur and his relations? Possibly.

Ben looked at the screen: L. Bana. Not necessarily Arabic. Not unless it was spelled a different way.

He keyed in "el-Bana."

"Shit!" The search yielded nothing. He tried another variation: el-Banna.

The computer punched up a story from the *Times* of London. El-Banna, a globe-trotting Jordanian businessman suspected of terrorist ties.

There was his picture. The handsome face meant nothing to Ben. He read on.

El-Banna present in cities at the same time as political assassinations were carried out. Strong suspicion but no proof to connect him to these killings.

But there were reports that el-Banna was close to Hafez Jamal, a well-known terrorist who opposed the Mideast peace talks.

The current whereabouts of the two men were unknown.

Ben's mind worked furiously as the pieces spun and fell into place.

Manshur and his relatives, the man who had died in his arms, Samir el-Banna, and Hafez Jamal—all of them were from the Middle East. Was it possible that either el-Banna or Jamal or both were responsible for the killing of Mustafa Manshur and his kin?

Suddenly, Ben realized where he was going with this. He wanted to stop, but couldn't.

Manshur was connected to Sid Poltarek. If Manshur had told Sid something, would that have placed Ben's father in jeopardy?

Damn right—if either el-Banna or Jamal was responsible for Manshur's murder.

Which meant that one or both of the terrorists could have followed Ben and his father back to the United States, waited for the right moment: *outside the Kennedy Center on a cold, wet night.*

Dear God, what did you do in Paris, Sid? What did Manshur tell you that got you and Rose killed?

Ben remembered his talk with Henry Blake, how he had interpreted the crime scene to infer that the driver of the sport utility vehicle could also have been a cold, deliberate killer.

El-Banna? Maybe. Jamal? Absolutely.

Ben took a moment to compose himself. He set aside everything he had learned and deduced. The next question related to Sid. What else had Sid done besides lawyering? What was he involved in that a man would die trying to reach him with a message about an American?

Ben had no doubt that the stranger who'd died in his arms had come not for him but for Sid.

Sid was the connection to Landau.

Who was Landau? The only thing Ben was sure of was that Landau had to know about an American.

Who was the American? Would his father have understood the reference?

Ben shivered. What he knew about terrorism he'd gotten from sound bites and the occasional magazine article. He needed to know more. If he researched el-Banna and Jamal, maybe he would come across a reference to Landau.

And he had to work quickly. The meaning behind the stranger's words, "They are bringing in an American," was clear: Whatever the terrorists were planning in the United States necessitated using a native. They could not do it themselves. Ben imagined a small, dusty room, empty except for a cheap alarm clock, ticking away. *A timetable.*

What was the terrorists' mission? How much time had already elapsed? How much was left?

Concentrate on Landau. He's your key—

"Freeze!"

Ben's last action was instantaneous: His little finger tapped the DELETE key and the screen went blue.

He stared at the woman holding the gun on him. "Who are you?"

"Special Agent Reece, FBI." She held out her ID. "Are you alone, Mr. Poltarek?"

"Yeah."

"Are you sure?"

"The seal and tape were unbroken when I got here."

"What about *after*? Don't leave this room. I'll be back in a minute."

Ben heard her heels strike the hardwood floors, disappear whenever she stepped on the rugs. He heard the soft shuffle of her feet on the staircase and wondered if she had stepped into the tape-drawn figure or skirted it.

Doors opened and closed and after a time Reece was back. Ben was leaning back against his father's desk, his arms crossed.

"What are you doing here?" he asked.

"I was about to ask you the same. You're trespassing on a crime scene. It's an indictable offense."

"This is my parents' home. I was staying here before—"

"You still shouldn't be here."

"And you? Since when did hit-and-run cases interest the FBI?"

Ben watched Reece approach the desk, look at the blue screen.

"What were you doing here?"

"My father did a lot of work at home. I was going through our case roster to see what would have to be farmed out, to whom. You still haven't answered my question."

"Mr. Poltarek, I'm here because that's where your office told me I could find you. One of your late father's clients was Kaiser-Agfa, which has a government contract for defense-related work. I'm here to ask you to give me access to that particular file so that it can be reviewed by our experts."

"For what—breaches of national security?"

"No, sir. It's just standard procedure in cases like this."

"Because my father was killed? If your people wanted to see the file, why didn't they ask him themselves?"

Ben thought Agent Reece's smile looked tighter than a suture.

"Maybe that's what would have happened. In any case, do I have your permission to take the file with me—assuming you have it here?"

Ben knew she was sinking in her own bullshit, but he didn't want her to cut and run just yet.

"Even if I had the file, I couldn't give it to you, not without the client's consent. I can call the head of Kaiser-Agfa legal and explain the situation to her. Under the circumstances, I doubt there'd be any problem."

"That's very kind of you, considering your situation. And I am sorry for your loss, Mr. Poltarek."

"Thank you. Does that mean I can stay here?"

"Let me talk to D.C. homicide."

"You'll want Detective Priestly."

Reece looked at him as she took out her cell phone. "Yes, I know."

Her conversation was brief. After breaking the connection, she said,

"It's okay for you to stay. Someone will be along to remove the seal and tape . . . and to clean up the stairs." Reece paused. "Just one thing. Detective Priestly mentioned that he'd asked you about the deceased who was found here. He said you might have remembered what he said to you."

"The dead man."

"Yes."

"Detective Priestly has it wrong," Ben said. "I told him that the dead man didn't tell me anything."

"I see. You're sure?"

"Absolutely."

"I'll mention that to the detective." Reece dipped into her jacket pocket and handed Ben a card. "Work, home, cell numbers. You can always reach me at one of them."

"Thank you. But I don't understand—"

"Kaiser-Agfa? In case there's a problem getting approval from their legal people."

Ben smiled awkwardly and walked her to the door. Agent Reece's handshake was cool and firm.

"Look after yourself, Mr. Poltarek. This time, lock the door after you. And again, my condolences."

Ben watched Reece go down the hall, then threw the deadbolt. He dropped both hands on the handle, trying to hold himself together.

He did not for an instant believe that Reece had talked to Priestly on the phone. She probably hadn't spoken to him at all. But she knew about Priestly's questions. Had Priestly mentioned them in his report? Is that where Reece had picked up on them?

It really doesn't matter, does it? The point was that Reece, like Priestly, was far more interested in the dead man than in the killing of Sid and Rose Poltarek.

Ben thought back to the connections he'd made. Had the police and the FBI made the same ones? Were they missing the same pieces that he was? And if so, did they believe that the dead man had had answers he might have passed on to Ben?

Ben felt a dull pounding at his temples, an incipient headache. He went into the powder room and fixed himself an Alka-Seltzer.

"Should I tell them?" he asked his reflection in the mirror.

The temptation was soft and sweet, like a lullaby, and Ben was very tired. But behind his bloodshot eyes, he saw a truth that continued to burn like a ship's lamp at sea: Priestly and Reece, and probably the people who stood behind them, did not really care that his mother and father were dead. They had their own agenda and it was centered around the dead stranger. Ben understood that if he gave them the little he had now they would not use it to help him, only themselves.

To hell with them. He would dig deeper, harder, longer, make more connections until he had the answers he needed. Ben splashed water on his face and went back to the computer.

*　*　*

Kaelin Reece found Landau in a most unlikely place: loitering at the end of the line of visitors who were waiting for a tour of the FBI building.

"I thought it was the one place where we wouldn't miss each other," Landau explained. After Reece led him into a restricted area, he added, "How did it go with Poltarek?"

"He's very shaky," Reece told him. "But still sharp. I think he saw right through the Kaiser-Agfa crap. When I asked him about Tarnofsky, he told me your man hadn't said word one to him."

"True or not?"

"Not. He was fiddling with Poltarek's home computer when I dropped in. The kid knows something, but he's not about to give it up."

Landau's eyes were black slits. "You're sure?"

"Give me some credit, Landau. I'm not saying Poltarek is an open book, but he's wounded, vulnerable. He tried real hard to hide behind the lie, but . . ." She shrugged. "I think we need to look into the father's computers, both home and office. Maybe there are filed-away notes about Paris."

"Can you do that?"

"With a court order? Sure."

"There may not be time for niceties."

"I know. I can get a Title VI tap order in about an hour. Our silicon cowboys can be in and out of Poltarek's equipment in no time." She paused. "What about your end?"

Landau turned just a little, so that he spoke directly to Reece and the wall behind her.

"You and I, we're good to go."

Reece was impressed. "That fast?"

"Whatever else my prime minister might do, he does not cry wolf. Your President knows that when Yakov Admony is ready for *tachless*, it's serious."

"*Tachless?*"

"'Business,' as in 'get down to.'"

"And what business are we getting down to?"

"Your Mitchell will be calling you very soon. Pretend to be surprised when he tells you that you will be paired with me. We have carte blanche on any resources we need."

"How far afield do we want to roam?"

"Until we find Jamal's nest."

"And then?"

"According to Admony, the President has agreed to allow me the privilege of having the first discussions with Jamal—as long as you are present."

"I see. You intend to take him alive. But your tone means you would rather not have me there."

"Kaelin, as a federal officer you are required to inform a suspect of his constitutional rights. I do not labor under any such onus."

"You want to torture him."

"No," Landau said softly. "I do not *want* to do that. But I will if I must. I am not going to allow Jamal to release his madness in this country."

"I know a part of you means that, Landau," Reece said quietly. "But don't you hold out on me or bullshit me. You're not doing this for the red, white, and blue. If Jamal were in Helsinki, you'd give the Finns the same spiel. Fact is, if Jamal does blow up something here and the casualty count is like Oklahoma City, Israel will take the heat—she and her supporters in Congress. That's what Admony is afraid of."

Landau looked at her keenly. "Yes, I'm aware of the consequences; yes, I will do whatever I have to to shut Jamal down. Believe me, Kaelin, when I tell you that whatever Jamal has in store for you, it will be much, much louder than Oklahoma City."

"Sometimes you frighten me, Landau," Reece said. "All power, no checks and balances."

"Then here are some checks for you," Landau replied harshly. "I am not going to survive Samarra—not politically. The crowd bays and Admony will have to deliver them my head. The only reason I am here,

Kaelin, is because Admony knows that there is no time to bring in some-one else. He's stuck with me. And given that, he knows it's suicide to handcuff me. So yes, it may seem I have all this power. But it is a chimera. It always is that.

"Now. We do this? Yes, no?"

Reece's cell phone chirped. *Mitchell.* "I guess it's yes," she said.

Nineteen

THE HUNT FOR HAFEZ JAMAL was headquartered not at the FBI's Hoover Building, a magnet for the media, but at the Washington field office in Buzzard's Point.

There were other advantages to this location. Buzzard's Point housed the Bureau's hostage rescue team. If Jamal was cornered and managed to take hostages, the HRT would be in play.

Because of its remote location and tight security, the media seldom assigned reporters to cover activity at Buzzard's Point. Even if some had been present, they would not have suspected that the delivery vans rolling through the gates contained sophisticated computer equipment, not food for the field office's cafeteria.

By midafternoon, Landau and Reece had organized their command post. While Bureau computer experts quietly hacked into Sid Poltarek's machines in his office and at home, Reece worked with an artist to prepare a composite of Hafez Jamal.

There were many photographs of Jamal available to Reece, some of them quite detailed. But the idea was not to define Jamal very closely. Jamal's sobriquet was Fast Walker. He would use his mastery of disguise to camouflage himself. Reece had the artist concentrate on the eyes and the mouth, on the slope of the cheekbones and the slant of the jaw, elements that Jamal could work around but not really change.

The cover story to be given to local and state law enforcement, and to the media, was that the suspect was wanted in connection with the wounding of a federal officer during a tractor-trailer hijacking gone bad.

The story pushed the wounded-lawman button for cops, but the part about a shipment of illicit cigarettes from North Carolina was a yawner for the media. The TV stations would run the composite out of civic duty and leave it at that.

Reece and Landau reasoned that this was the best way to get a close facsimile of Jamal's actual appearance into the hands of law enforcement throughout the southeast and northeast corridors. Cops would pay more attention, be more aggressive in pulling over people, because the call involved one of their own.

Meanwhile, Landau had turned out all his Washington embassy resources into the street. Men and women scattered throughout the city, concentrating on the ethnic neighborhoods where their appearance would not give them away and where they could eavesdrop in several languages. Their orders were specific: If they spotted Jamal, they were to contact Buzzard's Point immediately. They were to shadow Jamal, but make no attempt to apprehend him. Depending on the circumstances around Jamal, that would be the job of either the HRT or Landau's handpicked squad, which would be immediately pulled off its current assignment, the surveillance of Benjamin Poltarek, and sent after Jamal. The objective was to fall on the terrorist hard and fast, sweep him up before he or anyone else realized what had happened. Landau's private nightmare was a hostage situation that would involve the HRT and the publicity it would attract. He did not want to give Jamal a forum to talk to the world. He did not want lawyers wrapping Jamal in the Constitution or in the accoutrements of a politically persecuted victim. That way lay failure, and Jamal would laugh at him even as the handcuffs were slapped on.

Reece brought in coffee and shut the door.

"You know, we could be totally screwed if he's run to ground at one of the embassies—Syria, the UAE, even Jordan."

Landau shook his head. "They wouldn't take him, couldn't afford the risk. Whatever Jamal is running, it's an independent strike. That makes him a leper."

"They could still help him under the table."

"Before Dent Place, maybe. Not now. Word travels fast among the

Arabs. They know that two of their own died in that house. It wouldn't take much to discover who the victims had worked for. The trail leads back to Jamal and . . ." Landau spread his hands.

"Won't the Arabs recognize the composite when it's shown on TV?"

"Naturally. And they'll keep their mouths shut. They see it, it means your government is onto Jamal. No one will want to get in the way. They'll be scrambling for some kind of deniability."

"Maybe someone will think they can score points with us by turning Jamal in."

"Don't count on it. Betraying Jamal means creating a lifelong enemy. You don't do that unless you're certain Jamal will never live to see the light of another day. There's no guarantee of that."

A computer expert knocked, poked his head in.

"We've finished our run."

Reece cocked her head. "And?"

"Zip. The Paris hits pertained to legal files—Kaiser-Agfa—to airline flights and hotel reservations. Oh . . . And a reminder to bring back a special kind of foie gras."

Reece looked at Landau, who shook his head. "Sometimes goose liver is just goose liver."

"Now what?"

Landau appeared not to have heard her.

"What is the boy looking for?" he asked himself. "What's he found that he's digging in the father's files?"

"Looking for whatever Tarnofsky told him to look for?"

"Say that's true. Why won't he share it with us?"

Reece shrugged. "No idea. I think the way to go is to get someone close to him, someone he trusts and will open up to."

Landau nodded as if he agreed. He didn't mention that he already had someone close to Poltarek. Closer than Reece could have suspected. But for now, there was no reason to tell her about Rachel.

Instead, he asked, "Any ideas as to whom that might be?"

Reece went to her computer and pulled up Ben's phone records for the last few days.

"We know he has a fiancée, Dr. Rachel Melman. Calls to the hospital where she works, her apartment . . ."

"I don't think a fiancée would work with us, do you?" Landau suggested delicately.

"Nope. But here's something. A couple of calls to D.C. Internal Affairs, a Detective Henry Blake."

Reece pulled up Blake's 202 personnel file.

"There's the connection to the Poltareks," she said, running her finger down the screen. "Sid Poltarek did some civil rights work for black policemen."

She scanned ahead. "And here's something interesting. Henry Blake decides to have a peek at the report Priestly filed."

Landau was at her side instantly. "When?"

"By the looks of it, not long after Poltarek called him." She looked at Landau. "Our boy has a friend. A cop friend."

Landau knew exactly where she was going with this: Blake, a law enforcement officer, could be induced to cooperate. In the worst case, ordered to do so.

But there was more.

"Why would Poltarek want to know what's in Priestly's report?" he muttered.

"Let's have a look at it."

Reece called it up and they both read.

"Sounds pretty much cut-and-dried," Reece started to say.

"Yes, it does," Landau agreed softly. "Except something's not right. Read again the part about Priestly's asking Poltarek if Tarnofsky said anything to him."

Reece did. "I'm not getting it."

"Priestly says that *on three occasions* he asked Poltarek about Tarnofsky. Each time Poltarek claimed that Tarnofsky had told him nothing."

"So?"

"So why three times? Priestly's chief concern should have been with the body—whom it belonged to, and how it got there. And he addressed those questions one by one, right here, got rid of them with a simple 'Unknown.'

"But when it came to what the dead man might have said, Priestly became more insistent, even though it was a peripheral issue. The witness had already told him he didn't know Tarnofsky. Why belabor the point of what Tarnofsky might or might not have said?"

"What are you getting at?" Reece asked.

"I think you know."

"Priestly was asking not for himself, but because someone else wanted to know, *had* to know." She drove it home. "Hafez Jamal wanted to know because Tarnofsky had been the only survivor at Dent Place. He was in the basement, which means he was the interrogator. If Samir el-Banna had said anything about Jamal's operation, it would have been to him. And that's what Tarnofsky, thinking that Poltarek was the *sayan*, would have passed on."

Reece looked at Landau. "If this hangs together, that means Priestly is Jamal's boy."

"Oh, it hangs," Landau said grimly. "And Priestly is exactly that. Which also means that Jamal knows where Poltarek is at any given moment—"

"—And he doesn't *need* to come out of his hole to find him," Reece finished. "You've been hanging Poltarek out like a chum carcass, hoping Jamal'd come close so your people could take him. That's not going to happen."

Landau's lips creased into a bitter smile, as if he'd bitten into rotten fruit.

"True. But now we can use Priestly to lead us to Jamal, can't we? Priestly will get the hot sheet along with everyone else. He'll take one look and recognize the composite as being Jamal. He'll have to make contact right away, won't he? Either by phone, in person, through a *mishlashim*, a dead drop. Either way, he *will* lead us to Jamal."

* * *

Within the hour, a Bell Atlantic repair truck pulled up two doors down from Priestly's townhouse in Loudoun County, near Dulles airport.

Two technicians set up wiretaps on the detective's home line and installed a microtransmitter on the cable hookup. Now Priestly's bigscreen TV became a giant listening device.

Priestly's office line presented certain difficulties. Unable to gain direct access to the phone at his desk, the agents had to go to the main switching center in the basement. It took almost an hour and a half for them to isolate Priestly's lines and hook up the tap.

Acting on Landau's suggestion, the technicians left behind a cat's paw. On the very slim chance that Priestly discovered the taps, his investigation would eventually lead him back to Detective Henry Blake. This way Priestly, although angry, would not panic. His thoughts would focus on IA. Such investigations were common enough and were always run sub rosa, with the target never being told he was under suspicion.

By late afternoon, roving teams of surveillance specialists had Priestly in their sights wherever the detective went. They were supplemented by Landau's people, who provided an ethnic mix to the watchers.

At Buzzard's Point, Landau and Reece tore open Priestly's personal and professional lives. They rolled out his MBNA bank account for the last ten years, checked his Schwab account and pension plan, sniffed for safe-deposit boxes and offshore nests.

"He seems squeaky clean," Reece observed.

"No one keeps money in coffee cans buried in the backyard," Landau told her. "Priestly would want his money working for him, not rotting. Try the relatives."

After three hours of grinding, they found it.

Priestly had a married sister in the Vermont ski country. She and her husband had put a down payment on an old Colonial and turned it into a bed-and-breakfast. The carrying costs and the renovations were onerous, yet the bills were systematically being paid down.

"Not from tourist business," Landau said.

"No," Reece agreed. "But look here: deposits every March and October for the last six years. Like clockwork. Checks written against the deposits immediately. In and out."

"Priestly's contribution?"

"You know how the Arabs work. Would they have him on a retainer? Pay him twice a year, regardless of how much or how little he'd worked for them during that period?"

"Yes, they would—if Priestly wanted it that way."

"It's not bad," Reece said. "His sister is using her married name, so Priestly's doesn't appear anywhere. The infusion of capital isn't large enough to attract the attention of the IRS. Even if it did, it could be explained away as a gift or an investment." She paused. "This is smart. Priestly keeps his money close, in the family, buying into a business that will eventually make a potful of money."

Landau caught something in Reece's tone, like a woman criticizing another's dress out of envy. But this was different. Reece's bitterness sprang from betrayal by a fellow law-enforcement officer who'd turned rotten.

Landau steered them into Priestly's social life but there was little to mine. The detective dated often but seemed not to be the marrying type. Nor did he appear to have any interest in politics of any stripe.

"Why would he take from the Arabs?" Reece asked, more to herself than to Landau.

"Because they were the first with an offer," Landau replied. "Listen. There are people who have no moral or ethical backbone. They just don't know it until someone comes along and makes an offer. Then it's like they were waiting for this moment all their lives."

"But Priestly would know something about Jamal, that he'd be working for a killer."

"Maybe not. Curious thing about Americans. You can't really relate to the miseries of other people, what happens to a Somalian or Afghani half a world away. Charity does not reach that far.

"Priestly doesn't give a damn about Arabs or Israelis. He probably thinks that both sides are filled with lunatics. But as long as one side pays him, as long as he has no personal stake in the consequences, he'll play."

"I think it would be enlightening to talk with him," Reece said tightly. "When this is all over."

Landau checked his watch. "It's coming up on six o'clock. When is the first news cycle that will show the composite?"

"Half past." Reece looked at him. "Which is when Priestly gets off work. Maybe he'll stop by his favorite watering hole. There's bound to be a TV. Want to go and check out the expression on his face?"

"Love to. But if Jamal is anywhere nearby, he might recognize me. You go."

Besides, Landau had a call to make, to one of the few women in his life who might have come to love him had he given her the chance.

* * *

At that moment, the object of Landau's single-minded interest was seated at the bar in the lounge of the Holiday Inn on Rhode Island Avenue.

The hotel was a modest affair, catering to foreign tourists, families on package deals, and businessmen. It was a safe place for Hafez Jamal to lose himself in. The babble of different tongues soothed and the evening buffet was actually quite good.

The bar had a television perched in one corner. Jamal was watching it as he sipped his two-dollar Coke.

He listened with keen interest to the story about the Middle East peace talks—no progress—and the American shuttle diplomacy—quickly running out of steam. He lost interest when the commentator turned to the ethnic slaughter in the Balkans.

Chewing on the orange slice that had come in his Coke, Jamal reckoned he could teach the Serbs and Croats a few things about "cleansing."

But that would have to wait. He had heard from Manar—Judith, as he had to call her now. A sealed envelope had been on the carpet when he'd opened the door to his room. The note inside contained information he'd expected.

Jamal looked at his disguised features in the bar mirror and sighed lightly. One could not expect *everything* to fall together neatly.

After reading Judith's message, Jamal had used the lobby pay phone to make some inquiries. Passing himself off as a union representative with a dues-rebate check for the person in question, he was given the details he required.

That, in turn, had allowed him to form a plan he would put into effect an hour or so from now.

"Cocksucker!"

Jamal turned to the pale, beefy man on the stool beside him, his sausagelike fingers wrapped around a glass of beer.

"I beg your pardon?"

The man nodded his chin at the television. "Some son of a bitch shot a trooper."

On the screen, a pretty, young reporter was doing a stand-up in front of the Virginia state trooper barracks.

The story was about a hijacking that concerned cigarettes. Jamal snorted softly. Only Americans would shoot one another over cigarettes.

But his breath caught in his throat when he saw the computer-generated composite of himself as he appeared without the disguise. Here was the reporter droning on about the suspect, giving out a hot-line number that also crawled in yellow letters across the bottom of the screen.

"Anybody who shoots a cop? Send the fucker right to the chair. Am I right?"

Jamal decided to find out here and now if he had anything to worry about. He swiveled in his seat and faced his neighbor.

"I couldn't agree with you more."

He watched the man's eyes roam over his face as he nodded. If the tourist showed even the slightest recognition, Jamal would know it. The knife in Jamal's jacket sleeve would be in his heart before he'd had a chance to squeal.

The big man took a sip of beer, shook his head.

"Hope they get him. It's a good picture."

"Yes. Very good."

"I'm Bobby Ray Price, Huntersville, Georgia."

"Frank Yardani, Baltimore. I'm an accountant."

Bobby Ray told Jamal more about furnace installation than he ever wanted to know before sliding off the stool to join his equally porcine family.

Jamal thought that if a naturally suspicious, xenophobic redneck hadn't recognized him from the composite—at a distance of two feet—his disguise was safe enough.

Jamal felt elated by the news piece and left a dollar tip for his soda. He was not surprised that the Americans were onto him. They would have been talking to Landau and his Mossad. Connections between Issim Hassan and Jamal would have been outlined and explained. The Americans might be infuriated by the events at Dent Place, but they would listen to the Israelis, who would connect the massacre to Jamal.

Jamal walked across the lobby and into the wide corridor that led to the convention rooms. In a tiny recess to the left of the Mayflower Hall was a pay phone, which rang forty-five seconds after he arrived.

"This is James."

"I got stuff on your boy."

Jamal heard Asian voices in the background. Priestly must have been in a restaurant of some kind.

"Go ahead, please."

"He got into the office early, under his own steam—"

"I beg your pardon?"

"Alone. No escorts. It means that nobody thinks he's important."

Oh, he had escorts, Detective. You just couldn't see them.

Priestly detailed Ben Poltarek's few movements during the day. "Far as I know, he's still in that apartment," he concluded. "You want me to stay on him?"

"That won't be necessary. I will call you later if circumstances should change."

Jamal hung up and left the alcove. He stepped on the escalator and considered various possibilities while riding to the mezzanine level.

Benjamin Poltarek was being covered. Jamal was sure of this. With two *sayanim* dead, Landau would protect the survivor. Priestly had been looking for the kind of surveillance he was familiar with. He did not appreciate how Landau and his people operated.

But why didn't Landau go in and interrogate the boy?

Because after Dent Place, the Israelis had no currency left. Blood had been spilled in American streets. Landau would have to be very careful approaching Poltarek. And he could afford to be, as long as he kept the boy covered.

"The kid doesn't know anything."

Priestly's words echoed in Jamal's mind. He wished he could believe the detective absolutely, but that was not the case. The boy had to be considered a threat. And Jamal had to get to him before Landau did.

Tomorrow. The day after at the latest.

But not tonight. Tonight something else needed tending to.

*　*　*

The sound of the phone startled Ben. He looked up from his work and saw the last daylight fleeing the sky.

When he picked up, the concierge told him that Rachel was on her way up.

Ben rose from the kitchen table where he'd been working. On his way to the foyer, he closed the door to his father's study, where the computer screen cast a blue light across notes exposed on the desk.

"Ben . . ."

She went to him, shaking her head, looking around as if she'd never been there before. He caught the reproach in her eyes even as she cupped his cheek and kissed him on the lips.

"Ben, what are you doing here?"

"What needs to be done. Coffee?"

He sat her down in the country kitchen with its polished Amish antiques, brass cookware suspended from wrought-iron racks, framed samplers all in a row over the triple sink. Warm memories and familiar scents sailed out every time he opened a drawer or a cupboard.

"Are you okay?" Rachel was asking.

Ben turned from the counter, mug in hand. "Yeah." He pointed to the pages that littered the table. "I pulled out Sid's will. And Rose's. Checked the financials and the bequests. Talked to the bank and the brokers." He paused. "Called Paperman's. Did you know that Sid had prepaid all the funeral arrangements?"

It was a rhetorical question and Rachel let it go by.

Ben passed her the mug, sat opposite her, and watched as she drank.

He wasn't lying to her. The documents, some of them neatly typed and bound, others yellow with age, covered in Sid's scrawls or Rose's penmanship, had been the focus of his attention for the last few hours. Not only did the pedestrian issues surrounding death have to be dealt with but Ben had had to put aside, for a little while, the dark treasures and revelations he'd come upon in his father's study. He knew himself well enough to understand that if he didn't do this, those truths would overwhelm him. Only time could reduce their seeming enormity and importance and allow him to handle them.

"How did it go for Cheryl?"

"Well. Very well. The guy from Cedars in L.A. was very good."

Ben recalled the blond, blue-eyed child who'd been so captivated by his illusions. He knew only one thing about her—that she had a pinprick of a hole in her heart—yet right now he felt intensely close to her.

"I'm glad," he said.

"I wish you'd left me a note this morning. Or called later on. I would have helped you with this."

Rachel indicated the papers on the table. Her tone carried no reproach, only concern.

Ben nodded toward the answering machine on the counter.

"It was full. Half of official Washington must have called."

Rachel did not ask about relatives. As far as she knew, neither Sid nor Rose had any kin left.

"When is the funeral?"

"Not for a couple days. Maybe Monday."

In Jewish tradition, the funeral always takes place as soon as possible after death. But in this case there was the weekend to consider. Ben thought he could have all the arrangements ready for interment on Tuesday.

"Do you want me to speak with the rabbi?" Rachel asked.

"I'll see him Saturday. But I could use help with *shivah*."

Rachel found a pad and pencil and began making a list: How many people to expect; what to serve—deli and an open bar would be best; a caterer; a pianist to play suitable pieces on Rose's beloved Steinway; arrangement with the concierge to handle the overflow of cars and limos.

By the time Rachel was finished, the antique lamps swathed the kitchen in a soft glow. Ben read through her notes and couldn't find anything to add.

"I'll get started on this first thing in the morning," she said. "What do you want to do about dinner?"

"How about Chinese? That way no one has to cook."

Rachel called in the order. When she turned around, Ben was holding up two glasses of red wine.

"*L'chaim*," he said softly.

"*L'chaim*."

The wine was a great, billowy burgundy from Sid Poltarek's cellar. It whispered of faraway places and things yet to be discovered.

Rachel noted how quickly Ben emptied his balloon glass and refilled it.

"Not so fast on an empty stomach," she chided him.

They went into the family room, where a fire was laid in the hearth. Although it wasn't very cold, Ben stooped down and got it going.

Rachel found some quiet Sinatra, and they sat side by side on the floor, staring at the fire, using the snap and crackle of the wood instead of words.

I could ask him now, Rachel thought. *He's not much of a drinker, and two glasses would be more than enough to make him woozy. He'll tell me if I put it to him the right way.*

Rachel tried hard to make herself believe that she would be doing this for Ben, not Landau. This was the way to protect him. Give Landau the dirty knowledge, and let him use it to cut off Jamal's head. Then Landau would leave them alone, taking with him the nightmares he spawned.

Seeing that his glass was empty, Rachel poured him more.

When the concierge called to say the delivery had arrived, Rachel told Ben to stay put and went to pay for it. She put the food out and set the plates on the coffee table.

Ben was standing in front of the fire, head bowed, as though mesmerized by the flames.

"Honey, come and eat, before it gets cold."

Ben did not turn around. He kept his eyes on the fire as he said, "There's something I have to tell you."

Her bare feet were soundless and he did not sense her until she touched him.

"What is it, Ben?"

"They're bringing in an American."

The words seemed to carry a little bit of his soul out with them. Ben wondered if that was how it felt to die, to be emptied, leaving nothing.

"Ben, what are you talking about? Who's bringing in what American?"

Unable to look at her, he spoke over her shoulder to a small but violent Turner seascape.

"The man who came to the apartment, who died in my arms, he said they were bringing in an American. The detective, Priestly, asked me about that, and that FBI woman. I don't know why I didn't say anything before. Something was holding me back. I don't know what . . .

"I still don't know who that man was. Nobody else seems to either. Or else they're not telling me. But I know other things. Things that began when Sid and I were in Paris . . ."

Ben talked without pause, even when he went to the sideboard to retrieve the bottle and replenish his glass. He tried to maintain a level tone, but sometimes a ragged shrillness cut up his words. He was talking quickly, as though he had only so many minutes in which to get it all out, and after that, what had gone unsaid would be lost forever. He wondered if this was what penitents of the confessional faiths felt like before their absolvers.

"Do you believe me?" he asked, spent.

Rachel felt clammy, the way she knew heart attack victims felt at the beginning of the onslaught. But hers was not a physical threat.

"Yes, I believe you. But now, you *have* to go to the police. If terrorists are involved—"

Ben leaned against the mantelpiece. "I won't do that. I need to find out who killed Sid and Rose. And why. I need time."

"Ben, I think the police may be watching you." He looked at her sharply, and she knew she had to give him the half truth to his face. "I overheard Priestly talking. He doesn't believe you. He thinks you're holding back on him. So he was going to put you under surveillance."

"I need your help."

"Ben—"

"Without questions. I've found out a lot, Rachel, but the rest isn't here. I think I know where to look for it, but I need to do it alone—no one following me, no one trying to stop me."

Her tears were for him, but they were born of her rage at Landau.

I could tell him about Landau. Who he is and why he needs him. I could tell him and maybe save him.

The words rose in her throat and died on her lips. Others that sounded right and familiar took their place.

"What do you want me to do?"

Twenty

MISS ABBY BUFFETT had been a fixture in the Nineteenth Street neighborhood of Dupont Circle for sixty of her seventy-two years. Longtime tenants of the prewar buildings as well as the newest immigrants who ran the grocery stores and dry cleaners all knew her. In a city where night made people move a little more quickly, Miss Abby kept to her staid gait, smiling at her neighbors as she walked her route home every evening.

Miss Abby had been teaching geography and history at Paul Revere Middle School on N Street near St. John's for more than forty years. Some time back, there had been talk of pushing her into retirement—until Miss Abby appeared at a school-board meeting with the Democratic House majority leader. She had been a Sunday school teacher at St. John's for almost as long.

"Evening, Miss Abby."

"How are you, Sam?" She called back to the evening-shift laundromat manager who stood smoking in the doorway.

She continued along Nineteenth Street, receiving and returning greetings, until she reached a red brick townhouse bordered by a freshly painted black gate. Miss Abby owned the townhouse outright and rented out the upper two floors to transient professionals, young men or women who kept late hours and the peace.

Miss Abby slipped her key into the lock, turned the deadbolt. The small foyer and the staircase were both well lit, but the intruder was up high enough on the stairs that he didn't cast a shadow where she could see it.

Miss Abby was turning the lock on her door when she heard the creak of weight on a stairstep. She sensed movement behind her and half-turned, was about to call out, when something terribly hard smashed down on her right forearm. Before she hit the floor, a second blow broke her left arm at the elbow. The pain was so powerful that she uttered only a weak cry before she lost consciousness. She never heard the razor slice through the leather strap of her bag, nor the fall of soft-soled shoes and the rattle of the door as the mugger slipped out of the building.

Two blocks away, Hafez Jamal shoved Miss Abby's purse into a city garbage can. He'd rifled through it and taken the fourteen dollars in a small beaded change purse. Maybe the police would find the purse, maybe not. It didn't matter.

Jamal had intended to kill the old woman but had reconsidered. Even a random murder would draw a closer investigation, whereas in America's capital, muggings were commonplace. Plus, injuring her the way he had was perfectly effective. The old crow would miss many a Sunday school class waiting for her brittle bones to knit.

* * *

The ERT response was fast. More of a surprise to the neighbors who'd gathered in front of Miss Abby's home was how quickly the police got there, detectives and all.

Henry Blake of Internal Affairs was surprised, too—not as much by the alacrity of the response as by who put in an appearance.

Blake was standing catercorner to the townhouse, watching the comings and goings of paramedics and police with the same interest as the neighbors. Except he was focused on one particular man: Detective Priestly.

Blake had heard the dispatcher's squawk but thought nothing of it until Priestly's response had come over the air. The detective was only two blocks away. He would go in and secure the scene.

You were pretty close to the Kennedy Center that night too, weren't you? Blake thought.

He watched Priestly step aside as the paramedics carried Miss Abby out on a stretcher. Then Priestly flipped out his notebook, gave another investigator the information he'd gleaned so far, clapped him on the shoulder, and moved off to his car.

Maybe Priestly was just a conscientious cop. Maybe his being in the area was coincidence.

Henry Blake remembered what Ben Poltarek had told him, and the thread of coincidence seemed pretty frayed.

Blake had been on his way home. Now he thought he might tag along behind Priestly and see what else the homicide detective had planned for the evening.

* * *

In her room at the residential hotel, Judith Sawyer moved the lamp a little to the right to eliminate the glare on the laptop computer screen.

She had been at her desk for most of the night, gliding through the Internet like a silent bird of prey. She had alighted at the Smithsonian, the National Historic Register, and the Episcopalian Heritage Foundation; now she examined original construction drawings courtesy of the Architectural Landmarks Society.

Occasionally, her printer hummed as she found something worth keeping.

Judith sat back in her chair and rubbed her eyes. She had as much as she needed. A lot of the information was duplicated, but that was all right. When she showed it to Jamal, he would appreciate how thorough she'd been.

Judith printed out a final schematic and turned off the machine. She gathered up the pages and reviewed them. What she had was a kind of treasure map, one that had been there for anyone with enough curiosity or imagination to find. But no one had, because the map pertained to a minor landmark in a city filled with far more grandiose attractions.

Judith smiled to herself. Ford's Theater had been just another show-house before Lincoln; Dealey Plaza, an anonymous space in an unremarkable town before Kennedy.

Judith would now create a new shrine, the name of which would be spoken only in low tones. The only difference was that the Ford and Dealey Plaza still stood. This building would be razed to the ground. Given what it was, such could be its only destiny.

Twenty-one

"YOUR SNITCH IS TAKING his sweet time," Kaelin Reece said over the top of her coffee cup.

Landau did not disabuse Reece of her assumption that the person he claimed to have close to Benjamin Poltarek was male. Instead, he sipped his coffee and thought it had been considerate of Reece to bring good European-style beans with her. Reece had gone home for the night and now appeared rested and refreshed. Landau could have returned to the embassy but had chosen to bunk in the barracks at Buzzard's Point. The accommodations reminded him of the spartan facilities at the *midrasha*, the Institute's training center.

"Patience," he said, poking through the remains of bagels, cream cheese, and overly salty lox.

Privately, Landau had his own reservations. Rachel should have called by now.

"We need a backup plan," Reece said. "I assume you have one."

"If you are ever asked what it was, it might be better if you can honestly say that you didn't know," Landau replied dryly.

Reece sighed and let her anger carom off the cinder-block walls, painted matte white. The array of telephones, tape recorders, and notepads mocked her by their silence.

"I know you won't be wrapping Poltarek up in a wet sheet and letting it dry," she said.

"You're right, Kaelin. But only because it's a painful procedure. Young Mr. Poltarek has had enough pain for a time, don't you agree?"

The red phone rang softly before Reece could reply.

"Yes," Landau said.

"It's me," Rachel Melman said. "Is anyone listening?"

"No."

Landau glanced at Reece, pointed to the earphones connected to the telephone, and shook his head to remind her that this conversation was privileged.

"Where are you?"

Inadvertently, Rachel looked over her shoulder. She was in the kitchen, by the windows, close enough to the glass to feel the cold of the day outside.

"In the apartment."

"Where is he?"

"Upstairs, in the shower."

"Go on, then."

"There's nowhere to go. He doesn't know anything."

"You asked him?"

"Not in so many words. But we talked about Priestly asking questions, and that FBI woman. They spooked him. He's beginning to wonder why it's so goddamn important what the dead man might have told him."

"So something *was* said."

"If it was, he's not telling me. But I don't think so."

"Why?"

"Because he's exhausted and his nerves are shot. Under those circumstances, either you spill everything because you're careless or tired, or you suffer from stress-related amnesia."

"You don't think it's the latter, do you?"

"Nor the former. Why can't you accept that he just doesn't know anything?"

"Because I don't believe it."

Landau looked at Reece, who was nodding, her signal that she was getting the gist of the conversation.

In the kitchen, Rachel studied the design on a pretty white-and-blue sampler without focusing on the words.

"I think you're wrong. I know it."

"That may be, but time is pressing. I might have to consider alternatives."

Her voice came back at him with the sting of a bullwhip: "Are you still a Jew, Landau? Don't you know that it is time to bury and to sit *shivah*?"

"I understand—"

"Then listen to me! I will be here to help him—calling people, getting the caterers and cleaners, whatever I can do. *He* still has to deal with the funeral arrangements. All of which means he will be going out. I want you to protect him, Landau. You promised me you would."

"It will be that much harder when he is outside."

"I'll try to keep him in the apartment as much as possible."

"I imagine you will be staying with him."

"You imagine correctly."

"Let me know before he intends to leave the apartment. And about those caterers and cleaners—"

"The same ones the Poltareks have used for years. Get a pencil."

Rachel rattled off names that Landau could check out simply by opening the Yellow Pages.

"Let me hear from you soon," Landau said, then hung up.

Across the table, Kaelin Reece did not say a word. Not out of professional courtesy—a comment burned on her tongue. But because Landau had tried to do an end run around her and had failed. He'd been very careful in his conversation, very judicious about his choice of words. But for all his vaunted abilities, Landau was still a man. Men did not speak to women as they did to other men. They were unaware of this because they had a tin ear.

Landau's snitch was a woman. Given the limited number of possibilities, Kaelin Reece thought she knew exactly who it was.

*   *   *

In the Poltareks' kitchen, Rachel heard the click of Landau hanging up and put down the phone. She was so relieved to have this conversation behind her that she never heard the second click, which came just as her hand hovered over the cradle. She did not remember that there was an extension in the upstairs bathroom Ben was using. She could not imagine him standing there, water dripping off him as he listened to her talk to Landau, the expression on his face breaking apart like that of a man being stoned.

Rachel was still going over the list of things to do when Ben came downstairs. He kissed her on the back of her neck and she turned to look up at him.

"Something wrong?" he asked, pouring himself juice.

"I'm fine." She pushed the list toward him. "I thought we'd split it up. I'll go to the cleaners and caterers, you make the calls."

Ben looked at the thirty-odd names on the list, longtime friends of his parents. His eyes strayed to the answering machine. Its counter stood at zero.

"I rewound it after you went to bed," Rachel said. "The callers were most of the people on the list."

"I think I'd like to handle the outside stuff," Ben said. "I need to get some air."

"It's still pretty miserable out there."

"Doesn't matter."

"Let me call the cleaners and we'll do the rest together, okay? You can do the callbacks when we return."

"If it's all the same to you, I'll cab it."

His cool tone brooked no argument, so she let the matter drop.

Because the Poltareks had been longtime residents of the neighborhood, the merchants knew Ben on sight. All offered condolences, assured him that they'd provide anything he needed. By noon, he'd taken care of the undertakers and the florists, met with the rabbi, and contracted with the caterers and the cleaners. At every stop, Ben collected more condolences. He felt like he was being accosted by pitchmen handing him flyers in the street. When he thought like this, he felt ashamed. These people meant him only heartfelt goodwill.

But neither their words nor their hard embraces dampened the drumbeat of questions in his heart. Who was this Landau whom Rachel had spoken to over the phone, their tones as thick and soft as thieves' whispers? What was he to her that she had tried to worm knowledge out of him for Landau?

Rachel, why did you betray me?

The wail in his soul made his eyes water, which those who embraced him mistook for tears of a different kind of grief.

When Ben returned to the apartment, the cleaners were waiting.

The foreman was as familiar with the Poltareks' home as he was with his own. He greeted Ben with a bear hug, then he and his crew went about their business quickly and efficiently.

Three hours later, the lingering odors of blood, laboratory chemicals, and clumsy strangers were replaced by the scents of lemon and beeswax. The cleaners had bundled the equipment into the service elevator, and ridden down with it.

A half hour later, a yellow taxi returned Rachel from her last errand. In the lobby, the concierge informed her that the caterers had dropped off a menu for Mr. Poltarek's approval. Rachel took it up with her.

*   *   *

Landau was glad when Reece had to go to FBI headquarters to brief her boss, Mitchell, on the progress of the hunt for Hafez Jamal.

Since the alert had gone out almost twenty-four hours ago, there had been only thirty "hits" on the Bureau's terrorist hotline—calls from various law-enforcement officials in the northeast and southeast corridors calling in reports of possible sightings. These were almost evenly divided between tips that eventually proved to relate to an innocent person who had the misfortune to resemble Jamal (although in one case, the suspect turned out to be wanted on home invasion charges), and reports from the police pulling over Arab-looking drivers, which, in New Jersey, resulted in a harassment suit being filed.

Landau was the high priest of patience. On the rare occasion that he lectured at the *midrasha*, this was the virtue he extolled above all others. Yet now, Landau chafed. Somewhere in this diverse and noisy land, with its porous borders and melting-pot immigration, Hafez Jamal had gone to ground. In the Middle East, North Africa, even Europe, Landau would have known which rocks to knock over, what doors to break down, which informants to intimidate. Here, he had nothing. The *katsa*'s contact list was prodigious, but it was compiled of names found in the *Diplomatic List* and the corporate version of *Who's Who*. As for the *sayanim*, the *katsa* would not go near them. Nor would he hand the list over to Landau, preferring to take his chances with a court of inquiry in Tel Aviv for disobeying a superior's direct order. Not that it would come to that. The bluebloods on the list were much like the Poltareks. Jamal would not move in their circles. Landau needed contacts who worked in the under-belly.

Landau reached out to Jamal with his thoughts.

Where have you gone? You do not know America. You have never operated here. Who could have taught you what you need to know to remain invisible? Or do you simply have the devil's own luck?

"Communing with your ancestors?"

Landau pulled a fresh cigar from his pocket. Reece had taken great pains to inform him that smoking was prohibited on federal property, and he had studiously ignored her.

"How's Mitchell?"

Reece threw her sling on the table. "Nervous. He's expecting to hear a set of unreasonable demands followed by a very loud bang."

Landau puffed. "Won't happen. Jamal couldn't bring explosives into this country. Other, more portable, things, yes. But if that were all—demands followed by a demonstration—we'd have had them by now."

"Maybe the demonstration will come first, an example."

"No. Listen to Jamal's broadcast again. He won't take the time."

"Like you in Samarra? No warning?"

Landau looked up at her with the curiosity a viper might have for a chick.

Reece didn't apologize, but she changed the subject.

"What about your boy?"

Landau gestured at the printed field reports. "At home preparing for a funeral and to sit *shivah*."

"*Shivah*'s like a wake, right?" Reece said, looking over the surveillance reports on Poltarek.

"Like a," Landau agreed.

The first thing that made Landau's antenna shiver was the silence—except for pages being flipped forward, back, then forward again. Landau did not want to turn around.

"What is it, Kaelin?" he asked quietly.

"You have three reports, Melman leaving, coming back."

"Yes."

Reece was kind to him. She did not look at his face.

"The first time she goes out, she's driving her car. She returns, drives out again. *But then the last time, she returns in a taxi?*"

*   *   *

Things that Rachel did not know: that Kaelin Reece had the siren howling all the way from Buzzard's Point to the city, that Landau was riding shotgun, his eyes straight ahead, his rigidly held body rolling this way and that as Reece took the corners on the stink of burnt rubber.

Rachel hadn't witnessed these things, but she saw their aftermath in Landau's bright, angry eyes and tightly pressed lips. She had never seen him struggle so to maintain his self-control.

When Rachel opened the door and saw them standing there, all she said was, "Come in." She started to walk into the living room, then turned and saw that they had remained in the foyer.

"Where is he, Rachel?" Landau asked without preamble.

"I don't know."

Landau looked away, as though following her words to some distant horizon.

"Why did you betray me?"

Now it was Reece's turn to look elsewhere. She wore the tight, embarrassed expression of someone who has overheard a lovers' quarrel or a marital spat in a crowded public space.

"I didn't—"

She stopped when he held up his hand.

"Dr. Melman, we know you took your car the last time you left this building," Reece said. "We know you returned in a taxi. We've asked you about Mr. Poltarek's whereabouts and you say you don't know. Is he here?"

"No."

"We'll have to search the premises anyway."

Landau opened the door to reveal three silent, competent-looking men who brushed by Rachel like a strong wind.

"You have no right—"

"I have a standing search warrant, Doctor." Reece held up a dog-eared court document.

"Where did he go, Rachel?" Landau pressed. "How long ago did he leave?"

Rachel would not avert her eyes from his.

"We ran your name through DMV, Doctor," Reece said. "Your car's description and tag number are out in every state east of the Mississippi. Pretty soon some trooper is going to spot it and call it in. Now we underlined that the driver does not necessarily pose any immediate danger, which means the troopers *might* keep their guns holstered. They might not. Why put Mr. Poltarek in jeopardy, Doctor?"

"I'm not the one who put him in jeopardy," Rachel replied, looking at Landau.

"There's nowhere for him to run, Rachel," Landau said. "Nowhere for him to be safe except next to me. I and my men are the only ones who can keep him alive until Jamal is taken. Has it not occurred to you that Jamal might also be after him—might be a little closer than we are?"

Landau caught the flicker of fear in her eyes. Rachel was quick and gifted, but in extreme conditions even the best tend to overlook things or fail to think them through completely. He detected the tiniest fissures in her resolve and began to burrow into them.

"You told him, didn't you? You told him who you were that long time ago. Did you tell him *everything*? How it began, in Israel? How it ended, here?

"He listened and bled but in the end he forgave you. Because you had come to him saying I was using you to deceive him and that you had chosen him over me. You would show him your faith by betraying me, helping him to escape.

"Except there is no escape, Rachel. Poltarek is an amateur drawn into a situation not of his making. I know you did what you thought was best for him. I know you did this out of love. I think *you* know that it was all wrong.

"Help us bring him home, Rachel. Don't make him spend one more minute on some lonely highway than is absolutely necessary."

Rachel sat down in one of the chairs in the foyer. Her fingers were like claws around the armrests.

"Dr. Melman?" Reece moved close to her. "It's finished. You see that, don't you? Mr. Poltarek was holding out on us. Otherwise, why run? The man who came here that night, who died in his arms, he told Ben something—"

"I don't know." Rachel shook her head violently.

"I'm not saying you do," Reece said soothingly. "You helped him without demanding to know, maybe without even asking. You did this because you love him." She paused. "Bring him *home* because you love him, Doctor."

Landau thought Reece was very good. He could almost hear Rachel's resolve cracking, like old shellac exposed to the sun.

"Years ago, Ben's brother drowned while the two of them were at summer camp," Rachel said. "I know he goes there when . . . whenever he needs to be alone, to think. It's a kind of refuge for him. The camp is just over the Pennsylvania–New York border. It's called Timberland."

"A summer camp," Reece said, her tone flat.

"It's close to a river. Apparently, there are cottages all around. That's where the Poltareks stayed when they went up. I don't know any more because I've never been up there."

"That's fine, Rachel," Landau said. "We can take it from here."

He drew Reece aside. "He has a two-to-three-hour lead. Traffic would still be light before the weekend. How long before he reaches the camp?"

"A couple of hours, maybe more. He'll have to stop for gas, maybe food." Reece fished out her cell phone. "I'll get an exact location for the place."

"And a helicopter."

"Couldn't we use state troopers to pull him over?"

"We could. And he might jackrabbit on them. I don't want a chase. We pinpoint him from the air, create a traffic bottleneck ahead of him—some kind of phony accident—and winnow him from the pack."

Reece nodded toward Rachel. "What about her?"

To Landau, Rachel was as still as a statue.

"She has nothing left to give."

* * *

As Landau and Reece were climbing into a helicopter on the roof of the FBI building, a metallic silver BMW was crossing the Chesapeake Bay Bridge, forty-odd miles east of Washington, nowhere near Pennsylvania.

Ben had stayed on U.S. Route 50 and had watched his speed. Coming off the bridge, he glided through the small town of Stevensville on Maryland's upper Eastern Shore. He passed Grasonville, then turned south on Perry's Corner Road and headed for the Horsehead Wetlands Center.

Stopping shy of the 310-acre nature preserve, he took a cracked, pitted, single-lane blacktop to the border of the preserve, and turned into a half-mile drive that led to a rambling cottage set high on the dunes overlooking the bay.

Ben got out of the car and took deep breaths of the briny air. He looked at the cottage, with its salt-silvered wood, dormers, and four brick chimneys, and knew that for a while, at least, he was safe.

If Rachel had not held up under the questioning, the hunter she called Landau would have been here by now.

If she hadn't told Ben the dark truths about herself back in the apartment, and hadn't been a willing accomplice in his flight, he would never have made it here.

The Shore was the last stop for answers. Either he would find them here or he would have to surrender.

Ben reached in the trunk for the duffel bag he'd packed, hefted it, and walked toward the house.

Twenty-two

The Reverend Winslow Garrett sat behind his desk in his office at St. John's School, absently rubbing the leather blotter with his tobacco-stained fingers.

A short while ago, he had returned from the Georgetown University Medical Center, where Abby Buffett lay in the intensive care unit. The doctors weren't worried so much about her broken arms as about the concussion she'd received when she fell, her forehead striking a decorative marble slab set in front of her apartment door. There was pressure on the cranium, they said; drilling the skull to drain the fluid might be necessary.

Garrett shuddered at the thought. This was no longer a city he cared to know. But neither would he ever leave his beloved church. To that end, he turned his attention to the four applicants' files before him.

All were qualified. Two were currently employed part time in a private school in Virginia. That left two who were available to start immediately.

Derek Broad, a severe, prune-faced man of fifty, had a strong résumé but a glacial attitude. His teaching experience consisted solely of boys' boarding schools and was reflected in the emphasis Broad put on discipline.

Judith Sawyer was much warmer and Garrett found himself smiling at the thought of her. The children would cotton to her immediately. Garrett imagined how much rich, personal experience she could bring to the Sunday classes, and how lively these would be.

The only issue was security. The other three applicants had already been vetted by the Secret Service, in case Garrett had to hire them right away. The full background check on Sawyer would take at least a few days. It would be easier to hire Broad.

Garrett tapped the eraser-tipped pencil on the file. An image floated up to him: Judith Sawyer folding a ten-dollar bill and slipping it discreetly into the collection box.

Done.

Garrett dialed the number of the Secret Service agent at Treasury with whom he'd dealt for years, gave him Sawyer's name and the bio she'd brought in.

The agent ran the name through the current Threat List as well as the standing Service records on all people who had ever threatened the President. Judith Sawyer's name appeared on none of these. Neither had John Hinckley's.

The agent told Garrett that he would prioritize further checks but that at first blush Judith Sawyer was clean.

Garrett's next call was to the residential hotel that Judith Sawyer had given as her Washington residence.

*   *   *

The Chesapeake house was built in the early 1930s, the summer home of a minor chemical baron. The baron's fortune had been wiped out in the Depression. Ben Poltarek's grandfather had bought the property and used it as a family retreat.

Ben did not have many childhood memories of the house. For reasons that had never been explained, his parents never cared for the place. Visits were few and short. But neither was the house ever put on the market. The family owned it outright; taxes and maintenance were minimal. It was like a beautiful necklace or tiara, waiting for the right woman to come along and breathe life into it.

Instead, after Samuel's death, the house became a refuge for Ben. He went there on long weekends and holidays, and with only the gulls and terns as his audience, worked on new illusions or perfected old ones. As he became more proficient and pushed the limits of his imagination, the house became an extension of his craft. The big double parlor to the right of the center hall, the dining room on the left, and the game room behind the staircase all appeared normal—testimony to Ben's carpentry skills and constant pursuit of perfection. It was what one *didn't* see that created magic, and in this house there was much that never registered in the eye as anything but ordinary.

Inside, Ben turned up the heat and got a fire going in the parlor. The water and electricity were always on, part of the housekeeping agreement with a local realtor who also paid the handyman's bills.

Ben fixed himself a cup of instant coffee on the mammoth cast-iron gas range and took it outside.

He was certain that no one—not even Rachel, who'd never visited—would find him there. There was no longer any connection between the house and the Poltarek family. Five years ago, when Sid and Rose had updated their wills, they agreed, in consultation with Ben, to sign a quit-claim on the property in favor of Mary Nash, his father's secretary and confidante. Sid had promised that when he retired, Mary would not have to work a day after that, if that's what she wanted. But instead of a cash or pension plan arrangement, Sid put the Chesapeake house in her name, an interesting maneuver that eliminated gift, inheritance, and capital gains taxes all in one swoop. The only proviso was that Mary would not take possession of the property until Sid Poltarek's retirement or death, whichever came first.

Ben finished his coffee and went inside. The house had warmed up nicely. He spread out his papers and set up his computer on the stressed-pine dining table that could seat twelve.

Landau. Ezekiel Landau. Mossad. Israeli Secret Service.

The light coming through the tall, lead-lined windows was the silvery gray of a fish's belly. Ben thought it was very much like the light that had been cast across Rachel's face when he had confronted her.

She had returned from her errands, her cheeks flushed from the wind, to find him sitting in the living room, facing the fireplace. She said something, the words not registering with Ben—then went to him. He remembered how her eyes widened when she had looked into his. Her lips parted and a low moan escaped them because she recognized the knowledge he held. When she reached for him, he caught her by the wrists.

"Who is Landau?"

Her every word was burned into Ben's mind. He had thought Rachel incapable of fear, yet that was all there had been in her eyes and her voice. It had taken Ben a few minutes to appreciate the real reason for her terror: It was not fear of Landau's retribution; rather, by telling him what she did, she ran the risk of losing him forever.

Ben stared down at his hand. The flesh of his palm was still tender where her nails had dug in.

As one part of him had opened up to her deluge, another had stood by wondering how it was possible that there was this whole other side to Rachel he'd never seen or suspected. This was a woman who had given freely of herself, whose love had graced his world and filled it with light, a woman who had been embraced by his parents and made part of the family.

Neither her soft, halting voice nor her tears could drive away the feeling of deception that had crawled over him. Twice Ben had pulled away from her grasp; twice he had shouted at her to stop talking. But she'd refused, continuing until the very last possible word that could damn her did so, until she was as spent as he.

Ben remembered the silence that had descended between them, the way she sat curled up in a corner of the sofa, staring at the wall, he by the fireplace, watching sparks fly up the chimney, sparks that were like the white-hot slivers of anger within him. And after the anger had run its course, something cool and wonderful washed over him. Because he did not know what to call it, he thought it might be forgiveness, not only for Rachel but for himself. Somewhere in their deceits, a new truth about themselves had been forged. They reached out to each other, tentatively, seeking to balm the wounds with whispers, then resolutions against those who would do them harm.

Landau.

The name rippled across Ben's consciousness like a flat stone skimming a still pond. Rachel's lover. Rachel's blackmailer.

Landau, whose lot in life was terrorism.

Landau, sharing wedding bands of terror with Hafez Jamal.

Jamal connected to Samir el-Banna.

Who was connected to the murders of Sid and Rose.

And to Manshur and his kin.

The connections were almost complete, except for the one he needed most.

Ben rose from the table and went into the cellar—clean, well lighted, the walls and floor finished in fieldstone. In one corner, among ancient suitcases and wooden crates, was a trunk. It was small and appeared light, but Ben needed both arms to lift and carry it.

In the dining room, he undid the clasps, threw back the lid, and discovered that the trunk was empty. But not really. It was a magic trunk, the first prop he'd ever bought. After his skills had outgrown its use, his father had asked to use it. For Sid Poltarek's purposes, the trunk was just as secure as a lockbox and much more accessible.

Ben stared into the seemingly empty cedar-lined cavity. He had never had to ask his father why he wanted this trunk because in his heart he knew the answer. Whatever Sid's secret life was, Ben had not found it in places that might be destroyed or which, in a sudden twist of fate, might suddenly become accessible to strangers. Not at the office, not at home. Not in some bank or trust company vault which, in an emergency or by happenstance, could be opened by the wrong parties.

That left only one possibility: a place no one could track back to the Poltareks, on the fringe of a cloistered, closemouthed community mistrustful of strangers.

Ben reached down into the trunk and carefully pried loose the false panels. He expected to find grainy old papers whose edges would crumble in his fingertips, yellowing photographs with curled tips and, on the back, references in fading ink.

Ben began to laugh. He should have known better. Instead of decaying treasure, he found four CD-ROMs in hard-shell containers. Somewhere over his shoulder, he thought he heard his father chuckling.

*   *   *

The FBI helicopter was fast, but lousy on fuel. The pilot had to set down at the municipal airport in Harrisburg, Pennsylvania, to gas up.

Landau looked at the landscape around the field, a forest that reeked of decay as a wet winter grudgingly gave way to a raw spring that had not yet dried out the earth. In spite of the navy blue FBI windbreaker Reece had found for him, he still felt the sting of the wind as it skimmed down the runway like a scythe.

Landau turned to the small, squat building that served as a waiting lounge. Through the window, he saw Kaelin Reece on the cell phone. Their eyes met and she waved at him to come inside.

The lounge was vacant except for a private pilot arguing in the corner with an FAA official.

"The state troopers are at Timberland's front gates. They say it doesn't look like anyone's been around. No tire tracks. What do you think—should they go in?"

"Aren't there supposed to be cottages? They should go there first, I think."

"We'll split the difference."

Landau had no idea what she meant until he heard her tell the trooper to get over to the cottages, but to leave one car at the camp gates, in case Poltarek happened to appear there, coming in or going out.

The pilot poked his head in the door, beckoned to them.

"How much longer?" Landau called out, trotting after him on the tarmac.

"Thirty minutes tops," the pilot answered over his shoulder. "We've got a tailwind to help us out."

"What's the matter?" Reece asked as she climbed in.

Landau slipped in beside her, bolted the flimsy door. He pointed to the sky.

"This is taking too long."

"Don't start bitching now, Landau. Even money says we'll get there before Poltarek does."

So Landau took her up—fifty dollars' worth. It was one time he hoped he'd lose.

* * *

The old ships' lamps, whale oil converted to electricity, threw the light of a false dawn across the dining room. The blue glow of the computer screen washed across Ben's face. He finished reading the last file in the last CD-ROM and slumped in his chair.

"Alice," he said aloud, thinking how strange that one word sounded in the stillness of the house.

But that was the image that came to him, from an illustrated children's book he'd read so long ago. Alice chasing the rabbit down the hole, tumbling end over end into Wonderland. Just as he was now falling into lives his parents had carefully hidden from him, whose existence he'd never suspected.

Sayanim.

Assistants.

Part of Israel's secret army abroad, soldiers who held no rank, wore no uniform, received no recognition save a kind word or two from their embassy handlers.

Sid and Rose, assistants for forty years. Travelers who, when the occasion warranted, had a quiet chat with a quiet man about things they'd seen or heard.

Rose, the university professor and adviser to governments, who sometimes met an individual at academic seminars who did not belong there. Or "accidentally" bumped into an old "friend" at an embassy function who would take her aside to catch up on old times they'd never shared. Sitting at a Kalorama dinner party, the hostess on her right, and on the left, an ebullient musician accredited to the Israel Philharmonic—except his training in the oboe consisted of a two-hour crash course that same morning.

Sid had trolled in different waters, where two-thirds of those qualified to practice law in Washington never did so. They were lobbyists, spin-control specialists, special advisers, deputy assistants. But by virtue of a law degree, they all spoke the same dialect, belonged to the same clubs, gathered at the same watering holes. Whenever Israel came calling for a special piece of information, Sid had known where to look, whom to ask, and how—so that nothing ever came back to bite him or the Jewish state.

Yet, Ben's father had felt compelled, probably against standing instructions, to keep a running diary of his and Rose's service.

Ben understood why. As a lawyer, Sid would demand some kind of paper trail, an accounting he could refer to if anything ever went wrong. There was also the issue of history. Both the Poltareks and Rose's family had lost relatives in the Nazi caldron. The oral tradition of passing down history could no longer be trusted. Everything had to be committed to paper—or, in later years, to the silicon chip, preserved because the service to Israel would not cease with the Poltareks' retirement or death.

In notes dating as far back as twenty years, Ben found references to Samuel. Even though he was then only in his teens, the older son was being groomed to join and eventually replace the father. There was mention of Samuel's education, the career paths available to him, the time off needed for trips to Israel so that he would absorb the beauty and uniqueness of the land he would be called upon to serve.

There were comments about the younger son as well. Ben wondered if, given the chance, his father would now take some of them back. Ben was painted as a quiet, hardworking soul with a touch of his mother's artistic flair. But he was not *sayan* material. He lacked inner strength and conviction; he was too honest, too generous with his opinions. Guile was not his forte. To be a *sayan* required a certain ruthlessness that was not part of Ben's fabric. It was not a vocation for the contemplative or the imaginative.

Well, Pop. I'm all you've got left.

Preferences and choices no longer mattered. Ben was the survivor, the last Poltarek, the "assistant." Here, among Sid's notes, written down and cached only hours before his death, was the fallen standard.

The Paris trip should have been straight business—the Kaiser-Agfa account. It had become more than that when Mustafa Manshur had contacted Sid with information on Jamal.

According to Sid's notes, the connection was obvious: The Israeli raid on Samarra had been based, at least in part, on Manshur's intelligence. But either the information was bad or incomplete, or the Israelis had made a terrible mistake. Hafez Jamal had survived; Issim Hassan, the warrior for peace, had perished.

Along with his two-year-old son.

But what about Hassan's wife?

This was the question Sid Poltarek had worried.

She had not been mentioned by Hafez Jamal in his declaration to the world. Why not? Surely the widow of a newly minted martyr was a potent public-relations weapon.

Nor were there any references to her in the anti-Israel diatribes from Benghazi to Tehran. No one spoke of her. It was as though she didn't exist.

Sid had had thoughts about this. Maybe it was Arab mores. A woman was chattel; a wife, property. For the most part, women had no voice, no influence. Why be surprised that she was, in effect, a nonperson?

"Because she can be a *tool*," Ben muttered, treading along his father's logic. "She doesn't have to be seen as an equal, only a means. To some end. Why not parade her across the news cameras of the world and garner sympathy that you couldn't buy for love or money? It's too perfect an opportunity."

Ben started. Delicately, he replayed the words he had just uttered, plucking out *means* and *tool*. He set these aside and weighed them.

Means to what end?

Tool for what purpose?

Why would Jamal hide—

"They are bringing in an American . . ."

A dying man's words.

Who is Hassan's wife? An American? The American?

The possibility intrigued.

Ben reached for his laptop. His father had gotten as far as Hassan's wife. Had he tried to uncover her identity and failed? Had there not been enough time? Although there was nothing on the disk to indicate where Sid had begun his search, or the trails he'd blazed and discarded, Ben thought that the issue was, more likely, time. His father had been murdered before he could string together any clues.

Ben would start at the beginning, with the most obvious references— magazines, journals, newspapers, any source that might have carried a picture of Issim Hassan. The older the pictures, probably the better. The more Hassan molted from terrorist to diplomat, the more likely it was that he'd keep his wife in the background. Arab politics was, with few exceptions, no place for a woman.

Good.

As night stole through the windows, all that was heard in the house was the creaking of floorboards, the clicks of keys beneath fingertips, and the steady breathing of a man pacing himself toward a destiny he could not possibly imagine.

*　*　*

"I can set 'er down in that clearing," the helicopter pilot said over tinny speakers. To Landau's ear, the man had an atrocious accent— Southern, he guessed—and the headphones made it even more difficult to understand him.

Landau tapped Reece on the shoulder. "Tell him to hover and use his light."

Reece looked at him askance until Landau pointed down.

Night was falling quickly over the woods. State trooper cars were pulling up to the dozen cabins set in a semicircle facing the lake. Landau and Reece watched toy figures race from toy cars.

Reece got on the headphones. "Light 'em up. Start with the one farthest to the right."

The helicopter's belly lamp was rated 32 million candlepower. When the beam hit its target, the cabin appeared to be sitting in a block of ice.

Reece did not have to tell the pilot his business. He coordinated with the troopers on the ground, moving the beam from cabin to cabin as each one was searched.

"You don't think he's down there, do you?" Reece said. When Landau didn't reply, she added: "You think we missed him. That's why you didn't want the chopper to set down. It'd be a waste of time getting it back in the air."

Landau kept his own counsel until the final cabin had been searched. The state trooper commander wanted to know what to do next. He sounded unhappy, like a man who's been hound-dogging a chase that might go on half the night.

"Call it, Landau."

"It's your—"

"Yeah. My hunt. But it's *your* man. The son of a bitch should be here, right? But he's not. He's either hiding down there, which means it could take all night to find him, or else he came and went . . ."

Landau squeezed her shoulder. It was the first time he'd touched her, and Reece was startled.

"He's not down there," Landau said. "He never came, he never went."

Reece was confused by Landau's soft, sad tone, as if Poltarek's eluding them was somehow a personal affront. She understood when he finally found it in himself to complete his thought.

"Rachel fronted for him. She gave herself to us and gave him time to go God-knows-where. She loves him, you know, so she lied to us."

* * *

Ben organized his Internet search as a gold miner might arrange the panning of a streambed, with multiple sieves.

He began with popular weekly magazines and the big newspapers, including the European English-language dailies. The references to Issim Hassan were his signposts.

When those yielded nothing, he moved on to more esoteric publications—*Foreign Report, Foreign Affairs Intelligence/Counterintelligence, Stanford Review*—and others that carried scholarly pieces about terrorism.

Next, he moved on to publicly available information from the State Department and the Pentagon.

Nothing. No references to a wife. Not to any woman. It was as though Hassan had been some mythic, celibate warrior.

Ben turned his search to Hafez Jamal and repeated the process.

Nothing.

He sat back, stared at the screen. The clue was there. He just wasn't hitting the right area.

Unless it's hidden away in some source written in Arabic or Farsi, neither of which you can read.

The whisper of a possibility suggested itself.

Ben punched up the unclassified publications of American embassies in Egypt, Jordan, Saudi Arabia, and Israel. He threw in Hassan's name and started the search again. The computer chimed.

An article published in conjunction with the University of Chicago about archaeological research in Egypt. Here was a list of the academic members who had made up the team. And the embassy advisers who had worked with local authorities to expedite permission for the dig. And the names of the Egyptians representing the University of Cairo.

Credit also to: Issim Hassan, a part-time employee of the university, whose knowledge of the Valley of the Kings was invaluable to researchers since Hassan had grown up in the area.

Fine. Hassan, as the new Howard Carter. Wife? Ben's eye drifted back to the Americans from Chicago. Four men. One woman.

Pictures, please.

The university alumni archives were happy to oblige. Ben found himself looking at a three-quarter profile of a homey, academic-looking woman in her mid-twenties.

He would have clicked back to the Cairo material had he not spotted something.

The bios for the men ran on for several more lines. Three were now comfortably ensconced in academia; the fourth was at the Met in New York.

But there was no such continuity for the woman. Her blurb ended with the expedition to Cairo, as if—

Judith Sawyer had never come home.

"They are bringing in an American."

Had not come home until now.

Twenty-three

BEN MADE GOOD TIME against the suburbs-bound Washington traffic. As soon as he'd cleared the Chesapeake Bay Bridge, he telephoned Henry Blake at Internal Affairs. The detective returned the call when Ben was less than twenty miles from the city. Ben's instructions were precise and Henry Blake did not question them.

"Has anyone been looking for me?" Ben asked him when he was finished.

"Officially? Not that I've heard." Blake paused. "Should they be?"

"If you haven't heard, it doesn't matter. I'll see you in a bit."

The temptation to hurry was overwhelming, but Ben forced himself to stay just above the speed limit. A few minutes either way would not impact the information he was carrying. It would remain as good or as useless as it had been the moment he'd unearthed it.

He felt oddly at peace with himself, as if he were floating, free of all restraints. The questions he had carried to the Chesapeake had, he believed, been answered. His doubts about the answers diminished with every mile marker he passed.

"I'm coming home, Sammy," he said aloud, in the darkness. "I'm not going to screw up this time."

Ben felt as though his whole life had been leading up to this moment. Finally, he would be able to make the kind of contribution his father had never believed him capable of, the kind his mother had never asked of him. Not that it would bring back Samuel or Sid or Rose, but just maybe it would lay to rest the constant murmurs of his conscience, to measure himself against those who had never called upon him, and not to be found wanting. Hearing the handcuffs snap on the wrists of the son of a bitch who had murdered his parents would be his gift to his family and to himself.

Ben had thought out his moves as carefully as he could. There were only two people he trusted completely: Rachel and Henry Blake. He would not go to Rachel yet. To do so might put her in harm's way.

Henry Blake was his insurance. He had to be told about Judith Sawyer, made to see all the connections and how, ultimately, they led to the dying man who had burst into Ben's life. Then Ben would tell him about the FBI agent, Reece. And Landau—oh, how much he could say about him!

After that, the matter would be in Blake's hands. Ben imagined there would be hurriedly arranged meetings at the FBI, where the hunt for Judith Sawyer, and the men who'd made her their instrument, would begin. He could sense it all, like the sharp whiff of ozone from a distant thunderstorm. He savored what he imagined would be the thrill of the hunt and knew that no one would want him to be a part of it.

Good luck.

Ben crossed into Washington proper, going up Connecticut Avenue, passing the main entrance of the apartment building, taking the corner, and slowing at the side entrance to the garage. A long time ago, he'd given Rachel a key card, which she kept in the glove box, and now it came in handy. He could enter the garage, then take the elevator that bypassed the lobby and ride it directly to the penthouse.

Tires screeched on the polished concrete garage floor as Ben took a hard turn. He eased into a parking space, killed the engine, and stared at the dashboard clock. Henry Blake would be here by now.

* * *

"Say, Jack."

Priestly was on his way out of D.C. Homicide's bullpen when the voice snagged him.

"Yeah?"

"Got something here you might be interested in."

The uniformed sergeant's name tag read BARNES. He was a fixture who'd squandered the last of his promotion possibilities long ago. Now, to supplement his income, he did favors for detectives he knew he could trust. Valuable favors, because Barnes had made it a point to learn about computers. He regularly surfed the internal police net, trolling for hits that might be worth something to fellow officers. He believed he had one such nugget now.

He steered Priestly into an alcove by the coffee service.

"You know IA has been sniffin' around you?"

Priestly hitched up his pants. "Random shit, or has someone taken a special interest?"

"Special, I'd say. You ever heard of a guy called Henry Blake?"

"Yeah. A geezer from Narcotics way back when. I thought he'd been put out to graze."

Barnes held up a folded piece of paper between himself and Priestly.

"He's grazing at IA—and seems to be munching his way to you. Awful lot of interest in that John Doe mess up at Woodley. Blake's popped everything, including your interview with the witness, Polansky or whoever."

Priestly made a show of scratching up dandruff.

"The fuck he did that for?"

"I'm not a mind reader, Jack. Just the messenger."

"I'll check it out. Any idea where I can find Blake?"

Barnes's dentures were wet behind his grin. "Thought you might want to know. Log shows he left to go to that apartment."

The folded paper disappeared into Priestly's pocket. "I owe you," he said, and headed out the door.

Barnes did not take offense at Priestly's abrupt departure. He knew what it felt like to have IA chewing on one's ass. And he didn't have any concern about Priestly not taking care of him for having provided the tip. Jack was a go-around, come-around kind of guy.

* * *

Although the helicopter cabin was well insulated, the incessant pounding of the rotors was driving a headache between Kaelin Reece's temples.

She glanced over at Landau, who was still wearing the headphones and talking into the microphone. Yiddish or Hebrew, she couldn't tell. Not that it mattered. Landau would assume rightly that all outgoing and incoming transmissions were recorded. He wouldn't say anything that he might have to eat later on.

Landau caught her looking and removed the headphones.

"There's no answer at Poltarek's apartment. Now might be a good time to get a couple of my men inside."

Reece shook her head. She had anticipated that he'd ask this.

"If anyone were to go in, it'd be Bureau agents. And that won't happen because we don't have probable cause." She paused. "Don't piss me off by looking at me like that. As far as the law's concerned, that's Poltarek's home."

"I don't want to 'piss you off.' I was just asking."

"Besides, do you really expect him to pick up the phone? What makes you think he's even anywhere near D.C.?"

Landau shrugged and patched through another call. This time he spoke English, asking the operator at the Children's National Medical Center to page Dr. Rachel Melman.

When the reply came back, he said, "No. No message."

"She's finishing up in surgery," he told Reece. "We will pick her up on our way to Poltarek's. She has a key to the apartment." He noted the way Reece looked at him. "What? It's not like I'm asking *her* to break into the place."

Reece appreciated the frustration Landau was drowning in. There had been no sightings of Hafez Jamal, no hits off the all-points that had gone out on Rachel Melman's car. The trip to Timberland had been a colossal waste of time and energy. Landau might have been able to deal with that had it not been for the good doctor's betrayal. The unkindest cut of all, Reece thought.

She wondered how Landau would handle Melman, how much of the humiliation and anger would, despite himself, seep through. Reece thought she might learn something true and valuable about Landau in the next few hours.

She caught him staring at his watch, and when he noticed, he said, "Can't this thing go any faster?"

Reece slipped on the headphones to talk to the pilot.

* * *

Ben found Henry Blake sitting in a chair in the foyer, one slim leg draped over the other, the pant crease razor-sharp.

"Hello, Henry—"

"The key was just where you said it'd be. Now, you mind telling me what kind of car you been driving?"

The question was put casually enough, but Ben detected pinpoints of concern—or anger—in Blake's eyes.

"A BMW. It belongs to my fiancée."

"Know the tag number?"

After Ben gave it to him, Blake rose and went to him.

"There's an all-points out on it," he said quietly. "Local *and* state. You were lucky you weren't pulled over." He paused. "You want to tell me what you've done to deserve such attention? You *did* tell me you weren't going to go off half-cocked."

Ben held up his briefcase. "This will take a while. Why don't I make us some coffee."

"You don't seem surprised that you've gone to the top of everyone's hit parade," Blake said, following Ben into the kitchen.

"Nope. And you didn't mention the FBI."

Blake pursed his lips. "Them too, hmm?"

"Them too."

While the coffeemaker gurgled and dripped, Ben set out his notes, disks, and laptop on the kitchen table. It took him the better part of ninety minutes to walk Blake through all the material.

"That's it," Ben said, sitting back in his chair. "All of it."

Blake had listened without comment, even though some of the things Ben recounted were outrageous. Nonetheless, the boy had proof to back up most of his conclusions.

"I think," Blake said slowly, "that major shit is going to hit the fan. But before we make that happen, I have a few questions."

*   *   *

Hafez Jamal had questions of his own and he spat them at Priestly one after the other.

"I'm telling you, there's nothing to worry about," Priestly said.

As soon as he'd cleared police headquarters, Priestly had called Jamal on the emergency number. Twenty minutes later, he picked up Jamal in the parking lot of the Safeway on Wisconsin and Thirty-fourth Street.

"You keep repeating that—" Jamal started to say.

"Look. Internal Affairs has a jacket on *everyone*. They're like the fucking IRS. Their sniffing around? It's like a random audit."

Random at this particular time? I don't believe so, Detective.

Jamal did not voice his conclusion. Right now, he needed Priestly's cooperation and his detective's shield.

"But you agree that this Blake poses a"—Jamal was about to say "danger" but finished with—"a problem."

"As far as your boy is concerned, yeah."

"Then I think it best that we remove Mr. Poltarek from his consideration."

Priestly braked hard at a traffic light. "Look. I get paid to provide information. End of story. I don't 'remove' anybody."

"I am not asking you to do that," Jamal replied smoothly. "Believe me, it is not my intention to harm the boy. But I do need to speak with him privately."

Priestly shook his head. "You're talking about kidnapping—"

"No, I am not. All I am requesting is that you get me to his door. After that, you go your own way." Jamal paused. "Of course, there would be a bonus for this extra service."

Priestly had the car moving again. He drove three blocks, turning the offer over in his mind.

"What's the extra?"

"One thousand dollars."

"What do you have in mind that leaves me in the clear?"

Jamal had been thinking furiously. He needed to satisfy Priestly's demand for safety; he had to make sure that whatever he proposed would get him through to his target. One solution presented itself—if Priestly could be induced to go along.

Quickly, Jamal explained his plan. For thirty anxious seconds, he sat waiting for Priestly's reply. When it came, Jamal knew he had him.

Priestly pulled into a minimall and pointed at an Indian restaurant.

"You can get what you need in there. Oh, and grab me some tandoori chicken while you're at it. I'll eat it later."

*   *   *

The pilot received clearance from the Medical Center for the helicopter to touch down on its rooftop pad. Reece and Landau scrambled out of the passenger compartment, crouching under the rotor wash, hurrying to the double doors where a pair of orderlies were standing by, a stretcher held between them.

"Where's the victim?" one of them asked. "Downstairs, they said it was an emergency."

"Not that kind of emergency," Landau replied as he and Reece brushed by.

* * *

Henry Blake had more than a few questions. He had taken off his jacket, and whenever he reached for his coffee, the butt of his gun, riding in the exposed shoulder holster, tapped the edge of the table.

"I'm all out of answers, Henry," Ben said. The adrenaline that had kept him going had all but dissipated. "Jamal, his plan—whatever that is; Judith Sawyer's role; we need help to figure it all out."

Blake nodded silently.

Ben asked: "So who do we go to?"

"The FBI's already sniffed around you, right?"

"That woman, Kaélin Reece."

"You still have her card?"

"Somewhere. You don't want to use any of your contacts at the Bureau?"

"What I want is to find out exactly what division Ms. Reece works in."

"Because . . . ?"

"Because I think we'll end up talking to her at some point."

If Ben hadn't been tired, he'd have made the connection sooner. "You're saying she's with the antiterrorist division."

"In light of what we have, what we know, that would seem to make sense, wouldn't it?"

Ben rose. "Her card's in the study. Let me get it."

* * *

The concierge saw the doorman step aside to allow a tall, rangy man to pass. As he came closer, the concierge recognized him as the detective who'd been there before.

"Evening," Priestly said. He saw the concierge reach for the house phone. "Don't bother. I'm expected."

The front door opened a second time. This one was all bundled up, his face obscured by several brown paper bags resting in a cardboard box that he clutched against his chest with both hands.

The concierge crinkled his nose. The smell of Indian food made him hungry. Now he heard the deliveryman mumble a suite number. And the detective was in the elevator, holding back the door.

"I'll take him up," he called out.

The concierge waved his hand at the deliveryman, shooing him along.

*   *   *

Rachel still had on her surgical greens when Landau saw her. She saw him standing there in the surgeons' prep room, reached up and slowly pulled off her cap, pulled out the pins letting her hair tumble to her shoulders.

Rachel had only to take that one look to understand that he had figured out her deception. Figured it out long enough ago so that, for the moment, he could park his anger and get on with business.

Rachel reached down and pulled off the booties that covered her sneakers. She saw Landau's legs approach; the FBI agent was holding back.

"Where is he, Rachel?"

She tossed the booties into the burn bin. "I don't know. That's the truth."

"The truth. How refreshing. You should know that there's an all-points out on your car. We tried the phone but either it's dead or he's disconnected it. I don't have any way of warning him not to run when the troopers spot him."

"Ben's not stupid. He won't run."

"Maybe he won't, but he's still stupid."

"What do you want, Landau?"

"Your duties here are finished, yes? I would like you to invite Agent Reece and myself to Ben's apartment, where the three of us can wait for him together. Maybe talk a little."

"And if I have other plans?"

"Then Agent Reece will be obliged to take you into custody as a material witness in Ben's disappearance."

"That's a chickenshit play."

"It is. But I'm certainly prepared to use it. Contrary to what you may think, Rachel, I don't want to hurt him. But as you know, there are those out there who are not of like mind."

Rachel considered. She could fight Landau on this, raise such a stink that Reece might think twice. But there was nothing to gain. Ben had asked for this time and she had become his coconspirator in order to help him buy it. He understood that he could not evade Landau forever. Either Ben had gotten to the information he needed or he would come back empty-handed. To let Landau and Reece wait for him changed nothing.

Actually, Rachel thought, it might be better to have them close. Who knew what they might let slip?

"Five minutes to change," Rachel said, and gave Landau her back.

Reece started after her as Rachel disappeared into the changing room. She was surprised when Landau warned her off by shaking his head. This one, Reece thought, still had at least the tips of her claws in him.

*   *   *

"Here it is," Ben called out, coming out of the study.

Henry Blake was standing by the sink, staring at the samplers, but his eyes weren't moving. Ben walked up to him and handed him the card. The doorbell sounded.

Blake looked at him.

"Probably Rachel," Ben said and turned to leave.

*   *   *

Out in the hall, Priestly shifted from one foot to the other. He knew exactly what would happen next and what his role would be.

Priestly believed that the Arab wanted to talk to Ben Poltarek, but that was all he believed. The Arab knew that Henry Blake was inside that apartment, and that Blake would not let him get near Poltarek. So, Henry Blake would die.

Priestly had no problem with that. It wasn't any coincidence that Blake was shagging up his ass at this particular time. Blake wasn't sniffing for payolas or dope disappearing from the evidence room. He and Poltarek had met. The kid had told him something that keened his interest—probably Priestly's questions about the dead guy. Now Blake was bird-dogging. If he went far enough—and Blake's reputation spoke for itself—he might just come across Priestly's off-the-books arrangements with the Arabs.

So, Blake has to die. The Arab would be the triggerman. Now came the best part: Priestly would shoot the Arab and come out looking like a hero. That, plus the fact that the only two who could speak against him would be dead. Perfect.

Priestly had his detective's shield in his hand, ready. The Arab was behind him and to the left. The smell of curry was intoxicating. Priestly thought that that bit about getting the Arab to order extra food for him had been a nice touch. The victim doesn't expect his executioner to ask him to get takeout.

Such was Priestly's last thought. He heard the crinkle of paper bags but not the tiny report of the silenced shot. The explosion that blew apart the back of his head never registered in his consciousness as the .22 bullet rattled around in his cranium, chewing up brain matter.

"Who is it?"

Jamal heard Poltarek's muffled voice behind the door. He scooped up Priestly's ID and held it close to the peephole. He said, "Priestly," between two hacking coughs.

*　*　*

"It's Priestly," Ben said over his shoulder as Henry Blake approached. Blake stopped, frowned.

Ben's fingers flipped back the deadbolt.

"No!" Blake shouted.

It was too late. The door burst open, slamming hard against Ben, sending him sprawling against the secretaire.

Blake saw flashes of dark clothing. He was reaching for his gun, bringing it out in that practiced draw. But he was just a little too old, a little too slow. The barrel hadn't even cleared the leather when Jamal's bullet ripped into his rib cage, nicked bone, and buried itself in his heart.

Jamal was all motion. Even before Blake hit the floor, Jamal was hunched over the boy. A judicious blow to the head opened his scalp, stunned him but did not knock him unconscious.

Jamal then dragged Priestly into the foyer, returned for the food, and closed the door. He arranged Priestly close to the other detective, kneeled, and jammed his .22 into Ben's limp hand. Now the fingerprints were where they should be.

Careful to avoid the seeping blood, he tied the boy's hands with plastic cuffs and jerked him to his feet. He prodded him with Priestly's big Sig Sauer.

"I have come a long way to talk to you," he hissed into the boy's ear. "Now we will go where we can have privacy, you understand?"

Ben was swaying on his feet. His knees threatened to buckle and his head felt as though it was about to explode. Something warm and sticky was leaking down the back of his neck.

"Never make it . . ." he managed.

Jamal pushed him to the floor and raced toward the only lighted room, the kitchen. He saw his bounty on the table—the notes and CD-ROMs, car keys—and scooped them up into the bag the boy had conveniently left there.

He ran back into the foyer, checked the hall through the peephole, and pushed Ben through the door.

The elevator came within seconds. Inside, Jamal pressed the button for the garage level.

"You will show me your car," he said.

Ben was slumped against the wall. "Fuck you."

"Colorful, but rude. You think you can still play me, don't you?" Jamal said. "Wait, boy. I think I will surprise you."

Gripping Ben by the collar, he steered him toward a mesh cage that housed part of the building's electrical controls. Ben heard his breath whistle through his nostrils as he struggled to stay on his feet. What was Jamal waiting for? Then he heard the squeal of car tires taking the corner of the ramp and realized what Jamal had to do. In desperation, he flung himself at the terrorist, but Jamal had anticipated his move. Ben saw the blur of Jamal's arm, felt the back of his skull explode as the gun in Jamal's hand caught him behind the ear.

He was falling now, slowly, through galaxies of red haze. His cheek touched something cold and hard, and grit scraped his skin when he moved.

Just before the haze rolled over him completely, Ben saw Jamal walking away, toward the car that was slipping into its designated slot, the gun hidden behind his back.

Twenty-four

KAELIN REECE WANTED to whistle up a car from the Bureau pool, but Landau pressed for a cab. He was in a hurry. He didn't need any of the standard-issue paraphernalia the FBI carried in the trunks of their cars—bulletproof vests, AR-15s, and Remington shotguns. His own team, whom he'd called from the helicopter, and which would be close to Poltarek's building, had such equipment—and better.

Landau wanted to get over to the apartment because he believed that, if Poltarek hadn't already arrived, he would do so very soon. Rachel had not offered much, but in talking to her, Landau had come away with the impression that Poltarek had not bolted. Rachel had helped him buy time—time to do something privately, away from the city, then return.

Landau reckoned that was why the police hadn't picked up Rachel's car. Poltarek had made his getaway, arrived at his destination, and hidden the car. If what he had to do took no more than half a day, he would be on his way home at nightfall, when there was less chance of the car being spotted.

Landau figured that Poltarek hadn't yet returned; Rachel's demeanor would have been different if he had. She was not so accomplished an actress that she could hide her relief. Which meant that Landau could be waiting on Poltarek when he stepped into the apartment. He could throw him off balance by his presence, bully him a little. Poltarek would be nervous and tired. He might be more inclined to give up information because Rachel was there, seeing her in the glue because she'd helped him.

The cab was a big station wagon. Reece rode up front, Landau and Rachel in the back, on seats that smelled of mildew. From time to time, Landau glanced at Rachel, but her eyes were always averted, looking out at traffic. When the cab took sharp turns and their bodies touched, she shifted away.

The concierge recognized Rachel as soon as she stepped through the doors. The other woman was also familiar, in a distant sort of way. He did not know the man who moved very softly, like he was skimming, not walking, his compact body coiled like a snake's.

"It's a regular party here tonight," the concierge said. It was a silly, almost rude comment, prompted by nervousness.

The concierge caught the sharp look in the man's dark eyes. *Oh, shit!* He was about to apologize when the stranger whispered to Rachel.

"What do you mean, a party?" Rachel asked.

"Look, Doc. No disrespect, right? All I was saying is that there's been a lot of traffic up to the . . . the Poltareks' place."

"Who?"

"Well, first one detective went up." The concierge checked his log. "Henry Blake's the name. Mr. Poltarek called on his car phone to ask me to let him in, which is exactly what I did—after checking his ID."

"What about Ben?" Rachel asked urgently.

"I know he's there because I saw the elevator go up. But I didn't exactly *see* him. He went directly from the garage."

"Who else?"

"Well, then there was *another* cop." Another quick glance at the log. "Detective Priestly. And a delivery guy with some food."

"Describe the deliveryman!" Landau snapped.

"Looked like an Arab to me. I didn't see much of his face because of the food packages. Frankly, he seemed a little old for the job, but—"

The concierge's mouth hung open as Landau pulled Reece aside.

"Your team or mine? Mine are just down the street. Quickly now!"

"Jamal?" Reece whispered.

"Who else?"

"Yours."

Landau turned to the concierge. "Has the deliveryman come down? Has *anyone* left the building?"

The concierge swallowed. "Not that I know."

Landau was talking quickly into his cell phone. When he was finished, he said to Reece, "Get him"—he gestured at the concierge—"to close off all the elevators except one."

Reece flipped open her ID and huddled with the concierge while Landau took Rachel aside.

"I'm going to ask you this once: Will you stay down here, behind that desk, and let me do my job?"

"He's up there, isn't he? Jamal—"

"Will you, Rachel?"

She nodded, and went around the concierge's desk. Seconds later, a dark sedan screeched up to the front doors. Four men got out, carrying hard plastic shells that looked like they'd been molded for band instruments.

"Landau!" He was already in the elevator, had to look over his shoulder at her. "Bring him to me."

The elevator rose swiftly but Landau's men worked even faster. Clasps and snaps were flipped open, plastic rattled against the marble floor, harsh clicks and ratcheting noises filled the small space as ammunition clips were slapped into place, safeties flicked off.

Looking at the firepower, Reece felt naked holding her Sig Sauer.

"Kaelin?"

Landau's soft voice drew her back. "Yeah?"

"We are doing this on a wing and a prayer, correct?"

"Yeah. Especially the prayer part."

"My team hits the door first. You stay back. This will be a hard takedown. Jamal gets no warning, no time to grab hostages."

"What about Priestly?"

Landau's voice became very cold. "I don't care about Priestly. If I have to go through him to get to Jamal, that's what I do."

Reece realized that Landau was using these same words to issue instructions to his men.

"What about the other detective?"

"I don't think he's a part of this."

"So you won't shoot him?"

"Not unless I have to. Here is the play: Priestly and Jamal go down first. We aim for shoulders, legs, anyplace that makes them drop. I want Jamal alive. You want him that way, too. He has things to tell us."

Out of the elevator, moving swiftly and silently down the carpeted hallway. One of Landau's men tapped him on the shoulder, pointed. Reece followed his finger to the blood spots on the carpet.

Blood and the smell of tandoori chicken . . .

Reece held back as Landau and his team crowded both sides of the door. She missed the prearranged signal because in the next instant, there was the popcorn sound of silenced automatic weapons. The heavy wood around the ornate brass lock and bolt was shredded, heavy boots hitting the door so hard that it shook in its frame as it hit the wall.

For a moment, Reece saw nothing but bodies piling inside, heard men calling out softly, footsteps pounding. Then the foyer was vacant, and there lay two bodies: one white—Priestly; the other black—had to be the second detective. And two heavy-duty paper bags of food, stapled at the top.

Reece stepped inside, careful to skirt the blood. Deep in the apartment, men still called out to one another, but she knew that they knew the carnage was done. There was no one left to take by the throat, no one to bludgeon. The coppery stink of blood was Jamal mocking them.

"How long?" Landau demanded harshly as he clattered down the staircase. "How long have they been dead?"

Reece gazed into the dead men's eyes.

"Not long." She touched the black man's palm. "Still warm."

But too long for Landau. Enough time for Jamal to have done his work and left.

"What about Poltarek?" Reece asked. "You found him upstairs?"

When Landau didn't answer, she looked at him. "He *was* upstairs . . ."

Landau shook his head. "Gone. Jamal took him."

It was then that Rachel, standing in the hall, screamed.

Twenty-five

B EN TRIED TO GET TO HIS FEET, fingertips scraping the pillar, the stubble in the rough-textured concrete cutting through skin and nerves, tearing at blood vessels. The moments of lucidity were camera flashes going off in his mind. The pain did not so much hurt as stun him.

He twisted, slamming his back against the wall, thighs trembling as he fought to support himself. That was when he saw old Mr. Connelly, apartment 6E, elderly widower, writer of detective stories. Connelly, in his old cashmere overcoat and houndstooth cap à la Sherlock Holmes, fussing with grocery bags. The Jeep Cherokee's tailgate was down, Connelly, leaning into the storage compartment, never hearing, never seeing Jamal coming up behind him.

Ben's lungs burned with every breath he drew. The shout he wanted to hurl across the empty garage came out a whispery rasp. He wanted to warn Connelly. He wanted to scream at Jamal that he didn't have to kill the old man. A gentle tap on the head would be enough.

But the knife was already in Jamal's hand. Ben watched as in one motion he swooped down, grabbed the hem of Connelly's coat, pulled it up to reveal a wool sweater over corduroy pants.

Jamal did not pull his arm back to drive home the knife. With the thick coat out of the way, he slid the knife into Connelly's left lower back, twisting and digging like a butcher fleshing meat off a bone. When he re-moved the knife and started in on Connelly's right side, Ben realized Jamal was carving out the old man's kidneys.

Ben thought he heard Connelly utter a sharp gasp, but nothing more. The killing was over in seconds. Jamal gripped Connelly by the shoul-ders and flung him away, Connelly's body rolling, streaking the polished concrete floor with red.

Jamal reached inside the Cherokee and hurled the grocery bags. Then he was back, grabbing Ben by the scruff of the neck, thrusting him to-ward the vehicle.

Connelly was a prudent driver. Next to the spare tire was an emer-gency road kit. Ben felt the tip of Jamal's knife on the skin of his back as the Palestinian rummaged inside the kit and came up with a roll of thick adhesive tape, the kind used to temporarily patch a hole in an engine hose. Ben felt the tape go around his wrists, another piece across his mouth. Jamal pushed him into the cargo compartment and told him to curl up. Then he threw an old picnic blanket over him.

"Do not struggle, do not move," he heard Jamal say. "If you kick at the windows, I will cut your tendons."

An electric motor whined as the tailgate window was raised. Ben felt the Cherokee move, tires squealing as the rubber floated on the concrete floor.

Why keep me around? Why not kill me too?

The questions pounded in Ben's mind, clambering over the rocky out-crops of his terror to the answer: Jamal wanted to know what the dying man had told him. Jamal, a Swiss-trained physician who could carve out a man's kidneys like they were so much offal. Jamal, the patriot and free-dom fighter who sent adolescents with bombs into the streets of Israeli cities. Jamal, the charismatic, the fanatic, who, Ben knew, would cut and hurt him until Ben was screaming out his words. Not that the words themselves would matter. Jamal would kill him as soon as he was con-vinced that Ben had given up everything he had.

Ben could tell that Jamal was not yet comfortable behind the wheel. He was taking the corners too quickly, and the truck's swaying motion made the blanket shift. Ben saw streetlights and the lit offices of govern-ment towers. He thought that Jamal's driving might attract the attention of a roving patrol car. A part of him ached to hear the wail of a siren, to see the reflection of spinning gumball lights. Then he remembered Priestly and Henry Blake and understood exactly what Jamal would do to any policeman who tried to interfere.

Landau, Ben thought. *Landau and that FBI agent, Reece.* Soon they would realize how he and Rachel had tricked them, sending them off to Timberland. They would be furious with Rachel. They would come to the apartment and discover—

But how soon? And did they have any idea where Jamal might be going? *Don't think so.* If they had, they would have tagged Jamal by now.

The Cherokee was speeding along, the tires hitting tar strips in rhythmic intervals.

A highway?

Ben had not expected this. He thought for sure that Jamal would have a bolt-hole somewhere inside Washington proper. Staying on the road would be a great risk once the alarm went up.

Ben shifted slightly. He had to get into a position to see a landmark—something that would hint at the direction in which they were headed. He needed to believe that it was important to do this. It was all he had to believe in.

*   *   *

The two dead detectives created an unforeseen problem for Landau in the person of the grim chief of homicide, Abbott, who had arrived on the scene. Landau knew he would have to deal delicately with Reece if he was to get what he needed. He needed to coach and prod her in her dealings with him. Abbott, he knew, would see him as an interloper, a foreigner who had brought his bloody business across the ocean and deposited it on D.C.P.D.'s doorstep. He had to make Abbott understand what else was at stake.

The apartment and the lobby were filled with police technicians, plainclothes, and uniforms. The first units had begun arriving even before Reece had put out the squawk, before Landau had had a chance to pull her aside and set her straight. Where the panic call had originated was still a mystery, but Landau suspected the concierge or one of the other downstairs staff.

Abbott was slender, middle-aged, with a soft voice that carried a sting when he needed to make a point. By the quick, efficient activity in the apartment, Landau recognized that Abbott was accustomed to command. His investigators worked swiftly and silently, reminding Landau of a seasoned rowing crew.

"Reece, is it?"

"Special Agent Reece, Captain."

Abbott turned to Landau. "And Mr. Landau. No rank."

Reece caught the anger in Abbott's cool tone.

"Captain, Mr. Landau is here at the invitation of our government. What happened here . . . We believe it's part of a national security consideration."

Reece didn't think "national security" would cut much ice with Abbott and she wasn't wrong. But at least the captain was polite. His body language indicated that he was willing to listen.

Reece returned the courtesy, giving Abbott the details she thought he needed to know.

A suspected terrorist, Hafez Jamal, was believed to be in the D.C. area. He was thought to be responsible for the deaths of Sidney and Rose Poltarek, owners of the apartment. He might also have targeted the Poltareks' son, Benjamin, whom Reece and Landau had come to see.

At that point, Abbott held up his hand and looked at Landau. "You're Israeli."

"Yes, Captain."

"Those were your men the downstairs staff saw coming up to the apartment?"

"Yes."

"Under federal authority," Reece added quickly.

Abbott ignored her. "Which means you expected this Jamal to be here."

"Might be here, Captain."

"*Was* here. You're thinking Jamal killed my men."

"I know he did."

Abbott stuffed his hands in his pockets, rocked lightly on his heels.

"You had a description out on Jamal for the last few days, didn't you?"

"We wanted to bring him in for questioning," Reece said.

"'Questioning'? But you come in here with a commando force."

Reece was about to answer, but Landau cut in.

"Captain, I am very sorry about the deaths of your men. Somehow —and we *don't* know how—they either walked in on or otherwise became part of this situation. Our concern was and remains Benjamin Poltarek."

"What's his connection to Jamal?"

"That, Captain, is what we wanted to ask him."

Abbott thought about that. "You've been running your operation very quietly," he said at last. "No alerts, no postings, no interagency communiqués. Someone battened down the hatches on this thing."

He left the question unspoken.

"The White House," Reece said.

Abbott's eyes went dead. "You understand that I don't give a rat's ass if the President sends the AG and his entire staff to camp on my door, no one's taking jurisdiction away from me. Not with two of my own laid low."

"We both want the same man," Landau said softly.

"Yes. But I want to put him on trial here. Not in some courtroom halfway across the world."

"Captain, you must know that men like Jamal seldom allow matters to proceed that far."

Abbott looked him up and down. He had met men like this Landau, phantom warriors who dwelled in the shadows of the conventional army. There was a certain granitelike finality to them. Abbott believed that Hafez Jamal had injured Landau, probably killed some of his people. So Landau would trap him and hurt him and extract what he needed. Only then would those who demanded vengeance have it.

"Captain, you need to see this."

It was the fingerprint tech, holding up a sheet. Landau caught something in his voice—was it triumph?—and he didn't like it.

"Jamal's prints," Reece said under her breath after Abbott had moved off. "Gotta be."

Landau wasn't so sure. He got a better idea of just how wrong Reece was when Abbott came back to them, obviously struggling to contain his anger.

"You have fingerprints off the gun used to kill your men," Landau said. He wanted to reach out to Abbott, work with a positive, work to keep him calm.

"Fingerprints I have," Abbott said abruptly.

"Jamal's," Reece broke in. "They'd be on the antiterrorist hotline, linked to the NCIC—"

"They most probably are, Special Agent Reece. But that's not where I got these." Abbott took a deep breath, through his mouth, like a man standing over putrefaction. "These came off the .22 used on Priestly and Blake. But they don't belong to Jamal. They didn't come off the NCIC. They're from the Justice Department. All lawyers are fingerprinted when they pass the bar or go to work for the government, right? These are Ben Poltarek's prints on the gun."

Abbott looked from Landau to Reece. "What—no surprise?"

"Poltarek didn't kill your men, Captain," Landau said quietly.

"Jamal must have taken him down, put his prints on the weapon," Reece added quickly.

"Okay. So Jamal not only manages to take down two experienced officers, at the same time he subdues Poltarek, gets his prints on the .22. That's what you're telling me?"

"The concierge says Priestly and the deliveryman went up together," Landau said. "There was no reason for the concierge to recognize Jamal. But Priestly? In the confines of an elevator, the time it takes the car to reach the penthouse . . ."

"Don't even *think* of going down that road," Abbott said softly. "If Priestly didn't make the guy—"

He stopped short when he saw something in Landau's eyes.

"Priestly *knew* it was Jamal? They were *connected*? Fuck you, mister!"

Landau did not drop his steady gaze but neither did he press on. The details he and Reece had on Priestly could rest undisturbed a while longer. Later, he'd let Reece pick the time, when Abbott had cooled off, when they needed something from him.

"Something else you didn't tell me," Abbott was saying. "That you had a silent alarm out for Poltarek."

Landau noted the slight crease in Abbott's lips, the satisfaction he was getting out of this. Someone had scored big points bringing him the all-points on Poltarek.

"We weren't hiding anything and there's not much to tell," Reece said flatly. "We had Poltarek under surveillance, in case Jamal came calling. Then Poltarek jackrabbited on us. We wanted to find him, but without a fuss."

"Fuss is what you've got now," Abbott replied. "Far as I'm concerned, Poltarek has just gone platinum. The APBs out on the Jeep stand."

"But you don't think he killed Priestly and Blake," Reece persisted.

"His prints are on the weapon. Priestly and Blake were murdered while Poltarek was on the premises—"

"Do you think he killed that man down in the garage, too?"

The three of them looked in the direction of the haunted, wavering voice. Rachel stood in the doorway of the study. Reece had taken her there immediately after Rachel had seen the carnage and screamed. A few cops had poked their heads inside, but Reece had made sure no one had gone near her.

"Well, do you?"

"Dr. Melman?" Abbott queried.

"Yes. Now tell me. Do you think Ben killed Mr. Connelly? I overheard some of your men talking, Captain. Their account was quite graphic. 'Laid out his kidneys like they were a couple of fried eggs' was one of the more imaginative phrases."

"I don't know what to tell you about Connelly, Doctor," Abbott replied. "Maybe I'll have a better idea about Poltarek after I talk to you. But right now, Poltarek is my number-one play. If he and Jamal are joined at the hip—"

"You think Ben is cooperating with him!"

"I think, Doctor, that if we find one, we find them both. Now, if you're up to it—and no one has any objections—let's you and I chat. Maybe you can tell me something about Poltarek that will help him out. What do you say?"

Rachel gave him a barely perceptible nod and disappeared back into the study.

"What do *you* say, Captain?" Reece asked as Abbott brushed by her. "Hold off making Poltarek out to be a killer until you've talked to her."

"Not even if 1600 Pennsylvania asks."

Reece felt Landau tug at her elbow. She pulled away sharply and walked down the hall to the kitchen. Two patrolmen were talking quietly in the nook. They took stock of Reece, and of Landau, who followed her in, and left.

"It's our fault. All of it."

Landau took two Cokes from the refrigerator, put one back when Reece shook her head.

"What's our fault?" he asked.

"Henry Blake . . . the rest of it." She pivoted on the ball of her foot, like a dancer. "We made Blake the goat. Somehow, Priestly cottoned onto that—probably an in-station snitch who thought he was doing Priestly a favor. So Priestly knows IA is on his ass. He makes a play for Blake."

"And brings Jamal along? Jamal was using Priestly, but he wouldn't become his triggerman. Jamal wouldn't jeopardize his own operation that way."

"That's the part that doesn't stretch," Reece admitted.

Landau chugged his Coke. "It might stretch if you look at it another way." He paused until he had Reece's attention. "Let's say that whatever Jamal's here to do is heating up. He's in the endgame. If that's the case, the last thing he needs or wants are loose ends. Priestly has helped him. But in doing so, maybe he's learned a little too much, connected a few too many dots.

"But Priestly has problems of his own—Blake. Jamal sees an opportunity. He offers to help Priestly, to get rid of Blake for him. No reason for Priestly not to accept, right? Except he isn't aware of Jamal's agenda."

"So Jamal comes up with Priestly," Reece joined in. "He kills Blake, then Priestly too. Now he's home free, and there's Poltarek."

"I think that's the way it happened," Landau said. "More or less. In this situation, Priestly was a bonus."

Reece poured herself a glass of water. "Sounds good. And right. But it doesn't change the fact that we basically set up Blake."

Landau said nothing. Reece wanted to hate him for a little while and that was all right, too. He needed her to purge herself of anger and self-blame. He needed her keen and ready for what was to come.

"Let's go get Rachel," he said. "Abbott has had enough time with her."

*　*　*

The shock Rachel exhibited in front of Abbott was not feigned. She had gotten past the images of carnage. What she could not accept was the fact that Ben was gone.

But another part of her was cool to the touch, the part that had listened to Landau explain what the police would ask when they got here. He would make it easy for her, he'd said. She could give the detectives everything she knew, except for her being a *sayan*. She was a doctor, a fiancée, someone who knew that her lover was in trouble and had helped him, without asking questions.

Given everything else that Homicide had to deal with, they would accept her statement at face value. At least for now.

Rachel had taken Abbott's measure as soon as he'd stepped into the room. She recognized the intelligence behind his quiet demeanor, caught the way he'd forced himself to calm down before approaching her. He was poised to notice everything, so Rachel gave him the truth, knowing that a lie or even a half truth would resonate like a spiderweb struck by a fly. She was pleased that Abbott couldn't quite hide his smile when she described how she and Ben had conspired to send Landau and Reece off on a wild goose chase to Timberland. Clearly, Abbott had found Landau's social skills wanting.

"We'd like to put a tap on your phones—at your hospital office and at home," he said.

"Of course." Landau had warned her that the police would request this.

"And you'll let me know—immediately—if Mr. Poltarek contacts you in any other way, through e-mail or something like that."

"I will."

Rachel looked over his shoulder, and when Abbott turned, he saw Landau in the doorway.

Abbott finished his thought while keeping his eyes on Landau.

"I want to be very clear on this point, Doctor. Whatever other agencies may be involved, D.C. Homicide has jurisdiction in this matter. Your responsibility is to contact us, no one else."

"Absolutely."

"We'll do our best to find him, Doctor, and bring him back safely."

"Ben's innocent, Captain."

Abbott was about to reply but thought better of it. He nodded to Rachel and slipped past Landau, who closed the door.

"Jamal took Ben because he thinks he knows something," she said flatly.

"Yes."

"He'll hurt him, won't he? Ben will tell him what he knows, but Jamal will still torture him." Her voice rose in panic. "That's the way it's done, isn't it? You torture someone because the truth can never come too easily. If it does, it's suspect. Pain is the convincing thing, isn't it?"

"What does Ben know, Rachel? There's no point in hiding it now. Maybe it will help us find him."

Rachel caught the lethargy in his voice. Landau wasn't trying to fool with her. He was grappling with defeat, looking for a way to turn something—anything—to his advantage. He didn't care who had lied to him or had hidden things from him. He needed to make something happen. To help himself meant helping Ben, if only by proxy. Because she felt this to be true, Rachel could now give him what he wanted.

"'They are bringing in an American.' Those are the exact words Ben said your man used. That's all of it. That's all he knows."

Landau was very still. "'They are bringing in an American.' Was the American Priestly?"

"Ben didn't know. But I don't think so."

"No . . . If it were Priestly, Jamal wouldn't have kept him so close. He wouldn't have killed him. It's somebody else."

"Then do what you do so well, Landau. Go find him."

* * *

The ride was much longer than Ben had thought it would be. He heard the whoosh of cars streaming in the opposite direction, felt the Cherokee rock when the big semis hurtled by. He tried to maintain a sense of time, but that was hard because he'd forgotten exactly when Jamal had taken him. The best he could do was count off the minutes. Later, when they stopped, he would guesstimate the average speed and use that to figure out how far they might have traveled.

The problem would be direction. Ben twisted around to try to see the night sky. He caught a glimpse of it, the moon a wavering bluish shadow obscured by clouds. No stars to steer by, either. Jamal could be heading to any point on the compass.

Tires purring on metal—crossing a bridge. The smell of ocean seeping into the Cherokee. Jamal was slowing down, the road becoming winding, with the occasional hairpin turn. Rattling over washboard grates left by the winter, dipping into potholes, the shocks protesting. The engine whining as it labored up a crest, the truck lurching forward, rolling, and the engine was cut.

Ben heard Jamal get out of the truck fast. The tailgate was pulled open and Jamal grabbed him by the ankles, pulled him forward, stood him up, steadied him because his hands were bound behind his back.

Ben whipped his head back and gagged as the tape over his mouth was torn away. He coughed, doubled over, and was almost sick until he could straighten up and breathe normally.

The night sky was very clear on the Chesapeake. The moonlight made the tree branches look like a crèche of bones behind Jamal. There was the old house the Poltareks had never been able to bring themselves to love, which Ben had left just hours ago.

Ben stared from the house to Jamal, who stood before him, triumphant, his eyes black jewels framed in white.

"You are surprised."

Ben nodded. "How did you know? How could you find it?"

Jamal gripped him by the elbow and steered him to the porch.

"The detective, Priestly—he found it. He was a thorough man, a good and valuable servant."

"So valuable you killed him."

Jamal ignored the interruption. "He checked on all the property your parents had."

"But this house isn't registered in their names."

"Something Priestly discovered. I mentioned that he was a thorough man. He examined records not only of what they owned but what they had *bequeathed*—as a precaution, you understand. That was how he learned about your father's arrangement with his office manager, how title to the house had been placed in her name."

"Priestly knew I was up here?"

"He suspected. But I did not act on his information because I knew you would return to the city. What I did was have Priestly gather all the necessary information—how to get here, the proximity of neighbors." Jamal paused. "I can see why you would choose to come here, the isolation, the ocean and the wilds. It is quite beautiful."

He looked at Ben. "I understand what it is you are thinking: If Priestly could draw such conclusions, so can others. Maybe Landau? Your fiancée? The police? But Rachel Melman doesn't know this place even exists, correct? And Landau? He is not nearly as well versed in your property laws as Priestly was. He will have to rely on the police to run such checks and they will not be as thorough as Priestly.

"No, my friend. This haven will serve us equally well as it recently served you. Besides, we will not need it for very long. Now, where do you hide the key?"

It was underneath an empty flower pot in a corner of the covered porch.

A puff of warm air greeted Jamal when he opened the door. He turned on the lights and quickly oriented himself.

To the left of the foyer was the dining room and, behind the staircase, a parlor. To the right was the living room. The kitchen was behind the dining room and ran all the way to the back of the house and the rear porch.

Jamal steered Ben upstairs, glanced briefly into the guest bedroom to the right of the landing, then walked his prisoner into the master, on the left.

"This is where you slept?"

"Yes."

Poltarek was not lying. One of the twin beds was still rumpled from use.

Prodding Ben ahead of him, Jamal checked the bathroom and the adjacent study.

Returning to the master bedroom, he opened the century-old armoire and chuckled when he saw the contents. Hanging on tenpenny nails were sets of handcuffs, soft ropes, and several knives. Clothing in plastic dustproof bags hung on the rack; several boxes and bags were stacked on the bottom shelf.

Jamal held up a pair of handcuffs. "For your girlfriend?"

He pushed Ben over onto one of the beds, made him lie facedown, and ripped off the tape. Then he secured one ring of the cuffs to Ben's wrist, the other to the decorative wrought-iron headboard, checked the locks, and pocketed the key.

He sat down on the edge of the bed, brought out his knife, and laid the blade flat against Ben's cheek. When Ben blinked, he felt the knife point prick his lower eyelid.

"There's nothing for you to be afraid of," Jamal said soothingly. "You see, I am a doctor by training. I know the landscape of pain. I can cut a nerve here"—the knife point dug under the soft skin, making Ben scream—"and you shall suffer. Or I can touch you here." He touched a spot behind Ben's ear, flooding his senses with blissful relief.

"You understand, Mr. Poltarek? Good."

Ben steeled himself for the next cut, but instead Jamal rose.

"No. We will talk later, after you have had a chance to reflect and to rest. I want you to be alert so that you will answer me truthfully and we can avoid unpleasantness. Is that not what you wish, too?"

Twenty-six

JUDITH SAWYER REPORTED to St. John's the day after she'd received the Reverend Winslow Garrett's phone call asking her if she could fill a Sunday school position that had suddenly become vacant.

She dressed carefully for the occasion, in a conservatively cut jacket and skirt with a high-neck blouse accented by a cameo. She wore almost no makeup and her fingernails were coated with clear polish. Winslow Garrett's frank appraisal of her wardrobe and his subsequent smile indicated she'd passed the appearance test.

"We started Saturday classes last year," Garrett explained as they sat in his cluttered office. "The intention was to offer things a regular school might not emphasize. Art, for instance. Music and theater. Hoe different rows in the children's minds, so to speak."

Judith balanced the chipped cup and saucer on her knee and sipped Garrett's watery tea.

"I think it's very important for a child to be exposed to the arts."

"The lovely thing is, we've had more success than we ever dreamed. The classes are enormously popular."

More with the parents than the children, Judith thought. This was cheap day care for Mommy's Saturday morning shopping.

Judith filled out the paperwork Garrett placed in front of her, then followed him to the classrooms. Strains of a violin filtered out beneath one of the doors.

Garrett's smile made Judith believe he was tone deaf. "Isn't it grand?" he said. "Those are Mr. Williams's students. He used to teach at Ridley."

Judith had researched all the schools in the D.C. area. Ridley was a solidly reputable private school. If the violin music was any indication of Williams's ability to impart knowledge, no wonder they had let him go.

Garrett guided Judith into the teachers' lounge and introduced her to the drama and art instructor, a thin, silent Hungarian.

As Garrett took her through the classrooms, knocking on doors, poking his head in, introducing her, Judith matched each room with its counterpart on the blueprint she'd memorized. The last available plans dated back twenty years and she was afraid that on her first visit she might not have noticed certain changes or additions. She needn't have worried. Apart from some modernizing—air-conditioning and updated bathrooms—St. John's had remained exactly as the architect's drawings indicated.

Now, she had to get rid of Garrett.

Judith glanced at her watch while Garrett rattled on. The minute hand slid across twelve o'clock and, on cue, a bell went off.

Judith expected every door to fly open, braced herself for the onslaught of rushing bodies and screaming voices. It didn't happen. The doors opened quietly, and approximately eight children came out of each classroom. Dressed in sweaters and khakis, they mumbled "Good morning, sir" as they filed past Garrett.

Judith saw Garrett's hand snake out to tousle a passing head, then freeze momentarily and slap against his thigh. Garrett was of the old school, in which it was not considered wrong to show affection or kindness to a student, but these were not his times. Judith recalled how painfully Garrett had explained to her that she could never, under any circumstances, lay her hand on a child without another teacher present. Not even if the child was hurt or in pain. Not even if he was screaming or burning. Or . . .

Judith forced herself to look away from the young faces swirling around her. In each one she saw only the features of her dead son.

"Are you all right?" Garrett was looking at her with concern. "You're white."

"I overdressed for the weather," Judith replied quickly.

"Nonsense. It's the heating in this place. Ancient, I'm afraid. We're hoping that next year's budget . . ."

His voice trailed off as a blond boy of six or seven straggled out of a classroom, looking as if he hadn't a friend in the world.

"And who's this?" Judith asked brightly. She wanted to get Garrett's attention off her.

"Oh. Jeffrey Waterstone." Garrett lowered his voice. "Parents are with the State Department, away for weeks at a time. Now there's a divorce. Not good, I'm told."

As the boy shuffled by, Judith said, "Jeffrey?"

He looked up at her with eyes that made her remember. It was all she could do not to sweep him up in her arms.

"Jeffrey, I'm Miss Sawyer. Can I walk with you to your next class?"

The boy's reply was barely audible: "I have a free period."

Judith glanced at Garrett, who smiled and gave her her rein.

"Well, I'm new here and don't know my way around. Would you mind showing me the school?"

The boy debated, then nodded.

Judith waited until Garrett disappeared down the hall. "Do they call you Jeffrey or Jeff?"

"My mom calls me Jeffrey but my dad, he says Jeff. It makes my mom *crazy.*" A hint of a smile appeared on his pink lips.

"Which would you like *me* to call you?"

"Jeff."

"Well then, Jeff. Where should we start?"

"Do you want to see a classroom?"

"That's a great idea. How about that one over there?"

She had not chosen that room by chance. That the classroom was vacant was a lucky coincidence. If it hadn't been, she'd have had to find an excuse to visit it later.

"The windows are kinda small," Jeffrey said. "That's why Mr. Garrett leaves the lights on all the time."

This classroom was, she imagined, identical to the rest. The windows were set a couple of feet below the ceiling, level with the ground outside. Even if they hadn't been matted with grime, not much light would have gotten through.

And, as Judith had suspected, they were small enough for a child Jeffrey's size to crawl through. An adult would never make it.

But wriggling through a basement window wasn't what Judith had in mind. She examined the classroom, with its watercolors and cutout art draped along the walls, the scarred one-piece desk-and-chair combos, the teacher's old oak slab with its alligator shellac. There was only one door to get in and out. No closets. No cloakroom.

Fine.

Jeffrey thought it was kind of strange that Miss Sawyer spent all this time looking around the classroom, like she'd never seen one before in her life. Maybe she was a new teacher and had never taught in a real school before. Jeffrey had overheard the other kids talking about old Miss Buffett, how she'd been mugged. Brian Lambert said that she'd gotten her face smashed in and looked like Godzilla.

"What's over there, Jeff?" They were back in the hall and Judith was pointing to a metal-sheathed door painted battleship gray.

"Dunno. Mr. Garrett says we shouldn't go there."

Something in the boy's tone warmed Judith. "But you do, don't you?" she whispered conspiratorially.

Jeffrey was about to protest, then saw the twinkle in her eye. He decided that Miss Sawyer was cool. He was beginning to feel a kind of icky warm, like he felt whenever he dared glance at Susie Tompkins.

"There's a way to get in," he said boldly. "Sometimes we play hide-and-seek, y'know."

"Want to show me?"

The door reminded Judith of a fire-escape hatch, except it had no red-stenciled warnings of instructions. What it did have was a substantial lock. She must have been frowning because beside her, Jeffrey laughed softly. He squatted beside the brick wall. The placement of the bricks appeared seamless until he wedged his fingernails into an almost invisible crack and pulled one of the bricks loose. Nestled in the dusty mortar was an old-fashioned, two-tongue key. His presentation to Judith was as solemn as an offering.

"Who else knows about the key, Jeff?"

The boy scuffed his shoe against the floor. "Just me."

"Then this will be *our* secret. I promise."

Judith was pained by the enormity of his gift. She'd known of the existence of the door from the blueprints, had known what lay beyond it, and that somehow she would have to get in there. She had steeled herself for obstacles, yet the answer she needed had come from a child's hands.

With a screech of rusty hinges, the door opened to a narrow corridor lit by naked, forty-watt bulbs. The concrete walls were damp, giving off the sharp tang of lichen. The floor was pounded earth.

"Do you know where this tunnel goes, Jeff?"

The boy shook his head. "I just hide in here, until I hear the other kids go away."

It didn't matter. On the blueprints, the tunnel was represented by dotted lines, indicating that it was defunct. Judith wished she had a flashlight, but there was sufficient light to indicate that the only footprints belonged to a child. There was no reason for anyone else to go in there. Neither the water pipes nor the electric lines extended that far. Whatever plumbing had once been there had been capped long ago.

"I'd like to see where the tunnel goes," Judith said. "Would you wait here for me?"

"Can I come, too?"

Judith hesitated, then decided it wouldn't matter. "Sure."

She kept a tight grip on the boy's hand as she moved deeper into the tunnel. The air became fetid and the boy coughed. Dust swirled around her feet and fell from the crumbling concrete ceiling like snowflakes.

There it was: a worm-eaten door reinforced by boards haphazardly nailed to the frame.

Judith gripped one of the planks and pulled, the wood protesting as it slid out from the nails. She handed the board to Jeff.

Five minutes of pulling and the boards were down and neatly stacked.

"Miss Sawyer?"

"Yes, Jeff?"

"What are you doing?"

"I want to see what's on the other side of the door."

"Oh."

Jeff thought the explanation perfectly reasonable.

Judith gripped the corroded handle, braced herself, and pulled. Given her life in the desert with Issim, she was far stronger than she appeared. It helped that the frames were rotten and the hinges could be pried out of the wood.

When she was finished, the door sagged inward, supported only by the bottom hinge.

"Jeff, I have to go in there for a minute. Okay?"

"I'll come too."

"Not this time. I don't know what's on the other side. If I get into trouble, I'll need you to go get help."

"I can do that. Miss Sawyer?"

"Yes, Jeff?"

"You be careful."

"I will."

The lie dug into Judith. She already knew what was on the other side of that door. The question was, could she make use of it the way she had explained to Jamal?

Carefully, so as not to tear her suit, she climbed through the crack and found herself at one end of an enormous subbasement. There was a lot of debris—concrete chips, pieces of pipe, tufts of old asbestos lining. Looking up, she saw light through the cracks in the floorboards. Enough light to make out an old, birdcage elevator car.

Judith picked her way across to it. The elevator had a crisscross accordion gate. She gripped the brass handle and pulled. Inside, the power button glowed red.

If it's working today, it'll work tomorrow, Judith told herself. There's nobody on the job site today. That means they either left the power on for the whole weekend or just forgot about it.

As long as no one thought to come by and shut it off tomorrow. If that were to happen, she'd have to use an alternate route, costing her precious time, leaving her vulnerable.

Judith returned the way she'd come. Jeffrey was waiting in the spot where she'd left him.

"What's it like?"

"Cold and spooky and dirty. Not a good place to play hide-and-seek. I think we'd better be getting back." Judith paused. "Jeff?"

"Yes, Miss Sawyer?"

"Do you think we could keep this tunnel our little secret?"

The boy seemed to think that over. "Okay. But the other kids'll find it sooner or later."

They won't find out about it soon enough.

*   *   *

At noon, two men arrived at the Chesapeake house. They wore L. L. Bean country clothes and drove an expensive Oldsmobile Silhouette van. Any local chancing to pass them would figure them for yuppie week-end warriors.

That was half-true. They were warriors.

The one called Hatem was whipcord-thin, his hatchet features deeply tanned. In Paris, he had been Jamal's point man and executioner, disposing of both the Paris *katsa* and Mustafa Manshur.

His partner was al-Rahim, a Palestinian who could trace his heritage into the mists of time. He was tall for an Arab and well fleshed. In the proper attire, he could pass for a prosperous merchant. In reality, he was a purveyor of a different kind. Al-Rahim had once been a member of Arafat's personal security force. His taste for blood had not lessened after Arafat turned politician and would-be statesman. Al-Rahim had made a new compact with Hafez Jamal. It was he who had brought Hatem—a second cousin and an expert in close-in killing—to Jamal's attention.

Jamal was on the porch to greet his comrades as they trooped up the steps. Kisses on cheeks were exchanged, rapid-fire Arabic detailing the comfortable if monotonous journey from Paris to Montreal, then New York, by air, Amtrak to Baltimore, truck the rest of the way.

Hatem and al-Rahim had brought nothing with them over the border other than a change of clothes and personal toiletries. Their papers made them out to be Canadian restaurateurs who were interested in opening an establishment in the revitalized Baltimore harbor area.

At the Amtrak station, the two had gone into a noisy, crowded sports bar. A man at the bar, wearing an Orioles jacket, finished his drink and vacated the stool next to Hatem. In addition to a pile of coins as a tip, he'd left behind a hard pack of Marlboros, which Hatem had palmed.

Inside were keys—one to a locker, and two on a separate ring to the vehicle parked in the metered lot.

Hatem opened the locker and handed gaily wrapped packages to al-Rahim, who handled them as though they contained children's toys and not the weapons specified.

Now, in the living room, the pair tore open the packages and quickly assembled the two submachine guns and two Austrian-made Keva pistols with factory-installed silencers.

"Is the prisoner here?" Hatem asked.

"He is upstairs."

"Have you spoken with him?"

"Not yet. I set up the apparatus this morning." He checked his watch. "It will be time soon to see how he is faring. But we should eat first."

The cold chicken and grilled vegetables tasted strange in the mouths of the new arrivals, but both men had eaten worse fare, and less of it. The bird was devoured to the gristle.

As they ate, Jamal explained exactly what would take place tomorrow and the roles Hatem and al-Rahim would play.

"It sounds like woman's work," al-Rahim grumbled. "Do you really believe there will be so little opposition?"

"If the thing is done correctly, there should be *no* opposition," Jamal said. "And remember, my friend, woman's work can sometimes be the most treacherous."

"I am curious about the American," Hatem said.

Jamal had suspected this. Hatem held a very special place in the hearts of the Israeli Defense Forces, especially in those who had seen the results of his handiwork on their fellow soldiers.

"Come then."

Leading the way, Jamal toggled a wall switch, then cursed softly when no light appeared. Half the switches didn't work. But this was an old house, Jamal reminded himself. There had been more important things to attend to than checking the electrical panels in the cellar.

The master bedroom was bathed in a dull, oyster-shell light. Ben lay on the twin bed, his right wrist cuffed to the headboard. Pillows propped up his back and neck so that he was half sitting up. His left arm was pointed to the floor, the wrist shackled to the bed frame by a second set of cuffs. Just below the elbow was an IV needle stuck in this arm. The thin plastic hose was filled with Ben's blood, dripping steadily into a large Mason jar. The jar was one-third full.

Jamal squatted to check the level in the jar.

"One and a half pints, Mr. Poltarek. Maybe a touch more. You're feeling light-headed, aren't you?"

Ben rolled his head on the pillow. He opened his mouth to speak, but the words came very slowly and seemed very far away. He turned his head back and his eyes were once again riveted on the jar, the dripping blood. The plop-plop of the drops was thunder in his ears. He imagined he heard his veins sing as blood dripped out of him.

"Drink . . ."

Jamal picked up a plastic glass, held the straw to Ben's lips, and watched him drink greedily. Jamal had found apple cider in the pantry and orange concentrate in the freezer. The fruit juices would help keep Poltarek conscious.

Jamal pulled back the glass. "The human body can replenish its blood supply at an astonishingly quick rate, Mr. Poltarek. But not, I think, as quickly as you are losing yours."

Ben rolled his head from side to side. He tried not to look at the jar but was transfixed by it. He wondered if this was the hopeless feeling drowning men had when they could no longer kick and thrash, when they surrendered to the waters and allowed themselves to sink, opening their mouths to flood their lungs. Was it at once so peaceful and so horrible as what was being done to him? Was the process so numbing that the brain, abandoning self-preservation, became a spectator in its own destruction?

Is that what you felt, Sammy?

Jamal became conscious of Hatem's breathing. He was quite excited by the tableau.

"Is your mouth still dry, Mr. Poltarek?"

Ben focused on the voice. He saw Jamal as though the Arab were standing behind a gauze screen. That couldn't be. His eyes, like his brain, were betraying him.

"No." The word came out like sandpaper on balsa.

"You have had a chance to reflect, Mr. Poltarek. Yes?"

Ben felt the weave of the pillowcase against his cheek.

"Then you understand there is no hope for you. No one knows you are here. No one is coming to save you. Of course, people are searching for you. I do not deny this. But do you think they will find you before that jar is full?"

"No . . ."

"You see? You still have all your faculties. Impaired to some degree, but functioning nonetheless. Do you think we can begin? I think we can."

"What do you want?"

"That much should be obvious, even in your state. I need to know what *you* know, Mr. Poltarek. What the dying Jew came to tell you."

Ben closed his eyes. He imagined he could feel the heat of the red haze that flowered behind his eyelids. But he was not thinking of the Israeli. He beheld only Samuel.

"He did tell you something, didn't he, Mr. Poltarek. Are you curious to know how I know this? It's simple, really. You have become such an important person to the Israelis, to our mutual friend Landau. Do you know anything about Landau? His first name, for instance? No? Well, it doesn't really matter. The key is that Landau *believes* you have been withholding something. He pressed tremendous resources into service to watch over you and keep you alive. Believe me when I tell you that life is not all that precious to Landau. Not unless he stands to profit from it. And in this case, Mr. Poltarek, so do I. You see, I have something very important to do tomorrow and I need to know if that meddling Israeli knew anything about it. If *you* know anything. And if so, did you pass any information along to Landau—or perhaps your own authorities?"

"You're not the same man . . ."

"I beg your pardon? Oh, I see. You mean my change in appearance."

"You're letting me see you . . ."

"And so you think that because I did so, I will have to kill you when we are done. No, Mr. Poltarek. Not at all. What needs to be done will be over with very soon, very quickly. I will be gone long before your friends find you. In fact, I may even leave a hint as to where you are—once I am safely out of reach, of course. Now. What did the Israeli tell you?"

Snapshots of the bleeding man falling in his arms. *Bleeding the way I am right now. Worse. No chance for him.*

No chance for Sammy.

No chance for me. You can bank on that. Jamal's a fucking liar. Don't tell him a thing. Let him sweat.

Something must have written itself across his face because suddenly Jamal was very close.

"You are not yet ready to talk to me, are you?" He tapped the IV tube. "Are you a healthy man, Mr. Poltarek? You appear to be. I hope so. Because after the loss of two pints of blood, the body begins to shut down. A craving sets in among the major organs—primarily the heart and the brain, but the liver and the lungs as well. The light-headedness you are experiencing will not intensify. You will be as mentally alert as you are at this moment. But the pain will come. Your flesh will feel prickly, as though ants are crawling under your skin. Your eyes will burn, and you may experience the sensation that your extremities have been amputated. It will all be . . . unsettling. Unnecessary."

Jamal drew back. "But clearly you need this extra time. Just do not take too much of it. Such a waste if you were to die in silence."

Ben watched them troop out of the room. The thin one paused and looked back. Ben registered the rictus of a smile, the click of the tongue against the upper palate as if Hatem, the connoisseur, was already anticipating his next course.

* * *

He lost consciousness soon after he was alone. The voices in his dreams, if that's what they were, were so clear that he didn't understand why he was unable to discern faces or even bodies.

I'm dead. When you're dead, you don't need to see people.

Ben opened his eyes. He was not dead. But the voices persisted. It took him a moment to understand what was happening.

Jamal was not familiar with the house. Because everything about it seemed ordinary, nothing had thrown him. He did not suspect that the house was much more than it appeared to be.

The heating system, for example. There were old-fashioned ornamental grilles set at the base of the walls at floor level. The ones in the master bedroom had the vent flaps open an inch or so. In a normal house, this would have meant nothing. But because of Ben's extensive modifications, the grilles acted as giant telephone receivers; the ductwork was the phone line.

Ben shifted as far as the handcuff attached to the headboard permitted. He had not been mistaken: The voice was a woman's. He strained to listen, and in a little while he stopped hearing his blood drip into the jar.

* * *

Judith Sawyer had a temporary driver's license from the Washington DMV. That and her passport photo were enough to rent a car from Avis.

The drive took longer than normal. Judith had not been behind the wheel of a car for many years. It took her a while to get comfortable with the stalk controls on the steering column. The same could not be said for the eastbound traffic out of the city, all roaring, bright metal punctuated by the din of horns as other drivers cut her off. She crept into the far right lane and stayed there, tailing a McDonald's Systems semi that cleared the way for her.

Despite Jamal's detailed directions, which she'd memorized, she got lost in the loops and twists of the Chesapeake country roads. But finally she had made it, tired and rattled.

Once inside the house, she felt better. It was a big, airy place, with a touch of mildew in the air but quiet and comfortable. Jamal offered her tea and was thoughtful enough not to question her until she had relaxed a little.

"It is perfect, Hafez," she said. "Just the way you said it would be. The blueprints were accurate, the passageway—"

"Please," Jamal interrupted gently. "Start from the beginning. Tell me about the school, the other teachers, the children."

Judith took a deep breath and, for the first time in years, craved a cigarette. She called up the images she'd filed away throughout the day, arranged them chronologically, and began her account. She talked about Winslow Garrett and how, briefly, she'd met some of the other teachers.

"No one who'll get in the way," she assured him.

"But you will still carry a pistol."

"Of course."

Jamal had raised the issue of her going in armed the first time he had presented her with the plan. Judith had raised no objection, so the matter was taken as a given. Now, she saw no reason to inform him that she would carry the pistol for a reason altogether different from the one he presumed. The weapon would be her only insurance that, in the event something went wrong, she would never be taken alive.

Judith told him about checking the classrooms, the way she had timed how long it would take to get from the classroom to the utility door, and where she had found the key.

Jamal frowned at the mention of the boy, Jeffrey. She could tell Jamal was not pleased about this unexpected third party, but he became intrigued when she described the passage on the other side of the door and where it led. After that, he didn't mention the boy.

Jamal listened without interruption. He was gifted when it came to dealing with, using, people—an ability that had nothing to do with his medical training. He recognized Judith's need to describe her accomplishments. He sensed how warmly she basked in them, so he did not disturb her. He knew, too, that she was presenting her efforts in the form of a gift, laying them out at his feet. He took care to honor them and demonstrate his appreciation by silence.

Twice he asked her if there was anything she wanted to add. Only then did he unroll the blueprints across the kitchen table, weighing down the ends with a saltcellar and a pepper mill.

Hatem startled Judith by his unexpected appearance when he came down to get juice.

"This is one of my associates," Jamal said quickly, introducing him. He also mentioned al-Rahim. "I thought they might still be asleep," he added by way of explanation.

Hatem moved closer to Judith, and she smelled the rank odor secreting through his pores, like the greasy-wool stink of a sheep about to be slaughtered.

Hatem bowed slightly and murmured, "It is a privilege to meet you at last."

When he was gone, Jamal touched Judith's arm. "You need not be afraid. They are here to protect you. They are prepared to give up their lives for you."

Judith said nothing. When she had first met Issim Hassan, he had been surrounded by such men, hard and jagged and merciless as flint. Over the years, as the gun gave way to the word, these men either changed or her husband culled them from the ranks of his followers. He had once told Judith that some fighters could not change. They had been born to the blood and could not conceive of life without violence. She thought Hatem was one of them. Probably the other, too.

"Hafez, is there anyone else here?" Judith asked. She felt him brush his hesitation away, but he wasn't quick enough. "There is. Who?"

Jamal told her about Poltarek, being held prisoner upstairs.

"Why? What does he have to do with any of this?"

Jamal had to be very careful here. Judith knew nothing about the murder of the Poltareks or the attack on the Israeli safe house. Jamal did not want to bring up violence now. He did not want the woman to become emotional.

So he explained away the kidnapping of Benjamin Poltarek as a necessary precaution, and gave her some carefully edited background.

"I will hold him until we are done," he said. "After that, he is harmless to us."

"But you said you took him because he was a threat," Judith said.

Her intimation was clear. She knew well enough how threats of this kind were dealt with.

Jamal explained that Poltarek was under sedation and would remain that way. He did not add that the door to the master bedroom was firmly bolted and that the only key was in his pocket.

The afternoon was fading and they spoke of the plan, going over the minutiae in exacting detail. Their voices were low, but the large kitchen was a natural amplifier. Neither Judith nor Jamal noticed the old-fashioned grilles that covered the heating outlets, located beside the counter cabinets and next to the refrigerator. Nor were they aware of the natural air currents of the house, that tenderly plucked each word and sent it spinning into the maze of ductwork that honeycombed the house.

* * *

Judith left the house at twilight. Jamal had offered to have Hatem follow her, at least as far as the freeway, so that she wouldn't get lost on the Chesapeake's poorly lit, winding roads. Judith's distaste was evident when she said no.

Jamal waited until he could no longer see the taillights of her car from the second-story window, then went into the master bedroom.

Ben's eyelids fluttered when he heard the key in the lock. The woman must have left. Now Jamal was back, wanting answers to his questions. Ben understood that no matter what happened later, Jamal would eventually kill him. He had turned ways to play the Arab over and over in his mind until the options had blurred into a single, fragile possibility.

Jamal came to him with a glass of lemonade and Ben sipped through the straw. He watched Jamal inspect the level of the blood in the jar.

"We are approaching the critical amount, Mr. Poltarek. Do you feel pain yet? No? You are on the cusp, I think."

Ben wet his lips with his tongue, licking away a stray bit of pulp. "His name was Tarnofsky."

"Whose name?"

"The Israeli who escaped."

Jamal's eyes narrowed and he moved closer to the bed. "And?"

"Tarnofsky made it to my parents' home alive . . . Wounded, dying."

"Get on with it!"

"He said I should tell Landau, 'They are bringing in an American.'"

Jamal was very good at hiding his reaction, but Ben realized he had struck a nerve. A fissure in Jamal's quiet confidence appeared, and there was a hesitation in his voice.

"What else?"

"Nothing. Tarnofsky died after telling me that."

"And what did this mean to you?"

"Nothing." Ben hesitated. "I'm not a *sayan* like my parents."

He had Jamal off balance now and kept on. "They worked for the Israelis, but I didn't know anything about that."

"What else?"

"First, you stop killing me."

Jamal's expression was a mask in the pale lamplight. "You lie to me and you will not live to see midnight."

With practiced movements, he removed the handcuffs and the IV, taped the incision in Ben's arm, and shifted him, placing a pillow beneath the arm to elevate it.

"What was Landau's reaction when you told him about this Tarnofsky?"

Ben shook his head. "We trade. Information for food and rest."

Ben never saw Jamal's hand move. There was only the blur of steel and the cold edge of the knife at his throat.

"You demand *nothing*!"

"Then kill me. That way you will never know about the American." Ben closed his eyes and played his last card: "Landau's looking for a woman. The American, she is a woman, isn't she?"

Ben felt Jamal's hot curse on his cheek. "You know nothing!" he spat.

"Why? Because the woman hasn't been picked up yet? It's a matter of time, isn't it? You know Landau. You know how hard he will look. He'll never stop looking."

The exertion of speaking made Ben's head spin. The knife disappeared, and Jamal seemed to tower over him.

"What are you to Landau that you know such things?"

Ben shook his head. "Food."

For an instant, he was convinced that his gambit had failed. He felt as though Jamal's eyes were roaming the back of his skull, gleaming with delight because he had ferreted out the half truth that Ben had used to bait him.

Ben didn't have the strength to care anymore and welcomed the onrush of exhaustion. The last thing he saw before blackness closed over him was Jamal reaching out to him, his eyes bright with panic.

Twenty-seven

THE FOREIGN INTELLIGENCE BRANCH of the Secret Service maintains up-to-date files on terrorist groups and individuals around the world who might pose a threat to the President.

The Service was notified of Jamal's probable presence in the Washington area as soon as the President and the Israeli prime minister had hammered out their decision to slip Landau off the leash. Security around the Chief Executive was automatically notched up a grade, although there was no evidence to suggest that Jamal would make a play for fifty-six-year-old Charles Woodbridge, currently in the third year of his first term.

The word was also passed along to Steve Casey, the agent in charge of the detail protecting the First Family, which included Mary Woodbridge, the President's wife of twenty-two years, and their son, Kimball—"Kim"—age seven. Born late into the marriage, the boy, named after his maternal grandfather, was an only child.

Steve Casey was a sixteen-year veteran of the Service. A former Special Forces officer, he was thin and weathered like split-rail fencing. Like many bachelors, Casey was very good with kids. Ten years ago, his boss had assigned him to the First Family as part of a routine posting cycle. Then President Bush had been so pleased with the way Casey handled his grandkids that the assignment became permanent. When the Clintons, including daughter Chelsea, took over at 1600, Mrs. Clinton personally requested that Casey stay on at his post.

Casey had a slightly different perspective on the bad boys than his fellow agents. His living nightmare wasn't the explosives-strapped fanatic peeling away from the crowd, or the cool-as-snakeskin marksman in a perch. Casey dreaded the kidnapper. Hurting or killing a member of the First Family would be a terrible wound to the President, but it would not be a fatal blow to national security. Even the most demented "freedom fighter" understood that there was no mileage in incurring the wrath of the most powerful man in the world. Osama bin Laden, architect of the embassy bombings in Nairobi and Dar es Salaam, had found that out the hard way after he'd placed a *fatwa*, a death warrant, on a former First Lady's head.

No, keeping the crazies out of range was not what Casey dwelled on. It was something much more subtle and ultimately more pernicious. He was studying it through one particular prism right now, just as he did every Sunday.

Casey wouldn't say that Woodbridge was a particularly religious man. Certainly not like Carter, or Clinton when he surrounded himself with clergy while trying to stave off impeachment. Woodbridge attended St. John's Church two or three Sundays a month, he and his family taking their regular places in pew 54. They also attended special services at Easter and Christmas.

Each Sunday, two hours before the church opened for business, before a single parishioner or even the Reverend Winslow Garrett had arrived, Casey's men were inside. St. John's was old and small as churches go. It had a lot of nooks and crannies and the search teams knew them all by heart. Even the bomb-sniffing dogs didn't have to be told where to go. From choir loft to basement, the process took less than ninety minutes, after which a contingent of five agents remained stationed inside.

The school next door was even easier. The President seldom went there, although twice he'd almost caught Casey off guard by wanting to go watch his son rehearse for the Christmas pageant. Now Casey told his agents to air out the school each and every Sunday, even if the latest word was that only the First Lady and Kim would be in attendance.

At exactly seven o'clock, the phone purred. Casey sat back in an orthopedic chair he'd shelled out for out of his own pocket, sipped light brown coffee, and listened. Over the next hour, all the command posts checked in, not only those at the church and school but Woodbridge's personal bodyguards as well. Word from the family quarters was that the President wanted to get to St. John's by nine. He planned to stay for an hour before returning to the White House to prep for his meeting with the British prime minister. The First Lady and her son would stay for the duration of the service.

Casey dialed the White House meteorological room and got an update on the weather. The met guys thought this was hilarious, Casey calling to get the weather report. They razzed him about it, telling him to look out the window, even though they knew that his office was in the basement, with a fine view of flower beds.

* * *

The first limousine, a bullied-up stretch Cadillac with a chase Suburban and four outriders, left the White House compound at exactly 7:45.

At the same time, Judith Sawyer came out of the subway station at McPherson Square. Low, gray clouds scuttled across a murky sky, making everything a little darker.

Judith was properly dressed for the weather: a tan, lined raincoat over a dove gray pants suit. In one hand, she carried a rolled-up umbrella, in the other, a small briefcase. She walked just quickly enough to be in concert with the weather, a woman trying to stay warm.

The ride to and from the Chesapeake last night had not so much tired her as it had jangled her nerves. Back in her room, she had fixed a cup of instant hot chocolate and tried to erase some of the things she'd seen in Jamal's face. A long time ago she had seen them in her husband's face. But over the years, her love for him had softened and then finally erased them altogether.

But she did not believe there was a human being alive who could reach down far enough to touch Jamal the way she had touched Issim. Hurrying along Fifteenth Street, she could admit to herself that Jamal frightened her. Not because of what he might do to her—Jamal would never dare to place a finger on her. But what would happen hours from now, when he held true, raw power in his hands? How deep would his intoxication be? How great the temptation to deviate from the plan they had painstakingly thought through?

Judith had questioned him minutely on every facet before agreeing to become his partner. She had his promise that as soon they had exacted revenge for her husband and her child, it would be over with. There would be no corrupting the purity of their mission.

Hafez will not betray me, Judith thought as she rounded the corner to H Street. *He wants glory for himself, to take over Issim's leadership. To do this, he needs my support. So he will give me what I want, the way I want it.*

On H Street, in the tiny parking area between the church and the school, Judith saw a black Suburban. Jamal had explained what was behind the smoked-out windows. She felt a shiver pass through her, knowing that invisible eyes behind the glass were raking her. Soft voices were speaking into microphones as she took the steps to the school.

Judith raised her hand to the doorbell, but never got to touch it. The door opened and a Secret Service agent loomed in front of her.

She heard Garrett's voice behind the agent: "That's all right, Jimmy. It's Judith Sawyer. She's on the list."

The agent scanned the list. The way he scrutinized her face, Judith thought there must be a picture next to her name.

The agent stepped aside and Garrett was beside her, helping her with her coat. "Come, my dear. Let's get you out of the cold. *So* nice to see you again."

"Excuse me, Reverend," the agent rumbled. "I'll need to check Miss Sawyer's purse."

Judith didn't hesitate. She watched as the agent carefully removed her wallet, cosmetics case, a travel-size package of Kleenex, a key, and half a pack of gum. Judith sensed that a second agent had stepped up behind her, close enough for her to smell the soap on his hands. She did not turn to acknowledge him.

"Okay, Miss Sawyer. Thanks very much."

"We all go through this," Garrett apologized. "A necessity brought on by our times. Come along, now. The children are excited to meet you."

* * *

In classroom B-6, Kim Woodbridge finished the last crease on the wing of his paper airplane. He was absorbed in his task, oblivious to the chatter and horseplay around him. Kim made the best planes in the class—the other guys had told him that—but this one was special. It was a new design, shown to him by the naval officer who always followed his dad with a briefcase handcuffed to his wrist. The guy was so good he could take a piece of paper and make a plane out of it using *one hand*.

Kim wasn't about to tell his friends about the officer. Before he'd started at St. John's, his dad had taken him aside and solemnly reminded him that house rules applied. Kim could recite them in his sleep: What you do here, see here, hear here, leave it here.

Kim Woodbridge knew that he wasn't like any other kid. He was *the President*'s kid, with his own Secret Service escort, living in a place that had a lot of adults and few children. His parents tried hard to make his life as normal as possible. He was allowed to go to other kids' homes, play sports for Greenfield Park School, where he was in fourth grade, and have his pals over to visit. Of course, it was impossible to sneak out to Fat Mac's, across the street from Greenfield Park, to buy jawbreakers and toffee, or to get a few minutes alone with Susie Tompkins when she walked from class to the school bus. But Kim knew that Susie was sweet on him—the guys swore up and down that she was.

Kim pressed down hard on the two creases that created the delta-type wings, looked over his shoulder, and, with a practiced flick of his wrist, sent the plane streaming across the classroom.

Right into Susie Tompkins's thick blond hair.

Kim pretended not to see Susie pluck the airplane out of her hair and shoot him a dirty look—except that her eyes were twinkling and she couldn't quite hide her smile.

Kim wondered if it'd be okay for him to ask her if she wanted a ride home with him. He'd have to ask Jeb Rawlins, his personal bodyguard, who was a pretty decent guy.

"Nice shot, Kim. Planning to be an airplane designer?"

Judith stood in the doorway, arms folded, looking at Kim Woodbridge with his halo of curly red hair, Irish green eyes, and spray of freckles across his nose.

She walked over to Susie Tompkins's desk and examined the paper airplane. "Not bad. With a lot of hard work, you might just make NASA proud."

The hoots and hollers from the class made Kim blush.

"All right, ladies and gentlemen—and I presume we are that?"

There was a murmur as the class settled down. As Judith approached the blackboard, Kim watched her stop to whisper to Jeb Rawlins. The Secret Service agent shrugged and smiled, and Kim thought he saw him give Miss Sawyer the once-over. Then Rawlins moved to the back of the classroom, where a full-size desk and chair had been installed for his benefit.

"For those of you who don't know," Judith said, writing her name across the board, "I am Miss Sawyer. I'm filling in for Miss Buffett, who had an accident and is in the hospital."

"Is she, like, going to die?" Roddy McGowan piped up.

Kim rolled his eyes. Roddy's dad was a big shot over at the State Department. His uncle was a comedian who had his own sitcom, which made Roddy think he was funny, too.

Lame-o.

"No, Roddy. Miss Buffett was mugged and is in the hospital with two broken arms." *That* quieted things down. "And I think it'd be nice if you, Roddy, wrote a get-well note on behalf of the class, hmm?"

Roddy doodled on his notepad, eyes downcast. "Sure, Miss Sawyer."

"Fine. I'll bring the card next Sunday and you can work on it then. In the meantime, let's all take our history books and turn to page sixteen, the chapter on Moses." Judith lowered a rolled-up map and looked across at the class. "Has anyone here visited Egypt?"

Kim glanced around furtively. He'd been to all *kinds* of places with his dad. He hated being the only kid who'd gone anywhere. But there was Roddy raising his hand, and Dwight. No problem.

"Dwight," Judith said. "Why don't you go first, then Roddy and Kim."

Kim sat back and fiddled with his pen. He thought his bud, Jeff, had been right: Miss Sawyer was pretty cool—*and* a dish. Definitely an improvement over old Miss Buffett.

* * *

Jamal had arrived in the city in darkness, in the first slipstream of traffic. He was driving the van that Hatem had rented at the Baltimore-Washington airport. That particular model had no side windows and could pass as a construction or delivery vehicle. Especially after Jamal had taped the logo of a plumbing-supply company on the door panels.

He parked the van beside the fenced-off area of the office building that was being gutted. A canteen truck had already arrived to service the demolition crew, and Jamal bought himself a coffee. In his steel-toed boots, heavy denim pants, dirty windbreaker, and hard hat, he blended into the landscape.

Finding out that the rehab was going on seven days a week had been easy enough. An obliging foreman had told Jamal everything he needed to know when he'd come looking for a contractor's job.

Finding parking for the van had proved more of a problem. Access to the site was union-regulated. Jamal had gotten around that by slipping the security guard a hundred dollars, Jamal saying that he wanted to be on-site to get an early bid in on the new plumbing that would have to be done.

Jamal forced himself to sip the watery coffee. He wandered back to the van and, in the large sideview mirror, studied the reflection of St. John's Church.

Judith. Ninety minutes.

Jamal had brought along the day's fat edition of the *Post*. He read through it slowly, eyes darting to the side and rearview mirrors, keeping track of the construction pickups and double deuces that slowly filled the lot. The security guard who'd let him in went off-shift. The new man presumed that the plumber's van belonged there and didn't bother with it.

The canteen truck came around again as Secret Service sedans pulled up in front of the church. Standing in line to buy an apple, Jamal listened to hard-hat comments about the "boys with mikes coming out their ass-holes." For its part, the Service must have become used to the construction activity: no agent came over to talk to the crew or check IDs. The rehab was just another backdrop that had been noted, investigated to the required degree, and deemed no threat.

Good.

When most of the crew had disappeared into the building, Jamal moved the van to the side of the building. On his right was a sagging Cyclone fence that separated the site from the church and the school. On the other side of the fence was the tiny parking area for clergy. Jamal walked down a ways and, using cutters, snipped a section of the fence. He left the metal strands intact at key stress points so that the cutout section wouldn't collapse under its own weight. The momentum of the van would bring it down flat.

From the back of the van, Jamal brought out lengths of new copper pipe, tools, and a pair of sawhorses. Now, if anyone looked, all they would see was a workman's layout.

Jamal turned up the collar of his jacket and checked his watch. Judith would be in the school by now.

All that was missing was the preeminent member of the congregation.

*   *   *

Landau was back at Buzzard's Point by 6 A.M., having gone to the embassy to sleep.

On his way, he'd stopped to pick up Rachel at her house. A polite good morning was the extent of their conversation during the drive.

Kaelin Reece was in the ready room, talking quietly with the duty officer and a couple of members of the hostage rescue team. She nodded to Landau, then drew Rachel aside to the coffee machine.

Landau picked up the overnight reports from the duty officer and made a show of flipping through them. He knew there wouldn't be anything because his sleep had not been interrupted.

Out of the corner of his eye, he saw Reece and Rachel talking in low tones. It would have been easy to take offense, so pointed was their exclusion of him.

The women approached him together.

"Tell me what's happening with the search for Ben," Rachel said.

Landau wondered if Rachel had taken a little something to soften the edge to her voice.

Landau tapped the overnight reports. "Our friend, Abbott, was as good as his word. He's thrown a fine net over the area between here and Baltimore, south to the coast, west into Virginia. Every sheriff and highway patrol station has been alerted." He pulled out a blowup of Ben's driver's license. "It's a good likeness and now it's posted on the hotsheets and on the dashboards of the cruisers. Every officer on the 6 A.M. to 4 P.M. shift picked one up with his coffee."

"But no one's seen him," Rachel said.

Landau let her bitterness slide off him like old snakeskin. Reece surprised him by speaking up.

"Rachel, you've got to believe that the all-points will shake something loose. Jamal is very good, but he doesn't know that his hostage is a wanted man. Someone will see something and call it in. When they do"—she nodded toward the HRT agents in the room—"we're ready to move."

"You talk as if Ben's still alive." Rachel looked from Reece to Landau. "Do you think he is? Why would Jamal keep a hostage around once he got what he wanted out of Ben?"

"For insurance," Landau replied. "Ben's alive—"

"*Possibly* alive."

"No, *probably*. Probably, because Jamal has been moving very quickly. He has a lot on his mind right now. Yes, Ben gave up what he knew. And I hope to God he did it quickly. But it's exactly his confession that might make him valuable. Think about everything Ben could say. Suddenly, Jamal sees him as someone who might carry weight. The son of dead *sayanim*? Not a bad ace to have if things turned ugly. Jamal could force both Israel *and* the United States to listen if he threatened to bring the *sayanim* issue to light."

Maybe, Rachel thought. Maybe this time Landau wasn't lying. Or not as much as he usually did.

"The truth is that you won't know if he's alive until that damn phone rings," Rachel said. "You find Jamal, you'll find Ben. That's the way it will play."

Landau did not disabuse her of the notion. If the phone rang, it meant a solid sighting of Jamal. But that could be *after* Jamal had accomplished what he had come here to do.

The feeling that he—that everyone—had overlooked something gnawed at Landau. Washington and its suburbs were not the easiest place for an Arab to hide. His own teams had been scouring ethnic neighborhoods without pause and still nothing. The police and FBI had taken the more upscale and lily-white areas with similar results. Yet Jamal could not have gone to ground too far away. Every mile he had to travel increased his risk of being spotted and—disguised or not—recognized. The terrorist had found a safe nest, some place where he felt secure, where no one would bother to look.

Not a warehouse or a loft or an industrial space. Not an abandoned building. These had all been combed by D.C.P.D. The tenants or owners of recently leased or purchased apartments had been questioned by detectives. The FBI's legal division had waded through the real estate records and files in the recorder's office with nothing to show for its efforts.

Detectives . . . Records . . .

"Rachel," Landau said. "I've asked you this before, but indulge me. Besides Timberland, is there any other place Ben could have gone? A special place that he might have mentioned?"

Rachel stared at him over the rim of her cup. "Are you asking me if he had a treehouse when he was a kid? No, I don't believe he did."

Her sarcasm seemed not to register.

"Okay. Let's try another tack: You knew the Poltareks pretty well. Did *they* have a place somewhere? Some cottage or retreat they no longer used, and so maybe didn't talk about it very often."

"Sid and Rose were city people," Rachel said. "When they traveled, they stayed in upscale resorts—"

"Sometimes resorts sell time-shares," Reece broke in. "Even the ritzy kind."

"If they'd had something like that, I would have known about it," Rachel insisted. "The Poltareks were hotel people. Vacation time was precious to them. They wanted to relax and be pampered, not cook for themselves. Landau, where are you going with this?"

"Nowhere, it seems. But here's the thing: Jamal has gone to ground where no one can find him—even though the authorities are doing everything short of tearing up the streets. Jamal took Ben with him. No, that's not right. He deliberately went back for him—"

"But that's because he wanted to . . . to question him."

"That's *one* reason. But what if there's another? What if Jamal is hiding somewhere that belongs to Ben? Here we are, eavesdropping on *schwarma* cooks in chickpea-paste restaurants, checking suspicious-looking busboys. If I were Jamal, that's what *I'd* want the police to be wasting their time on."

"You think he's using Ben as a cloak?"

"Not Ben himself. Something that Ben has or knows about . . ."

Landau's voice dwindled into silence. Rachel watched him lose himself in the myriad of possibilities, pouring them through the sieve of his fine-meshed intuition.

"You're headed in the wrong direction with this," she said flatly. "Even if Ben had such a place, it doesn't make sense that Jamal would take him there."

"It does if you remember that we can't find Ben, either."

Landau steered Reece by the elbow into a corner. "We need to do something."

"Fine. You're just a little short on the 'what.'"

"Yes. So what have we missed?"

"Jesus, Landau. Don't you ever take a breath? We're hunting *two* now. You said so yourself: find one, find the other. Short of asking the President to declare martial law—"

"It's more simple than that. Jamal is not dealing in complexities. He is operating on foreign terrain. His operation depends on simplicity."

"He has the American to help him."

"Yes. But help him only so far. Maybe the American is the close-in operator, or the triggerman, someone who can't help Jamal with logistics. Logistics is what's keeping him alive, why he doesn't have to show his face any more than is absolutely necessary."

"You sound like you're about to grub, Landau."

"I don't understand."

"'Grub.' To bow and scrape before asking a favor."

"I don't think that the head of Homicide is enamored with me."

"I don't imagine Abbott's alone in his feelings."

"I need to see some files."

"Whose?"

"Priestly's."

"Priestly's?" Reece's voice was rich with wonder.

"And his file on Poltarek. Everything from the minute he stepped into that apartment."

"We've been down that road, Landau. We know Priestly was bought and paid for. He was the one who made sure that Jamal knew where Poltarek was—"

"But what else did Jamal buy and pay for? If Priestly was bird-dogging Poltarek for Jamal, what other information was he providing?"

"You're saying that Priestly did a more detailed report than the one we pulled up."

"One way to find out. But I can't do it."

Reece held his gaze for a moment, then reached for the telephone.

Twenty-eight

AT 8:15 A.M., THE PRESIDENTIAL MOTORCADE left the White House for the 5-minute ride to St. John's Church.

At the same time, in classroom B-6, Susie Tompkins, pointer in hand, finished outlining the Israelites' flight from Egypt on a map of the Middle East.

She handed the pointer back to Judith Sawyer and, while walking back to her seat, grinned at Kim Woodbridge.

A minute later, as Judith was assigning reading for the following Sunday, the bell rang, signaling the end of class.

In the construction yard, Jamal lifted his head to the sirens from the outrider escorts in the motorcade. From where he stood, he caught flashes of black cars sweeping by.

Jamal opened the rear doors of the van and checked his handiwork.

* * *

"Gum?"

Jeb Rawlins had watched Judith Sawyer approach him, a pack of gum in her hand. He noted that it was half-full and had seen her pull out a piece for herself and pop it in her mouth.

"Thanks."

Protecting the First Kid was easy duty and was not without its perks. Rawlins got to meet a lot of young teachers, nurses, and doctors, one-stop shopping as far as dating went. He thought Judith Sawyer looked pretty good, though maybe a little stiff in that suit. But there was a lot of potential in those wide, smiling eyes.

Rawlins was focused on Judith, but he didn't miss her smiling at Kim and offering him some gum, too.

What the hell. Kim was a good kid, not like some brats the old-timers had had to baby-sit during previous administrations. The First Lady was a little over the top when it came to what he ate—a lot of granola bars and fruit. Rawlins remembered Kim's long face when the other kids high-tailed it over to Fat Mac's for a snack. A piece of gum wouldn't kill him.

Between the distractions of Judith Sawyer and his ruminations, Rawlins wasn't as focused on Kim Woodbridge as he should have been. The problem was one of routine. Every Sunday was the same. Rawlins could recite the sequence in his sleep.

The class was finished. In two minutes, he and Kim would go upstairs, where the boy would meet his parents as they entered the church. There'd be some chitchat before they took their seats, then more whispers before the reverend appeared.

As soon as Rawlins was upstairs with the boy, Kim would become the responsibility of other agents, who covered the First Family as a three-some. Until then, Kim was completely his charge. But that was fine. The only other adult in the room was a good-looking woman who seemed fascinated by his White House anecdotes. Her fingers were conspicuously devoid of rings, and her attitude suggested that she wouldn't mind if Rawlins segued into asking her out.

Rawlins had tucked the gum behind his left molar, sucking more than chewing it. The taste of mint flooded his mouth, made his tastebuds tingle pleasantly.

Then he became aware that his voice sounded faraway, as if it were an echo. The skin on his face and neck was very hot, as though he had a fever. Rawlins shivered like a dog shaking off water. His eyes glazed over as the woman reached for him. In the back of his mind, a voice born of training screamed. Rawlins opened his mouth, but no words came out. The image of a dying fish, flopping in the bottom of a boat, flashed through his mind.

The woman guided him to his desk and helped him sit. The narcotic soaked into the gum had not yet gripped him completely, so Rawlins could still think about the boy, panic about not being able to protect him.

He lurched to one side, looked past Judith Sawyer, and saw Kim by the classroom door, talking to a friend.

He's okay. I'm the one . . .

Rawlins found it impossible to complete the thought. The drug was now inducing confusion as well as paralysis. He forgot about hitting the emergency button on his wrist mike or drawing his weapon. He watched the woman's lips move, heard none of the words. He sat rigidly in the chair, as though his buttocks and spine were glued to its seat. His limbs were numb and he felt his heart racing. Jeb Rawlins knew he was dying. What terrified him was not why, but how—how quickly, how painfully?

Judith moved away from the agent, keeping her body between Rawlins and the boy.

"Miss Sawyer?" This was Dwight. "Kim doesn't look so hot. I think he's sick."

The President's son was exhibiting the same symptoms the Secret Service agent had, but in a milder form. The stick of gum Judith had given him had been treated with less of the toxin than Jeb Rawlins had ingested.

Judith glanced at her watch. Two minutes until the bell rang for the church service.

"Dwight, why don't you go to the bathroom and bring me some paper towels?"

"Sure, Miss Sawyer."

"If I'm not here, then look for me in the reverend's office. Know where it is?"

"At the end of the hall."

"That's it. On the left side. Go on now."

Judith draped an arm around Kim's shoulder. "You'll be fine. Promise."

She locked the door to the classroom and stepped into the hall, which was teeming with children. A smile was pasted on her lips as she clutched Kim's hand, steering him through the mass of small bodies. Twice Kim stumbled and Judith had to jerk him up sharply so that he didn't fall. When he looked up at her, his face so flushed that it appeared swollen, she thought he might die.

Judith pushed on, silently cursing Jamal. He had assured her that he knew Kim's exact height and weight and that, from what he had gleaned from publicly available sources, the boy was in good health. On that basis, Jamal had determined how big a dose to give the boy, enough to anesthetize him, make him malleable, but not so much as to bring about collapse.

What if it was too much? What if he's having some kind of reaction?

Judith reached the gray fire door that Jeffrey had shown her. She had already taken the key out from under the brick. She was far enough down the hall that no one noticed her and Kim disappear.

In the corridor now, with its earthen floor and weak overhead bulbs. Kim mewling, dragging his heels. It was no effort at all for Judith to scoop him up in her arms without breaking stride.

Up to the opening where she had pried off the wood. No one had noticed the damage or fixed it. The air colder now, the wind gliding under her sleeves along her skin. Goose bumps. Into the elevator, closing the gate, the car rising to street level.

"Here!"

More of a hiss than a call.

Judith stepped out of the rehab, glimpsed Jamal as he jumped into the van and drove it to where Judith and the boy stood.

She had the rear doors open even before he came to a full stop. Jamal climbed back, hauled the boy in, and laid him on the blanket-covered floor. Then he gripped Judith's hand and pulled her in.

"Stay with him!" he ordered.

Climbing forward to the wheel, Jamal slipped the parking brake, and drove straight into the cut-up Cyclone fence, flattening it. He edged the van through the narrow alley out to Fifteenth Street.

Over Jamal's shoulder, Judith saw that the street was relatively clear. The presidential motorcade and escorts parked along H and Sixteenth Streets.

Jamal swung left and headed up Fifteenth Street. Less than four minutes had elapsed from the time that Judith had stolen the President's son from the classroom, where Agent Jeb Rawlins now took his last, labored breath.

* * *

The bell for the church service rang. Dwight braced himself against the rush of bodies headed for the staircase and upstairs to the connecting hall that led to the church. He still clutched a bunch of brown paper towels in his hand and looked around to find Miss Sawyer.

The din passed into silence. Dwight went over to the classroom and tried the door. Locked. Where could Miss Sawyer and Kim have gone?

He tried the bathroom. Nope.

Dwight wadded the towels and thrust the ball into the wastebasket. As he trotted down the hall, he thought that Kim and Miss Sawyer were already upstairs. Dwight may have been only seven years old, but he'd hung out with Kim long enough to know that when the Prez's kid even sneezes, *everyone* snaps to. Kim was okay.

*　*　*

At the church, the President and the First Lady were in the vestibule, talking to the director of the Kennedy Center and his wife.

"Everybody seems to be going in," the President observed.

The First Lady touched her husband's arm. "Where's Kim?"

The President glanced inside, where children were making their way into the pews where their parents sat.

"You know Kim," he said. "Always has a question for the teacher. I'm sure she's bringing him up." He took his wife's elbow. "Why don't we go in."

But the President didn't move. Two Cabinet officers came up to say good morning. Ninety seconds passed before they were finished.

Hovering half an arm's length from the President, Agent-in-Charge Steve Casey had overheard the exchange between Charles and Mary Woodbridge. While the President chatted with his advisers, Casey kept one eye on the staircase. Any second, he expected to see Kim and Jeb Rawlins step up onto the landing.

When they didn't, he whispered into his wrist mike. Then again.

The third call sent the agents outside scrambling into the school.

Come on, Jeb. Don't do this to me . . .

Rawlins's mike was down. Things like that were known to happen.

Casey did not have to imagine the scene taking place downstairs. He got the play-by-play even as he and his men escorted the President and his wife to their pew. He winced when a sharp report rattled his earpiece. Casey's number-two told him that they'd had to go through a locked door to get into one of the classrooms.

Silence.

Number-two again, his account succinct but his voice hoarse, as though he were choking. Rawlins was down. The boy, code name Brave-heart, was gone. A search was under way.

Steve Casey allowed himself one nonprofessional thought. He remembered the first time he'd been introduced to Kim Woodbridge. He'd explained to the boy that he'd need a code name and asked if he had anything special in mind. The boy's face had lit up and he'd answered instantly: Braveheart, after the hero in the movie of the same name.

Reports were flooding in as agents searched every classroom, the teachers' lounge, canteen, and washrooms.

A message crackled in Casey's ear: "We got a door here we can't find a key for."

"Pop it."

The Secret Service always had two demolition specialists on the squad. It would take them a minute or so to blow the door. Casey could do something in the meantime.

The Reverend Winslow Garrett was walking into the sacristy, and the congregation was quieting. Usually at this point, the agents retreated up the aisle, except for Casey, who always sat beside the President.

He leaned over, cupped his hand around the President's ear, and whispered, "We have a Q-level message."

Q-level relates to a terrorist event somewhere in the world that affects U.S. interests.

Charles Woodbridge stiffened. He was very quick, leaning in to his wife, whispering. She too was a pro, smiling, giving him a reassuring pat on the arm. Anyone watching would think nothing was amiss.

Casey was talking to his men at the school even as he hustled the President into the vestibule.

"What's going on?" Woodbridge demanded.

Casey shushed him by holding up his hand. The door had been popped, agents were in a tunnel that seemed to lead to the adjacent building.

Casey talked to the agent being held in reserve outside the church.

"The rehab next door. Shut it down. Nobody moves. Get the cadaver dogs over here."

Casey saw the President pale at the word "bomb." He switched frequencies and spoke to the duty officer at 1800 G Street N.W., requesting the dispatch of cadaver dogs and their trainers.

Charles Woodbridge gripped Casey's arm. "What the *hell* is going on?"

Woodbridge was a well-read man. He knew all about cadaver dogs, hounds trained on pig fetuses or chemical human decomposition to find buried bodies.

Casey's breath poured into the President's ear: "The agent guarding your son has been found dead. Kim is missing."

Casey felt the President falter, go limp. He saw the terror and the questions explode from Woodbridge's eyes.

In this situation, Casey could go one of two ways. He could assume that Kim Woodbridge had met with foul play that was part of an overall plan to kill the President. A bomb would be the most likely weapon. In that case, his responsibility was to get Woodbridge and his wife the hell away from the church *now* and, as soon as they had been evacuated, sound the alarm to evacuate the rest of the congregation.

But there was a problem. Such an evacuation would create a public spectacle that would immediately be seized upon by the media. This result could have severe, if not terminal, repercussions on the second possibility, Casey's worst nightmare.

Kim Woodbridge had been kidnapped.

In this scenario, it was absolutely imperative that there be no public or media knowledge of the incident. Not even a whisper. Not if Woodbridge and key members of the government were to have any chance to negotiate with the kidnappers. The pressure would be intense; it would be unbearable with the country looking over their shoulders.

Call it.

Casey pulled Woodbridge closer. "Mr. President, they took your son. I do *not* believe that this is part of a greater threat against you at this time. But we have to get you out of here right now. The kidnappers will want to establish contact. There's only one place they'll be calling."

Woodbridge shook off his daze. "Yes. Of course. But my wife—"

"If we pull her out now, people will wonder what's going on. They'll assume it's a personal matter, and we don't want them going down that road." Casey paused. "It's a lousy thing to do, Mr. President—and your wife will be very pissed off with you when she gets back to the House. But leaving her here maintains the illusion. It gives us and you time."

Woodbridge shook his head. "I want her with me."

"It's your decision, sir."

"Tell her that it's her brother. He's in a Florida hospital with a kidney infection." Woodbridge paused, his distaste for the white lie evident. "It'll be better than . . . than the other thing."

Forty seconds later, Casey had the President in the back of the limousine. While Woodbridge waited for his message to be hand-carried to his wife, Casey was talking to the teams that had, by now, found the cutout section of Cyclone fence and tire marks nearby. The second-in-command sketched out a scenario.

"The kidnapper takes out Rawlins. We don't know exactly how, but she didn't—"

"She?" Casey interrupted.

"All the teachers are accounted for except for a Judith Sawyer. Get this: She was hired just this week."

The hell? "Give me the rest."

"Someone cut a section of fence at the construction site, flattened it when they came through. I'm thinking a sport utility vehicle or a van. Maybe a pickup. We'll get good prints off the dirt."

"How many involved?"

"At least two. The woman and the van driver. Could have been more, though."

"What do we have on the woman?"

"We busted into the good reverend's office to get into his files. We have a picture, some background."

"Is it possible the woman—Sawyer, right?—is it possible she was picked off, too?"

"That would mean at least two guys, Steve. One to take out Rawlins, one for her and the boy. I don't think they could have done that without spooking the other kids, no matter how slick they were."

"To get to and past Rawlins, they were pretty slick."

"You want an all-points on Sawyer?"

Casey noticed Mary Woodbridge hurrying out of the church. He thought about how much lead time the kidnappers had—going on twenty minutes. Casey had no ID on the getaway vehicle, which had probably been abandoned by now anyway. He had information on one possible perpetrator but no idea in which direction she and her partners were headed. In short, the little he had was almost useless. Putting out an alarm now would only bring on a media frenzy. Which meant that

Casey and the Service would be second-guessed on every step they took. They wouldn't be able to do their jobs, nor would the President be able to do his.

"No all-points," he said to his second. "Get a crew over to Sawyer's house or apartment and look for her there. Get it done *quietly*."

Casey lifted the wrist mike to his lips. Drivers in the motorcade shifted gears, ready to move.

When Casey jumped into the back seat of the presidential limousine, it was Mary Woodbridge who spoke.

"What's this about my brother? What happened to him?"

Casey took it on the chin. "Your brother's fine, ma'am. We're not aware of any change in his condition."

"Then what *is* it?" She turned to her husband. "Charlie?"

"It's Kim," he managed.

The motorcade was moving fast, sirens bleating. No one outside the armored limousine, with its tinted windows and Lexam soundproofing, saw or heard Mary Woodbridge scream.

Twenty-nine

TRAFFIC WAS NEGLIGIBLE SO EARLY on Sunday morning. Hafez Jamal had the van parked near the subway stop at L'Enfant Plaza just as Casey's men were discovering Jeb Rawlins's body.

The vehicle he had stolen in the early hours of that morning was common enough in Washington: a dual-axle, twenty-four-seat minibus. It was painted a deep blue, with the tour company's name in red lettering along the side. The oversized windows were coated with antiglare material, which blurred the passengers' faces.

Hatem wore a windbreaker with the company logo that he'd found behind the seats. As Judith stepped in, holding Kim between them, he handed out Orioles baseball caps.

Judith slipped Kim onto the bench seat at the very back, which ran the width of the bus. The boy was groggy, barely able to stand. If anyone had been watching, they would have seen a boy being half-dragged, half-carried to the minibus. Fortunately, the area was deserted.

Judith laid Kim down on the seat, using the seatbelts to strap him in as the minibus shuddered and moved off. She touched his forehead, felt how warm he was. She ripped away his tie and undid the top button on his shirt. She noticed the slim gold chain around his neck, felt something beneath the fabric of his shirt, tugged the chain until she saw what she thought was a piece of jewelry.

When Judith turned it over, she realized it was a MedicAlert bracelet. "Hafez!"

Jamal was beside her instantly. He frowned when she showed him the bracelet, turned it over in his fingers.

"He's asthmatic. The medication in the gum—"

"Won't hurt him at all." Jamal ran his fingers over the boy's throat. He pressed his ear to Kim's chest and listened to his breathing.

"His lungs are clear. He'll be all right as long as he doesn't have an anxiety attack. You will have to soothe him, tell him that all will be well."

"Will it be well?"

Jamal pulled her onto one of the seats. "Remember in Amman and Cairo, how we planned this out? Woodbridge is the President, but he is also a father. And a husband. His wife will pressure him to get the boy back. When she learns we are not threatening annihilation, that all we want is an admission of guilt and an apology, she will become our ally. Woodbridge's political advisers will find it difficult to fight her."

Judith considered the logic. It was still as clear and simple as the first time Jamal had outlined his plan. What else *could* Woodbridge do except acknowledge guilt and make a show of humility?

"It will all be over quickly," Jamal was saying. "Woodbridge will never allow this . . . incident to become public. How safe would America feel if it knew that the President's son could be taken? No. Woodbridge will need time to create a framework for what he has to do, find a reason or an occasion to make the announcement. But after that, matters will proceed quickly."

Judith glanced at the boy. "He may need medicine. We don't know what kind—"

"When I make contact, I will ask," Jamal promised. "Such a gesture will reassure the mother, and indicate to Woodbridge that he is not dealing with animals."

The image of the Israeli helicopters flooded Judith's mind. The streaks of orange and red, the black smoke and crackling flames. Men, women, and children burning. Her child. Her husband. She had thought the Israelis animals, to stalk innocents like that. If so, how was she different, stealing away with this child?

"Manar," Jamal whispered, using her Arab name. "Manar, the boy will be returned unharmed. I swear it. When the Woodbridges learn of your sorrow and suffering, they will realize how their God has favored them."

Judith returned to the boy. She sat with him, wiping away the sweat as the toxin worked its way out through his pores. In time, she heard nothing but his breathing and the soft, reassuring hiss of the tires taking them to sanctuary.

* * *

Mary Woodbridge followed her husband into the Oval Office. Thank God it was Sunday, she thought. There was only a skeleton staff on hand, squirreled away in the small offices around the Office.

She sat on the couch, watching Charlie do what he did best. Her husband had a rare ability to compartmentalize tasks. Looking at him behind his desk, one would never suspect that his child had just been kidnapped, unless one noticed the slight tremor as he reached for the phone.

Mary Woodbridge listened as he got Yakov Admony, the Israeli prime minister, out of a family dinner. The conversation was terse and strained, Woodbridge driving questions across the satellite link.

"I'm keeping it contained on my end, Yakov," she heard. "No, I'm *not* interested in doing that. The fewer people who know—"

The Israeli must have been persistent—and persuasive—because Woodbridge changed his mind, grudgingly.

The President finished his call and went to his wife. Her skin was cold beneath his touch.

"The Israelis are scrambling everything—and I mean everything— they have on known terrorists. Every contact, informant, deep-plant agent will be touched. Nobody's going to get any sleep over there tonight."

He paused, stroking her cheek with his knuckles. "I need you to back me up here, Mary. We gotta ride this out together."

Mary Woodbridge looked into the eyes of the man who had stolen her heart when she was a senior at the University of Chicago. She'd known way back then that he was destined for greatness. She also told him that while he dueled in politics, she would continue in the fine arts and education. Mary was a gifted painter as well as a skilled teacher. She had none of the wiles or guile of that other Chicago-area native, Hillary Clinton. As far as Mary was concerned, the Queen of Denial and Doublespeak had helped make feminism a dead, bankrupt religion. Her popular children's book should have been titled *It Takes a Village to Raise an Idiot*.

Mary had her child, her husband, her painting, and the students who came to the White House once a week for her tutorials. She knew enough about life to realize how beautiful hers was. She never asked for more, just as she never believed that what she most prized and guarded could ever be wrenched away from her.

She gripped his hand. "Do you have any idea who they are, Charlie? What they want?"

There was a soft knock on the door. "I suspect we're about to find out." He called out, "Come in."

Steve Casey had a file in his hand and anguish in his heart. He did a quick scan of the pair on the couch. They were tough, he decided. *They'll make it through this if it doesn't drag.* And it couldn't drag because then the boy would be dead.

"We have preliminary information on the teacher, Judith Sawyer." The Woodbridges needed his details, not his condolences.

"A *woman* was involved in this?"

"By the looks of it, yes, ma'am."

Casey walked them through the file. "The reason we have so much information so quickly is because Sawyer didn't bother to cover her tracks. She just came back from the Middle East and became an American again. One thing: Her passport is original, but the renewal date was dummied up. Someone wanted her back here fast."

"And she's disappeared," the President said.

"Vanished."

"Maybe someone hurt her . . ." Mary Woodbridge began.

"I think that's unlikely, ma'am. This thing came down so fast, there would have been no time to hide the body. And no point for the kidnappers to ride around with it."

"Do we know what she was doing in the Middle East? Specifically?"

"We're piecing that together right now. First reports indicate that she spent time as a gopher for an archaeological dig outside Cairo, then went native. Never finished the dig, never returned home. Until now."

"That's a big chunk of her life missing," Woodbridge said.

"We're filling it in, sir. The Israelis have had their hotline open. I take it you talked to them."

"They won't be holding back anything. Admony gave me his word." The President seemed to flinch, as if what was coming next was too painful. "Could this be connected to Jamal?"

"Who's Jamal?" Mary Woodbridge asked.

Her husband told her that a known terrorist was suspected to be in the capital area, that security had been upgraded as a result.

"Was he after you, Charlie?" she demanded. "Was he intending to use Kim to get to you?"

"We have no evidence of that, ma'am," Casey said hastily.

"Then what *do* you have evidence of?"

"Mary—"

"No! You don't tell me there's this . . . this creature out there and now Kim is gone!"

"He is gone, Mrs. Woodbridge. I believe Jamal took him. Jamal and this Sawyer woman."

The First Lady whirled around at the voice. Landau and Reece stood in the doorway, framed by a pair of Secret Service agents.

"My name is Landau, and I have something to tell both of you. Mr. President, you have spoken to Yakov Admony. He mentioned me, yes?"

"Yes."

"You must be Steven Casey," Landau said. "Has anyone briefed you?"

"No." Casey was clearly unhappy.

Landau nodded to Reece. "This is FBI Special Agent Reece. She will tell you everything you need to know."

"Mr. President—"

"It's all right, Steve. Mr. Landau and Agent Reece are known to me. Just be sure to give him everything, Miss Reece."

The door closed and the President said, "You have something to tell us, sir?"

Landau had pieced together his words during the brief, furious drive from Buzzard's Point to the White House. Word that the President's son was missing—probably kidnapped—had come not from within the United States but from five thousand miles away. Landau's number-two had talked to him even as Yakov Admony had been on the phone with the President.

Admony's subsequent instructions had been precise: Landau was to brief the Chief Executive on any and all events relating to Hafez Jamal. That included the reason for and planning of the raid on Samarra. Admony did not want the Americans to discover anything for themselves after the fact.

Landau thought that the Woodbridges were all right—so far. The wife settled down. She asked short, tight questions about Jamal, about Israeli suspicions as to why he was in the United States, about the Samarra raid.

"The truth is," Landau concluded, "*no one* believed Jamal would go through your son to get to you, Mr. President."

"You mean blackmail," the First Lady said.

"Yes."

"Does Jamal want money? Does he want to threaten us with a suitcase bomb?"

"No, ma'am. It is something else. What exactly, well, we will learn soon enough when he contacts you. Let me say one thing here. It is of small comfort, I know, but still . . . Jamal will not hurt the boy. It is not in his interest to do so. He is clever enough to appreciate that if Kim is harmed, there is nowhere he can hide. No country will harbor him; informants will be falling over themselves to turn him in."

"What if I can't give him what he wants?" the President asked.

"I believe that Jamal thought that part through very carefully. He would not have taken the boy if he believed you *couldn't* or *wouldn't* give him what he will ask for. No, that will be in your power.

"He has also anticipated that you will not make the kidnapping public. Such a decision is in both your favor and his. Jamal is hiding, but not too far away. If you do not let loose your police, he does not have to move. If he doesn't feel threatened, the danger to your son diminishes accordingly."

"The question is *what*, Mr. Landau. What does he want? I'm told you know him better than almost anyone. Tell me what he wants."

"I will not guess, Mr. President. As I said, we will know soon enough."

Landau broke off as Casey reappeared with an update. The White House switchboard operators had been alerted to forward any unusual calls to the family quarters.

"Where two of my people will be sitting on the phones. As soon as we get a hit—"

"Won't you have to screen for cranks?" Landau asked.

"You'd be surprised how few of those we get," Casey told him. "Cranks think we have superinstant tracing facilities—which is fine with us. Plus, we've made it known that such calls to 1600 constitute a felony."

Casey handed the President a note. "A short list of those people who have to know on my end. You'll want to add your names, Cabinet officers—"

"Not until the call comes in," Woodbridge said. "Not until we know exactly what we're dealing with. Then I'll decide who to bring in."

"We also checked the place Sawyer was staying at, Mr. President. I'd like to take a minute and bring you up to speed."

Landau wondered why Mary Woodbridge shook her head when her husband asked her to join him. She continued to sit on the couch, her face to the windows, a faraway expression in her eyes. To someone else, she might have seemed to be in a state of mild shock, confused, disoriented. Landau thought it was something else. There was a hard, working intelligence behind those eyes. The First Lady sliding into self-pity, she was thinking. Somewhere, just beyond her grasp, was something she needed to grab hold of, something too important to ignore. Landau knew better than to disturb her.

Mary Woodbridge surprised him by saying, "You're waiting for me, aren't you, Mr. Landau? How clever of you."

Landau said nothing.

"You know what I think, Mr. Landau? Why no mention of a woman?" Landau didn't stir. "Yes, a woman. Here you are telling me how your people attacked Samarra. Your account is vivid, even graphic. You have a flair for details. You talk about Issim Hassan, his son, how they were killed." She paused. "But you never mention Hassan's wife, the child's mother. Why is that? What happened to her? Did she die? Disappear?"

It was the word "disappear" that galvanized him. Judith Sawyer had "disappeared" from Cairo—that's what Casey had said. "Gone native . . ."

With *Hassan*?

As Hassan's *wife*?

"You didn't think of that."

Landau jerked his head toward Mary Woodbridge. Her words came out as a statement, not an accusation.

"That Judith Sawyer could have been his wife? No."

"I don't understand."

Landau's mind was racing. He wanted to snatch up the phone, not explain himself to this woman. But he owed her some consideration.

"Arab mores are different from Western ones," he said. "When it comes to wives, women in general, they are not so enlightened."

"Clitoridectomy and infibulation. I have done my share of traveling, Mr. Landau."

"We have documented that, as a young man, Issim Hassan knew many women, Mrs. Woodbridge. We had some photographs, some background reports. Hassan favored tourist girls—Germans, Scandinavians. There would be romp and romance and then they would go home. Admittedly, this was curious to us. Hassan was a very intelligent man, well educated, from a good home. Yet, he was not a part of Cairo society. The Arab equivalent of debutantes held no interest for him."

"So after a while, you didn't watch him anymore. Or not as closely."

"Hassan disappeared for a while. Afterward, when he surfaced in Palestinian politics, our interest in him changed."

"Was he married by then?"

"Yes."

"But you don't know to whom."

"Hassan kept his wife well away from his politics. In and of itself, this is not unusual. Most Arab leaders keep their families away from the office, for security if nothing else."

"What 'nothing else' would that be, Mr. Landau?"

"Women do not play a large role in politics. It is an arena in which they are not heard, much less seen."

"So in all this time, you knew that he had a wife, but not who she was—or is." Mary Woodbridge paused. "What if she turns out to be Judith Sawyer?"

Landau dreaded the question. Hassan's child had been burned alive by the Apaches. His father with him. The woman of this man and child had watched, helpless. Then she had come home, to America, and took for herself another's child.

Eye for an eye? Could a mother become so demented by grief that she would destroy another child? Of course.

"Will she hurt Kim, Mr. Landau?"

"I do not believe she will. If Jamal were not involved—if this were the work of a lone sociopath—I would not hold out much hope. But Jamal is political. He would not commit time, resources, and risk to such an operation only to squander everything. Your son is meant to be traded for something Jamal wants."

"And Sawyer? Does she want the same thing?"

"She would not be here otherwise. Jamal would have made sure of that before he brought her in."

"But she might still hurt him."

Landau would have touched her had it been possible for him to reach across such a barrier.

"He will be frightened, but not hurt. He must be returned to you whole."

Mary Woodbridge nodded. "You seem antsy, Mr. Landau."

"'Antsy'?"

"Anxious. Desperate to get on with something."

"A call, Mrs. Woodbridge. There is a very important call to make."

"To Tel Aviv?" Landau nodded and she continued. "Use the phone on my husband's desk. I'll go tell the others what we've come up with."

Dressed in her Sunday best, Mary Woodbridge rose and took a moment to compose herself. Then with her head high and shoulders back, she left, vaguely conscious of Landau on the phone talking in soft, urgent tones.

*   *   *

When they arrived at the Chesapeake house, Jamal scooped up the boy and carried him upstairs. This time Judith followed him. Jamal did not care because Ben Poltarek was asleep. A blanket covered him up to his chin, hiding the gauze taped to his arm.

Jamal laid Kim Woodbridge on the other twin bed. From the armoire, he plucked another set of handcuffs and bound the boy's wrist to the bedpost.

"Is that necessary?" Judith asked.

"We don't want him wandering around, do we?"

"What about the drug?"

"It will wear off in an hour, maybe less."

"He needs a bath, and fresh clothes. We should have thought of the clothes."

Judith's eyes never left Ben. Jamal had talked about him, but this was the first time she had seen him. She thought he looked all right, pale, but otherwise unharmed. Maybe Jamal hadn't had to do too much to induce his cooperation.

She felt Jamal touch her elbow. "There is food downstairs. You should eat."

Judith took a last look at the captives. "I want to take a bath, and rest."

She shook off his hand, as if his touch made her feel even more dirty.

*   *   *

Kim Woodbridge opened his eyes and took stock. The first thing he did was listen to his breathing. Good. No wheezing. His parents had drilled it into him: As soon as he was short of breath or heard wheezing, grab the inhaler.

With his free hand, Kim checked his jacket and pants pockets. No inhaler. Either he'd dropped it or that dickhead who called himself Jamal had taken it. That was okay, for now. He'd just have to be careful.

Next, the room. Smelled like camp, all musty. The pink rose wallpaper was awful. But at least he was warm and dry.

Okay. His stomach. Bad guy Jamal had said the drug—whatever it was—would be out of his system in an hour.

Jerk. Kim still felt a little nauseated, but no worse than that. Whatever they'd given him had been awful, but it was wearing off fast.

Jeb. What happened to you, dude? Kim liked his Secret Service escort. Jeb was pretty funny when no one was around, more one-liners than Seinfeld. *Hope you're okay.*

Now, for the guy on the next bed . . . Kim turned on his side for a better look. Whoever he was, he didn't look good, pale like a fish belly. And so quiet that Kim would have thought he was dead if not for the faint rise and fall of his chest.

Not much hope there. Kim rattled the cuffs. *Not there either.*

He understood exactly what had happened to him. His parents had explained kidnapping to him, how careful he had to be, how he could never slip away from Jeb or whoever else was assigned to protect him.

Kim remembered Jeb telling him that no one had ever kidnapped a President's kid. Never. Like it was against the rules.

Obviously, this Jamal hadn't read the rules.

Something else came to him: Jeb telling him about backup plans, in case they should become separated; Jeb saying that Kim should stay very cool. He had to remember that hundreds of Secret Service agents would be out looking for him. Every policeman in the country would have his picture. He had to stay calm and—what was it? Yeah, focused. Don't give the bad guys any excuse to hurt you. Go along with what they want you to do and hang on. Help is on the way.

Although the boy was unaware of it, it was his knowledge of who he was to the world, plus his implicit faith in the adults around him, that cooled what could have become anxiety and panic. He was cognizant of his circumstances, but for the time being at least, he maintained faith in those who always protected him. It had not yet occurred to Kim Woodbridge that those who could mastermind the kidnapping of a protected person were also clever enough to keep him hidden as long as circumstances demanded.

"Hey, kid."

Kim nearly jumped out of his skin. He stared wide-eyed at the guy on the next bed. His eyes were still closed and he didn't seem to be breathing. But he *had* spoken. Unless Kim was hearing things.

"Too weird," he muttered.

"You don't know *how* weird."

Ben opened his eyes and rolled over. He blinked, then stared at the boy. "I know you. I've seen your picture. Kim Woodbridge?"

"Yeah. Who're you?"

"Ben."

"They got you too, huh?"

"Me, too."

"Why?"

"They think I know something."

"About me?"

Ben saw that the boy was confused, trying to place him in his world.

"You don't know me. I'm a lawyer . . ."

"That's why you're here? Because you're a *lawyer?*"

"You make it sound like I'm pond scum."

Kim shrugged, like, *You said it, not me.*

"Tell me what happened to you."

Kim was instantly wary, his imagination kicking into overdrive. Who knew who this turkey was? Maybe that Jamal guy had put him there to try to get information out of him.

"You first."

The lack of blood had left Ben weakened. But he'd had a chance to rest, and a few hours ago an Arab had come in with something that tasted like very sweet lemonade. Ben had almost gagged on his first sip, but forced himself to drink it all. The sugar was fuel for his system.

Ben looked at the boy. He still could not believe that the plan he'd overheard had been carried off. How in God's name had Jamal and the woman kidnapped the President's son?

"Mister?"

"My name's Ben," he reminded the boy. "You don't have to call me 'mister' or 'sir.'"

"What's your last name?"

"Poltarek."

"Is that Jewish?"

"Yes."

Ben had never heard that question from a child. He liked the ring of innocent curiosity, devoid of innuendo.

"So tell me what happened to you."

Ben had never been anything less than honest with a child. Children gave in to illusion, but they could spot a con or a fib quicker than any adult.

Ben was careful not to be graphic, but neither did he shy away from the facts. People had been killed. The boy had to understand and appreciate that. Ben talked softly, not only to avoid being overheard but so that he could still listen for anything that might rise out of the vents. For the time being, the house was quiet and he was grateful that he did not have to stop. As he talked, he gauged how much strength he had. The boy would have questions later.

"That's it. That's all of it. Your turn."

For a moment, Ben thought there was something wrong with the boy. His eyes were glazed and he was breathing through his mouth.

"Is it true?"

"Yes, it's true. Now tell me what happened to you."

Kim's head was still spinning from what he'd heard. This guy was something out of *Mission: Impossible.*

Unconsciously imitating the adult, Kim poured out his story slowly, carefully, making sure he described things exactly as they had occurred.

"How do you think they managed to knock Jeb out?" Kim asked.

Ben doubted that the Secret Service agent had been "knocked out." But there was no reason to strip the boy of the notion that his friend and protector was still alive.

"What was the last thing you and Jeb did together?" Ben asked.

A wrinkle appeared between the boy's eyes. "I don't know."

"I think you do. Close your eyes. Imagine Jeb and you entering the school. You're in the classroom. He's sitting in the back." The boy nodded. "Okay. Now class is over. You're ready to leave—"

"No, we're not. I mean, we are, but we don't." Kim opened his eyes. "Miss Sawyer went up to Jeb. She gave him some gum, then me, too."

"Was she chewing any?" Kim nodded energetically. "So what do *you* think happened?"

"Jeb's gum was poisoned?"

"And yours?"

"Sure. But only a little bit because I'm not as big as Jeb."

"And Miss Sawyer was chewing a piece she didn't poison."

"That's gotta be it," Kim agreed. He glanced at Ben, puzzled and clearly hurt. "Why would she do that? I mean, she was new. It's not like I ever did anything to make her mad."

How to explain to a child that people have reasons that are the stuff of nightmares?

"I don't know," Ben said.

"I don't think she's a bad person," Kim said somberly. "The other guy, yeah—he's a creep. But not Miss Sawyer."

Ben was not inclined to agree. He shifted to prevent the cuff from chafing his wrist. Talking had scorched his throat and he desperately wanted something to drink.

"Ben?"

"Yeah?"

"What are we going to do?"

Ben grimaced. The kid had chutzpah—and that beautiful, innocent belief that an adult always has a way out of any problem.

Ben had been thinking along those lines for a while now, a way out. When he was listening or talking to Jamal, when he watched his blood ooze from his body, one part of him was focused on escape.

But he had been alone then. Planning escape for one was easier and simpler than for two. And for all his composure and poise, Kim Wood-bridge was still a child. He could not lead, only follow; he could not share a burden, only become one.

"Are you going to leave me here?"

Ben wasn't sure which startled him more, the boy's matter-of-fact tone or the question itself.

"No. I'm not going to leave you here. I was thinking how the *two* of us could get out."

"You were planning to escape?"

Ben wondered if Kim had it in him to be sarcastic. Sounded like it.

"Of course."

"But you didn't do it."

"I was a little busy." *With Jamal making me a one-man blood bank.*

"I don't think you could go anywhere. I don't think you can even get out of those handcuffs. You would have done it if you really could."

Ben fixed him with a stare. "You think so?"

"Yup."

Ben never took his eyes off the boy as he jiggled his wrist lightly, then curled his fingers over the ratchet. The nail of his forefinger marched across the teeth on the ratchet. When it reached the fourth one, Ben gave a slight tug. The handcuff snapped open and fell into his uplifted palm.

The kid's eyes were larger than full moons.

"I'm outta here, partner," Ben said.

"Hey, wait a minute—"

"Shh. Kidding, all right? Want to learn how to do it? Here, give me your finger."

It took Kim a few tries, but finally he mastered the intricate motion.

"Magic!" he whispered.

"Yes, it is. That's what I do."

"You're a magician? I thought you said you were a lawyer."

"What—I can't be both?"

"Why didn't you get out of here before?"

"Because I was tied up. Now listen. We have to put these back on, in case someone comes up."

"But—"

"Nobody's going anywhere yet. We need a plan first. We need to know what they're up to."

"How are we—?"

Ben pressed a finger against his lips. "Listen. What do you hear?"

Kim strained to listen. What he heard were soft voices, the kind you heard in scary movies, when you didn't know where they were coming from. He cocked his head, then slipped quietly to the floor and put his ear against the duct grille.

Then he looked up at Ben, who gave him a thumbs-up.

What is this place? Kim asked himself. He stole a glance at Ben. *And who is this guy?*

Thirty

DOWNSTAIRS, OTHERS WERE ALSO LISTENING.

Sitting at the kitchen table, Jamal kept one ear tuned to the faint splash of water in the bathroom directly above him. What he would say to Hatem and al-Rahim when they finished eating was something Judith could never be privy to.

Maybe it was the sound of the water or the scraping of forks on cheap china, but Jamal never heard the stirring of small bare feet on the floorboards upstairs.

Kim Woodbridge looked over his shoulder at Ben, lying on the bed. He felt exposed and afraid, his feet cold on the wood.

"Open the closet door," Ben called softly.

He wouldn't have sent the boy if he hadn't felt light-headed. Ben did not want to risk blacking out, stumbling, or worse, falling. Also, the boy weighed much less than he did and this was a house that betrayed footsteps.

Kim opened the closet. It smelled of mothballs. There was nothing in it except old clothes on rusty hangers.

"Look behind the clothes. There's the door."

Kim remembered what Ben had told him. He lifted the hangers, didn't scrape them along the pole. Here was the door.

He reached for the half-moon grip and pulled. The shrieking of ancient hinges met his ears. He turned fearfully to Ben, who gave him the okay. Was he crazy?

"Close . . . the . . . closet . . . door."

Kim got it. He didn't much like dark places, but he sucked up his fears and closed the door. This time, he slipped both hands through the grip and yanked back, hard. The shriek wasn't so bad and now he had his opening.

"The light switch is on the left of the first step."

Yup. There it was.

The bulb was weak and covered with dust, but it gave enough light for Kim to see the short staircase to the attic.

"There's another switch at the top of the stairs, also on the left."

There'd better be. Kim thought how good a baseball bat would feel in his hands right now.

He edged his way up the stairs, tentatively reached out, and slid his fingers along the two-by-four support beam. The light switch.

The attic rafters were high enough for Kim to stand up straight. He breathed the stale air through his mouth. Ben had told him it would be dusty up there and not to sneeze.

A series of low-wattage bulbs cast shadows over large rectangular pieces of wood. Kim was in the drama club at school. The wood reminded him of theater sets, the kind that were rolled into place to provide background scenery.

There was a lot of wiring; Ben had warned him about that too. Why would a house need so much? Maybe because it was old? There was the junction box.

The panel cover came away with a shower of dust. Inside were rows of circuit breakers.

"Flip all the ones on the left."

Okay.

Nothing happened. Kim didn't know what he was expecting—lights, sirens, loudspeakers. Anything to get somebody's attention.

"Don't waste time. Grab the bag and go."

Kim spotted it easily. It was shaped like those doctor bags he'd seen in Westerns. This one was three times the size, and heavy. Kim hauled it to the stairs and bumped it one step at a time. At the bottom, he gripped the handles with both hands and set the bag gently on the floor.

"Got it?"

Kim peeked out of the closet. "Yeah. But I can't carry it all the way over to you."

"Don't have to. Look inside."

Ben's description was good. Kim tiptoed across the floor carrying a black rectangular box. Ben popped open the top, checked the batteries, and frowned. He couldn't remember when he'd last changed them.

"Do they still have juice?" Kim asked.

"We'll find out." He placed the box under the bed, as close to the vent as he dared. "Pull the clothes back into place. Hide the bag as best you can."

Kim was closing the closet door when Ben motioned for him to get back into bed. There was just enough time to reset the handcuffs and dive under the covers before the whispers drifted into the room.

Downstairs in the kitchen, Jamal watched Hatem and al-Rahim smoke cigarettes. He had promised them important news and he enjoyed their anticipation.

"The ransom demands have been modified slightly," he said.

Hatem stirred. "I thought the issue had been settled in Amman."

"As did I," al-Rahim rumbled.

Both men were part of Jamal's inner council. While most of the tactical planning belonged to Jamal, their quick, savage skills had been invaluable in Paris and elsewhere.

But in Amman, Jamal had not told them everything. Manar—Judith—was too close, swathed in her widowhood, revered, party to all discussions and decisions.

Jamal sat back in his chair. "Did you really believe I would settle for contrition, squander this great opportunity on apologies that would be nothing but lies?"

"What is it you wish, Hafez—exactly?"

"Exactly this: The American President will force the Israelis to withdraw completely from the territories they currently occupy. Building of new settlements will cease. America will guarantee the Palestinian existence just as over the decades she has guaranteed the existence of Israel. She will match foreign aid to our homeland with what the Israelis receive, dollar for dollar. And the President will embrace me as the new prime minister, the only legitimate authority, of Palestine."

Hatem and al-Rahim exchanged glances. Jamal saw the doubt in their eyes, but also the blazing light of possibility. For years, leaders like Arafat had kept such men sustained on promises, until the promises had become hollow, the words worthless and ridiculed. But neither Arafat nor anyone else had ever had the leverage Jamal now possessed; no one had ever gotten even close to the elusive goal. Instead of perpetual stones, Hatem's mouth now watered with the taste of milk and honey.

"Will the American do this?"

"We have his child." Jamal gestured at the radio on the counter, tuned to an all-news station. "No mention that the boy is missing."

"So the President agrees to all your terms," al-Rahim said hoarsely. "What is to prevent him from going back on his word once we have returned the boy?"

"Woodbridge will give his word in front of the whole world, at the United Nations. He will never be able to renege. If he tried, who then could ever trust him or America again?"

Jamal looked away, his voice becoming dreamy. "There is more. The President will also give me Jerusalem."

In the silence of shock, Jamal heard water gurgling in the pipes and the flush of a toilet. Judith must have finished bathing.

"Jerusalem!" Hatem whispered.

"The capital of the new Palestine. And I will be the soldier who returns it to the Arab people."

"The Jews will eat toads before they surrender Jerusalem!" al-Rahim said.

"Then they had best acquire a taste for them. Because, my brother, Jerusalem *will* be ours."

Hatem looked up, hearing the shuffle of feet on floorboards. "Does she know any of this?"

"No," Jamal replied. "Nor will she ever know. This is understood."

"I still do not see how—" al-Rahim began.

"It is quite simple," Jamal said. "If the President does not give me Jerusalem, I will give him back his son—one piece at a time."

Judith appeared in the kitchen, dressed in jeans and a sweater. Strands of wet hair were plastered to the back of her neck, and her face was flushed pink from the warm bath.

Jamal moved to get her a cup of tea. "Are you feeling better?"

"I wasn't sick, Hafez," she said, accepting the cup. "It was an . . . unsettling experience."

Hatem glanced up and Jamal registered the contempt in his eyes. Other than to marry Issim Hassan, this woman had done nothing to earn her stature. Hatem had a frontline fighter's disdain for such people.

"How is the boy?" Jamal asked. "Did you look in on him?"

"Just for a moment. He was asleep. The other one, too. Hafez, we should discuss exactly how to phrase our demands."

Jamal inclined his head. "Of course. But we are agreed on the major point: the President must acknowledge that America was directly responsible for the deaths of your husband and child, and that she will support the establishment of a Palestinian state."

"Through dialogue," Judith added. "By seeing that Issim's work is completed, peacefully and for all time."

"Peacefully and for all time," Jamal echoed. "The words have a statesman's ring to them."

"Words are all I have left to live with," Judith said. She looked from Hatem to al-Rahim. "Would you leave us, please?"

"How will you deliver our demands?" she asked when the two were gone.

Jamal took his time explaining, allowing Judith to consider every step.

"Very good," she said finally. "Which method do you think is better—a letter or a tape?"

"Tapes provide better security."

Judith smiled sadly. "For my protection? We are beyond that, are we not, Hafez? By now the police and FBI have discovered that I'm missing. They will have searched my room and run my name through their computers. They are ninety-nine percent certain that I kidnapped the boy. They will show me no mercy. In fact, they will hate me more than if I were an Arab, since I am one of them. A traitress."

Jamal's eyes narrowed. "What are you saying?"

"I wish to write our letter to the President in my own hand. And sign it. Let Woodbridge—let the world—know that this is the grievance of a wife and mother."

"Woodbridge will never allow the world to see your letter."

"Not now. But later, when our demands have been met, he might release it, to justify his actions."

She is insane, Jamal thought, staring at Judith's dreamy expression. *Truly, she believes she can raise the dead.*

"What if Woodbridge *never* tells the world about the letter?"

"Then I will. I will write out a copy. It will be Issim's last testament."

And the ax upon my neck. Such a letter would make Judith the most powerful woman in the Arab world. No! The most powerful *individual.* She would transform herself into a combination of Mother Teresa and Indira Gandhi, a long-suffering martyr melded with a shrewd, charismatic political leader. The idea of having to seek her council, her *permission,* to rule revolted him.

But all he said was, "I agree. What you propose would be a powerful testament—and a fitting tribute. But it needs to be done quickly. Woodbridge must hear from us tonight."

In the bedroom upstairs, the boy stirred and rolled over on his side. Kim Woodbridge had heard every word percolating up the duct. Jamal's cold promise resonated: *". . . I will give him back his son—one piece at a time."*

"They're gonna kill us, aren't they, Ben?"

"No. They'll trade."

"No, they won't. That Jamal guy's a liar. You heard what he told Miss Sawyer. That's not what he's gonna do." Kim fell silent for a moment. "You know, I hear a lot about what goes on in the White House. Most people, when it comes to kids, they're really lame. They think that just because you're small, you can't see or hear. I remember my dad talking with some guy from the CIA or something, saying how we'll never negotiate with terrorists, never give them what they want."

Ben saw the boy's lip tremble, his eyes glisten with tears. "Your father will come for you," he said with as much conviction as he could muster.

The whole friggin' government is hunting. But Jamal is moving fast. And the woman . . .

Ben had hoped that Judith Sawyer would act as a counterweight to Jamal. But after listening to her, he realized that she was swathed in her own particular insanity.

"Nobody's going to die," Ben said, more to himself than to the boy. "You and I, we're getting out of here."

Kim stared at him, angry. He didn't appreciate anyone trying to con him.

"Getting out of the cuffs was a neat trick—"

"Not a trick. An illusion. Remember: The cuffs were never really closed."

"So *what?*"

"So maybe we have a few more illusions."

Kim's eyes darted to the closet door. He imagined the big, heavy bag sitting there in the dark. He looked back at Ben, who nodded.

Thirty-one

THE NATIONAL SECURITY ADVISER was in Mexico City, discussing drug-traffic interdiction with Central American counterparts. Landau and Reece made his office their temporary operations center.

Landau had pushed for the arrangement. Besides access to the Oval Office, only three doors away, the adviser's office gave him absolutely secure communications. Landau had open lines to Tel Aviv, to the embassy *katsa*, and to the FBI hostage rescue team at Buzzard's Point. Reece had her own channels with Bureau headquarters and the special agents in charge in Baltimore and Quantico.

At the President's express instructions, the hunt for Hafez Jamal was scaled down. Media alerts that made every news cycle were quietly dropped. Interim reports and queries meant to jog memories no longer appeared on police hotsheets. Charles Woodbridge did not want his son's kidnapper to feel too pressured. If Jamal were spotted and captured—or, worse, killed—what would happen to the boy then?

The hunt for Judith Sawyer was equally furtive. Since she was an American, Landau was content to let Reece take point. The FBI has hundreds of superbly qualified investigators. Those on duty or living within a hundred miles of Washington were not enjoying the Sabbath rest.

"When do you think he'll make his move?" Reece asked. She was intrigued by Landau's seeming fascination with the national security adviser's collection of Franklin Mint antique pewter cars.

"*Tchotchkes.*"

"I beg your pardon?"

"Nothing. When will Jamal come? Soon. I think he may be on his way now."

"And you're playing with toys."

Landau blinked. "It's not *my* collection. Please, what would you have me do? I don't even have my sidearm in case we have to move fast."

That was true. The Secret Service did not allow a foreign national to carry a gun in the President's presence. Landau had argued, and even Yakov Admony had intervened. Both had been told pointedly that the Service didn't care if Landau was the Messiah—no gun.

"Be patient, Kaelin. Jamal will establish contact. We need that first step."

Landau did not have to explain. Both he and Reece knew about the vast arsenal of locating and eavesdropping equipment the security forces had marshaled. At great expense, two of the newest KH-14 satellites had been reprogrammed to maintain a geosynchronous orbit over the capital. The images they sent back were so fine that they could capture a man smoking a cigarette. If the way he held the cigarette was opportune, the cameras could make out the brand name printed on the rolling paper.

Nightwind helicopters—the army's newest and quietest machines—were also airborne, equipped with heat-imagery cameras and other devices that had not been discussed in Landau's presence. Landau imagined that if Jamal made contact via phone, fax, or computer, the Nightwinds, working with the techies at the National Security Agency, would fix his position in less than a minute. The helicopters would then alert the ground units, and Jamal would be in the fishbowl. Still untouchable, but constantly in sight. Landau thought the Americans would, under the circumstances, take great pains to remain calm. The temptation to snatch Jamal, drug him and sweat the truth out of him, would be close to overwhelming. But they would wait, allow Jamal to lead them to his nest. Once they determined that the boy was there, they would decide on the best way to extract him.

But now, the waiting. Landau felt Reece strain as though she were on an invisible leash. The whole damn government—at least those who were privy—was straining. In a brief moment of indulgence, Landau allowed himself to pity Jamal. To have such power massed against you and not even know it . . .

"What does he *want*?" Reece pressed.

"Want? I don't know."

The question was still being debated, intensely, ceaselessly by those involved in the situation.

"Not freedom for political prisoners," Landau mused. "There aren't any left. Money? Maybe, though not likely. There are a number of enlightened statesmen in the Middle East who have adopted terrorism as their charity of choice. What else *can* you give him?"

Reece frowned and remained silent. Landau wondered if she knew but didn't want to say, or she just didn't know.

For most Americans, the dispute between the Arabs and the Israelis was a tiresome canker. After a while, you put on more balm and hoped that this time, the sore would go away. Because you didn't live there, with fanatics strapped with explosives getting on buses or going into restaurants. You were tired of watching limbs fly on the evening news, of Arab homes being bulldozed, of Israeli children in gas masks practicing air-raid alerts. The world was problematic enough without the Jews. So no—intelligent, capable people like Reece might not think it through. There was only one thing Hafez Jamal could want, that the Arabs had always lusted for. Now, one of them had the wherewithal to realize the dream.

"Jamal must want *something*," Reece said, worrying the issue as if it were a hangnail.

"I always said that you should let me get close when we tag him," Landau replied. Reece thought his smile would intimidate a reptile.

"I don't think anyone ever gets close to you," she shot back. "They don't live long enough to do that."

*   *   *

Through that strange connection that binds ancient enemies, Hafez Jamal was thinking of Landau. His thoughts were not ragged with trepidation or anxiety; rather, he experienced an exuberance that left him almost light-headed. Here he was strolling among the crowds in Union

Station, and he felt invisible. The boy was his talisman. As long as Jamal had him, he was invincible.

Two hours earlier, Jamal and Hatem had arrived at Baltimore-Washington International Airport in the minibus. Jamal had gotten off at the international terminal. He waited until a group of Spanish tourists trudged out of baggage claim, then slipped in among them and boarded the express coach to Washington. He got off at the first stop, Union Station.

Dressed in the casual clothes of a tourist, Jamal swung down the wide halls to the rows of pay lockers. His sharp eyes surveilled constantly, settling on faces, evaluating, moving on. The pattern broke when he noticed repair work being done on some marble columns. The gouges were unmistakably bullet holes, evidence of the gun battle between the fleeing Jew, Tarnofsky, and Jamal's men. Good men, dead now, martyrs waiting to be avenged.

And so you shall be.

Jamal fed coins into the slot, retracted the key, and opened the locker. He placed the envelope containing the letter inside the cavity. On the envelope, written in black felt pen, was a series of numbers. Meaningless to others, they would instantly be recognized by the President or the First Lady.

Jamal walked to a bank of telephones and dialed the general switchboard number.

"Good afternoon, the White House."

"I wish to speak with Kim Woodbridge."

"Excuse me . . ."

The Secret Service agent monitoring that bank of the switchboard was very quick. She transferred the call to her line, at the same time disconnecting from the switchboard. Now, the operator would think that the caller had hung up.

"You wish to speak to Kim Woodbridge?" the agent asked, watching the trace timer count down.

"You are not the operator," Jamal said.

"No, sir. Whom do you wish to speak to?"

"Let me save you the trouble of trying to trace this call. I am at Union Station. Tell your people to go to the B. Dalton bookstore. In the third aisle on the left, halfway down, is the political-history section. On the second shelf from the bottom is a book called *The Illustrated History of Torture*. Inside, you will find a key to a station locker; inside the locker will be a message. You need not worry about explosives or booby traps. It is in my interests—and certainly yours—for you to read the message. Now, the book containing the key is not a best-seller, but I would hurry, in case someone else finds it as entertaining as I did."

Jamal hung up and walked away. He entered the bookstore and slipped the oversized volume from the shelf. The illustrations were gruesome, depicting methods of torture dating back to the Dark Ages. Jamal found them tame. He had already placed a piece of clear tape across the key; now he placed the key in the center of the book and pressed the tape firmly to the page. Carefully, he returned the book to its place on the shelf, making sure to push it all the way back so the spine was less visible.

Jamal checked his watch. Seven minutes had passed since he'd hung up. He exited by the doors that opened onto the National Postal Museum across the street. The cab he got into was pulling away from the curb just as the first of the black Suburbans caromed around the corner.

"Where to?" the cabbie asked.

Jamal glanced through the rearview, envisioning the impending chaos. "The Hilton."

He remembered that the Hilton advertised a nice all-day buffet on Sundays.

* * *

The Secret Service communications specialist needed another sixteen seconds to complete the trace.

"It doesn't matter," Landau said, listening to the playback. "That's Jamal's voice."

"How can you be sure?" Reece demanded.

"Because he wants us to find what he's left for us."

"I still have to send the bomb squad in," Casey said.

"A waste of time. Where are your men?"

"They should be at the station now."

"May I suggest you tell them to pick up the key. Then let me open the locker."

Casey shook his head. "You have a death wish?"

"No," Landau replied. "But bringing in the bomb squad would cost us valuable time. The sooner we know what Jamal wants and how he wants it, the more time we have to fashion a response." He paused. "If Jamal lied, if the locker is wired, he will be very pleased that I was the one who took him at his word."

Landau glanced at Reece. "If I should be blown into the next world, promise me you will slap Jamal's face. Just a slap. It's a terrible insult. It will be like me spitting at him from the grave."

Casey continued to shake his head. "Slapping, spitting—you people are crazy."

"Then get me down there and let's do this thing."

Casey turned to Reece as Landau swept out of the room. "*Is* he crazy?"

"As a loon. But he's *our* crazy."

The ride to Union Station took less than fifteen minutes. The two agents sent in to retrieve the key were waiting outside. One held the key by its edges between thumb and forefinger.

"In case you wanted fingerprints," he said.

"We know whose we'll find." Landau turned to Casey. "Tell them to give me the key."

Casey stamped from one foot to the other. "Collins, Johnson, get everybody away from the locker area. Fifty feet minimum. And out of those stores. Too much damned glass."

The station was strangely quiet when Landau finally walked inside. Yellow tape cordoned off the locker area. The surrounding retailers were empty, doors locked. The slap of leather-soled shoes sounded like gunshots.

"The media are on the way," Casey said conversationally as he walked beside Landau. "It'd be nice if you could get the damn thing before they arrive and we could all get out of here."

"I see. So now it would be nice."

"You know what I mean."

"Ten minutes."

Fifty feet from the lockers, Casey put his hand on Landau's shoulder. "Good luck." He handed him the key.

Landau examined the key as he walked on. It looked like any one of a million others, no special cuts or abrasions, no filaments or coating to indicate that it had been tampered with.

In front of the locker now, the keyhole almost exactly at eye level. Had

Jamal chosen this locker deliberately, for its height? *If he wants to blow my head off, yes.*

Landau thought there was something Jamal wanted much more than that: Landau alive to hear or read the demands, to feel sick and outraged—above all, helpless. This was mother's milk to him.

Once in motion, Landau did not stop. The key went in and turned smoothly. Landau pulled open the door, saw the envelope, picked it up, and turned on his heel.

He did not check the envelope, but the thought occurred that Jamal could still toy with him, coat the adhesive in the flap with a minuscule charge, enough to tear off Landau's arm.

"At least let me put it through a fluoroscope," Casey called out.

A portable version of the machine had been wheeled in and set up next to a candy store. The technician was bulked out in protective gear that made him look like an astronaut.

Landau placed the envelope on the tray and watched the technician roll it through the machine. The buttons lit up one by one, all green.

Using a three-inch stiletto, Casey slit open one end of the envelope and, using gloves, pulled out legal-size sheets that had come off a laser printer.

"What are those numbers on the envelope?" Landau asked.

Casey's voice was dead. "The kid's MedicAlert registration. Only one of its kind. I guess we're hearing from the right people."

* * *

Al-Rahim had no respect for the woman. Neither did he fear her. To him, Manar Hassan was a Western whore, the kind he saw occasionally in the white-slave-trading cellars throughout the Middle East. Only she was uglier.

But some time had passed since al-Rahim had been with a woman. Watching her move about the kitchen, preparing food for the prisoners, stirred him.

Al-Rahim's next act almost cost him his hand. The woman was by the sink, bent over slightly. The Arab reached out and ran his fingertips along her buttocks. He felt her twist, was ready to grab her hand when she tried to slap him, as he anticipated she would. What he didn't anticipate was the ten-inch chef's utility knife she snatched up as she whirled around, the blade slicing the dust motes, flashing by his eyes.

Al-Rahim looked down at the bracelet of blood on his wrist, saw the sinews in her arm tauten like cables as she poised to cut deeper. He could not hold back his terror, saw its reflection in her eyes, the satisfaction it gave her, the shame it heaped on him.

"Get out!" Judith hissed.

When he was gone, she put down the knife and ran cool water over her wrists. Although her mind raced, her hands were steady. This was not the first time she had handled a knife, and Issim had taught her well.

Judith dried her hands and finished making lunch. She wondered how people could eat such spongelike bread, and vegetables that were artificially colored and tasteless. When the soup was ready, she placed everything on a tray, along with plastic spoons and forks. Jamal had been clear on that: no metal cutlery.

Ben heard the creaks on the staircase. He glanced at Kim, who nodded. Ben had hoped that he would get one shot at the woman when she was alone. It was the only real chance he and the boy had.

Ben had heard the exchange in the kitchen between Judith and the Arab. He tried to put images to the angry words and thought that the Arab might have made a pass at her. Whatever had happened, it had created a fissure between the kidnappers. Kim had told him as much as he could about Judith Sawyer, comments and impressions that Ben folded into what he already knew. Now, Ben thought hard about how he might exploit this new antagonism.

Judith set the tray on the dresser. Ben watched as her eyes flickered over him, as though she didn't want to linger, then settled on the boy. She remained silent, but her movements around the boy were tender, maternal. She felt his forehead, then reached around and fluffed his pillow.

"Hello, Kim."

"Hi, Miss Sawyer."

"Are you feeling better? Your temperature is almost normal."

"I'm okay. Thanks."

Ben was pleased. The boy was playing it just as they had scripted it: polite, but not too friendly.

"Would you like soup first, or the sandwich?"

"The sandwich, please."

Judith set a paper plate where Kim could reach it with his free hand.

"What about me?" Ben asked.

His voice seemed to startle her, as if she'd been pretending that he didn't exist. Wordlessly, she set a paper plate within his reach.

Ben took a bite and spoke to her back. "This is good. It'll help with the blood."

That got her attention. When she turned her head, Ben locked eyes with her.

"You didn't know? Jamal never told you that he tried to bleed me dry? An inducement to get me to talk." She turned away, and he hurried on. "Don't believe me? See for yourself." He rattled the cuffs, then heard Kim say, "It's true, Miss Sawyer. That's why he looks so white."

For a moment, Judith didn't stir. She rose to remove Kim's plate, then hesitated before picking up the soup. Turning to Ben, she lifted his arm as if it were a slab of meat. But her mouth fell open when she saw the gauze and tape.

"Go ahead, remove it. Jamal was a doctor, wasn't he? He knew just how far he could bleed me before I'd lose consciousness. He was careful not to let that happen."

She let go of his arm as though it were maggot-infested.

Judith returned to the boy, sat him up, and began spooning him the soup. Ben forced himself to eat half a sandwich.

"How does it feel to be back home, Judith?" he asked, his tone light. He let a beat go by. "Lots of changes, I bet. Were you planning to stop off at the university, see if your pals are still around? How surprised *they* must have been when you didn't show up for the flight home—what was it, eight, nine years ago?"

He tossed the questions as lightly as he would a softball. When she kept her back to him, he knew he had to prick her deeper.

"Was he everything you ever dreamed of, Judith?"

He saw the spoon stop in midair. At last, she turned around.

"What could you possibly know?"

"Maybe not so much. But more than you think." She went back to feeding the boy. "I'm sorry for your loss, Judith, as long ago as it was. I'm sorry for what you're doing now."

Jamal had warned her not to talk to either of them. Yet, a part of her revolted against this. Maybe if she hadn't seen the bandage on his arm . . . He wasn't lying about having been bled. Jamal was perfectly capable of inflicting such cruelty.

"I'm doing what is necessary," she heard herself say. "What is just."

"Because of what happened to your husband and son?"

"You don't know what happened to them!" she said fiercely. "You know nothing!"

She returned to the dresser, rattling the spoon against the soup bowl, and was ready to pick up the tray when Ben called out: "Samarra. Israeli helicopters coming out of the night. Your home on fire, your life burning away."

Judith swept the tray from the dresser. *"Who are you?"*

"An orphan," Ben told her. "Jamal murdered my parents."

She hadn't known that, he was sure. Her shock was genuine. Ben spoke quickly now, not knowing how long he could hold her attention.

"Did you know a man called Mustafa Manshur?"

"No."

"Your husband never mentioned him? Maybe Jamal did?"

She shook her head.

Ben sketched out for her what had happened in Paris and then later by the Kennedy Center.

"Why are you telling me this?" Judith cried. "It's meaningless—"

"No, it's not. Because Mustafa Manshur told my father that Jamal would be in Samarra that day."

"Ridiculous!"

"My father kept a record, on disk. He was a careful, organized man."

"Even if he knew about Samarra, what difference does that make?"

"A lot. Because it wasn't Jamal who was killed, was it?"

Color drained from her face as the realization slammed into her consciousness.

"Why, Judith?" Ben asked softly. "Why was Jamal not in Samarra when *Manshur* knew he would be? When my *father* knew? When the *Israelis* knew? There was no mention of Issim Hassan anywhere, by anyone. No one expected him to be there. Certainly, no one thought he would be." He paused. "Where was Jamal, Judith?"

She looked away, as though staring through a window into the past. "Riding. I saw him coming out of the sun. He was riding and then the helicopters came."

"My father never figured out why your husband was killed. There was no reason for the Israelis to get rid of him. He was a moderate, someone they could actually talk to at the peace table. So why would Israeli helicopters go to Samarra if Issim Hassan wasn't supposed to be there—if there was no reason to hurt him or his family? Who *was* supposed to be there, Judith?"

"Stop it!"

"Jamal. Only Jamal. But he wasn't alone. He brought along his best friend, his comrade, his brother-in-his-arms. And the brother's wife, their child. How did he manage that, Judith? What did he say to get Issim down there? The reason must have seemed innocent . . ."

The words were like acid eating away at the mistruth in which she had clothed herself. Judith felt its fabric dissolve, felt the sting of the words on her flesh. It was the sting that forced her to remember. Here was Jamal speaking.

"Tonight, but later. When we reach our destination."

Now she: *"Destination? Where are we going?"*

And Jamal: *". . . this may be an unnecessary precaution. But old habits . . . Arrangements have been made in another place . . ."*

A place called Samarra.

"The reason must have been innocent." The reason was a precaution, an old habit. An excuse Issim would never have questioned, suspected, or doubted.

Because Jamal was like a brother, and one brother would never betray another.

"Judith, listen to me."

She started, glancing over her shoulder at the far corner; she could have sworn that the voice had come from there.

"Judith . . ."

Throwing his voice had worked, unsettling her enough so that when he spoke a second time, Ben had her attention. Now, it was his timing, her vulnerability.

"It was Jamal. It couldn't have been anyone else. Jamal does not believe in what your husband did, but he craves what Issim Hassan possessed—the power and charisma. He craves to become the leader Issim would have become. Now, having the boy, he can satisfy that craving. Jamal wants to *be* Issim Hassan. But he couldn't be, not as long as Issim was alive!"

She flinched, as though his words pummeled her.

"He lured Issim to Samarra. He *knew* whom he left on the tether. And he was careful, wasn't he? Careful with you. There were horses for you in Samarra. He knew you loved to ride in the dawn, alone. He told you about the horses the night before, didn't he? He wanted you away from the house. He offered you something irresistible . . . Then he let the Israelis come and kill for him."

"Stop it!" Judith screamed.

Ben heard voices downstairs, then pounding feet. He had only seconds left.

"You are a prisoner, Judith! As much as Kim and I. Test me on this. Tell them you want to walk along the bay shore. The path goes on for miles, no one around. See if they let you—"

Al-Rahim burst into the room, his pistol looking like a child's toy in his hand. "I heard shouting."

Judith picked up the tray. "It's nothing. This one"—she tossed her head in Ben's direction—"was rude to me. But now he, like you, knows better. Come, take this for me."

She thrust the tray at al-Rahim, who had no choice but to take it.

After the door closed, after a moment's silence, Kim said, "Ben, you're crazy."

"But did I get through to her? Will she at least try?"

"Take the walk?"

"Yeah."

"She will."

"How—?"

"She's a teacher. I know about teachers."

Thirty-two

THE FBI HAS SOME of the best hair and fiber and latent-prints experts in the world. They were set up and waiting in the subbasement of the White House when Jamal's three-page missive was delivered.

The technician had a long sheet of fine white paper spread across his worktable. Above it was a row of powerful spotlights. He draped each page, one at a time, over a dowel and peered at it through a powerful magnifying glass. Then he lightly tapped the paper with a spatula to dislodge any debris—hair follicles, tiny grains of dirt, carpet or upholstery fibers.

"Your boy was very careful," the technician pronounced. "The only thing left behind was some cellulose fiber that came off the envelope. Sorry."

Latent Prints struck out too.

"The laser pulled up two skin-oil smudges," the technician told Casey. "But they're old. I'm thinking that someone besides your guy handled the paper—maybe the clerk who sold it to him, or another customer. You know how this stuff is displayed at copy shops, piles of it. I wouldn't bet the skin oils would match those of your guy. But we'll test him when you break his ass."

Casey appreciated the vote of confidence.

The Secret Service Documents Section took over from there. The paper was identified as a Hammermill brand manufactured especially for laser printers—in this case, a Hewlett-Packard desktop model. The ink was blended by Lippincott.

"Not so good," the Service tech told Casey. "The paper is made in lots of a hundred thousand sheets and is distributed cross-country. The printer can be picked up at any Office Depot or variation thereof. The ink comes in standard cartridges and is brewed in sixty-thousand-gallon vats. Your boy could have gotten this stuff anywhere."

Casey went to the conference room and presented his findings.

"Nice try," he told Landau.

Landau had pushed for the scientific analysis on the off chance that Jamal had gotten careless and let one of his accomplices handle the letter. Landau had quietly pointed out that Jamal and Judith had to have operational support. Two people couldn't possibly manage everything that needed to be done. It would have been useful to narrow down the number and identities of the supporting cast. Quite possibly, Landau might have had prior dealings with them.

Casey led Reece and Landau into the Oval Office. Charles Woodbridge and his wife were sitting side by side on the couch. He was holding her arm as she read the letter.

Casey cleared his throat. "Forensics can't help us, Mr. President."

Woodbridge seemed not to hear him, then stirred. "We didn't expect they would, did we? We know who we're dealing with."

Mary Woodbridge let the pages slip from her hand to the carpet. The President leaned down and picked them up.

"You can't give him what he wants, can you, Charlie?" the First Lady said. She looked at Landau. "And you can't find my son, so Jamal will kill him."

"Mary—"

"Don't bullshit me, Charlie. Okay? Not where Kim's concerned."

To Landau, the President seemed to deflate. His fine political skills counted for nothing. His powers of persuasion, debate, and horse-trading were useless before the woman who probably knew them better than he did.

"We have something, Mrs. Woodbridge," Landau said. "Not much, but something."

She gazed at him as though he were an interesting but repulsive specimen in a zoo cage.

"And what would that be, Mr. Landau?"

"Jamal has given us a timetable. Certain demands he makes can be met without compromising your government—and doing so would demonstrate good faith. This would help keep your boy safe."

"Go on."

Landau proceeded carefully. Yakov Admony had warned him that the Americans would bridle at being told what to do. Landau's job was to advise, not dictate.

"Jamal wants the President to issue a statement for the early evening news," he said. "To the effect that a major policy announcement will be made tomorrow, Monday. He also wants both the United Nations and its Security Council alerted to an emergency session to be held no later than Tuesday."

"Where are you going with this?" Charles Woodbridge demanded. "I can't make any damn 'policy announcement.'"

"Mr. President, Jamal has left us some . . . I believe you call it 'wiggle room.' He does not specify the exact text of the announcement. I believe that is an oversight on his part. He would have made it harder, if not impossible, for you to act if he had included a text. As it is, would it not be possible for you to issue just the kind of statement he desires? You announce the unveiling of a new policy. Period. No details of any kind. No defining whom or what part of the world this policy will affect, when it will be implemented, or its purpose or duration."

"Keep it vague," Charles Woodbridge murmured.

"Exactly."

"There will still be questions—not from the media, but from members of Congress."

"It's Sunday night, Mr. President. Certainly, your congressmen will be curious, but will they badger you for details? I think not. After all, you might be referring to the political situation in the Balkans or the financial troubles in Asia. Who's to say?"

"Nonetheless, I'm still committed to say *something* the next day."

"There are a lot of hours until then," Landau said softly.

"I see where you're going with this, Mr. Landau," the First Lady spoke up. "You're holding out the carrot of a rescue operation. But you don't know where to begin. You haven't a clue as to where Jamal is hiding, do you?"

Landau steeled himself not to glance at Kaelin Reece. Priestly's report on the homicide in the Poltareks' apartment had been delivered only an hour ago. There hadn't been time to get to it and now he was sorry he hadn't done so.

"No, madam. I don't know where Jamal has your son."

"Tell me, Mr. Landau. Would it be such a terrible thing for Israel to give Jamal a part of what he wants?" Mary Woodbridge demanded, her voice rising. "Wasn't the creation of a Palestinian state the reason behind the Oslo Accords?"

It came, just as he'd known it would. Landau hurried to say his piece before the President, pained, found a gentle way to quiet his wife.

"The Oslo Accords, yes. Mrs. Woodbridge, imagine Fifth Avenue in New York. Imagine that east of it live a people who, in fifty years, built up the thriving area they now call home. Then other people arrived, settled on the West Side, demanded to call it their home. But that was not enough: They wanted to cross Fifth Avenue, take the East Side, too.

"I do not exaggerate. The boundary between Israel and the West Bank is not much larger than Fifth Avenue. Terrorists, killers, saboteurs cross it every day. Would you stand for such an arrangement, Mrs. Woodbridge? Would you allow your kin to live under such a threat? Because that is exactly what Hafez Jamal is—a threat. He will not go away, he will not be reasoned with, he will not be appeased. He has told you what he wants, but believe me, these are only his first demands. If your husband were to cloak him in America's power, if he were to legitimize the man and his aspirations, he would be planting the seeds of so much terrible bloodshed—"

"That's enough!"

Charles Woodbridge's voice sounded like a gunshot. He settled back a little when his wife touched his arm.

"Your input and expertise are appreciated, Mr. Landau," he said formally. "As are yours, Agent Reece. However, dealing with Jamal's demands is my responsibility. Yours is to find out where he's holding my son."

Dismissal was implicit in his words.

Using his bulk like a tugboat, Casey steered them out.

"You were out of line in there," he told Landau.

"People who haven't had personal experience with terrorists have no idea what they're dealing with," Landau replied harshly. "I didn't want her to think Jamal was some carpet merchant she could haggle with."

"No, you wanted her to know that Jamal is the Antichrist. That's your agenda: to paint him black. For God's sake, Landau. He's holding her son!"

In his mind's eye, Landau saw a barbwire perimeter fence running along the West Bank, swinging around by south Lebanon, encircling Israel like a noose, slowly squeezing, choking . . .

"I wanted her to know that no Jew is going to sit at a conference table and let someone sell out other Jews. End of agenda."

In the Oval Office, Charles Woodbridge stood beside his desk, gazing out across the lawn. The weak sun caught and cast shadows of the roving guards.

"You never answered me, Charlie," Mary Woodbridge called to him. "You can't force the Israelis, can you?"

Woodbridge ran his fingertips over the telephone console. Touch one button and he could have the best minds in the nation either inside his office or on the line. Except that no amount of advice could sever the Gordian knot under which his life and his wife's lay. Advisers would propose, argue, debate, bleat, scream, and for what? He knew what *could* be done. He knew what *had* to be done. The tragedy was that they were mutually exclusive.

"Jamal is asking me to carve up a country, this from a terrorist kidnapper who also wants me to sponsor him as a statesman."

"Couldn't you go along for a little while, at least until we get Kim back?"

"Jamal won't give Kim back until I stand up in front of the whole world and support him. Do you realize the political firestorm that would unleash—here and around the world?"

Mary Woodbridge held back the obvious retort. Her husband didn't deserve it. He wasn't putting the nation's interests before those of his child; he just couldn't find a way to give them equal footing.

"If I go to the U.N., bully Israel, I might be able to get Kim back. Then I could announce that everything had been done under terrible duress, that none of the agreements were valid. Our credibility would be finished. Oh, sure, most people would make all the right noises, but what would be going through their minds the next time we sat down to bargain or sign a treaty?"

"I want Kim back, Charlie. I know the rest of it. Just tell me how we get him back. Do that and I'll support any decision you make . . . that you can make."

The President looked across the row. "Jamal is like a water moccasin living in your boat shed. Landau is our king snake. He's the only play we have, Mary. He has to find out where Jamal has hidden Kim."

"After that?"

"After that the SEAL team goes in to get him."

*   *   *

The Americans liked him even less now, if that were possible. Landau saw it in the set expressions of Casey and the others. Even Reece was keeping her distance, telling him she had a meeting to attend at the Hoover Building, pointedly giving no details. Clearly, his presence was neither required nor desired.

"The Service will notify us as soon as Jamal makes contact again," Reece said as she and Landau walked to her car in the underground garage.

Landau thought she might be trying to mollify him. He watched her dig the key into the door lock.

"Priestly's file," he reminded her.

"It's in the back seat."

Landau got it out himself and was surprised when she fired up the engine. "Aren't you going to take me back to the embassy?"

Reece pointed at the Service agent who'd escorted them out and who, Landau now realized, had never left.

"He'll take you. I gotta run. I'll call if I hear anything."

The Service agent swung the car onto Pennsylvania when Landau told him, "I've changed my mind."

Ten minutes later, he found himself standing in front of Rachel's century-old townhouse in Georgetown, with its brass vase, filled with flowers, where the knocker was usually affixed. The door opened even before he touched it.

"Are you going to stand there, or do you want to come in."

Rachel stood framed by the doorway, in jeans, sweatshirt, her red hair a flaming ponytail. Landau thought she looked exquisite.

"Anything?"

"No, I'm sorry."

Landau followed her into the living room. Shaker furniture and cheerful Indian rugs, flowers and plants in gaily painted ceramic vases. A private side of Rachel he'd never seen: her refuge. The television was tuned to CNN.

"I've been watching the news," she said. "They're saying it was an attempted robbery gone bad."

Anger tinged her words; Landau could feel their heat.

"They have to say something, Rachel."

"But why say Ben is 'missing'? How could he be missing when you know Jamal has him?"

Landau measured exactly how much she didn't know. He understood that nothing but the truth would work here, if he wanted her help.

"Would you make us tea? This will take a little while."

He told her about Kim Woodbridge as she fussed with the tea. He wanted her hands busy, her mind focused on minutiae as he laid out the terrible facts as impassively as a blackjack dealer servicing his players. He monitored how deeply the horror bit into her, how much poison it secreted, how she fought to expunge it. By the time he was finished, the tea had cooled. He sipped it slowly, measuring her stillness.

"The news people haven't connected Ben to the President's son," she said at last.

"No."

"They're hunting for the boy."

"With difficulty."

"And so Ben doesn't matter a whole lot, does he? Jamal has him, but no one cares. He might be dead, but no one cares."

"You care. So do I."

Rachel laughed bitterly. "No, you don't. You think that if you find the boy, you'll find Ben. If it comes to a choice—who lives, who dies—you would sacrifice Ben."

"The President has the best troops standing by. It doesn't take much imagination to figure out what their orders are." He paused. "But maybe there's still a way for us to help him."

She was wary of him, like an animal who's been abused too many times but can't refuse the proffered hand. *Not if it means helping Ben.*

"What are you saying?"

Instead, he showed her Priestly's file, pages thick with glued photographs, rife with bad grammar and spelling mistakes.

"I don't understand," Rachel said as she riffled through it.

"Priestly did a lot of background on Ben," Landau said. "Here's the problem: I don't know Ben. Neither does Reece. I think Priestly discovered something that Jamal is using, but I can't recognize it. I'm hoping you can."

* * *

Jamal finished his brunch at the Hilton, paid, and went to the meeting rooms and conference halls on the second floor. Two hours had passed. More than enough time. He found the bank of telephones.

"I wish to speak with Kim Woodbridge."

The White House operator answered smartly, "Yes, sir." Jamal knew she wasn't an operator at all. He surmised that after his first call Secret Service agents would have replaced the switchboard personnel.

"This is Robert Stone."

"And who might you be, Robert Stone?"

"Would you please tell me what you sent, sir, as well as the alphanumeric code."

Jamal recited Kim's MedicAlert ID numbers. "There are no letters," he added. "Now. Who are you?"

"My name is Robert Stone. I'm a Secret Service negotiator."

"Hostage negotiator."

"In this case, yes."

"Am I to understand that the President will make an announcement in a few hours?"

"Preparations are under way. But we need—"

"Something in return? You already have it, Mr. Stone. The boy's MedicAlert number."

"We need to know the boy is alive. *I* need to know what your name is, or what you want me to call you."

"Don't waste time, Mr. Stone. You know who I am. You know that the woman who abducted Kim Woodbridge is Judith Sawyer. That is all the confirmation you get until I hear the President speak. After that, I will provide evidence that his son is alive and well."

"We need assurances—"

"No more than I do, Mr. Stone. You are familiar with my message to the President. It is not in my interest to hurt the boy. Surely you have concluded that much. Give me what I want and I shall return the gesture. Goodbye, Mr. Stone. I will speak to you after the announcement."

In the White House crisis room, three stories beneath the swimming pool, Robert Stone peeled off his featherweight headset. He was a middle-aged man who, because of his sedentary job, was starting to run to fat. His voice was as gentle and calm as a baby's breath; his eyes were as blue as arctic ice. Robert Stone had been a negotiator for fifteen years, first with the FBI, now with the Service. During his career, he'd lost only three prisoners in hostage situations. He considered each of these failures a personal affront and swore that he would never experience another. He would get Kim Woodbridge back, no matter what.

"What do you think, Bobby?" Casey asked.

Stone rolled back his executive-style chair. He was surrounded by monitoring and tracing equipment, lines to Quantico, the SEAL force, and the Oval Office. Too damn much equipment.

"Tell the President to make the announcement," he said softly.

Casey shifted uncomfortably. "I don't mean to tell you your business, Bobby. But you've spoken to the guy only once. We have psyche evaluations coming—"

Stone held up his hand, gestured at the files stacked like a parapet around his desk. "I'm knee-deep in profiles. A lot of them are based on the same sources, most are repetitive. This guy knows exactly what he wants, Steve. He has the means to get it. If the President tries to do an end run, Jamal will spot it and send us the kid's thumbs."

Stone studied the perforated soundproof ceiling tiles. "He's thought this through so well. He knows we won't go public with the kidnapping. He knows that if the President refuses his demands, he kills the boy and crows about it later."

"Crows?"

"You bet. If Jamal doesn't get his nation-state, he'll make sure the world knows that he waltzed into D.C. and plucked the kid right from under our noses. In one stroke, he'll be the most feared and admired terrorist in the world. A lot of wannabes will think that if Jamal could get away with it, well . . ."

"He'll be feared and admired until we drop his ass in a grave," Casey said tightly.

"You probably will. But by then it'll be too late. Jamal will have set an example, a precedent for the rest of them."

"Are you saying you won't be able to negotiate this guy down?"

Stone shook his head. "What I can do is help keep Kim Woodbridge alive. But Jamal will never let me get close enough to go one-on-one with him. He'll never stay on the line long enough to give us a location. So unless you have some magic up your sleeve and can get a hard fix on him, you tell the President that the only way his son stays alive is if he starts to give Jamal what he wants."

Jamal was following very much the same logic pattern, except his focus was on Stone and the men around him. His years of medical training had included a generous amount of psychology and clinical psychiatry vineyards in which hostage negotiators toiled. As he strolled to the Hilton's front entrance, Jamal was quite certain he hadn't left any bolt-hole for Robert Stone to escape into, then circle back and pounce on him. Stone would recommend that the President obey Jamal's directives. There was no other choice.

The thought of possessing such leverage over the most powerful man in the world thrilled Jamal. His mood bordered on euphoria as he slipped into a taxi under the hotel portico. There was plenty of time to get to Union Station and catch the train to Baltimore, where Hatem would meet him. Then it was back to the Chesapeake house to wait for the inevitable.

* * *

Judith washed the dishes from lunch and set them out to dry on the rubber draining rack. The task had taken her longer than usual because she scrubbed each plate and glass thoroughly, sometimes cleaning the same piece twice. She was not conscious of doing this. All she could think of, all she heard, was Ben Poltarek's voice in her head, a gristmill grinding away at her belief in Hafez Jamal.

Judith dried her hands and stepped out onto the front porch. Al-Rahim sat on a dusty rocker at the end of the porch, gnawing on a left-over piece of mutton. In front of her were stairs to a dirt path that swung away from the house and disappeared into the tall grasses. Beyond, she made out part of a dock and some of the rocky beach Ben Poltarek had described.

The wind felt cool on her face, and the sea salt beckoned her. All she had to do was step off the porch and head down the path. Then she would be certain that Poltarek hadn't lied to her.

The wide planks covering the dirt path creaked beneath her weight; the grasses and reeds brushed against her legs like cats seeking attention. She could see the whole of the small dock now, the beach, and the shoreline. It was just as Poltarek said it would be, so peaceful and lovely—

"Stop! Do not go further."

The guttural voice startled her. Judith turned and saw Al-Rahim standing on the porch.

"I am going for a walk."

"You cannot. Jamal does not permit it. He wants you to stay in the house."

Involuntarily, Judith laughed. "He does not permit it? How stupid of him."

She took two more strides before an overhanging tree branch snapped off and fell at her feet. The second shot from al-Rahim's silenced pistol spun by her ear and buried itself in the tree.

Trembling, Judith faced him. "Hafez will kill you for that."

She couldn't believe that he was laughing at her.

"Kill me? No, slut. When Hafez has completed his mission, he will *give* you to me. Then I will teach you to be useful and obedient."

Her shock and fear amused him. "Oh, yes. You think of yourself as the famous grieving widow of a noble man. Fool! Issim Hassan is only a memory. His name will be like dust upon the wind when Jamal is finished. The memory of a slain hero will no longer protect you. Now, go back into the house and prepare food. Jamal and Hatem will return soon. Do it swiftly if you wish to keep your knees."

Because Judith knew he was mad, she obeyed. Inside the house, she gave silent thanks that he did not follow her. She forced herself to move quickly about the kitchen, setting the food out on the counter so that if al-Rahim looked in, he would be satisfied. Next, she filled a water jug, set it and two plastic glasses on a tray. She held her breath as she passed through the foyer, relieved to hear the creak of the rocker on the porch. The squeaks masked her footsteps all the way up to the master bedroom, where she looked at Jamal's captives and in their eyes saw herself.

Thirty-three

Upstairs in the bedroom, Ben looked across at Kim Woodbridge. The boy's face was pinched white, his eyes rolling in fear.

"Do you think she's dead?" Kim whispered.

Ben shook his head. "Listen . . . The door, the footsteps."

The porch door had a peculiar squeak and the footsteps were light. Judith Sawyer was still alive. And with her, the plan he'd fashioned out of spit and desperation.

With Jamal and one Arab gone, that had left only two people in the house. Using the swinging porch door as his guide, Ben was able to judge when Judith and the second Arab were outside. He used the interval to creep into the closet and take inventory of what was in the bag Kim had lugged down from the closet. Ben removed certain items and hid them in the bedroom dresser, where they would be within easy reach when the time came. There were other things in the attic he could use, but they were bulky. If the opportunity presented itself, he would get to them.

Ben had been walking Kim through the plan for a third time when they heard the Arab on the porch shouting for Judith to stop, and her contemptuous response. They did not hear the muffled shot, but the cracking and falling of the tree limb was distinctive and clear. The Arab's curses and threats followed. That was when Kim had asked if Judith was dead.

"Listen," Ben whispered. "Water running in the pipes. She's in the kitchen."

Then footfalls in the foyer and steps on the staircase.

"Close your eyes," Ben said. "If you don't, she'll know you over-heard."

Ben pretended to be startled when the door opened. Judith entered as a night nurse might glide to the bed of a sleeping child. When she touched Kim's forehead, the boy stirred but did not open his eyes.

Silently, Judith held up a glass of water in front of Ben, who nodded. He forced himself to sip slowly through the straw.

"Thank you."

No response, and now she was turning to leave. Ben wondered about the fortitude it took to maintain her dignity in the face of a big, crazy man with a gun who, when the time was right, would take pleasure in brutalizing her. He asked himself how much of it Judith had already expended, how much she had left. Maybe it would be enough.

"Judith."

She caught a different timbre in his voice and responded to it. Ben cleansed his eyes of fear before he looked up at her.

"Under the bed, by the post."

She was wary, coming around and kneeling by the bed in such a way as to always keep his free arm in sight. Her fingers curled around something hard, made of plastic. When she pulled it out, she found herself holding a small, executive-style tape recorder.

*   *   *

The FBI had sent "bullets" to every field office in the nation. The subject was Judith Nancy Sawyer, an American citizen born in Laguna Beach, California, wanted for questioning. Calls had poured in after that. Was the "bullet" incomplete? There was no mention of what Sawyer was wanted for or where she had last been seen. The reply from the Hoover Building was terse: Sawyer was wanted—period. The SACs in the field offices were to dig deep and hard, pulling in as much manpower as they needed.

The break came in the big New York field office. The computers didn't strike on Judith Sawyer immediately, but they lit up a Lester Sawyer. Sawyer had made it into the federal data bank because years ago, in a Manhattan federal court, he had blown his brains out on the witness stand.

Within minutes, the computers had made the correlation and the results were flashed to Steve Casey at the White House.

"Shithouse mouse!" Casey muttered, staring at the fax sheet in his hands.

His heart rate had rocketed when the Bureau warned him that hard information about Judith Sawyer was on the way. Now he wished he'd never seen it.

Casey walked out of the communications room and took the elevator to the family quarters. Charles Woodbridge was in his study, watching the winds sweep away what was left of the gray afternoon. Casey had hoped to see the President alone, but Mary Woodbridge came out of the master suite just as he was about to close the study door behind him.

"You have something," the First Lady said, her back against the closed door.

Casey winced. He hadn't had time to prepare himself for her.

The President gestured toward the faxes. "Steve?"

"Background on Judith Sawyer."

Hope sprang into Woodbridge's eyes. "Something we can use?"

"Mr. President . . . Sir, do you remember your days with Watson, Frick and Marshall?"

"My old law firm. I started with them right out of law school, back in the early seventies."

"Do you recall a case you handled in January 1975?"

"Steve, what the hell are you talking about?"

"Do you remember, sir?"

Woodbridge swept his fingers through his hair. "Jesus, 1975."

"A case you second-chaired . . ."

Woodbridge snapped his fingers. "The embezzlement case. Who was the guy?"

Casey pitied both of them as the awful realization leeched the color of the President's face, as his wife, set to miss nothing, was at his side, her questions shrill, insistent.

"What's he talking about, Charlie? What case?"

Woodbridge didn't take his eyes off Casey. "Sawyer?" he managed. "*Lester* Sawyer?"

"She's his daughter."

Woodbridge took a moment to compose himself. When he could, he described to his wife the grisly events that had occurred when he had Lester Sawyer on the witness stand. Casey saw that she, too, remembered.

"Oh my God," Mary Woodbridge whispered. She turned to Casey. "She's the daughter. There's no mistake?"

Casey shook his head.

The First Lady gripped her husband's arm. "*She* has our son? Why . . . ?"

"Because her father was set up. Sawyer was innocent, Mary. He was *co-operating* with the feds. He wasn't an embezzler . . ." His voice broke. "But it was my business to paint him as one. The people he was accusing would have gone to jail unless I broke Sawyer's credibility."

"You never told me *any* of this," his wife shouted. "You said he was sick, deranged. You never said his daughter was in the courtroom!"

"What did you want me to tell you?" Woodbridge whispered. "That I had deliberately destroyed an innocent man? A man who, by virtue of his suicide, *became* guilty in everyone's eyes? A man I could have saved, but didn't? Jesus, Mary. I was terrified of what you'd think of me. I kept asking myself how—or even if—you could still love someone like that. So no, I couldn't tell you. I didn't have the courage. I wouldn't take the risk."

"But she has," Mary Woodbridge said stonily. "After all these years, she's come back to punish you. Us. She came and took our child, Charlie! Knowing what we know now, do *you* think we'll ever see Kim alive?"

Casey moved because of training and instinct, but he stopped just short of laying a finger on Mary Woodbridge. The sound of her palm striking the President's cheek was like a gunshot. Then she was running, the echoes of doors slamming in the hall.

Immediately, agents started calling Casey, who gave them the code word for a domestic spat. He kept his eyes averted as the President slumped down in his chair.

"I'll make the announcement, Steve," he heard Woodbridge say. "I'll do any fucking thing I have to to keep my boy alive. Give me five minutes, then send up the chief of staff."

*   *   *

Rachel had never had a problem concentrating. She'd had roommates in college and med school who cranked up the stereo or the television. None of it had ever gotten to her.

With Landau, it was different—and he wasn't even in the same room. She was in the kitchen, working on her second cup of tea; he was in the living room, she assumed. That's where she'd last seen him, but just because she hadn't heard him didn't mean that he hadn't moved. She didn't think that anyone had ever really heard him move.

She was on her third pass through Priestly's thick file. The detective had a lot of background on Ben—school records, legal experience; trips, domestic and foreign, holidays and business; real estate records on his townhouse, including information on the contractors who were doing the rehab.

To Rachel, it seemed excessive, even in the context of a homicide investigation. Of course, it was a great deal more than that, as Landau had pointed out. But whatever Priestly had been looking for, it must have been something particular—something that might prove useful and maybe had.

Rachel looked up from the file to rest her eyes. Everything she'd known about Ben and his parents was in here. She knew a whole lot more, too—Rose's favorite perfume, Sid's preferred brand of cigars, the way Ben cupped her below the small of her back when they made love. Making love the day he'd bought his townhouse, before the remodeling started, on an old sofa that shook and wheezed.

Rachel smiled. She looked down at the page, but the words were blurred. Her mind was elsewhere.

Ben's townhouse . . . Not the renovations. Him buying it. The transaction. Something odd he'd said when he was going through the process. *But not about himself. This had nothing to do with him.*

Rachel brushed the air with her fingers, as though shooing away a fly. What she wanted was circling just beyond her grasp. She knew better than to press.

Rachel read three more pages, trying to ignore her frustration. Then suddenly she flipped back to the part about real estate. Ben joking that he would leave it to her in his will because that way . . .

She snatched up the phone and dialed the Poltareks' law office. Mary, the office manager, answered on the second ring.

"Mary, it's Rachel."

A moment of exchanging condolences, another taken up with Rachel fibbing that Ben was fine, he was out of the city for a few days, she was joining him tonight. And by the way, Mary. . . .

Rachel hung up the phone and was very still. In her mind's eye, she beheld what Mary had told her, turning it this way and that, seeking flaws the way a jeweler would search for clouds or splinters in a diamond.

She did not turn around because she knew that Landau had come into the kitchen, although she hadn't heard him.

"I know where Ben is."

*   *   *

Kim wanted so badly to break the silence, but he didn't dare. The room was almost dark. In the next bed, Ben lay still and silent, reminding Kim of a picture in a history book, a sculpted crusader lying on his tomb.

Kim had heard Ben tell Miss Sawyer to listen to the tape. Despite what Ben had said, he had opened his eyes and watched her. The tape recorder volume was very low and she'd held the instrument close to her ear. Twice her eyes had fallen on him and he had met her gaze. He wanted her to believe what she was hearing, needed her to believe. But in the end, she said nothing. She listened, and when the tape played itself out in a hiss, she placed it in her pocket. What terrified Kim was the utter lack of expression on her face, as though she were beyond reach. At that instant, Kim thought she was the scariest thing he'd ever seen.

"Ben? Did I mess up? Was it my fault? I couldn't just lie there. I couldn't help looking . . ."

"You didn't mess up. No one did." Ben shifted so that he faced the boy. "She just didn't buy it."

There, he'd said it, the ugly truth. She'd come in, listened to a betrayal from the mouth of the betrayer, and said nothing. No reaction. Nothing but cold and blackness where her heart should have been.

Ben heard them talking downstairs. Jamal and the other Arab were back. Most of what was said was in Arabic, but the back-and-forth was animated, the way ballplayers talk after winning a close game. Ben gleamed what he could whenever Judith broke into the conversation. Then Jamal switched to English. Yes, the White House had been contacted and by now the letter she'd written would be in the President's hands. Proof of this was an hour away, on the early news programs. Jamal was confident that the President would make the announcement.

To buy time, Ben thought. *How the hell can anyone think he'd really carve up a sovereign nation—even if he could?*

Jamal thought that way, for sure. The two Arabs as well. And Judith? As far as Ben was concerned, she was as crazy as the rest of them.

"Ben?"

"We stick to the plan," he said, staring at the ceiling. "It'll be a nice night. Maybe one or two will be outside. It'd be easier if they were. Either way, we go." He looked over at the boy. "We don't have to do this if you don't want. We can wait—"

"No, we can't." Kim remembered Miss Sawyer's masklike face, like that creepo in *Halloween*. "We gotta go."

"All right, then."

"All right."

Kim shivered. One part of him knew for a fact that they would never make it. Get outside? Maybe. But not much farther.

But another part told him that there was nothing to wait for except for those terrible things that Miss Sawyer carried around inside her. Kim didn't want any part of them.

"All right," he repeated softly, and said nothing more.

* * *

"You have a problem?"

Rachel was seated in an overstuffed leather chair, leaning forward, elbows on knees. Landau stood leaning against the fireplace mantelpiece. The tableau struck her as absurd; he reminded her of some matinee idol lothario, the "gentleman caller."

Landau ran his fingertips over the mantel, as if checking for dust.

"A problem?"

"Yes. About what to do."

Almost an hour had gone by since Rachel had told Landau about Mary, the house on the Chesapeake, how one time—at an anniversary party?—the subject had somehow come up. She recalled Sid Poltarek hugging Mary, describing the arrangement, Mary beaming, proud but a little embarrassed.

She had walked Landau through her reasoning, made sure it stood up to his scrutiny. Landau poked and probed, but he could not break it. Rachel knew he believed her when he asked if she had a map of that part of the Chesapeake. She had dug out an old but still serviceable ADC guide. The relevant grids were now smudged from Landau's fingers.

"About what to do?" Rachel prompted him.

"What would you have me do, Rachel?"

His tone was very soft, as if he were whispering during funeral rites.

"Tell the President? Set things in motion to rescue them?"

"It's not so simple," Landau said. "For one thing, we're not *certain* that Ben and the boy are at the Chesapeake. Ground reconnaissance could confirm that . . ."

Now, in his faraway gaze, she saw the possibilities unfold, the combinations and permutations he juggled, waiting for each piece to fall into its designated space.

"You don't want to tell the Americans, do you?" she said suddenly. When he didn't instantly deny it, she realized she was right and plowed on. "You want to take Jamal yourself. Why? Are you still smarting over the way he tricked you in Samarra?"

"I have the resources I need, Rachel. My men and I know Jamal better than the Americans ever could. We know how he thinks, the way he's set himself up, the booby traps and other little surprises he'll have waiting."

"This isn't the Middle East," she retorted. "This isn't your turf. It's not your child." She bit off the words about Ben. She wouldn't let him that close to her heart. "You don't have a choice, Landau. If you don't tell the President, if you go after Jamal and Kim Woodbridge gets hurt, Israel will become a pariah. Congress will see to it that she never gets another dime of aid money. Are you willing to risk that, all because of pride and revenge?"

"It's not pride and revenge. You know I don't travel with that Semitic baggage."

You're so clever, Rachel. There is something else, but if I told you, you would become old before your time.

"I will tell the President," Landau said. "You have my word on that."

She listened very carefully to the inflections of his voice, seeking any hint of a lie.

"Is there anything I can do?"

Landau made to leave. "Have you ever been to the Chesapeake house? Do you know the area?"

"No, on both counts."

"Maybe the President will still want to hear how you came up with this. Will you be at the hospital?"

"I'll be right here waiting. Landau. When they're ready to go, call me. Call me as soon as it's . . . finished."

"I will."

* * *

At five o'clock, the press secretary stepped up to the podium and faced the press corps assigned to the White House. He opened by saying that he had a brief but important statement to make. He would not be taking questions afterward.

The media were fidgety; this last-minute summons played havoc with their dinner schedules. Their interest was piqued when the press secretary announced that the President had just completed the last details of a bold new plan for peace in the Middle East. The initiative would be unveiled at the United Nations tomorrow.

That created a stir and raised questions because no one in the room had had any inkling that such a plan had been in the works, nor that it was far enough along to present to the world.

The secretary maintained his best Cheshire cat smile as he kept up a steady stream of honeyed assurances that more details would be forthcoming first thing tomorrow morning. He made as gracious an exit as the barrage of questions allowed.

Most of the reporters took the story at face value and ran with it in order to make the early evening news cycle. Those who had a little more lead time made some calls and discovered that the secretary-general of the United Nations had no idea what the President had been talking about. A presidential appearance before the full assembly was not on the agenda.

The spokesman for the Israeli ambassador spoke guardedly, saying only that his government "was giving serious consideration to the initiative."

On the West Bank, Yasser Arafat proclaimed the declaration "a possible breakthrough in the stalled peace talks" but would reserve judgment until more details were available.

"What the hell is going on?" Yakov Admony demanded, speaking to Landau over the secure satellite link between Jerusalem and the embassy. "The Americans aren't talking to Laudenberg—hell, even *I* can't get through to Woodbridge."

Laudenberg was the ambassador, a political appointee with an abrasive personality. The Americans didn't speak to him even in the best of times.

"Yakov, listen to me."

Landau walked the prime minister through the minefield, slowly, carefully, elaborating when he had to. He finished by saying that he was almost certain he knew where he could find the President's son.

Admony was very quick. "Have you told Woodbridge yet?"

"No."

"You want to go in and get Jamal yourself."

"I think that would be best, yes."

Admony's sigh was like the soul escaping the lips of a dying man. "I can't let you do that, Landau."

"Yakov, my team is here, ready. It's night. We could reconnoiter, then move in—"

"*No!* Listen to me. If something were to go wrong, if the boy is injured, or killed—"

"I know, Yakov."

"Tell the Americans. Let it be on their heads."

"*When* do you want me to tell them?"

The faint crackle of the connection sang in Landau's ear.

"Am I to understand that you're not a hundred percent sure that the boy is there?"

"That's right."

"I think you should be certain of your facts before you speak, no?"

"Absolutely."

"Even if it took you, say, two hours to carry out reconnaissance, the Americans would still have all night for their operation."

"They would."

"Check out Rachel Melman's story. Make sure she isn't imagining things. It would be equally embarrassing if American Rangers or whoever descended upon an empty house. This is a delicate situation. We must be sure of all the facts."

"Yes, sir. All the facts."

Landau replaced the phone and turned to the men standing around him. All six were dressed head-to-toe in black, their faces smeared with camouflage paint.

"Weapons and communications gear?" Landau asked.

"Already in the truck, sir," the lead commando replied.

"Then let us take a ride in the countryside."

* * *

The odor of dinner cooking wafted up through the ducts, snuck underneath the door.

"If it's like before, they'll bring us our food first," Ben said. "Don't eat anything. Push it around on your plate. Slop some under the bedcovers if you have to."

Kim nodded. The cuff had chafed his wrist and he tried to move as little as possible.

"When are we gonna do it?"

"After they finish eating. Hopefully, they'll be relaxed. Maybe one or two will decide to take a walk—"

He cocked his head. New sounds traveling up the ducts—a drone, actually. Then Jamal shouting in Arabic, undisguised triumph. Breaking into snatches of English.

". . . told . . . he would do it! He *had* to do it! Do you . . . what this means, Judith?"

Then the woman's voice, oddly subdued, as if she couldn't share Jamal's exhilaration. Or maybe she was just stunned.

"What's going on?" Kim whispered.

Ben thought he knew: Charles Woodbridge had given Jamal a piece of his demands. *But he'll never give him the whole loaf. He's buying time.* Then something else occurred to him: *A rescue operation! Should we wait?*

Ben almost missed the creaking on the staircase. Judith, carrying a tray, entered and turned on the lamp in the corner. She set down two bowls of canned stew on the beds. Ben tried to catch her attention, but her gaze was as vacant as the dark windows of an abandoned house.

As soon as she was gone, Ben placed his bowl on the floor. Kim followed suit. From downstairs came the sounds of men eating, talking in Arabic with their mouths full.

A little later, the clatter of dirty crockery in the sink and the smell of strong coffee. The porch door opened and slammed shut, followed by voices trailing up along the eaves.

"Now that we heard the President, we need to talk," Judith said. "Let's take a walk."

Jamal's reply had an expansive ring to it: "Of course."

"Ben? Now? We gonna do it now?"

Go or wait? Is the cavalry on the way? Go, and die. Wait, and die.

A shadow snaked through the crepuscular light, slithering up the wall, as Ben reached up and sprang his cuff. Across the way, Kim did the same.

They slid off the beds and faced each other.

* * *

The blue van that boomed along U.S. 50 had the name of an electrical service stenciled on its sides. Landau had debated using one of the embassy vans—big, reinforced stretch models that could carry twelve and withstand a direct impact from a grenade. He had also considered one with diplomatic plates, which would keep the police from thinking about a speeding ticket, but had passed on that one, too. If Jamal was at the Chesapeake house, if the takedown didn't go cleanly, Landau didn't want the American reinforcements to find unmistakably Israeli property at the site.

Landau twisted around in the passenger seat and pulled back the cover on the peephole. His men sat on benches, facing each other, their bodies rocking to the rhythm of the truck. Several were busy with items they had pulled out from canvas tote bags; none of the items resembled electricians' tools.

None of the men carried ID of any kind. Their armament had been manufactured in a number of different countries, but not a single piece had been made in Israel. Each man spoke at least three languages. If, by some stretch of the imagination, any were taken, their captors would find themselves talking to a Frenchman, an Italian, or a Spaniard.

"Mordecai." The lead commando raised his head. "Ready?"

A flash of white teeth in a painted face. "Always."

"Do something about the teeth." Landau paused and added softly, "Luck."

He pushed the cover. Luck would have plenty to do with this, he thought grimly. He was sending his best people into unknown terrain against an unknown number of enemies. In the middle of the hostiles were two hostages whose faces his men now knew by heart. The trick would be to take the guards down first. That would provide the opening to Jamal and the woman, who could not be allowed to see death coming. One or the other would have a remote-controlled detonator for the explosives that would surround the hostages, Landau was sure.

He glanced at the digital clock on the dash, then at the speedometer. The driver had them moving along at sixty-five miles per hour, keeping up with the flow of traffic.

"How much longer?"

"Thirty-five minutes to the Chesapeake Bay Bridge."

Landau flipped open a panel cut into the floor of the cab, pulled out the silenced submachine gun, and began to check its action.

Thirty-four

B EN PUSHED ASIDE THE WINDOW CURTAIN. Judith Sawyer and Jamal were on the path leading from the house to the water. One of them must have found the right switch because both the path and the dock were faintly illuminated by lights set under rusty, weatherbeaten metal shades.

Ben's eyelids fluttered. He told himself that this was the best chance he had—the only one, with two Arabs in the house. Everything he'd planned revolved around there being only two people. Two, he could deal with. No more.

In his mind, Ben retreated to that cool, dark place where the magician in him dwelled. Carefully, he went over every aspect of the illusions he had prepared, checking timing, positioning, angles, and equipment. Still, doubts bombarded him. Images of things going wrong mocked his carefully constructed plans. Fear and uncertainty crept up his limbs like a strangling vine, choking his ability to move.

"Ben? . . . Ben, what's wrong?"

He dared not look at the boy, lest he infect him with his fear. But something in Kim Woodbridge's voice hailed to him, not the words but their intonation, as though it wasn't Kim's voice at all but someone else's.

The image of his brother rose, wavered, and settled before him. They

were kids again, and Sam was teaching him how to box, making Ben
pound the heavy bag until his muscles screamed.

"You're doing this to learn that you never have to run away," Sammy was
saying. *"You and I, we don't run. Now raise those gloves and give me your best
shots."*

Ben smiled at the memory. He hadn't recalled that specific moment
for years and now its return was a rare, precious gift.

He stepped over to the armoire and quickly slipped the black suit out
of its dry-cleaner's plastic. He put out of his mind the creaks made by his
movements; there was nothing he could do about them.

Ben felt as though he were moving through water, silently, purpose-
fully, filling his pockets with objects that, even if Jamal noticed them in a
search, appeared harmless: pieces of paper, some powder that looked
like dust, a pair of lightbulbs, other things.

Ben drifted across the floor to the closet. More props went from the
black doctor's-type bag into his pockets. Then he removed the panel and
climbed up to the attic. His fingers traced around the base of the electrical box and found an object the size of a television remote control.

Next, he pulled open the cover of the box, felt the familiar switches,
and snapped all six on the right side, finishing what Kim had begun. Now
he should be in control of all the electrical current in the house.

Ben climbed back down. "Ready?"

Kim nodded, his nose twitching involuntarily.

Moving as quietly as possible, Ben led him to the landing at the top of
the stairs. In magic, as in life, timing is everything. He needed to attract
enough attention to get one of the Arabs to come up. But only one.

He positioned the boy in the exact center of the landing. "Remember
what I told you: *Don't move.* I'll walk you through this."

"Bet you tell that to all your assistants," Kim mumbled.

"Only those who want to reappear. Now, stay still."

Ben reached for the remote unit and pressed one of the twenty buttons on the pad. Instantly, the lights in the landing and the upper half of
the house went out.

Al-Rahim was sitting in an old chair with musty upholstery over sagging springs. He felt sated and pleased with the state of affairs; his an-
noyance was with the television set, which tuned in only three channels
through a blizzard of poor transmission.

Al-Rahim was positioned in such a way that he caught a sliver of the sudden darkness upstairs. He frowned, pushed himself out of the chair, and walked to the foot of the stairs. The landing at the top, normally lighted, was dark.

Listening, he heard the rustle of newspaper in the kitchen, where he'd left Hatem. He debated calling his partner, then decided to investigate by himself. This was an old, drafty house. A bulb had gone, or maybe a fuse. He would find out.

Al-Rahim was halfway up the steps when he stopped short and his mouth fell open. In the darkness, far above the landing, a lightbulb suddenly appeared. But it wasn't attached to the fixture in the ceiling. In fact, al-Rahim was certain that it wasn't connected to anything. It was just floating. Yes. *Floating?* He blinked to reassure himself that his vision wasn't impaired. It wasn't. Because now, as Allah was his witness, the lightbulb was dancing, up and down, side to side. Entranced, al-Rahim climbed the remaining steps.

*   *   *

Judith's canvas slip-ons made no sound as she walked along the length of the dock. Beneath the bowed, warped boards came the sloshing sound of the evening tide spilling into the marshes, carrying nutrients for what lived in the grasses and the reeds. Judith walked halfway to the end, took a deep breath of the salt and decay, and turned to Jamal who had been following her.

"What will happen now?" she asked. "Will the President obey?"

Jamal zipped up his jacket against the damp chill. The woman had told him she wanted to talk privately. Now she was asking questions she could have put to him in front of a cheerful blaze in the living-room grate.

"He has no choice," Jamal replied, stuffing his hands into his jacket pockets. "He will give us exactly what we demand. Tomorrow, at the United Nations—"

"Don't you find it strange, Hafez?" she interrupted.

"What is strange?"

"That Woodbridge didn't mention that his son is missing. That all we require of him is an acknowledgment, an apology. Why would he go before the United Nations just to apologize to me?"

"Perhaps that is how he interpreted your letter. After all, you did say that he had to present his complicity in the tragedy at Samarra before the entire world."

"He could have done that just as easily, and as meaningfully, from the Oval Office."

Jamal stirred uneasily. "I don't understand what you are trying to say."

"Just that I find Woodbridge's response odd. No one has asked him for any kind of ransom, no one has threatened the life of his son, or forced him to do anything that is beyond his power." She stepped close to Jamal. "No one has done that, have they, Hafez?"

"Of course not."

"You're absolutely sure? I have your word on that?"

"You are not making sense!" Jamal snapped.

"No? Then maybe this will make sense for me."

Judith brought her hand out of her pocket. In her palm lay a small black tape recorder.

*   *   *

Al-Rahim was transfixed by the lightbulb. He was a brutish man who had great faith in his physical strength. But he was descended from the Jabal hill people, who lived at the base of mountain ranges populated by ghosts and demons. The specter of the demons prickled the hairs on the back of al-Rahim's neck.

He uttered a low moan. The lightbulb had moved to illuminate the impossible: a telephone booth.

Al-Rahim shuddered. He wanted to reach for his pistol, but his hands betrayed him. Because inside the phone booth, which could not possibly exist, was the boy. He'd been cut in half, and there was a series of multicolored lights where his torso should have been. He was staring at al-Rahim, unblinking, accusing.

A synapse fired deep in the primal cortex of al-Rahim's brain. He lunged up the last few steps, knees pumping hard, arms held out to crush the telephone booth in his powerful embrace.

Suddenly, all the lights went out. His arms flailed helplessly, finding nothing.

Four feet away, dressed in a black suit, standing in a black corner, Ben pressed another button on his remote control. The telephone booth had slid smoothly into a cavity in the wall. The center section had two forty-five-degree mirrors, reflecting the side walls and the lights, creating the illusion that the cube where Kim's torso should be was empty. Kim was actually *behind* the mirrors, quite whole. Ben's last tap on the control released a spring that enabled the boy to get out of the box.

The Arab's breath came in heaves and snorts. Ben raised his right arm and freed a luminous green silk. It weaved and bobbed like a giant leaf and made al-Rahim curse. He pounded after the silk into a seemingly empty black space that had once been a guest bedroom.

Now it was something more than it appeared to be. Two years ago, Ben had used the room to create an illusion that was a variation of the Egyptian Table of Death.

As the Arab staggered into the room, a section of the seemingly solid floorboards tilted up, sending him crashing onto his back and into a coffinlike cavity. Eyeball halogen lights, embedded in the ceiling, popped on. A long board with foot-long spikes detached itself from the ceiling and began its descent. At the same time, the section of flooring the Arab lay on started to rise.

Al-Rahim's eyes rolled like those of a steer about to be gored. He fumbled for his gun and managed to fire three sound-suppressed shots at the spikes before he felt the first one prick him.

* * *

In the kitchen, Hatem had looked up at his reading when he'd heard footsteps going up the stairs. It occurred to him to call to al-Rahim and ask what he wanted with the prisoners. An answer suggested itself immediately: al-Rahim was known to take a small boy now and then for sex. Hafez Jamal had said nothing about not molesting Kim Woodbridge.

Then came the soft whir of oiled machinery. Hatem cocked his head, thinking it might be the furnace. He jumped out of his chair when he heard the tremendous crash. He was taking the stairs two at a time when the shots were fired.

* * *

"The ransom demands have been modified slightly . . . Did you really believe I would settle for contrition . . . ? . . . the President will embrace me as the new prime minister, the only legitimate authority, of Palestine."

Another voice, Hatem's: *"Does she know any of this?"*

"No. Nor will she ever . . . If the President does not give me Jerusalem, I will give him back his son—one piece at a time."

The wind keened through the reeds as Jamal listened to himself on the tape recorder. He had managed to control his initial rage, but now it was being stoked by a single question.

"Where did you get this, Manar?" He kept his gaze fixed on a light far out on the Chesapeake, not trusting himself to look at her face.

"Does it matter?" She paused. "Your lack of protest condemns you, Hafez."

"Does it?"

"Before me, your people, and Allah. It condemns you before the memory of a man you called your brother."

She watched his anger rise, swelling the muscles of his back and neck. He could break her like a stick, yet she was not afraid of him. Judith felt very light, as though she were hollow, and, oddly, that made her happy. Happy in the way a person who has had everything taken away from her can feel, who has nothing more to offer or to lose.

"How *did* you come by the tape?" Jamal asked again. "You were not present when the conversation took place."

Judith told him willingly, pleased to skewer his smug invincibility and destroy the grandiose palaces he'd built for himself in his mind. It was Poltarek, she said, who'd made the tape. He was able to do so because voices traveled throughout the house in the ductwork. He had waited for the right conversation, then turned on the tape recorder.

"But how did he get the recorder?" Jamal interrupted her. "He'd been searched and was chained to the bed."

Judith shrugged. "Obviously an oversight on your part."

"And he played the tape for you?"

"Yes."

"You believed it?"

"What was there not to believe? It's your voice—and Hatem's."

Then she told him about other things Benjamin Poltarek had talked about.

"Is he right, Hafez?" she finished. "Did you want the leadership so badly that you led Issim and me and our child into Samarra to be killed?"

"So badly? I think that is not exactly accurate. It was *necessary* to re-

move Issim. He had grown too soft and too generous. He was giving away
our cause, piece by piece."

"The cause of death, you mean?"

"The dream of Palestine."

"Which now will never be anything more than that. Less, in fact. Because you have butchered it." She hesitated. "And I, in my foolishness,
helped you destroy it. May Issim forgive me." When she turned to leave,
he took her arm. "What, Hafez? Are you going to kill me, too? Drown me
here and let my corpse rot? That would be unwise."

"Why?"

"Because—"

Judith got no further before a scream sent the terns fleeing from the
rushes.

*   *   *

Hatem burst into the guest room, his pistol level, tight against his hip.
He had been well and thoroughly trained. That he screamed and fired
twice, the bullets gouging plaster and lath, were involuntary reflexes, un-
derstandable given what he'd witnessed.

In the center of the room, seemingly suspended in midair, was al-
Rahim's head. Hatem became aware of two things simultaneously: the
stink of gasoline and the presence of the boy. Kim Woodbridge was a
pale, ghostly figure in the dark. Hatem heard a scratch, then a lit match
appeared in the boy's hand. He stared in utter disbelief as the boy
brought the match close to al-Rahim's gaping mouth, smiled, and pushed
it inside. Al-Rahim's head ignited like a torch. Hatem screamed and fired
again.

In Ben Poltarek's house of illusions, nothing was as it seemed. A system of moving mirrors made Kim Woodbridge appear to be within arm's
length of al-Rahim; in fact, he was on the other side of the room.

Ben stepped up behind Hatem and coldcocked him with a length of
two-by-four.

"Help me!"

But Kim was enthralled by the sight of the burning head as its skin and
hair slowly melted to reveal a skull. Ben threw a heavy cloth over the
weak flames, which were nothing more than flash paper and a little
lighter fluid.

"Kim, I need you to help me!"

The boy snapped out of his trance. He and Ben each grabbed an arm and dragged Hatem to the landing at the top of the stairs. As Ben propped him up, Kim slipped a noose over the Arab's neck.

Shouts could be heard outside.

"Get to the back stairs!" Ben whispered.

He checked the braces, then followed Kim through an opening in what appeared to be a solid wall.

On the porch, Jamal drew back his leg and kicked in the front door. Training his gun on the empty foyer, he whirled around to check the dining room and the parlor. Nothing . . . except for the soft whir of machinery somewhere in the house.

Jamal was looking up the staircase, at the landing, when the lights flickered. He was a third of the way up when they went out altogether. Then the steps beneath his feet disappeared, folding into one smooth board. The wind went out of him as he fell forward, but he managed to grab hold of a railing on the banister to keep from sliding to the bottom.

He needn't have bothered. Beneath the staircase, gears and pulleys spun to straighten out the floor so that no Jamal lay on it. He scrambled to his feet, squinting into the blackness. Then eerie bluish green lights flickered above, a dreadful chuckle reverberated in the air, and a sudden draft swept into his face.

As did Hatem, swinging down from the landing, his body jerking as it dangled from what seemed a hangman's noose around his neck.

Jamal jumped to the side as Hatem's body reeled toward him like a mannequin tied to a clothesline. Except that this mannequin was alive, his fingers working frantically at the rope around his neck, a gurgle escaping from what was left of his throat.

Without warning, Hatem jerked savagely and collapsed to the floor, as though the rope had been cut by an invisible knife. Then came a mechanical cackle—a sound effect that made Jamal curse.

Ben and Kim Woodbridge burst through the door at the back of the house. Never breaking stride, Ben turned and pointed the remote control at the house. Instantly, high-intensity floodlights bathed the front of the house in searing white light. It would have blinded anyone who had his eyes open.

Reaching for Kim's hand, Ben ran on, to the flat, grassy area where the vehicles were parked. The keys he'd found in Hatem's pocket did not fit the Cherokee, but they opened the door of the minibus.

"Get down!" Ben ordered as he slipped behind the big wheel.

The engine caught on the first crank. Ben shoved the gear lever and mashed the accelerator, spinning the rear tires. The minibus bucked and shot forward just as the windshield to his right was riddled by automatic-weapon fire.

Ben spun the wheel and jammed on the brakes, sending the minibus into a shuddering slide. When it finally stopped, rocking on its springs, he saw Jamal in the headlights, holding a submachine gun.

"Get out now!"

Jamal, standing in the fringe of the lights, his face leeched like that of a corpse dredged up out of the water. Behind him, the house, bathed in hot white light, the grass sparkling silver, the trees liquid mercury.

Didn't make it. The thought speared Ben.

"Get out!"

He twisted in the driver's seat and reached behind the chest-high partition. Small fingers clamped onto his hand.

"He's not going to hurt you," Ben said as Kim stood up. "When we go out, stay behind me."

Kim Woodbridge was old enough, and frightened enough, to pick up the inflection in his voice.

"He'll kill you," he said.

"He's sure thinking about it. But he'll think twice."

"When—?"

"Come on now. He's pissed off enough as it is."

Ben had his hands up as he exited the minibus. "I'm not armed!" he called out.

Jamal was twenty feet away. He watched Ben move away from the ve-hicle. Now came the boy, blinking like a fawn caught in headlights, scur-rying over to the Jew. The boy's proximity to Poltarek was the only reason Jamal didn't fire.

"Tell the boy to come here!"

Kim looked up at Ben and shook his head. In a throwback to child-hood, he wrapped his arms around Ben's thigh.

"Tell him to move or I will shoot out your knees!"

"You better do as he says, partner," Ben said. He leaned down and pried away Kim's fingers. "Go on, now."

"I won't!"

Ben gripped Kim's shoulders, turned him around, and shoved him toward Jamal, but at an angle so that the boy wouldn't be caught in the line of fire.

"He's out of it, Jamal! Just you and me now."

Jamal stepped forward, seized the boy by the neck, and flung him behind him. The submachine gun rose like an extension of his arm.

As did a shadow, which only Ben saw. A shadow that seemed to detach itself from the earth, rise above Jamal, and silently fall upon him.

The sod tiller that Judith had found was old and rusted, but its three curved prongs at the end of a broomlike handle were still sharp. They cut through Jamal's jacket and into the meaty part of his shoulder. The Arab screamed and fell to his knees, firing, the bullets stitching the night sky.

"Run!" Judith shouted. "Take him and run!"

Ben moved toward her. Judith gripped the handle of the tiller in both hands, rocking back and forth to free the prongs that had caught in the fabric of Jamal's jacket. As Ben reached her, she gave the tiller a final wrench and shoved the business end in his face.

"Take the boy and go! Leave this to me!"

Judith raised and swung the tiller again. Hearing Jamal's grunts and screams only drove her to redouble her efforts.

With the exception of the first blow, which had set his shoulder on fire, Jamal felt nothing. The knife was in his hand as the tiller came off him. Jamal took advantage of the opening, scrambled to his feet, and lunged. Her breath was rancid on his face as the life went out of her, the knife twisting once, twice, before it pierced her heart.

Jamal stepped back and let the corpse fall off the blade. He did not need to look at her to know she was dead. Instead, it was a sound that caught his attention: the roar of the engine and the fierce grinding of gears as the minibus fishtailed down the dark road.

Thirty-five

THE MINIBUS AND THE TRUCK carrying the Israeli commandos converged on the intersection at Route 50 and Swallowtail Road. The minibus got there first, turned, and was roaring up 50 when the truck flashed by. Both the truck's driver and Landau were too preoccupied to take note of it.

Seventeen minutes later, the truck edged up the drive to the house, lights out. At the tree line, the driver killed the engine and the troopers piled out.

Landau, wearing Kevlar armor under civilian clothes, lagged behind. He was neither dressed for nor equipped to participate in the assault, much less lead it. Up front, he'd only get in the way.

The team covered the distance between the tree line and the front yard of the house in ninety seconds. A woman lay near the crushed oyster-shell driveway. She did not move when the laser sights of the raiders' submachine guns played over her face.

Voices could be heard from inside the house, which was bathed in white light. The commando leader looked at Landau, who'd caught up with the team.

"She's dead," Landau said with soft certainty. His night vision was better than an owl's. He'd noticed the dark trail from Judith Sawyer's midsection, darker than the shadows cast upon her, dark as blood by moonlight.

"How many inside, do you think?"

The assault leader raised two fingers. "Downstairs. Making a racket. And why is it dark in there?"

It all felt wrong to Landau. He sensed that something terrible had happened here, something he could not define, did not understand.

"Get inside. Take down whatever's moving. If Poltarek and the boy are alive, they're upstairs. Anyone tries to run that way, shoot to kill."

"Jamal?"

"Jamal, too."

Except Jamal wasn't here. Landau sensed it the way the blind can sometimes feel empty space in front of them. And if Jamal was gone . . .

He would know the answer soon enough. His men were at the door, then inside. The light coughs of suppressed fire punctured the silence, whispers of "clear" crackled over his headset.

Landau was standing over Judith Sawyer's eviscerated body when they brought out Hatem, supporting him under the shoulders because his right foot dragged uselessly behind him.

"Hatem," Landau said. "Greetings."

The Arab jerked back his head and covered the front of Landau's jacket with spit.

"The other one was al-Rahim," the assault leader said. "He was already dead."

"Shot?"

"Heart attack."

"No one else?"

The leader shook his head. "They are still searching. The house—it is bizarre. Like something you would see at a fair, a *golem*'s house."

"No violence?"

The leader understood that Landau was asking about blood trails or any other evidence that Poltarek and the boy had been killed.

"None."

Landau focused on Hatem. "The boy. Where is he?"

Hatem smirked. "Gone. With Jamal."

Landau regarded him thoughtfully. "You're a poor liar," he said at last.

"The boy is *dead*, Landau!" Hatem screamed as he was hustled away to the truck.

"No, I don't think so," Landau muttered.

The house, the lights, the carnage that had taken place outside . . .

Outside. Had Poltarek and the boy managed to free themselves? Could they have *escaped*?

Landau looked around. He was in the middle of nowhere. And in the middle of nowhere, deep into the night, his truck had been passed by . . . not a car, not a van . . . He closed his eyes and pictured the vehicle, pictured it against the brilliant blue and white of Ben-Gurion Airport. A minibus.

Seconds later, the raiders were piling back into the truck.

"Do we tell the Americans?" asked the leader.

"About Hatem? I think not. They haven't yet learned that putting terrorists on trial only invites reprisal. We will spare them such a consequence. Hatem goes to Tel Aviv."

The leader jerked his thumb toward Judith. "Her?"

Landau was silent for a moment. "Cover her. I'll tell Reece to come. She is theirs. She is home."

*   *   *

"Ben, where are we going?"

The wind sang through the spidery bullet holes in the windshield, snatching away words that Ben wished the boy had never asked. He was hunched over the wheel, driving as fast as he dared, the rear end of the minibus slip-sliding all over the highway.

"Give me a sec." He concentrated on the road as it narrowed at the approach to the Chesapeake Bay Bridge.

Ben's eyes kept flitting to the big side-view mirrors. So far, there was no one behind them. But he had noticed a Jeep parked close to the minibus.

The kid's right: Where am I going?

The process of converting the Chesapeake house into an experimental fun house where he could create, construct, and test illusions had taken several years. Ben had traveled this route often, but he was not familiar with it. Usually he set his mind on autopilot when he drove, so that the scenery and landmarks became a continuous blur. Now he had to look closely for some signpost or marker—anything that would direct him and Kim to shelter.

"Keep an eye out for those emergency phones along the highway."

"Why?"

"Because we need to get help."

"What about the radio?"

Ben followed Kim's finger. Tucked under the dash was a radio and a hand microphone. Ben felt very foolish as he reached down, flipped the switch, and was rewarded by squeaks and squawks.

"See that knob?"

Kim peered down at the tiny control panel. "The red one?"

"Yeah. Turn it slowly to the right, click by click. Give me enough time to talk, okay?"

"What are you going to say?"

Ben pressed the TRANSMIT button on the hand mike. "Mayday, Mayday, Mayday. Can anyone hear me? My name is Benjamin Poltarek, traveling on Route 50. I need help. Anyone?"

*   *   *

Maryland State Trooper Brian Tobin was six months fresh out of the training academy. He was sitting in his favorite radar trap, two miles from the west end of the Chesapeake Bay Bridge. Drivers coming off the narrow span tended to goose it once they were on dry land, and that was just fine with Tobin. But tonight's pickings had been slim, which was why Tobin still sat there instead of pulling into the nearby HoJo coffee shop for his break.

"My name is Benjamin Poltarek, traveling on Route 50. I need help. Anyone?" Then a pause. "I'm in a minibus—"

Tobin grabbed his mike and called back, but got only static. The caller must have flipped past the designated emergency channel.

Tobin was a conscientious recruit. He had a good memory and read all the posted bulletins before starting his shift. The name Poltarek was unusual enough to have stuck in his mind, and now he recalled the context in which he'd heard it—twice, in fact. The first time had been when a BOLO—"be on the lookout"—had come in from the feds. Nothing radical, just a guy wanted for questioning. The second reference was the one that had gotten Tobin's attention. It came straight out of the D.C. homicide chief's office. Two detectives had been wasted. An APB had gone out connecting Poltarek to a Jeep. *So where did the minibus fit in?* His fingerprints had been found on the murder weapon.

Tobin experienced an adrenaline rush that left him glassy-eyed. The son of a bitch was headed his way—he could feel it. He reached for the mike, then stopped. It was the minibus that bothered him. If that had been *the* Poltarek on the air, what was he doing in a minibus?

Tobin took a minute to scan the updated list of stolen automobiles. There it was—a minibus taken from the Capital Tours compound.

And there it went, cruising down 50 at a solid clip, passing less than sixty feet from the cruiser.

Tobin gunned up onto the blacktop. He drove with parking lights only, to keep his silhouette low. When he was two car lengths behind the minibus, he was able to read the plate number. It matched the one on the stolen vehicle.

Tobin pushed his speed up a bit. He remembered the details of the description given out on Poltarek. Now he would come alongside the minibus and get a look at the driver. He wanted to be sure it was Poltarek before he called his dispatcher and dropped the hammer.

Tobin increased speed a little more and pulled parallel to the minibus. There was the driver, in profile. It could be Poltarek. Suddenly, another face appeared, a young boy's. Then Poltarek looked directly at him.

*   *   *

The squeal of his cell phone startled Landau.

"Where are you?" Kaelin Reece's voice had a hard urgency to it.

"What is it?"

"A Maryland trooper just reported seeing Poltarek driving a stolen minibus toward D.C."

A minibus . . . Landau felt sick. "What else?"

"The trooper also saw a child in the bus, but he couldn't identify him."

"Reece, where are you?"

"The White House situation room."

"Does the President know any of this?"

"Not yet. Landau, where *are* you?"

"On Route 50, not more than a few miles behind Poltarek. Reece, listen carefully."

He walked her through the discovery of the Chesapeake house and what he'd found there. He told her about Judith Sawyer dead and Jamal missing.

"You must tell that trooper to fall back. Stay in sight, but make no attempt to stop Poltarek. Let me handle it."

"It's not going to happen that way, Landau. The trooper asked for backup and it's on the way. They still think Ben's a cop-killer. Remember Abbott's APB?"

Landau did. "Then at least tell them I'm coming up on the scene."

"No good. You have no jurisdiction, no authority." She paused, then gut-punched him: "You should have told me what you were doing, Landau, taken me along. You could use my badge right about now."

"I'm not going to stop, Kaelin," he said softly. "I don't give a damn if I create an international incident, I'm not leaving Poltarek and the boy out there alone."

"They won't be alone—"

Landau switched off his phone. He didn't even have to look at the driver before the truck surged forward.

*　　*　　*

"That was a cop!"

Yes, it was. Thank you, God.

"Get back in your seat," Ben said.

He switched on the blinker and began to slow.

It's a cop. He has a radio. A radio is help.

"We're gonna be okay now, right?" Kim said, squirming in the passenger seat. He was too short to see the entire side-view mirror.

"Just fine. We're going to be just fine."

Inside the cruiser, Trooper Brian Tobin adjusted his speed. He was still trying to figure out who the kid in the cab was. The BOLO hadn't mentioned a child. The word "hostage" flashed through his mind; but then why was Poltarek slowing down?

Tobin began to feel a little more confident. A suspect who bolted was the real danger. One who slowed down, even when there were no flashers or sirens, was usually manageable, especially with the business end of a 9-millimeter in his face.

Ben had the minibus on the shoulder. He lowered the window and heard the crunch of the trooper's car on the dirt. He placed both hands on top of the steering wheel. Once, in the emergency room at Rachel's hospital, a cop had told him that what an officer needs to see when approaching a vehicle are the hands. No hands causes suspicion and a bad frame of mind.

Tobin, too, was thinking of hands as he adjusted his spotlight to shine on the door on the right side of the minibus. He had the dash-mounted videocam running, but it wouldn't pick up much until the suspects were out of the vehicle.

Tobin didn't know it, but he was wrong on that point. He registered, but did not pay attention to, the sound of a big engine coming up the road behind him. He thought it was his backup. He climbed out, the safety snap on his holster open, his hand on the butt of his 9-millimeter. Intent on the minibus, he came around the open door, holding a mike in his other hand.

"Driver! Open the door and climb down!"

The bullhorn built into the roof rack lights punched the words into the night. The volume also drowned out what Tobin would otherwise have heard.

Tobin stood by the left fender of his cruiser; behind him was the open driver's door. He was trapped, but never realized it. A figure, arms raised, was stepping out of the bus.

Tobin heard the roar of the engine and turned, but much too late. His mind registered that the vehicle bearing down on him was a Jeep Cherokee. A split second later, the Cherokee smashed into the open door, spinning Tobin around, exposing his spine to the shredded metal.

Hafez Jamal was a good driver. He knew he had a strong vehicle and he used it well. He never stopped after hitting the cruiser's door, didn't turn around to see if the trooper was dead, because he knew he was. What Jamal did was lift the submachine gun off the passenger seat and, when he came alongside the minibus, sprayed the large driver's window.

The stairwell in airport minibuses is deep and wide to accommodate large suitcases. The well saved Ben's and Kim's lives, the bullets traveling over their curled-up bodies.

After the fusillade, Ben scrambled toward the driver's seat. He peered over the dash and saw the Cherokee screech to a stop up ahead. With startling clarity, he understood what could happen next.

Sweeping away the pebbles of safety glass, Ben jumped into the driver's seat and shifted gears. The minibus surged forward, its high beams pinning Jamal as he was getting out of the Cherokee. Ignoring the upraised submachine gun, Ben bore down on him and twisted the wheel, not to avoid hitting Jamal, who, at the last second, had leaped into a culvert, but to miss smashing into the Cherokee. The minibus was the only weapon he had; he could not afford to damage it.

Jamal scrambled out of the culvert and trained his gun on the fast-disappearing bus. If he could shoot out the tires—

He never had a chance. The blacktop around him exploded, asphalt chips like shrapnel striking and cutting his exposed skin.

Jamal whirled around and laid down a barrage at the big van thundering toward him. The driver must have anticipated this because he swerved left, the bullets disappearing into the night.

But the hail of gunfire had some effect. The van rocked to a stop. Jamal saw figures in black leap out, lay down suppressing fire, then begin to close in on him. He recognized the moves as classic commando tactics.

Landau . . . The realization tore at Jamal as he rushed back to the Cherokee and, killing the lights, screamed down the highway. The *pock-pock* of bullets striking the chassis made him keep his head down.

Jamal took two curves before he straightened up and searched the night for the minibus. If it was still ahead of him, he could not see it. But there had also been two turnoffs onto secondary highways. The minibus could have taken either one of them.

Jamal slammed his fist on the wheel in frustration. Poltarek and the boy had been so close . . . Well, maybe they could be made to come close again.

Jamal watched the exits for the one that would take him into the heart of Washington.

*   *   *

Outside the D.C. city limits, on either side of the Amtrak lines, lies a small rust belt that both the capital and the Baltimore city fathers try to ignore. It is a place of machine shops and car chop shops, of self-storage units surrounded by razor wire and derelict buildings with the names of old cotton interests fading on chipped brick. There is nothing here but desolation, broken only by the occasional, fortresslike enterprise. One is a small oil refinery; the second, a truck stop called the Shift and the parking lot that serves it.

Ben stared at the winking strobes of the refinery, the floodlights glaring off polished steel and glossy paint. Then he looked at the Shift, a creaky roadhouse with a year-round Christmas tree on a sagging awning, rockabilly music spilling out where it was ground under the engine roar of eighteen-wheelers pulling in and out.

Kim was staring at the trucks. "You said we needed a ride, right?"
"Right."

He pressed the boy close for warmth. They needed more than a ride. Safety, protection, people who could help them. But a ride would be a good first step.

The minibus had died two miles up the road, wheezing until the engine shuddered and quit. Ben suspected that a bullet had found its innards. So they had walked to this point, following the railroad tracks, not the road. Ben had seen enough death on roads.

He had no clue that Jamal had been so close. Nor had he witnessed the firefight afterward. He presumed that since Jamal had not given chase immediately, something must have happened with his vehicle. If there was a God, the Jeep had flipped, and exploded with Jamal in it.

Ben had taken Route 17 as far as he could before turning onto a two-lane blacktop that brought him close to the Baltimore-Washington Expressway. As though to mock his hopes, the minibus had died there, leaving them no option but to walk.

Ben had been worried about Kim. He was silent and wouldn't let go of his hand. Only when they were on the tracks had he relaxed a little.

When Ben asked him if he was okay, the boy had stopped and looked at him. "That lame-o was shooting at you. Are *you* okay?"

Ben thought the kid redefined the term "resilience."

Kim pointed at the roadhouse. "You gonna walk in there or what?"

Or what? Ben had no money—he'd already fished in his pockets. He imagined he looked like something that had crawled out of a Dumpster. Someone inside the Shift might, out of pity, give him a dollar for a cup of coffee. But a ride?

The kid was tugging his arm again. "Come on. Let's go. I'm cold."

Earl Tate came out of the Shift rubbing his hands briskly against the raw night air. He had sixteen ounces of T-bone and four cups of coffee in his belly. In less than forty minutes, he'd be dumping his load of five thousand pounds of Maine lobster at the D.C. food terminal. After picking up his check, he would crawl into the bunk at the back of his truck cab and sleep for a few hours before hauling back to Bangor.

In his early sixties, Tate was a big man, tall, with a generous gut and flowing white hair. Other truckers kidded him that he looked like Santa Claus or Jerry Garcia. Tate had seen a lot of things during his time on the road and there wasn't much that he was afraid of. But the voice coming out of the darkness somewhere between the parked rigs spooked him.

"Excuse me."

Tate had the door to his cab open. When he turned, there was a smooth-worn fish billy in his hand.

"What can I do for you, mister?"

The man approached him the right way, one arm away from his body, the other holding on to something that Tate realized was a young boy. Both of them looked tired and beat up, like they were on the run.

"If you're headed into D.C., we could sure use a ride," Ben said.

"Step out here in the light where I can see you better."

Tate looked them up and down. The man wasn't carrying a weapon, unless it was a knife taped to his leg. Probably didn't even have that. He had "city" written all over him.

Tate squinted at the boy, his face all smudged, clothes torn up. Something beneath the grime tugged at him, like the boy was familiar.

"Don't usually give rides to strangers," Tate said. He wanted to hear their story, but was surprised when the boy stepped forward.

"We need a ride," Kim said. He pulled up his sleeve to show a string of purple bruises. "Please."

Earl Tate knew more than he liked about people on the run. He was an arm's-length member of an organization that helped folks disappear. A phone call would come in, Tate would make a detour, and a woman and child—they were almost always women and children—would jump in. One suitcase for the two of them, a lot of makeup for the bruises, codeine or Valium to settle the child. The ride might last fifty miles or five hundred, depending. Rule of thumb was that the fugitives fell asleep after the first ten. There was something about Earl that allowed them to do that.

But these two were not runners—*on* the run, sure. But not from domestic violence.

"Why don't you tell me your name?" Tate said.

"Ben. And this is Kim."

"Ben, you want to slide up into the cab for a minute? Something I want you to hear. Come on, now. I don't bite. You worried about the boy, let him stand outside."

Tate turned the ignition key far enough to power up the radio. The all-news station was on top of a breaking story about the hit-and-run murder of a Maryland state trooper on Route 50.

"I was watching it on the television in the Shift," Tate said, studying Ben's face intently. "They say a guy called Benjamin Poltarek had something to do with this, that the cops are looking for him. Your name wouldn't happen to be Poltarek, would it?"

"It would," Ben said. "But I didn't kill the trooper."

"No one is saying you did. Just that they're looking for you, like you might be a witness."

They're looking for me because I have the boy, Ben thought. *The trooper saw Kim, recognized him, called it in. Then Jamal killed him. Except no one knows that. They won't broadcast that Kim is missing—they couldn't. But they'll hunt me to get to him.*

"If you believe I killed that trooper, or that you have to turn me in, then knock me over the head with that billy and get it over with," Ben said. "If you don't, the boy and I would very much appreciate the ride."

Tate thought about that for a minute. "Where is it you want to go?"

"Sixteen Hundred Pennsylvania Avenue."

"The White House?"

"Look at the boy—carefully."

Tate did just that. "You're shittin' me," he said softly.

"I'm taking him home. I'm taking him because there's no one else to do it."

Thirty-six

WHY WAS THAT COP AFTER YOU?" asked Earl Tate.
He had his truck in the center lane, moving a few miles above
the posted limit.

"They connected me to Kim," Ben replied. "They think I had something to do with kidnapping him."

Earl glanced over his shoulder. The boy was tucked away in the bunk,
his head sticking out between the curtains. He reminded Tate of a
prairie-dog pup.

"He didn't," Kim said. "Can I honk your air horn?"

"So we're just going to drive up to the White House and ring the front
doorbell," Tate said.

"Not quite. But I want them to know we're coming. Do you have a
phone?"

Tate tugged out a cell phone from his jacket pocket and was about to
hand it over.

"No," Ben said. "I want you to do the calling. That way, you'll know
I'm not steering you."

Tate looked at him approvingly. "Who do I call?"

"Directory assistance for the Children's National Medical Center.
When you get through, ask for Dr. Rachel Melman."

After a minute, Tate heard, "This Dr. Melman." He looked at Ben.
"Now what?"

"Listen." Ben took the phone. "Rachel?"

Her exclamation and subsequent words made Tate look away, as if he'd trespassed into a very private moment. But Ben had told him to listen, so he did. Twice in the course of what he heard, Tate found his knuckles tightening on the big steering wheel.

"She's going to meet us on Pennsylvania?" he asked conversationally when Ben looked at him.

Ben nodded. "When should I tell her to be there?"

"Ninety minutes tops."

Ben relayed the time, lowered his voice and spoke a little longer, then broke the connection.

"Sounds like a fine lady," Tate ventured.

"One of a kind."

"Think she'll be able to keep Lander and whoever else off our backs?"

"It's Landau. Yes, she'll do it."

They drove in silence for a while, then Tate said, "No one's said that Kim's missing."

"No one." Ben paused. "No one can *ever* know. I'm sure some people will be talking to you about that."

"I'm sure they will be," Tate said. "Thing is, even if I wanted to flap my gums, nobody'd believe me."

* * *

Kaelin Reece was in an FBI helicopter hovering two thousand feet above the Chesapeake house. Five hundred feet lower were two state police choppers with belly lights that illuminated the area around the house.

Through binoculars, Reece watched as two bagged bodies were hoisted into a morgue van. The van would not be going to Baltimore—the coroner's seat—but to the Bureau labs. Even now, all the paperwork associated with the events that had taken place on the upper Eastern Shore was quietly being expunged.

"Landau, where are you?" Reece said into her headset.

His reply danced on the crackle of static. "Approaching Washington."

Reece sighed. She was on secure communications, but she didn't want to get into what Landau had been doing there, what he'd left with. Initial reports indicated gunfire inside the house.

"No contact with Poltarek?"

"No. You?"

"We're chasing him down. Found the minibus in the rust belt with a hole in the gas tank. They hoofed it from there."

"Somebody must have seen them, a man and a boy walking at night?"

"If so, we haven't found them yet. Landau, what are you going to do?"

"Return to the embassy."

I bet you are, with whatever goodies you managed to get your hands on.

"What about Jamal?" Landau asked.

"What about him? He vanished, too. The key is the boy. Let's get him back to 1600, then we can hunt."

"Where will you be?"

"Headed back to the White House. The President has been informed. He and the First Lady aren't getting any sleep tonight."

"I'll call you there."

The connection sputtered away. Reece kept staring at the back of the pilot's head. Landau was holding out on her, she could feel it. She snorted. Landau *always* held out.

Now the pilot was looking at her oddly.

"Back to the White House," Reece told him.

* * *

The van carrying Landau and his raiders was in fact very close to the embassy.

Landau was on the line to the *katsa*.

"Anything?"

"She got one call, from a mobile. We backtracked the number."

The *katsa* rattled it off, along with the owner's name.

"Earl *Tate*?"

"We're running him down now."

"Where is she going?"

"Poltarek asked her to meet him on the Pennsylvania side of the White House. He has the boy."

"Why would he call her?"

The *katsa*'s tone changed. Landau realized he was enjoying this part.

"She's his eyes. Poltarek said he wouldn't go near the area if she told him you were there."

The *katsa* expected profanity. He was surprised by what he heard next.

"Can't really blame her, can we?" Landau paused. "We're six minutes out. Have the garage open and a car ready. And get an El Al freighter on the ground. I don't care where you have to divert it from."

* * *

They were in the city proper, Earl Tate concentrating on his driving now, his big hand working the gear stick. Other than the rattle coming from the refrigeration unit mounted on the end of the trailer, the cab was quiet. What needed to be said, shared, had all been said.

Ben recognized the landscape as the truck lumbered through the Sunday-evening-empty streets. Every turn brought the boy closer to home, to safety. With that thought, his exhaustion, held at bay by adrenaline, began to seep into his bones. He pictured Rachel, how good it would be to see her, to hold her. He had an absurd notion that he and she and Kim could all go out for pizza when this was all over.

Losing it, fella.

The phone in Tate's pocket trilled. Ben smiled: He'd been thinking of Rachel and here she was.

Tate passed him the phone. "For you."

Ben was still smiling until he heard Jamal's voice.

"Congratulations, Benjamin Poltarek. You know who this is."

Ben closed his eyes to keep the world from spinning away into hell. "Yes."

"I understand you have an appointment to keep."

"Put Dr. Melman on."

"She is safe. There is no reason for her to get hurt."

"What do you want?"

"The obvious. Her for the boy."

Ben found himself nodding. He looked at Tate, whose mouth had tightened into a grimace. The volume on the phone was set on high. The trucker had heard everything.

So had Kim, who had crawled out of the bunk and was staring at him.

Ben turned back to the phone. "Her for the boy?"

"That is all you have left to trade, Mr. Poltarek."

"How can you be sure I don't have an escort?"

"Then why call her? Please, don't waste time. Dr. Melman has so little remaining. She lives for yes, dies for no."

"*Yes.* Where?"

"Not Pennsylvania Avenue, no, thank you. The Lincoln Memorial."

"It's—"

"Yes, Mr. Poltarek?"

"It's far from where we are. I need some time—"

"Two hours. You and the boy only. I will find you." Jamal laughed. "Mr. Poltarek, under different circumstances I would have enjoyed those tricks at your country house. But not even you could manage a repeat performance on such short notice, hmm?"

The connection was broken.

"Ben?"

He shushed the boy with a wave of his hand.

"The Arab?" Tate asked finally.

"Oh, yeah."

"I overheard most of it. What do we do?"

"A detour," Ben said. "A really fast one so we have something to bring to the party."

* * *

Wanda, of Wanda's Witchcraft and Magic Shoppe on Vermont Avenue, lived in an apartment over the store. Her voice was low and throaty over the intercom.

"Who is it?"

"Ben."

"After all this time. Come up. Come up."

The light from the open door on the landing illuminated the staircase. Wearing a black silk robe, her raven hair curling over her breasts in ringlets, Wanda embraced Ben. Her perfume was subtle—homemade, he remembered—and her lips were painted as red as freshly spilled blood.

"You bad, bad boy," she said. "People have been talking about you."

"Hello, Wanda. You look wonderful."

Ben stepped into the apartment—large cushions, beanbag chairs, strings of floor-to-ceiling beads that served as room dividers. Fragrant trails of smoke rose from brass incense pots; two black cats rested like statues at the feet of Nefertari.

"What people?" he asked.

"It's all over the TV. Haven't you been watching?"

"I've been busy."

Wanda chuckled, throwing her voice so that it came at Ben from half a dozen directions. Wanda was one of the few female illusionists who stood on a par with the best of the men in the profession. At forty, she not only retained her ripe, desirable figure—a clear asset when it came to distracting an audience—but was acknowledged as the queen of the "haunted-house" illusions. Many of Ben's ideas for the Chesapeake house had been brought to life in Wanda's blueprints.

"Busy," Wanda said. "Ben, just what the hell is going on?"

He took three precious minutes to explain, then said, "I need your help."

"Oh, dear boy, yes, you do."

"The Lincoln Memorial is being cleaned up. Sand or air blasted."

"Yes."

"I'm thinking Omar's Maze."

Wanda's eyes gleamed. "Oooh, yes!"

Out of thin air, she produced pea-sized capsules of flash powder mixed with granules of phosphorus. The capsules were airtight.

"Flaming Seas," Ben murmured.

He had seen Wanda do this illusion only once, in front of close friends, fellow professionals who'd been scared witless.

"Yes," Wanda whispered.

"Time. That's the problem."

"Then why are we still here?"

Wanda furled a cape around her shoulders, then picked up the phone.

"Larry, Pete, load up the Maze. I want the truck ready to roll by the time I get downstairs." She grinned at Ben. "Lucky for you, dear boy, that my workshop is open tonight."

Ben raised his eyebrows. It was poor etiquette to ask another magician what he or she was working on.

Wanda laughed lewdly. "I plan to call it Bordello of Blood."

* * *

When Ben hopped back into the truck, Tate asked, "What's up?"

"Wanda is going to help us. Head for the Memorial."

Tate pulled into the street. "Wanda . . . Who's she?"

"A magician."

"And she's going to help you."

"All magicians are brothers," Ben said. "If I had the time, I could call a dozen more people and they'd all be waiting for us, no questions asked."

Tate drove in silence for a while, then said: "No offense, but I have to spit this out. If you made one call, couldn't you have the entire Secret Service or whoever on the spot in two minutes?"

"Yes, I could. And Kim would be safe, but Rachel would be dead."

"You're not seriously thinking of trading—"

"No. Kim won't be in danger. Not for a minute."

"But you think you can scam this Jamal guy?"

Ben looked down at his hands. They had caused thousands of coins, doves, silks, and other objects to vanish, sometimes not three inches away from an audience member's eyes.

"I can scam him long enough to get Rachel away from him."

"Then what? You gotta know Jamal will be armed."

"There's nothing I can do about that."

Tate dropped his hand into the space between the driver's seat and the door. He brought it back out holding a blued-metal .357 Colt.

"Now maybe you can," he said.

* * *

Looking at the Memorial, Ben understood why it appealed to Jamal. Behind it were intersecting loops and drives that led to the Arlington Memorial and Roosevelt Bridges. Either one of those would get Jamal into Virginia in less than two minutes. Or he could take Ohio Drive, hook up with I-395, and have a clear shot out of the city.

The Memorial was also good because of the season and time of night. There weren't many tourists around yet, and with no shelter against wind slicing off the Potomac, none would be wandering the wide expanses between the Memorial and the Washington Monument.

No tourists meant fewer police cars, and certainly no foot patrols. Park Service and D.C. cops would stay bundled up in their cruisers, heaters going strong.

But did Jamal know about the scaffolding?

The cleaning of monuments is a haphazard affair. One day, crews appear with diesel-powered generators on flatbed trucks, erect scaffolding, and start air-blasting.

He doesn't know. It's coincidence.

Coincidence that Ben remembered. Coincidence that had fired certain connections, their light illuminating a path to what he dared to call hope.

To Jamal, location was all-important. If the Memorial was covered with scaffolding, so what? It neither served nor interfered with his purpose.

"Wanda?"

She had had her helpers park the truck—a long, flatbed affair favored by moving companies—next to one of the generators. She glided to him out of the night, her cape billowing like giant wings.

"Where do you want it?"

Ben quickly outlined it for her.

"How much time do we have?"

"An hour, tops."

Wanda's breath sang through the tiny space between her front teeth.

"An adventure!" She nodded toward Earl Tate's truck. "Things'll go faster if the old dude in the rig pitches in."

* * *

Landau watched the lights wink out one by one in Rachel's house. He was in an embassy sedan, with diplomatic plates that gave him license to double-park. So far, the evening patrols hadn't been by and the street remained quiet.

The embassy *katsa* had taped Rachel's conversation with Ben Poltarek. Landau recalled the cascades of emotion in their voices, Poltarek being the more reticent, probably because there were people within earshot. Soon it would be over, he thought. Not quite as soon as Rachel and her lover expected, because there were debriefings to come. But soon enough for them to become happy again, to return to their lives never really knowing how close they had come to losing the future and—

Landau's eyes narrowed. Rachel was stepping out the front door, into the pool of light cast by the lamp over the archway. She had her car keys in one hand, the other behind her, as though she were holding on to something—

Someone.

Landau's scalp prickled. Hafez Jamal followed Rachel out, pushing her down the steps and the walkway. Rachel fumbling with the car lock, opening the door; Jamal pulling out his gun, training it on her as he skipped around to the passenger side.

Trying to get out of her parking spot, Rachel nudged the car behind her. Landau sensed that she was unfamiliar with the vehicle. Naturally. Poltarek had taken hers. This one was a rental.

She finally managed to steer it out into the street and drive toward the light at the intersection.

Landau dropped his car into gear and rolled toward her, using only his parking lights. He could ill afford to have Jamal see him; he would feel safer once they were in traffic.

Landau dropped his hand to the car phone, then changed his mind. Raising the alarm at the embassy was no good. He had no idea where to direct an assault force, nor even the number of men he needed or how they should be armed. For now, he had to follow alone.

"In the end, it's always like this," he said to himself, and was startled more by his frankness than by the fact that he'd spoken aloud. An image leaped into his mind, the prime minister's Execution List. There was number 34, Hafez Jamal, a shortcoming long in need of correction.

* * *

Jamal had told the woman doctor to drive carefully, but not slowly as to seem like a cautious drunk. She was doing exactly as instructed.

Lights from the bars and restaurants along M Street washed across Jamal's expressionless face. The plan he had conceived, nourished, and executed had almost come to a bloody end six thousand miles from his homeland. He knew now that he should have killed Poltarek as soon as he'd set eyes on him, never mind what Poltarek knew or how valuable it might be. By introducing an unforeseen element into so intricately crafted a plan, he had upset a delicate balance.

It had been, Jamal acknowledged, a sin of pride. By wanting to leave nothing to chance, he had, in the law of unintended consequences, risked everything. Unconsciously, he cursed under his breath.

"Excuse me?"

Jamal started. "What do you want?"

"I'm sorry," Rachel said. "I thought you said something."

"You have been doing well. Stay quiet and drive."

Jamal thought Poltarek's woman very good-looking. After the outrage at the Chesapeake house and the failure to stop Poltarek on the highway, Jamal had thought that all was lost. Hatem and al-Rahim were dead, Poltarek and the boy were loose, and the devil Landau was on his heels. Jamal's first thought had been to escape while there was still time and opportunity, and he was not ashamed of that. But there were different places to run to, different opportunities to be had.

Given all the information the late Detective Priestly had amassed on Poltarek, it was easy not only to understand how valuable Rachel Melman could be to him but how to find her. Jamal had never believed that he might need to remember Rachel Melman's address. But out there on the dark highway, with Landau shrieking behind him and only flight on his mind, she had strayed into his thoughts. So Jamal had changed direction, from BWI Airport to Georgetown.

Jamal shifted as Rachel bore right off M Street onto Pennsylvania Avenue. He was well versed in the psychology of hostages and hostage situations. She needed to hear this now.

"This is a simple trade: you for the boy. As long as Poltarek understands this, everything will go well." He paused. "It may be that *you* will have to encourage him to understand this. It will be in your interest and the boy's to do that."

"Yes," Rachel said, knowing that not a word of what Jamal was saying was true.

Her mind was rampant with images of men in black holding long-barreled rifles.

At Twenty-third and C Streets, Jamal began scanning for telltale signs of a trap. The Americans would be very good at this. Washington was probably the most protected city in the country; SWAT and counterterrorism drills were constantly conducted. But Jamal knew what to look for: shadows that were out of place, an intersection with no traffic, stationary vehicles such as public-service vans that could hide a dozen troopers, men in hard hats ostensibly working on a sewer or power lines.

He told Rachel to turn onto Constitution Avenue and take it to Seventeeth Street. Then right, and right again, past the D.C. War Memorial, all the way to the Lincoln Memorial. Jamal was pleased with his choice of site. The long Reflecting Pool and surrounding grassy parkland afforded no cover. The Memorial itself was spartan, with long wide steps and open areas between the columns. The scaffolding was an unexpected bonus. Anyone lying on top of those long wide planks would have no cover at all.

"Go around the back," he told Rachel. "I will tell you where to stop."

Ben saw them walking from the direction of Henry Bacon Drive and figured that's where they had parked the car. The two of them were so close together they looked like one person, the way lovers do, hips and shoulders rubbing together.

They came around the edge of the Vietnam Veterans Memorial, past the giant flag and the "last firebase," a rickety stall where, during the day, vets passed out leaflets about American MIAs. He could now see Rachel clearly. She was slightly ahead of Jamal, her head bowed as though she were on a forest path, watching for roots underfoot. Ben blinked away the image of Jamal's gun nestled in the small of her back.

He held his breath as they went right past him, along the base of the steps that climbed the Memorial, past the construction trucks loaded with tarps, humming generators that fed power to the floodlights swathing the Memorial. He let them walk until they were exactly where he wanted them.

"Jamal!"

Jamal whirled around at the soft call, at the same time pulling the woman hard against him. His night vision was excellent and he clearly saw Ben standing in front of the Reflecting Pool, the wind riffling the water, turning it into crêpelike skin.

With his hands away from his body, Ben took one step forward. He and Jamal were fifty, sixty feet apart.

"Rachel," Ben called out.

"Ben..."

"Are you all right?"

"Yes..."

"Jamal, look to your left."

The Arab waited a heartbeat before turning. There was the boy, coming out from behind the thick, rectangular columns that flanked the steps to the Memorial. Even at a distance of a hundred feet, Jamal's hunter's eye detected the teary sheen on Kim Woodbridge's cheeks.

"Kim. Stop." Then to Jamal: "Get her moving."

Jamal released Rachel's elbow and nudged her forward.

Ben watched her take one step, then another. She hesitated, looked directly at him.

Don't stop. Whatever you do, don't stop.

Ben willed her to continue, prayed that she would see what she had to do, and do it without hesitation.

"Kim. Move."

The words and the boy's motion distracted Jamal momentarily, long enough for him to miss Rachel's misstep as she made an abrupt left turn. She was in Omar's Maze.

Ben watched as Kim seemed to approach Jamal. Seemed to because he was in another part of the Maze, nowhere near Jamal.

The Maze . . . Ben, Earl Tate, Wanda's helpers, all of them unloading mirrors from the truck. Mirrors six feet by four feet, set in rough frames with ribbing in the back to brace them. The frames were set on casters so that they could be moved around like modular partitions in office work-stations.

The mirrors lined the Reflecting Pool, making sixty feet of it disap-pear. Another row was set at an angle to the Memorial, creating the illu-sion that the edifice was closer than it really was. Two more rows created a corridor through which Rachel and Kim were now walking. But to Jamal, it would appear that Kim was walking to him while Rachel was walking away.

The illusion of Kim was twenty feet from Jamal. Ben thought he could bring it a little closer before Jamal realized he'd been tricked.

At the same time, he caught a hint of Rachel's perfume as she passed him, her shoulders shaking.

"Go on," he murmured. "Follow the maze. Someone's waiting."

Kim's illusion was very close now. Ben saw Jamal focus both his atten-tion and his weapon on what he thought was the boy. Rachel was in the clear.

Ben shrugged one shoulder, and Wanda's capsules dropped into his hand.

Jamal was watching the boy when a gust of wind swept past him. The boy seemed to shiver. No. Something else. He trembled. His entire image trembled, as though a ripple, beginning at the boy's feet, rose up through his body, making it shimmy and shiver. When his features distorted and then righted themselves, Jamal knew.

The barrel of his gun, elongated by the suppressor, bucked. Fifteen feet away, a mirror exploded.

Jamal whirled around, squeezing off the second round even before his motion was complete. The image of Ben shattered as the mirror collapsed in shards.

Running through the maze, Ben squeezed the pellets and dropped them at the base of the mirrors. Oxygen met phosphorus and lit up the night.

Hearing a faint crackle, Jamal turned. His scream was involuntary as his brain registered the waves of flames cascading toward him. The Flaming Seas.

Ben grabbed Rachel's hand and together they raced around the back of the mirrors. There was Kim, standing stock-still, exactly where Ben had told him to be. Ben scooped him up in one arm on the dead run.

Left turn, right, another right, and into a slot that opened to the path to Henry Bacon Drive. Safety if they could reach the trees.

Ben stopped hard, jerking Rachel's arm. He nodded toward a mirror just as it exploded. Here was Jamal, crashing through the shards, rivulets of blood streaming down his face as he turned on them.

"Jamal!"

Wild-eyed, he pivoted in the direction of the voice. He could not know that Ben was throwing his voice, buying time to raise the gun that Tate had given him.

Ben and Jamal saw the image in the same instant: Landau. Two Landaus, stepping out of the raging inferno, each holding a gun, staring at Jamal.

Somewhere in Jamal's brain, the idea burst that he was about to be tricked one more time. He swung back to Ben, Rachel, and the boy, knowing that he had to kill them all, knowing this with the same awful certainty whispering to him that he would never get out of here alive, that he had to take as many as he could with him.

Mirrors shimmered as one of the Landaus stepped between Jamal and his targets. The gun and the rifle fired almost simultaneously, the bullets smacking into flesh and bone. Landau staggered, but remained on his feet long enough to spot the neat, round hole in Jamal's forehead. Pain flamed in his chest, but he knew he was smiling. Smiling even as he was falling. And here was Rachel leaning over him, lifting his head, her eyes wider than he'd ever seen them.

His voice was remarkably clear as he said, "Keep him well." Then he could no longer feel Rachel's finger on the pulse at his throat, and finally, nothing at all.

Epilogue

I SPEAK OF ARMS AND OF THE MAN. The man who surrendered his life for that of his brothers-in-arms. The one who did not return to us, who resides forever in the presence of the Lord . . ."

Ben thought the words of the soldier's prayer sounded pure and honest on Kim Woodbridge's young lips. It was always the young who dressed the dead and kept the vigil, for they were all that was left.

The big doors to the hangar at Andrews Air Force Base were open to the sky. Armed air police formed a perimeter outside; inside, near the El Al cargo jet, in front of the coffin resting on a makeshift bier, were the President and the First Lady, their son, and Ben and Rachel. Behind them stood the Israeli ambassador and members of Landau's commando unit who would accompany the body back to Israel.

The cargo jet would also carry the surviving terrorist, Hatem, who was being held under suicide watch in the base lockup and would be shunted on board when the ceremony was concluded. His presence anywhere near these last rites would have been sacrilege.

Kim Woodbridge stepped forward. His arm trembled slightly as he saluted the coffin. The moment brought to Ben's mind the image of another child who, long ago, had offered his salute at the grave of his father. Kennedy. *It was always the young . . .*

The wind coursed gently into the hangar, rippling the blue-and-white Israeli flag that draped the coffin. Members of the American honor guard stepped forward and, gripping the edges, began to fold it. Protocol dictated that since Landau had been killed on foreign soil, one ceremonial object remain behind to serve his memory. On board, another flag would be placed across the coffin before it was taken off the plane at Ben Gurion Airport.

Ben looked at Charles Woodbridge and his wife, their faces pale and drawn. He could not imagine how it must have felt to keep the death-watch, not knowing whether your child was alive, if all you would ever have left would be photographs and memories. Now, they had Kim between them, each with a hand on his shoulders.

To Ben, it seemed that moments after the deadly standoff between Landau and Jamal, the whole world had exploded. From out of the darkness came streaks of light and the shouts of men running hard. The mirrors that were still intact reflected the spinning lights on cruisers that were pulling up to the scene and the big belly spotlight of the helicopter that had arrived overhead.

The Capitol Police were the first to pile in, guns drawn. Ben still remembered their cursing as they stumbled through the maze. Then they found Jamal lying twisted on the ground, and Rachel cradling Landau, and Ben with his arms around Kim.

Dimly, Ben recalled saying something about needing to speak to the President. The officer in charge was writing him off as a crazy until he took a close look at Kim. Radios crackled furiously as word was relayed to the White House.

Steve Casey, in charge of the First Family detail, was on the scene in twelve minutes flat. He had the police seal off the area while he bundled everyone, including Wanda and Earl Tate, into Secret Service vehicles. The bodies went into the Service ambulance. Ben overheard Casey tell the police lieutenant that what had happened was a construction accident, related to the cleaning of the Lincoln Memorial. Kim Woodbridge had never been there. The rest of the people had never been here. There had been no shoot-out, no killings. If Casey heard anything to the contrary on the news reports, the lieutenant and his men could count on finding themselves on the night watch at the Smithsonian.

A full-blown medical unit was waiting at the White House. Kim Woodbridge was given a quick examination before his parents were finally allowed into the infirmary. At the next table, Rachel assisted the White House doctor who was tending to Ben. She would not leave him.

When the doctors had finished and the First Family had been spirited away, Casey came back, followed by an orderly pushing a cart of hot coffee and sandwiches. After reading the riot act to Wanda and Tate and having them escorted out, he went to Ben and Rachel and placed a tape recorder between them. The reels spun slowly for two hours.

At three o'clock in the morning the President reappeared.

"Kim told me and my wife everything. You saved my son's life, then risked it all over again, Mr. Poltarek."

For a moment, Ben thought the man would actually strike him.

"Jamal took my family," Ben said. Then he looked at Rachel. "I would not let him take more. For that, I needed Kim. You won't believe me, but he was never in danger."

"He says that right at the end, you stepped forward to shield him."

"He only *thinks* he was standing behind me. It was all an illusion."

"Then why—?"

"Because I was going to kill Jamal. Until Landau . . ."

"Yes, Landau." Woodbridge shook his head. "People have told me things about him, but nothing makes sense except that he had been tracking Jamal for a long time."

"Mr. President," Rachel said. "All anyone of us needs to know is that Landau saved our lives."

She didn't bother to add that Landau had never told the President about the Chesapeake house because he knew that Woodbridge would immediately order an assault—an assault designed only to save his son, making Ben expendable. This way, Landau had given her back the man she loved.

"Yes, I suppose." Woodbridge made to leave, then stopped. "My wife and I owe you a debt of gratitude. Everything that happened on the Chesapeake, you still brought our boy home to us." He paused. "Kim tells me you're a hell of a magician."

"An amateur."

"Sure. I hear you work with kids. Maybe you'd join us for the Easter egg hunt." Woodbridge smiled. "I think I'd like to see your magic."

Rachel remembered little Cheryl Pulaski. "Not magic, Mr. President. Illusions."

Then it was just he and Rachel, side by side on a lumpy cot, holding each other in the darkness, their breathing soft and slow as exhaustion finally overtook them.

A few hours later, a nurse shook them awake. Shower and breakfast were waiting, then the ride out to Andrews in the presidential motorcade.

Ben watched as the honor guard created the last folds in the flag and carried it to the ambassador, who accepted it on behalf of the country Landau had served.

The bier was rolled toward the conveyor belt that disappeared into the belly of the cargo jet.

Ben looked at Rachel, who smiled. "He would have liked that."

Ben held up his magician's black wand. Steve Casey had sent one of his men to Ben's apartment especially to get it. Ben stepped to the coffin as it was laid on the conveyor belt and, holding the wand high, broke it in half. Then he released the two pieces, but instead of falling, they floated above the coffin. As it rolled into the aircraft, the broken wand danced lightly, then suddenly vanished, and no one who was watching could ever say where or how.

ABOUT THE AUTHOR

J. Patrick Law is an international business
and government consultant. He now resides
in Hawaii.